Meg Hutchinson left school at fifteen and didn't return to education until she was thirty-three, when she entered Teacher Training College and studied for her degree in the evenings. Ever since she was a child, she has loved telling stories and writing 'compositions'. She lived for sixty years in Wednesbury, where her parents and grandparents spent all their lives, but now has a quaint little cottage in Shropshire where she can indulge her passion for storytelling.

Meg Hutchinson's previous novels, *Abel's Daughter*, *For the Sake of Her Child*, *A Handful of Silver*, *No Place of Angels* and *A Promise Given* are also available from Coronet.

Also by Meg Hutchinson

Abel's Daughter
For the Sake of her Child
A Handful of Silver
No Place of Angels
A Promise Given

Bitter Seed

Meg Hutchinson

CORONET BOOKS
Hodder and Stoughton

Typeset by
Phoenix Typesetting, Ilkley, West Yorkshire

Printed and bound in Great Britain by
Mackays of Chatham PLC, Chatham, Kent

Hodder and Stoughton
A division of Hodder Headline PLC
338 Euston Road
London NW1 3BH

For the people of the 'Black Country'. The coal they mined and the steel they forged built more than industries; it created a people of unique character. Theirs is a warmth of spirit and a depth of generosity that is unsurpassed, while their humour is second to none. I count myself fortunate to be of their number.

Chapter One

'Oh, yes, Father, *you* know best! You have always known what was best, both for Mark and myself. It has always been do what *you* say, do things the way *you* think they should be done. No thought to what Mark or I might want, no matter what our feelings . . .'

'Shut your mouth!' Luther Kenton smashed his fist on the table separating him from his daughter. 'I haven't asked for your opinion nor never will, no fear of that. There be nothing inside a woman's head that's worth the enquiry . . . just do what a woman be meant to do: keep your mouth closed!'

'Like my mother did, like she had to do all those years she was married to you, like you have forced Mark to do ever since he became old enough to think for himself!' Isabel Kenton stared into the face of her father, a man she had feared for almost all of her twenty-one years. 'Well, this time there is nothing you can do. For the first time in his life Mark is his own man, he is free of you . . .'

'I said, shut your mouth!' Eyes starting with the anger that raged inside him, Luther jumped to his feet, his heavy-set body leaning across the table, one hand coming close to her face. 'Shut it . . . or you'll feel the back of my hand across it!'

'It would not be the first time, nor would it come as any surprise.' Isabel sat perfectly still. 'After all, that is the only place either of your children has ever felt the touch of your hand. You are a bully and a bigot. You ruled my mother until the day she died, just as you have ruled my brother and me, but your rule is ended, Father. Mark is free of you and from today I will be too . . .'

'I told you to shut your mouth!' Luther Kenton's hand came flashing across the remaining space, smacking hard against her mouth, snapping her head back on her neck. 'You don't have enough sense to learn, you or that bloody brother you be so fond of defending. You will do as I say, the pair of you, and should *you* ever dare back answer me again, girl, it will be more than a smack to the mouth you'll get.'

Blood was oozing from the split in her bottom lip but Isabel made no move to wipe it away. 'I have no doubt of that, Father,' she said quietly. 'That has always been you strategy. If anything gets in your way, destroy it. If anyone opposes you, beat them into submission. Well, you have money enough to achieve the first and the physical strength to accomplish the second, especially where your opponents are your son and daughter. But I tell you this – for all your strength and all your money, you are not nor ever will be half the man your son is!'

Taking in his breath with a soft hiss, Luther stared at her, his hand already raised to strike again.

Across the small space Isabel's hazel eyes held his calmly though her heart thumped with fear. She had never defied him before, never questioned his word, accepting always that as her father she must do what he said no matter what the pain or unhappiness to herself, but feeling that hurt doubled whenever his anger fell on Mark.

'Go ahead, Father,' she said as his hand began its downward swing, 'add one more memory of your spite, one more reason for my remembering you as you are: a man empty of love but filled with ambition. You have already sacrificed your wife to it and would offer your children too. But you will not sacrifice me upon that altar, and when Mark returns I pray God he too will find the courage to throw the business back in your face.'

'Get out!' His raised hand crashed once more on to the table. 'Get out!'

Rising from her chair, she stood looking at the man now hunched over the table, his hands supporting his weight, his chin on his chest.

'That is exactly what I intend to do. This is the last time you will ever have to look on me, or I on you. I wish I could say that causes me sorrow, Father, but it does not. The only sense it gives me is one of joy.'

'You'll leave this house when *I* say.' His voice hard with anger, Luther did not look up. 'And that will be as Jago Timmins's wife.'

Isabel caught the back of the chair from which she had risen, her knuckles showing white. 'No, Father,' she said tightly. 'I will not marry Jago Timmins.'

'You'll do as I bloody well tell you!' Luther straightened up, his face purple with rage, the words exploding from his lips. '*I* be master in this house!'

'You always have been. My mother would testify to that were she still alive, but she is not. She gave up trying to live with your cruelty and meanness, and I will no longer live with them either. Nor do I intend to die because of them.'

Isabel felt a shiver of fear tingling along her spine even as she spoke. Luther Kenton had never before been confronted with the truth in his own house; now it was being thrown at him by the daughter who had always been quietly submissive, and his reaction could only be anticipated.

Across the room an ormolu clock ticked into a silence charged with both fear and rage. Isabel's hands still held on to the chair though she longed to turn and run from the room. But she would not. She had long awaited this day, each of the ones before filled with terror that her father would marry her off to Jago Timmins before she could make good her escape; but now her deliverance was here and nothing would make her consent to marry that man. Breath catching nervously in her lungs, Isabel kept her voice calm.

'I tell you again, I will not marry Jago Timmins and I am leaving this house today.'

The muscles in his neck standing out like thick cords, the left side of his face twitching spasmodically, Luther remained hunched across the table but now his face was lifted to hers. 'You leave this house and you burn your boats. You won't get a brass farthing from me, not so much as a bloody brass farthing! And who do you think will even look at you without it?'

'If you think that causes me worry you are wrong.' Isabel stared into eyes that still seemed cold and dead despite the anger etched clearly on her father's chiselled features. Money is the last thing I ever wanted from you. As for my boats, let them burn. When I come to a river I will swim across or drown in the attempt. Either way I will do it smiling, glad to be free of you.'

'Oh, arrh?' Luther snarled. 'You'll be glad to be gone from me. But how will you feel a few weeks from now? A few weeks of having nothing to eat save what you can beg will have you singing a different song. A month . . . I'll give you a month. But you'll be back long afore that, whining for me to get you out of the mess you'll be in, begging to be given back your home; and him, that brother of yours, he'll be mewling after summat else. Will already have forgotten this latest fad of joining the Army.'

Isabel walked to the door then hesitated, looking back to meet cold eyes that burned like grey ice. 'I cannot speak for Mark.' Blood still oozed from the cut in her lip, trickling down steadily to drip from her chin, but still she did not check it. 'But for myself, I vow that once I have left this house only your death of mine will ever bring me back to it.'

'Arrh, you be right.' Luther's anger flared anew. 'It will be the death of one, but that one won't be me!'

'I said I would not speak for Mark's feelings.' Isabel forced herself to stand firm as her father got to his feet, his face dark with rage. 'And perhaps before *you* do, you should know you can no longer exert any influence over his life. The fad, as you call it, will by now be reality. Mark left for Birmingham on the morning train. He has gone to enlist. And before you speak of buying his release, even should he wish you to do so, you might remember this country is now at war! If Mark has enlisted, and I am positive he will have done so, then there is nothing your money can do. He will be beyond your reach, for at least as long as this war continues, and if God sees fit to return him here then maybe he will continue to follow his own way. Maybe you will no longer dominate him!'

'Mark's gone to enlist?' His voice was thick with rage. 'After what I said to him!'

'Maybe it was *because* of what you said to him. Mark is no longer a child. You cannot go on ordering his every move, making every decision for him. You cannot *demand* he go into the business, he . . .'

'I can't demand?' Luther kicked savagely at the chair he had earlier sat on, sending it crashing sideways against a tall spindle-legged plant stand, toppling the aspidistra that crowned it. 'I can't tell him? I can tell him this: either he comes into the business *now,* or he can kiss goodbye to my money. Like you, he'll not see a penny.'

'Bringing Mark into the business will not be achieved by kicking over a hundred chairs.' Isabel felt her heart jump violently as the china plant pot crashed on to the floor. 'That is a matter you will have to discuss with His Majesty and the Prime Minister. Somehow I feel that given the present situation they will be less than impressed by your temper or your money.'

'Present situation!' Luther said scathingly. 'This war that everybody's going on about – how long do you think it will last? Six months and the Kaiser will be on his knees. By Christmas this war will be over and done with but the country will still need steel.'

'And that is all you care about, isn't it?'

'Arrh, it is all I care about. What else do I have? A daughter – what good be them to any man? – and a son whose bloody head be filled with daft notions. Well, hear this, any man who leaves the employ of Kenton's to go playing bloody soldiers will need to find himself a new place of work when he comes back.

5

Arrh, and a different home if the one he has belongs to me. And that goes for your brother too. If he has signed on then he be finished. Let the Army find him a place for good. He won't be welcome back here!'

Isabel sat in the small trap outside Wednesbury railway station. Mark would rather he were picked up in one of those racy motor carriages he loved to talk about, the machines their father dismissed as 'useless contraptions that would not last out the decade'. They were noisy, Isabel admitted to herself. At least the one that Joseph Hayden had bought was. It was the only one she had seen in the town so maybe she should not pass judgement, but if they all made as much of a racket as that or smelled so terribly of oil and fumes then she hoped the town would not be blessed, or rather plagued, with more. In this one thing at least she was in accord with her father: motor carriages were definitely no replacement for the horse and trap.

'Train be due shortly, Miss Kenton.' The station master, smart as new paint in his green uniform embellished with brass buttons and gold braid, had come out on one of his two-hourly checks of the exterior of the station, colourful now with the flowers of summer. 'Would you care to sit in the first-class waiting room and I'll 'ave you some tea sent in?'

'No, thank you, Mr Perkins.' Isabel smiled. 'I prefer to wait here and watch the world go by.'

'If Wednesbury be the world then it won't take a deal of passin'.'

'Yes, it is a small town.' Isabel's smile widened as she answered. 'But you know the saying, Mr Perkins: there can be some good stuff in a little bundle.'

Albert Perkins lifted his peaked cap, smoothing one hand across his grey hair before replacing it. 'That be right enough and no mistake, and I reckon old Kaiser Bill will find out just how good when a few of our blokes get set about him. He'll see then just 'ow much of a mistake it is to be at war with England.'

6

'War is a terrible business.' Isabel's smile faded.

'Now don't you be worryin'.' Across the town the clock of St Bartholomew's chimed four and Albert Perkins checked his pocket watch, giving it a shake and holding it to his ear before replacing it in the pocket of his waistcoat. 'Like I said, this little shindig with the Kaiser will be over afore it starts. We'll soon see 'im off, never fear.'

'I do not doubt that for one minute. It is the thought of the men who might be hurt in the process, maybe even killed . . .' Isabel shuddered. This was why she had tried to talk Mark out of his determination to join the Army . . . what if he were killed?

'Won't be no men killed.' The station master adjusted his cap, this time with an air of confidence as if already having seen off the enemy. 'And only ones to be hurt will be the Germans as they tumble over one another running away. No, Miss Kenton, this little tussle ain't worth getting yourself in a state over. Come Christmas you'll be wondering why you ever felt bothered in the first place.'

Why had she felt bothered in the first place? Isabel watched the station master return to his office as the blast of a steam whistle heralded the arrival of the four o'clock train. Mark, her father, Mr Perkins, everyone she spoke to seemed to think this war was no more than a childish prank, an escapade to be enjoyed. Why then did she feel so differently, why did her heart sink at the very thought of it?

'Hello, Bel!'

Isabel lifted a hand to her twin brother as he strode from the station, coming towards her with all the self-assurance of a man who had achieved what he had set out to do. His mouth was set in a wide happy grin, sand-coloured hair which always resisted every attempt at constraint flopping forward untidily. This was why her heart always sank at the thought of war. Mark, the only thing that mattered in her life, would be a part of it.

'Good of you to come and pick me up.'

'Did you think I would leave my baby brother to find his own way home?'

'Less of the baby!' Reaching up, he pulled her easily from the driving seat of the trap, whirling her around in his arms. 'Or I might have to teach you a lesson in manners, me wench!'

'Mark, put me down!' Isabel tried to sound shocked though the smile that came instantly to her face belied her tone of voice. 'What on earth would Father say?'

'Who cares what that old ogre thinks?' Mark dropped a kiss on her nose before setting her on her feet. 'Nothing he says can affect me, not now.'

Isabel winced as he kissed the side of her face.

'Bel!' Holding her at arm's length, he studied her closely and his smile disappeared. 'Not you too . . . it was him, wasn't it? He did this to you?'

'No, Mark, I . . .'

'Don't lie, Bel, not for him, he's not worth it. Though I must admit I never thought even he would strike a woman . . . But he will pay. As God is my witness, I swear he will pay.'

'Forget it, Mark, there are other things to worry about.'

Isabel settled back into the driving seat, watching her brother walk around to the other side of the smartly painted trap and climb in beside her.

'*You* are my main worry, Sis. Leaving you with that swine while I was away getting an education was bad enough, but now . . . now I know he uses his hand on you the same as on me . . . Oh, Bel! Why didn't you tell me before? Why does it have to be now when it's too late?'

'I said not to worry about me.' Taking up the reins, she urged the mare from the station, into Great Western Street.

'*How?*' Mark asked through clenched teeth. 'How can you expect me not to worry? I know just how easily that man loses his temper, how hard his hands can strike . . . of course I am going to worry for you. Oh, Christ, Bel!' If only I had known yesterday.'

Passing tradesmen's carts on their way to the railway goods depot, Isabel guided the pony trap left into Dudley Street before answering.

8

'I did not want to tell you yesterday, Mark, because I knew what would happen then. I knew you would forget about joining the Army, and if that had happened you might never have got out from under Father's thumb. He is so determined you should join the business, and I know how much you hate the idea.'

'It isn't that I hate the business so much as I dislike the idea of devoting myself to it, body and soul. Father would allow nothing less. Once I started at the works I would be given time for nothing apart from the factory – and there are so many things life has to offer. Is it wrong to want to live a little before devoting myself to Kenton Engineering Works?'

'No, there's nothing wrong in wanting that.' Isabel smiled at a young boy who trotted alongside the mare, one hand set lovingly on her neck. 'And neither of us *will* be sacrificed to it, not if you have enlisted. Have you, Mark?'

Lifting a hand, he ran it through his sandy hair, a gesture that displayed the worry he was feeling. 'Yes. Yes, I have. I put my name on the dotted line and now I wish to God I hadn't.'

Returning the wave of the lad who reluctantly left the side of the horse, Isabel turned on to the Holyhead Road and glanced at her brother. 'It was what you wanted, Mark?'

'Yes, it was what I wanted.' He dropped his hands, letting them both hang limply as he hunched forward, resting his arms on his knees.

'Then we both have what we wanted.' Isabel smiled, feeling a stinging pain in her lip over the cut. The price of freedom, she thought, was a price well worth the paying.

'How can you say that . . . and how can I believe you want to be marred to Jago Timmins, a man as old as your own father?'

Ahead of them the heath lay to one side and half-mown cornfields to the other. The vaulting sky above changed from blue to scarlet as the furnaces of a myriad distant workshops were opened for the tipping of molten metal and the drawing of bars of steel. Isabel stared at the spectacle, feeling as she always did the awesome, almost frightening, beauty of the sight, knowing the power that lay behind it: a power that would soon be turning raw metal into weapons of war.

'I will not be marrying Jago Timmins,' she said quietly. 'Today I have reached the age of twenty-one. From this day forth Father cannot force me to do anything I do not want to do. I am free of him, Mark, and so must you be. Do not let him bully you into giving up the Army or anything else you want to do. Live your own life, Mark, live it before it is too late.'

'But you will still be here, in his house . . . But it won't be for long, Bel. Four months at the most is all this war will last, everybody says it will be finished by Christmas. Just four months more and I will take you away from here, I promise.'

Her glance still on the scarlet bowl of the sky, Isabel smiled. 'I will not have to wait four months. My belongings are already packed. Once I have delivered my baby brother home, I shall leave. I have already told Father.'

'You have *told* him!' Mark jerked upright, surprise replacing the worry in his face. 'What did he say?'

'What I expected. He used the same weapon he always uses . . .'

'His money?'

'Yes.' Isabel nodded. 'His money. He thought to make me change my mind about leaving the house and refusing to marry Jago Timmins by telling me I would not get one penny . . . or as he put it not a bloody brass farthing . . . from him. But his threats and his bullying did not work. I *will* leave, nothing is going to prevent that.'

'But where will you go, how will you make a living?'

Isabel guided the mare past the fever hospital and along the path worn by miners and laden carts going to and from the Lodge Holes coalmine and which now linked the towns of Wednesbury and Darlaston.

'I have thought of that. I have money I've saved from my quarterly allowance – whatever else Father may be he has never been mean with my dress allowance. I can use that to pay for a room somewhere, and thought that with the war I might be given a job in a hospital. I don't mind if it is only scrubbing floors, at least I will have charge of my own life.'

'There's no need for that, Bel.' A smile breaking across his face, Mark was suddenly the boy she had laughed and played with in those long-gone days before their mother's death. 'I have no money saved, I'm afraid, but I will get my pay from the Army, which should be enough to keep us both. I will find a place and we will share it, you and me together, and Father can keep his money.'

'Then you will not let him talk you out of the Army?'

'There is less chance of that than there is of the Kaiser becoming King of England!' Mark laughed. 'You can pick up your belongings from Woodbank House and when you leave, I leave with you. Flying Office Mark Kenton and his sister Miss Isabel Kenton will begin their new life together.'

'Flying Officer!' Isabel's face took on a puzzled look. 'But you were hoping to be given a place in the regiment of the King's Dragoons.'

'A commission, Bel.' Mark laughed again. 'A man is not "given a place" in the Army, he is given a rank. Either private, non-commissioned officer or officer.'

'Well, whatever!' A frown settled on Isabel's brow. 'The fact is you said you were hoping to join the Army, and not five minutes ago you told me you had, and now you are calling yourself a Flying Officer, whatever that might be. Mark . . .' The frown faded, leaving a hint of concern in her hazel eyes. 'Was there something wrong . . . would the Army not take you?'

Mark's hoot of laughter momentarily drowned the crunching of the gritty coal waste beneath the trap's wheels. He threw an arm about Isabel, drawing her close and hugging her.

'Oh, they took me all right.'

'But how?' Wriggling free from his grasp, she stared at him. 'You called yourself Flying Officer Kenton. You did, Mark, I distinctly heard you say it. But men do not fly to war, at least not in the British Army.'

'They will from now on.' His voice became low and eager.

'Men will fly to war and I will be one of them. Oh, Bel, I can't tell you how I feel. It's all so exciting, so new. It's the start of a wonderful world.'

Was it? Isabel looked at the face of her brother, shining with enthusiasm. Was it the start of a wonderful new world or was it the beginning of the end?

'I can see how exciting it all is.' She forced away the doubts that filled her mind. 'But perhaps, Flying Officer Kenton, you will tell me just what occurred in that recruiting office. Do they have flying officers in the Army, and if so, just what is it they are required to do?'

'They do and they don't. Now don't frown at me like a displeased school mistress – I will explain everything while you coax this old hack into getting us home.'

'Janey is not a hack!' Isabel was suddenly indignant. 'You call her that again and you will find yourself walking to Woodbank.'

'Sorry, Janey. See, she has forgiven me . . . she knows I love her like a sister.' Mark laughed as, hearing her name, the mare's ears flickered. 'Though I wish it were a Bean we were driving in. Now *there* is a motor car a man can feel proud of.'

'Janey and the trap will do for me.' Isabel flicked the reins. 'I am not a lover of those awful motor carriages.'

'You will be, Bel, you take my word for it.'

'Like I took your word you were going to join the Army but you did not?'

'I did, Bel. Look . . .' Mark twisted in his seat, meeting her gaze as he explained himself. 'I was in the recruitment centre. There were queues of men all waiting to sign on . . . I tell you, Bel, the Kaiser is going to get such a belting . . .'

'Mark! Flying Officer?'

'Oh, yes.' The boyish grin widened. 'I had already signed for the Dragoons when in walked Goosey Gandere . . .'

'In walked who?' Isabel shot him an amused look, her indignation at his calling Janey a hack forgiven and forgotten.

'Goosey . . . John Gandere. We are . . . were , . . at Cambridge together. His father bought him a biplane, lucky blighter! He got his pilot's licence then used to take me up at weekends or whenever we could shove off to his parents' place in the country. Needless to say, I got the bug. I spent every moment and every penny I could on flying lessons – that's why I've got no money. But I have got my pilot's licence.

'Well, like I say, Goosey walked in just as I signed. Turns out the man he was with was his uncle, Field Marshal Sir William Gandere. Anyway, Goosey told me he had signed on with the Royal Flying Corps. He was full of it, said they were set to play a pretty active part in the fun to come and that good pilots would be like gold dust. So when he told his uncle I too could fly an aeroplane, the Field Marshal immediately seconded me to the Flying Corps. Hence Mark Kenton, Flying Officer, RFC.'

'Mark, you mean you have been in a flying machine . . . up in the sky!'

'They don't do so well anywhere else, Sis.' He chuckled.

'But you never said.'

'And you know why.' The chuckle ended abruptly. 'Because of what Father would have done. He'd have put the kibosh on my flying straight away.'

'Yes, he would have put a stop to it,' Isabel agreed. 'But I don't know that he'd have been wrong. Flying machines are dangerous Mark.'

'Nonsense.' Mark swivelled around, once more looking to his front. 'They're as safe as riding with old Janey and she wouldn't hurt a fly, would you, old girl?'

The mare's ears flickered again.

'Aeroplanes will not be just a part of fighting this war against Germany. They are the future, Bel. They're here to stay.'

'You said that about the horseless carriage.' She felt the pace of the trap quicken as Janey recognised home ground. 'Surely there will not be the same noisy machines over our heads? They would terrify Janey, not to mention me.'

'You'll get to love them, Sis, despite the noise. This war is going to change a whole lot of things. Aeroplanes being only one of those changes . . .'

Isabel felt a sudden chill down her spine, as though his words were prophetic, speaking not of fun and daring in flying machines, but death and twisted bodies and the weeping of widowed women. Would it be like that? She wondered. Would this war that Mark dismissed so flippantly leave the nation weeping?

'. . . but the first step is to find ourselves a place to live,' he went on as his sister turned the trap into the short drive that led to Woodbank House. 'I'll ask Mrs Bradshaw if she knows of somewhere just for tonight. Even if we drive back to Wednesbury there will be no train until morning. Who knows? Perhaps now we are at war Darlaston might reopen its passenger line. Lord knows, we could do with it.'

Isabel glanced at the house partly screened by tall conifers. She had planned so long, dreamed so often of leaving this place, yet had not thought of finding herself an alternative home. What if her father's housekeeper did not know of rooms she and Mark might rent . . . what if there were nowhere else she could go? How Luther would smirk, how he would revel in making her apologise. What was it he had said? That she would soon be back, begging to be given the shelter of her old home? Glancing again at the house as Mark helped her from the trap, Isabel set her teeth. That was one pleasure her father would never enjoy. He would never hear her beg!

Chapter Two

'When did it happen?'

Isabel seemed to hear the question from a long way off.

'About five minutes after Miss Isabel left for Wednesbury.'
Arthur Bradshaw gravely looked at the brother and sister he had
known from childhood. 'The master rang for me and ordered
his carriage.'

'Did he say where he was going?'

'It was difficult to tell, he was shouting and banging around.
Begging your pardon, Mr Mark, you know what he be like in
a temper, but seems he said something about going over to
Butcroft.'

Butcroft. Isabel heard the word through the mist that had
enveloped her, setting her apart from the discussion taking place
between her father's servant and her brother. Her father was
going to Butcroft . . . it could only be to Jago Timmins's home,
but to no avail. She would not marry that man. Her father could
not force her – not now.

'So then what happened?'

'I went over to the stables to tell them to bring the carriage
around to the front of the house.' Bradshaw shifted his feet
uneasily. 'Then I came back to see if the master wanted anything
else. He . . . he was standing over there, against the fireplace,
and when I spoke to him he shouted . . .'

'Well?' Mark asked as the manservant broke off. 'What did my father shout?'

'It don't be right for me to say in front of Miss Isabel.'

Mark crossed the spacious sitting room, overfull like all the rooms in this house with heavy ornate furniture, and placed an arm about his sister's shoulders.

'Miss Isabel feels as I do, Mr Bradshaw.' He addressed the manservant with the respect his mother had always demanded her children should show the servants. 'She will not take it unkindly. Just tell us exactly what was said.'

'He . . . he . . .' Bradshaw cleared his throat, obviously reluctant to continue, but when neither Mark nor Isabel spoke he went on. 'I asked the master if he wanted me for anything else and he said I was to tell Mrs Bradshaw there would be a marriage taking place in this house next week. He said what sounded like "special licence". Then he grabbed the ornament from the sofa table – you know the one, Miss Isabel, the Three Graces, it was your mother's favourite. Well, he grabbed it and smashed it into the fireplace. His face was sort of blotchy, purple and red, and his eyes . . . I ain't never seen him in such a paddy afore. He was fair screeching and throwing anything he laid hands on.'

'Think they can bloody well pull the wool over my eyes do they? Think they can tell me what they will and won't do! Well, they've got a bloody shock coming to 'em, a bloody big shock, the pair of 'em. They will do as Luther Kenton says. One will marry where I tell her, and the other will start in the business tomorrow . . .'

'He laughed then and followed it up with a fit of coughing but all through it he kept on ranting and raving. "They'll do what I tell them," he shouted, "all the days of my life. And when I've gone they'll be ready to reap their reward. Oh, and they'll reap it all right. One shilling each will be all they get of Luther Kenton's money. A shilling for my son and a shilling for my daughter, that will teach them to tell . . ." '

Bradshaw halted, his eyes on Isabel who sat unmoving, then

at Mark's nod he continued: 'That was when it happened. He stopped all of a sudden, like he'd been pole axed. His mouth was working but no words came out, and his eyes . . . his eyes was like gobstoppers. One second he was shouting and the next he was on the floor. I sent for the doctor right off . . . eh, Mr Mark, I'm sorry!'

'You must not worry, Mr Bradshaw, I am sure you did all you could.' Suddenly Mark sounded infinitely older than his years. 'Where . . . where is my father now?'

'We got him up to his room. Will I take you up to him, sir?'

'No.' Mark's fingers tightened on Isabel's shoulder. 'No, Mr Bradshaw, not for the moment. I think my sister needs to rest before . . . before we go to see our father.'

'Very well, Mr Mark.' Bradshaw nodded. 'Will I have Mrs Bradshaw send in a tray of tea?'

'Thank you, that would be most helpful.'

'It was my fault.' The door closed softly behind the departing Bradshaw yet the sound of it shattered the invisible wall that surrounded Isabel, driving away the mist that had wrapped itself around her. 'It was my fault. I should not have spoken out, I never should have told him.'

'It was no more your fault than it was mine.' Mark dropped to his knees before her, taking her hands in his. 'I could say I caused this to happen by telling him I wanted to join the Army. I could, but I won't. Neither of us was the true cause, it was his own vicious temper. His rages have been getting worse, you know that. Look what he did to you.' He lifted one finger to her mouth, gently touching the recent cut. 'And this isn't the first time he has struck you, is it, Bel? Is it?'

'No, but . . .'

'No buts, Bel.' Mark rose to his feet and walked to the fire-place where the remains of the lovely porcelain figurine still lay scattered across the hearth. 'No more excuses. He was a vindic-tive man who will tread anyone down who gets in his way, no matter who they are. Even his own children. We did right to stand up to him. From today we can go our own way.'

Watching Bradshaw set the tea tray on the pie-crust mahogany table their mother had always kept beside the sofa, Isabel thought again of the long years she had waited for this day to dawn, her twenty-first birthday. In any other household of their standing in the town there would have been celebrations planned, but not in Woodbank, not in Luther Kenton's house. It was almost as if he had hated them. Isabel heard the soft click of the door as the manservant withdrew. But why? For what reason could a father dislike his own children as much as Luther had disliked Mark and herself? Why nurse the spite he had vented so often on them both, and why have hated their mother so openly?

'God, this would happen now!' Mark struck one fist into his palm. 'What the hell will the Flying Corps say when I ask for leave before I even report for duty?'

'They will understand, Mark.' Isabel automatically poured tea for them both, adding milk and two spoons of sugar to her brother's cup. 'You must do what is right by Father regardless of how we felt about him.'

'He's managed it after all, hasn't he, Bel? I told you he would put the kibosh on my joining up!'

Older than her twin by two minutes, Isabel had always felt a kind of responsibility for him, often shielding him from their father's anger, even long before their mother's death. Now that instinct rose strong in her again. Luther Kenton would not win, would not destroy his son's hopes and dreams as so often before. He would no longer dictate Mark's life, or hers. 'No, he has not,' she insisted. 'This need not prevent your taking up your commission.'

'But the business . . .'

'It appears we no longer need worry about the business. One shilling each didn't Bradshaw say? One shilling for his son and one for his daughter. It seems our father has willed Kenton Engineering elsewhere. At least we will be free from that.'

*

Isabel smoothed the black taffeta skirts of her dress, touching a hand to the rich folds of auburn hair held back by a black ribbon. It had been a week since she had vowed to leave this house, a week since she and Mark had returned to find Luther Kenton dead of a heart attack.

She had tried to feel sorrow, or even remorse, but neither of those emotions had come to her. Nor did she yet feel relief. Her father was dead, could no longer rule her life; yet somewhere deep within her she feared he had not so easily released his grip. She trembled suddenly. Could he somehow, even now, have a hold over her?

'Ready, Bel?'

Outside her bedroom door, Mark's voice called. Tomorrow he would be gone. Seven days was all the time the Flying Corps had granted him. Seven days in which to bury his father and settle his affairs . . . and hers. Isabel walked slowly to the door. Seven days in which the town's industrial elite had paid their respects and followed her father to his grave. Now they were gone and soon Mark would be gone too and she would be left to find them both another home.

Downstairs in the room her father had kept strictly for conducting any business he felt could not be conducted at the works Isabel took the chair Mark held for her. Soon the last of Luther Kenton's words would be spoken to them: soon she could leave Woodbank House.

'Are you feeling up to this, Miss Kenton?'

Isabel nodded to the man seated behind her father's desk, heavy horn-rimmed pince-nez clinging perilously to a nose too thin to hold them.

'Would you perhaps care for a glass of water?'

'No, thank you.' Isabel gave a single shake of her head. 'I am perfectly all right. Please continue.'

'Very well.' Luther Kenton's solicitor cleared his throat as he unfolded a sheet of thick parchment.

'Being the solicitor acting for the late Mr Luther James Kenton it falls to me to read this, his last Will and Testament . . .'

His final words. Isabel's fingers clenched in her lap. What last act of spite had their father planned for them?

"'. . . To my manservant of many years, Arthur Bradshaw . . .'"

Isabel felt the flurry of expectancy behind her and the satisfied sigh as the solicitor related the bequest. She felt a mixture of pleasure and relief. At least Luther had not forgotten his servants.

"'. . . and finally to Mark Philip, son of my wife, Victoria Kenton . . .'"

The solicitor glanced over his pince-nez, catching the puzzled look that passed between brother and sister.

"'. . . I leave the thing he least wanted: the firm of Kenton Engineering, together with its subsidiary businesses. To Isabel Margaret, daughter of my wife Victoria Kenton, I leave this house together with the sum of five thousand pounds on the stipulation that she remains living in it. My name, however, I cannot leave them for they were not begotten of me. Signed this day . . .'"

'But there must be some mistake?' Mark interrupted. 'Luther Kenton was our father.'

'I am sorry, Mr Kenton.' The solicitor held the document out towards him. 'I can only read what is written here, which having been signed in the presence of witnesses is, I assure you, perfectly legal . . .'

'I don't damn' well care who witnessed it! That paragraph is a lie. My mother was married to Luther Kenton and we are his children.'

'Once again, Mr Kenton, I assure you the words are not mine. I read only what has been written. You can read it for yourself . . .'

Grabbing the piece of parchment, Mark scanned the contents. 'Damn him!' he muttered, throwing the document back on to the desk. 'Damn Luther Kenton to hell!'

'My father . . .'

Isabel waited while the Bradshaws withdrew then turned to the solicitor, now folding the will.

'. . . could not have left this house and all of his business concerns to my brother and myself . . .'

The solicitor looked over the pince-nez which was gradually losing its hold on his nose.

'You see, Mr Bradshaw heard him say we were to have no more than one shilling each. Those were his very words, you can ask Mr Bradshaw.'

'I can.' The pince-nez had reached the end of its journey and now teetered on the very tip of the man's nose. 'And should you so desire it, Miss – er – Kenton . . .' Realising he had left a most embarrasing gap before saying her name, the solicitor poked a finger at the spectacles, pushing them back on to the bridge of his long narrow nose '. . . I will do so. But it would have no bearing upon the bequest, I do assure you. Whatever your father . . . Mr Kenton . . . intended I cannot of course say, but unless a later will is found – and again you have my assurances that no later document was signed in or lodged at my chambers – then this,' he tapped the folded paper against the desk top, 'is the legal and binding wish of the deceased.'

'He *did* win.' Having seen out the solicitor Mark returned to Isabel, still sitting in Luther's study. 'We should have guessed he would.'

'Can it be true, Mark? What he wrote in that will. Are we really not his children?'

'Why would he write it otherwise?'

'To hurt us?' She looked up at her brother, her hazel eyes brimming with tears. 'He did it so many times during his life, could it be that he wanted one last stab in death?'

'Well, if so, it's a bloody good one!' Mark turned away, kicking angrily at the heavy walnut desk. 'Christ, fancy leaving something like that to be read out in a will! He might as well have hired the town crier. Sorry for the language, Bel, but the man was a thorough bastard!'

'It seems *we* are the bastards.' Isabel's fingers twisted together as she fought against tears. 'We are the ones who appear to have no father . . . but if not Luther then who, Mark? And why now? Why did he not tell us sooner? Was it to spare Mother's feelings?'

'Spare Mother's feelings!' Mark's laugh was heavy with bitterness. 'Since when did that man care about feelings, Mother's or anyone else's! It's my guess he intended to tell us but was waiting for a moment when it would cause us the most pain and give him the most pleasure. Yes, I think he intended to tell us, Bel. He wouldn't deliberately miss seeing our faces when we learned the truth.'

'But *is* it the truth?' She dabbed a handkerchief to her eyes, wiping away the tears. 'We have only the word of a dead man, one who cannot be questioned, cannot be called upon to prove what he has written. Where is our mother's word in all of this? Would she truly have left us to believe we were the children of Luther Kenton if it were a lie?'

'I don't know, Bel. If so there has to be a reason, and when this war is over I shall find it out.'

'What about our birth certificates?'

'There are those, of course, and they are certain to be among his papers somewhere though I have not looked yet. I suppose I am going to have to but, truth to tell, Sis, I feel I never want to touch anything that was his. And that includes his business!'

Getting up from her chair, Isabel went to stand beside him, her hand touching his shoulder. 'Let's forget this, Mark: our parentage, the business, everything. Forget it until the war with Germany is over, then we'll sort it out together. You will have enough on your mind until then.'

Mark turned to her and folded his arms about her. 'We won't be able to forget it, Sis, neither of us. It will be like a spectre sitting on our shoulders. But I reckon I shall have little chance to sort it out before I leave. Oh, Lord, I wish I hadn't signed on!'

'Don't,' she said gently. 'Don't wish that. The Army was what you wanted. Don't let Luther win, Mark, don't give up now. Take your life and fashion it the way *you* want it.'

'But what about Kenton Engineering? He may not have

been intending for it to come to me, but it has. I am stuck with it, Bel. He has hung it around my neck just as he always wanted to.'

Pushing away from him, Isabel looked into his face, her own set and determined. 'Then throw it off! Sell Kenton Engineering. I can't think of a better way to repay Luther.'

'Is that what you intend to do with his house?'

'Yes, Mark.' She glanced about the room, at the heavy desk and oppressive furniture.

'But you will lose the five thousand.'

'Yes, I shall lose the money but I shall keep my self-respect. I do not know whether Luther Kenton was in reality my father, but I hope he was not. I would sooner be the daughter of some passing tramp than carry the blood of that man in my veins!'

Isabel leaned her head against the hard padding of the leather chair set before Luther's desk. Mark had written several times in the two weeks since he had left for camp at Upavon and in each letter she had noted the underlying excitement. For Mark the whole business of war was a game, a time to be enjoyed, while for her in Woodbank . . .

She closed her eyes, the feelings of weariness and guilt almost too much to bear. She had felt no sorrow at Luther's death and it haunted her. He had not been the kindest of men to her or to Mark and she could never remember a time when he had showed them love, but even if he were not their father he had at least given them a home when the responsibility had not been his. For that she should feel something, even if it were simply gratitude. But she could not; try as she might she could feel nothing. It was as if all feeling had died within her.

Opening her eyes, she resumed the task of going through the contents of the desk. She had agreed to Mark's suggestion she should stay on in the house until he found a new place for them, and now she was following the request in his latest letter: that she should go through Luther's papers.

Opening yet another drawer, she lifted the contents on to the surface of the desk, the same flutter of trepidation scurrying along her nerves. Did she want to find her birth certificate. Did she really *want* to know her true identity? She took up a sheet of paper, releasing a long breath of relief when she read the words 'your order for'. Like every other paper she had seen, this was not the record of her birth.

Leave it! The thought rose in her mind as it had so often since her brother had left. Leave it. Who cares whether you are Luther Kenton's child or not? Reaching for the next paper, Isabel read it slowly through. She could not leave it. She cared.

There had been nothing in the desk. Rising to her feet she stretched, easing the tiredness from her spine, pressing a hand to her strained eyes. She had sat reading the papers stored in that desk for over four hours. Drawing a long breath, she walked to the window, a lovely half-moon bay that overlooked a garden heavy with slumberous roses, their beautiful coloured heads lifted to the late-afternoon sunlight. Soon the summer would be gone and the garden would be left bare of colour as her life had been left bare of love since the death of her mother. They had sat together in that garden so often during her childhood, when Mark had been away at school, and had talked of so many things, the passing years supplanting fairy castles and princes on white horses with fresh dreams of a home away from this house, a home Isabel could share with just her mother and Mark, a home where Luther could never hurt them again. But her own years had not passed quickly enough while her mother's had gone too soon, taking Isabel's dreams with her to the grave.

She would write to Mark this evening; she would have to tell him what she had told him before, that she had found no evidence to support Luther's words. Glancing one last time at the garden, she turned to leave. She would resume the search tomorrow. But where was there left to search, where else was there to look?

'Begging your pardon, Miss Isabel, but there is a man wishing to speak to you.'

Glancing across the room to where Bradshaw had entered, she gave him an enquiring look. 'A man?'

'Yes, miss. One of the men from the works along at Bull Piece'

'The works!' Isabel had forgotten them. They were still Mark's responsibility, he had not yet sold them. 'He will have to speak to Mr Mark.'

'I told him that but he said it couldn't wait till Mr Mark came home. Said he must see you.'

'But I know nothing of the works!' Isabel glanced over Bradshaw's shoulder as if expecting to see the visitor in the open doorway.

'I told him that an' all. But it made no difference. He said he had come to see whoever were in this house and he wouldn't be leaving 'til he had, short of being carted off by the bobbies.'

'Who is the man? Do you know him?'

'Arrh, I do that. Been your father's charge hand for ten years and more. What he don't know about the making of a good pistol don't stand the knowing.'

'Guns?' Isabel's consternation deepened. 'I know even less about them. I know only that Kenton's are engaged in their manufacture.'

'Locks and barrels, mostly.' Bradshaw smiled proudly as though the product were of his own making. 'And very good they be an' all, miss. Some of the finest gentlemen in the land have guns made right there in Bull Piece. Why, even the King himself takes a couple of Kentons up to Balmoral every year for the grouse shooting, then they comes back here to be serviced.'

'I . . . I have no idea of their construction.'

'No, 'course not, Miss, why should you have? 'T'aint a subject a woman be naturally interested in. Shall I tell him to come back when Mr Mark be next on leave?'

'There's no telling when that might be.' Isabel smoothed her black skirts, the movement more from habit than necessity. 'No, ask Mr . . . '

'Perry, Miss. Edward Perry.'

'Ask Mr Perry if he would join me here.'

'So you see, Miss Kenton, I don't rightly know how I can do that without your brother's say so.'

Isabel looked at the man perched nervously on the edge of the chair she had invited him to take. Middle-aged and greying slightly at the temples, his fingers twisting the flat cap whose colour had disappeared beneath layers of foundry dust, he stared at her with eyes almost startling in their blueness.

'I understand that,' she replied. 'But my brother has every intention of selling all of Kenton Engineering, including the works at Bull Piece. I will write to him this evening, telling him of the letter. In the meantime, you may tell all of the workers they are no longer required and have the place boarded up until my brother returns to see to the selling of it.'

'I don't 'old no wish to tell you or your brother your business,' the blue eyes held hers with no trace of nervousness, 'but the government has ordered five thousand gun locks and the same number of bayonet sockets and they won't take lightly to being told Kentons be closing down.'

'I do not see it is any of the government's concern. Kenton Engineering is my brother's property, to do with as he sees fit.'

'Arrh, it be your brother's.' The blue eyes regarded her steadily. 'An' in normal times the government wouldn't care if he sold it, give it away or set fire to it. But these ain't no normal times, this country be at war and them up in the House o' Commons could very probably requisition every one of your brother's 'oldings. If he don't keep it as a going concern then they will. They could well take it off him, every nut and bolt, lock and stock – and then come back for the barrel.'

'Can they honestly do that?' Isabel's look reflected her surprise.

'Oh, arrh, they most likely can.' Edward Perry nodded. 'They 'ave already got their 'ands on them motor carriages Samuel Hayden bought for 'isself and his son and them don't be the only ones. I hear Jago Timmins along of Alma Street give his or had it took away. Believe me, miss, I knows the Army. I was in the South African do. That was where I got this.' He touched a finger to his flattened nose. 'Catched a bloody Zulu shield full in the face then took the haft of his spear across the nose. Would have been killed if it hadn't have been for one of our chaps letting the black devil have it with a shot that nigh took off his head. That were when I made up my mind, if I got home in one piece I would take meself into the gun trade. It were a gun saved my life so I reckoned it were up to me to make a good job of as many as I could. That way I might save some other man's life should this country ever see itself in another war.'

Jago Timmins? Isabel's surprise increased as she realised she had not even thought of him since telling the man she would not marry him. 'And now it has.'

'Arrh, miss, it has. And that be why your brother has to keep the works going, if he 'opes to be the owner of 'em much longer.'

But Mark did not want to own Kenton Engineering. Isabel glanced at her hands resting in her lap. He wished the works to be sold. To retain them was to behave as Luther had wanted. But it would only be for as long as this war lasted and that could only be until Christmas, everyone was totally convinced of that, Mark especially. Four months. The fingers of her left hand pressed one by one against her skirts as though counting the months. Surely Mark could hold on to the works that long? But how? How could he run any part of the business when he was away in the Flying Corps?

Drawing a long breath, Isabel looked squarely into those blue eyes. 'My brother is now a member of His Majesty's forces. Until he returns I myself will take charge of Kenton's. That is, if you will help me, Mr Perry?'

27

'I'll help you, me wench.' The charge hand stood up. 'I'll help you all I can.'

'In that case,' she smiled, 'will you draw up a list of supplies we need to comply with the government's order? Meanwhile I will inform my brother of what is being done.'

The workman gone, Isabel glanced once more about the room. Luther, it seemed, was still an influence upon them, still directing their lives, imposing his will. 'You are master of the game, for now Luther,' she whispered. 'But it is not over yet. No, not by a long chalk.'

Her glance coming to rest on one of several glass-fronted bookcases, she walked across to it. To read in the garden while the sun was still warm would be a pleasant pastime after the hours spent searching through endless papers. It would relax her mind before writing to Mark.

Running a finger slowly over a line of red morocco-bound volumes, she idled over the gilt titles visible along each spine. *Bleak House*? Isabel rejected that. She had had enough of bleak houses living in Bankwood. *A Tale of Two Cities . . . David Copperfield*. None of them suited her mood. Tapping a dismissive hand against the spine of the next book Isabel made to turn away, but before she could the spine swung back revealing a small cavity. A hiding place, but for what?

Feeling a pulse pound in her throat, Isabel hesitated. Could what she was searching for be in there?

Slowly, more than half afraid of what she might find, she reached into the narrow space, her fingers closing over a sheet of paper.

Isabel felt her resolve harden as she looked at Jago Timmins. Bushy whiskers, more grey than brown, stood out from his cheeks, following the line of his jaw. Beneath his wide brow thick eyebrows ran in a single straight line, as if a section of his hair had fallen from his scalp and lodged above his pallid eyes.

'I tell you, no woman can go running an engineering works!'

'I see.' Isabel kept her voice evenly polite. 'You do, of course, have much more experience of the steel industry than my brother, and certainly very much more than myself . . .'

'Of course I do! That be why I'm telling you it be impossible for a woman even to think of attempting such a thing.'

'. . . but is it inexperience alone that you see as an insurmountable obstacle?' Isabel ignored his interruption. 'Or is it that in your estimation a woman does not have the brain for such an undertaking?'

'Tcha!'

He gave an impatient toss of his head, clearly unused to argument. Or was it just argument with a woman he was unused to? Isabel held back a grim smile. Jago Timmins was like Luther Kenton in more than years.

'It ain't a matter of brain,' he went on. 'Mauling about wi' steel takes strength, and no woman could stand working in front of a furnace twelve hours a day.' He laughed derisively. 'Five minutes would be more than one of you could manage. Five minutes and you'd be flat on your back with a doctor holding smelling salts under your nose.'

'While you, of course, have that strength?' Isabel said, making no effort to disguise the sarcasm colouring her voice. 'You are no doubt often to be found on the foundry floor, mauling steel alongside of your workmen. Or perhaps it is the twelve-hour shifts in front of the furnace that you work?'

'Don't try being bloody clever wi' me!' Jago Timmins's eyes turned to needle points. 'I don't take sarcasm from any woman.'

'But they must accept it from you!' she flashed. 'Well, *I* will not. I'm afraid your lack of manners is no excuse for your ignorance. I did not ask you to call here Mr Timmins, and nor did my brother invite your offer to purchase his business. Kenton Engineering will remain my brother's property and for the duration of the war it will be managed by me.'

Jago rose to his feet, coming to stand close to Isabel. 'That can be hard work – too much for a wench as pretty as you. You should leave that to a man. A woman don't be meant for worrying over a foundry. Her only concern should be how to please a man . . . how to please a husband.'

'I think you should leave!'

Isabel reached a hand towards the bell pull that hung beside the fireplace but Jago grabbed her wrist, twisting her sharply towards him.

'You could please me, Isabel,' he breathed thickly, pale eyes glazing over as his free hand fastened painfully over her breast. 'These would please me. There would be no need for you to bother about anything else . . .'

'Let go of me!' Isabel tried to push free but the hand that held her wrist twisted behind her back was merciless in its strength.

'You don't want me to let go.' Jago caught her mouth, pressing his flabby lips over hers. 'And once you have a taste of what I've got for you, you won't ever want me to let you go.'

Using his weight to press her backward he walked her to the sofa, pushing her down upon it, still without relinquishing his hold on her. Shock and outrage almost robbing her of her senses, Isabel found herself on her back with Jago sprawling over her. Her body pinioned painfully over one arm, her other hand caught over her head, she could only gasp: 'Let me go . . . please . . .'

'Oh, I know your little game.' Jago chuckled thickly. 'Women be full of 'em when they don't want to appear too eager. But that be all right with me. Play on if it pleases you, Jago Timmins won't refuse to take part.'

'Let me . . .'

Her cry was stifled as his wet mouth closed once more on hers. His weight was too much for her to shake off.

'That's it.' His mouth still against hers, Jago breathed hard and fast. 'Grind yourself into Jago, feel the pleasure of him, the pleasure of this.'

Taking the top of her blouse in his podgy hand he snatched it apart, dragging the delicate lace chemise after it.

Covering her mouth with his, cutting off her cries, he

cupped his hand over the soft mound of her flesh, his fingers squeezing the nipple until it stood proud.

'This be Jago's pleasure.' Releasing her mouth he grunted like an animal, lowering his head to her breast, flicking his hot tongue over her nipple. 'And this will be yours.'

Bringing her hand down from above her head, he eased himself half off her as he pushed it into his groin. Sickness catching in her throat, Isabel gagged as the bulge of hard flesh throbbed against her fingers.

'That be what will please you.' Jago's voice thickened even more, the pulse of his tumescent penis beating against her hand. 'There be enough there to keep you happy. You'll have no thought for aught else when you get that between your legs. Jago's wedding present will take your mind from foundry managing . . .'

'Get away from me!' Fear and revulsion lending power to her limbs, Isabel heaved him the rest of the way off her. Jumping to her feet and putting the width of the room between them as he fell heavily to the floor, she glared at him, dislike giving way to hatred.

'You are despicable . . . loathsome!' Too angry for tears, the strength of her feeling showed plainly in her face. 'You disgust me! You would disgust any woman, decent or otherwise. You are not a man, you are an animal . . . a filthy repulsive animal. I would never marry you, not if you were the last man on earth! I despise you, Jago Timmins, just as I always have!'

He struggled to his feet, face purple behind the encroaching whiskers. His pallid eyes now bright with fury, he let them rest on her as both his hands tugged viciously at his black waistcoat, pulling it neatly into place over charcoal grey trousers from which the evidence of passion had disappeared. Hands grabbing the lapels of his black swallow tail coat, he eased it forward as if only now putting it on.

'So Jago Timmins is an animal, is he?' The words were ground out from between gritted teeth. 'A filthy repulsive animal? But he is an animal with clout! In less than three months

Kenton's will be out of business and you and that brother of yours most likely on the Parish. You'll wish then you'd married that animal!'

'I will never wish that!' Isabel drew the remnants of her blouse together, holding them across her breasts.

'That be easily said.' Jago lowered his hands from the coat now sitting squarely on his shoulders. 'But you'll feel different when you have to ask for the money to buy your bread. You'll need to watch the way you ask too – the Parish Board won't take kindly to being called animals!'

Cheeks flaming, her whole body trembling from his attack, Isabel forced herself to stare back at those pale and spiteful eyes.

'Should Mark and I find ourselves relying upon the Parish for our living, Mr Timmins, then I am sure you will give yourself the pleasure of withholding your charity.'

'You be too bloody sharp-tongued!' Jago's face darkened still further. 'Luther should 'ave knocked the cockiness out of you.'

'As you intended to, no doubt?' Isabel reached for the bell pull, giving it a sharp tug.

'Arrh, as I would 'ave done – and still will when you find that begging for charity from the Parish don't suit you after all.'

Turning her back as a tap sounded on the door, Isabel answered as it opened. 'I might not have the brawn to maul steel, Mr Timmins, but thank God I have the brains to refuse to marry you!'

'We all 'ave brains.' His words came through clenched teeth as Jago made to leave. 'It could be some of us knows better how to use them than do others. There be more ways than beating to knock the cockiness out of you, and Jago Timmins knows 'em all!'

Pushing Bradshaw aside, he strode into the hall.

'Don't say I never warned you!'

Chapter Three

Isabel stared at the sheet of paper. She had pushed it into her pocket as Bradshaw had come into the study to announce the arrival of Jago Timmins; there it had stayed until now. For the remainder of the afternoon and throughout the evening it had lain in her pocket, pressing on her like a physical weight.

Would it tell her whose child she was? Would this paper she had found hidden in a book show who had fathered her?

Her hands trembling, Isabel turned up the lamp, driving back the shadows from her room. That was easy to do. She stared again at the single sheet of yellowing paper lying on her bed. But what of the shadows that filled her mind? Would this paper drive them away?

Why had it been hidden away in so secret a place, and by whom? It could only have been Luther. She sank on to the bed, eyes still on the paper. If it were the birth certificate of herself or Mark, why hide it away? He had made it known they were not his children so why hide the evidence? Unless, as she had thought, it had been kept in reserve as a final blow.

Her hand shaking visibly, she reached for the paper. Unfolding it she read the beautiful flowing copperplate.

My dearest love,
I pray God my letter reaches you before you sail for America.
I now know the fear of which I could not speak is a reality: I

carry our child within me. I did not tell you of my fear when last we were together for I would not have you worry unduly. But now I am certain. Please, my love, return for me. Take me with you to America. We can be married before the ship sails. I pray you come for me quickly.

Your very loving,
Victoria

Victoria! Isabel stared at the signature – her mother's signature. But to whom had the letter been sent? There was no other name and no envelope. Surely it had not been written to Luther? She read it again, slowly, this time, remembering the pain always present behind her mother's gentle eyes, the look of sorrow that never quite left her face. *I carry our child within me.* Isabel's eyes stayed on the words. Her mother had been pregnant and unmarried. How terrified she must have been, knowing the shame and disgrace that would bring. Her mother's lover could not have been the man she married for there had never been a pretence of love between them, so who was he, and why had he never returned? *Please, my love, return for me.* The words swam as her eyes filled with tears. But he had not returned. Whoever Isabel's father was, he had turned his back on them. The paper falling to the floor, Isabel buried her face in her pillow, the rustling of her taffeta skirts like dry laughter in the quiet room.

'His words as I remember were: "Kenton's will be out of business in less than three months and you and that brother of yours most likely on the Parish."'

'You never liked him, did you, Bel?'

Liked him! Isabel repressed a shudder. She detested Jago Timmins as she had once detested Luther. Once? The thought brought a smile, half rueful, half surprised, to the corners of her mouth. Was the memory of her father's unkindness already fading? Should she even call him Father? Once again she touched the letter in the pocket of her skirt. She had not yet shown it to Mark.

'Can't say I blame you.' He returned his glance to his dinner plate, cutting through a slice of beef. 'I never felt any particular regard for him on the few occasions I met him, and I must say I hold even less for him now. I have no doubt it would give him no end of a boost to see us engaged in a bit of crashery. As Goosey would say: "Let's go for him, old boy."'

Isabel smiled indulgently at Mark's phraseology. He had settled so well into the Flying Corps and looked so handsome in his uniform. God keep him safe, she thought, sudden fear snatching away her smile. God keep them all safe.

'You would like Goosey.' Mark glanced up again, eyes more brown than hazel glowing with enthusiasm. 'He's such a sport to be with, Bel, there's never a dull moment when he's in the Mess. And he's an absolute wizard in a kite!'

'Kite?' Isabel hid her amusement.

'Sorry.' Mark grinned. 'I meant an aeroplane. Really, Sis, you should see the things he can do with one of those machines. They say that on a recon' flight . . .'

'A what flight?'

'Reconnaissance.' The grin widened. 'Over Mons and Charleroi, well, Goosey spotted a German Taube coming straight at him. According to Lefty Wright – that was the chap with the camera taking shots of the German positions – old Goosey pulls out his revolver . . . a Kenton that had belonged to his grandfather, would you believe? . . . anyway, he grabbed it and let off a full chamber at the Hun. That not bringing the blighter down and he having no more ammo, Goosey turned and brought his kite head on for the Taube, throwing the revolver at it as the German pulled away in a tight curve. God, I would have given a week's leave to have been in on that!'

Isabel dropped her eyes. It was all such a game to Mark, something to enthuse about, provide a fund of tall stories. So why could she not laugh? She listened to him talk during the rest of the meal, heard the boyish excitement that turned each

35

frightening episode into a joke. But where was the excitement in men trying to kill each other, where was the joke in death?

Mark pushed away his empty dessert plate with a satisfied nod to Bradshaw. 'We must get Field Marshall Gandere to second Mrs Bradshaw to our Mess. With food like this we could have old Jerry back in the Fatherland by the end of the month.'

'I be glad you enjoyed it, Mr Mark.'

Since when had he not enjoyed Mrs Bradshaw's cooking? Isabel added her smile of appreciation to her brother's. 'Please tell her the meal was delicious.'

'Arrh, I will that.' Bradshaw's smile answered their own. 'It always pleases her to hear you two have enjoyed what her cooks. Always had a soft spot for you, the wife has, ever since you was little 'uns.'

'The feeling is reciprocated.' Mark touched a hand to his stomach. 'And I fully intend to do what I always said I would. Remember, Bel?'

'I remember.' Isabel laughed at a childhood memory of a small boy standing beside the large kitchen table, a sultana-packed scone in his hand, declaring: 'When I grow up I shall marry you, Mrs Bradshaw.'

'They say the way to a man's heart is through his stomach, and you were no exception!'

'And who could blame any man for giving his heart after dishes such as our Mrs Bradshaw makes? I warn you, Bradshaw, I will run away with your wife yet!'

'I reckon you would bring her back as quick as you took her,' he chuckled. 'Mrs Bradshaw's cooking be one thing but her tongue be another altogether. A dose or two of that and you'd soon have her home!'

'If you're trying to scare me off it won't work.' Still laughing, Mark stood up from the table. 'You just wait until I've seen the Hun off, then . . .'

'When you've done that, Mr Mark, I'll make you a present of her.'

Leaving the manservant chuckling softly, Mark ushered his

sister from the dining room. When she turned towards the sitting room, he caught her hand, leading her instead to the room Luther had always kept so strictly private.

'We still have Jago Timmins to deal with,' he said, seeing the question in her eyes. 'We'll shoot him down in flames before he even gets off the ground.'

Seating himself at Luther's desk, Mark took out two sheets of paper. 'I am setting it down in writing, Bel,' he said, dipping a pen into the crystal ink well. 'A copy for you and one to be kept by our solicitor. I am giving you full and total authority to administer the business of Kenton Engineering together with its subsidiary businesses as you see fit. In the event of my not returning, then you will become their sole owner.'

'Mark, please! Don't . . . don't talk like that.'

'I have to, Bel.' He looked up and his eyes had lost their laughter. 'It has to be faced. There is the chance I might not come out of all this . . .'

'No!'

'Bel, we have to face it and I couldn't if I thought I had not left everything straight for you.' He rose and came round the desk to take her in his arms. 'You are all that matters to me,' he muttered against her hair. 'The only one I have cared for since our mother died.'

'You mustn't die, Mark.' Isabel clung to him, her tears leaving a darker patch on his uniform jacket. 'I couldn't face life without you. You're all I have.'

'Hey! Who said anything about dying?' Holding her at arm's length he grinned at her – but the grin did not rekindle the laughter in his eyes. 'When I said I might not come out of all this, I meant I might choose to stay in the Flying Corps once this jape is all over. And I can't do that unless you relieve me of the burden of running Kenton's.'

He did understand after all. Isabel looked at him through her tears. Treating the whole affair as a game was his way of coming to terms with war, but beneath that façade he knew as well as she the horror war could bring.

'I love you, little brother,' she said quietly.

Watching while he finished writing, folding both papers into separate envelopes and writing an address on one of them, Isabel knew she must show him the letter she had found in that hiding place. She had thought of holding it back, not showing it to him until this trouble with Germany was finished, thinking he had enough to concern him and this new matter could wait. But now she realised that would be wrong. Mark had the right to see his mother's letter.

Taking the envelope on which he had written just her name she laid it aside then withdrew the yellowed paper from her pocket, holding it out to him and standing silently by as he scanned the elegantly penned words.

'Mother?' His glance as it was raised to her held obvious pain. 'Where did you get this?'

'I found it, hidden in the spine of a book.'

'Who was it written to?'

'I don't know. There was no envelope, and as you see there's no name written in the letter apart from our mother's.'

Mark read it through again. 'You don't reckon it could have been written to Luther?'

'No, I don't.' Isabel shook her head. 'Do you think it could?'

'No, Bel. But if it was not, why would Mother hide it in here where there was every possibility of its being found by him?'

'Was it Mother who hid it, though?' Isabel voiced the question that had lurked at the back of her mind since finding the letter. 'As you say, this would be a most improbable place for her to choose. Surely she would have put it somewhere less frequented by him?'

'That's my thinking too.' Mark folded the sheet of paper, holding it in his hand. 'So, Sis, at least we know the words Luther wrote in his will were not just another outpouring of spite. We know we are not his. The question now is, just who was our father?'

'We might never have the answer to that question, but whoever he was, our mother loved him.'

38

'Yes, she loved him!' Mark slammed the letter down on the desk top, his mouth white with the anger that suddenly raged through him. 'But he didn't love her.'

'You can't say that, Mark. You don't know.'

'I know this!' He slapped one palm hard down beside the letter lying on the desk. 'I have the evidence here. Some swine persuaded my mother that he loved her, then when she became pregnant he left her alone to face the music!'

'He didn't know.' Isabel tried to rationalise, to ease the hurt he was going through. 'The letter says as much. Our mother had not told him she might be pregnant.'

He got up from the desk, striding to the window overlooking the darkened garden. 'He should not have needed to be told. If a man is old enough to play with fire, he should expect to get burned. But he . . . he didn't stay long enough to burn, he left a young woman to do that. She did all the paying, she did all the suffering married to Luther.' He stopped as if hit by a sudden thought. Turning to face her across the study, his voice was calmer, quieter. 'Just where does Luther figure in this? Why did he marry a woman who was pregnant by another man? And if that letter were not intended for him, what is it doing in his private room?'

'I have asked myself those questions a thousand times,' Isabel answered.

'Show me, Bel. Show me just where you found it.'

Taking up the letter from the desk, Isabel took it to the bookcase. Opening the glass front, she touched a finger to one of the books, hearing Mark's gasp of surprise as it sprang open.

'I found it tucked in there. This was all there was, no envelope, nothing except this one piece of paper.'

'*Our Mutual Friend*.' Pressing the book's spine back into place, Mark read the gilt-lettered title. 'Appropriate. It smacks of Luther. That is just the title he would choose, especially if he and this lover of Mother's knew each other, and if Mother were aware of the fact.' *Our Mutual Friend*! He stared at the book. 'The mutual bit is unavoidable, but friend you could never be!'

'How do you think the letter came to be in Luther's possession? Always assuming it was he who put it there.' Isabel closed the glass doors of the bookcase as her brother turned away.

'I think it is safe to assume that, though how he came to have it is anybody's guess.'

'Mark . . .' Isabel looked at the letter still in her hand. 'Do you think he could have stolen it?'

'Stolen it!' He frowned. 'Why would he do a thing like that?'

'Jealousy,' she mused. 'Spite. Revenge. Luther was capable of all those emotions, he gave way to them regularly. What if somehow he came across this letter addressed to the man Mother was in love with, that he discovered her feelings and was jealous? He could have stolen it to prevent it reaching whomever it was addressed to.'

'It all sounds a bit like a penny dreadful, Bel.'

'But not unlike Luther. You knew him as well as I. He would not think twice about doing something like that, especially if he wanted Mother for his wife and she had refused him.'

'He could never have loved her!' Mark returned bitterly. 'A man who felt any trace of love for a woman would not have treated her as Luther treated our mother.'

'He could have wanted her for his wife without feeling any love for her.'

A silence settled on the room, holding brother and sister in its suffocating folds. It was Mark who spoke first.

'A man who has no love for a woman can't be jealous of her feelings for someone else, Bel, it doesn't make sense.'

'I agree.' She spoke softly as if only now understanding some long-harboured thought. 'But what if he were jealous of the man?'

'Hell, Sis, you can't think Luther was in love with the chap himself!'

'Of course not. But maybe he wanted what Mother had to give.'

'Meaning?'

'Meaning the money she would bring with her when she

married. She told us that her parents settled a large sum on her to be hers when she married; and that money would automatically become her husband's on the day the marriage took place.'

'That part sounds feasible enough, but how does the letter fit into it?'

'We can only surmise, obviously. But what if Luther had been visiting the house where Mother lived, and had seen the letter waiting to be posted and stolen it; not because he knew what it contained but simply as an act of spite. Perhaps he even hoped that on receiving no answer, Mother's feeling would be one of disappointment that would become anger, possibly causing her to turn away from the man to whom it was written and accept Luther instead.'

'It is a bit far-fetched but, as you say, feasible. But guesswork won't help us. We can go on fabricating ideas but we will still end up not knowing who fathered us. Lord, Bel! When I think of how Mother must have felt, I would like to wring the man's neck!'

'Try not to feel too badly.' Going to where he stood, Isabel threaded her arm through his. 'It is all in the past, Mark, let us leave it there.'

Yes, it was in the past, she thought as they left the room together, but would it stay there? Would the question of their parentage remain hidden, or would it rise up from the sad ashes of yesterday to cast its long shadow over the future?

'It'll be a bit of a shock to 'em, but they'll get used to the idea.' The cap he had hastily pulled from his head screwed up in his hand, Edward Perry looked at the young woman who had called him from the foundry floor.

'How do you think they will take to it?' She held the man's blue gaze, her own eyes anxious.

'It'll be as I said. The men will find it more than surprising, but once they sees what your brother wrote, they'll accept it.'

'But to be accountable to a woman! I can see that will take a deal of adjustment on their part.'

'Arrh, so it will.' Edward nodded. 'Be you wanting me to tell 'em?'

The walls of the small office seemed to close in around her. Through its dust-grimed windows the clang of metal bars being drawn along rollers rang like distant bells, and the shouts of men warning of the tipping of molten steel from the crucibles resounded like rifle shots against the brick walls. How could Mark believe she could run a business such as this? How could he expect a woman to handle what was so obviously a man's job? But she had told Jago Timmins that brawn was not the only factor necessary in the successful operation of a business; it needed brain too. Brawn she had none of, but what she possessed of the second she would assuredly use.

'What time will the men be taking their break?'

Edward Perry cast a glance through the murky window. 'Tipping will be over in a couple more minutes, and rods 'ave been drawn. That leaves the furnace. But that won't be opened afore three. I guess the bull will blow in a five minute.'

Isabel nodded. Bradshaw had long ago explained the strange terminology. 'When the steam horn is sounded, do the men congregate in one place to eat their meal?'

'No.' He lifted a forearm to his brow, wiping away a streak of sweat with his shirt sleeve. 'Most of 'em just sits against wherever it was they was working when the bull went, but some goes outside to eat their dinner, 'specially if the weather be clement.'

'The weather is clement today, Mr Perry, so will you ask all the men to give me a little of their dinnertime? I will see to it that they are recompensed in their wages.'

'Ain't no call for you to go telling 'em, if that be what you be planning on doing. Some of the men don't exactly have a pretty turn of speech. Yes, best let me do it, Miss Kenton.'

Miss Kenton. Isabel suppressed a grim smile. Some of these men were going to find it difficult enough to work for a woman.

What if they were to find out that woman was not even a Kenton, that she was not Luther's daughter?

'Thank you, Mr Perry.' Isabel drew a deep breath, her head coming up decisively. 'But this is something I prefer to do myself. The men have to know sometime that it is myself who is now in charge of this foundry. That time might as well be now . . .' She broke off as the deafening blast of a steam horn drowned out all other sounds. Ear-drums vibrating madly, she calmly hitched up her skirt as the sound faded. 'Please have the men assemble in the yard.'

'That be a bloody lie!'

The shout came even before Isabel had finished speaking to the group of men gathered about her in the foundry yard.

'Wouldn't no lad of Luther Kenton as would leave the running of this place to a woman. It be a bloody lie!'

'It be no lie, Ernie Griffin.' Edward Perry turned sharply in the direction of the speaker. 'And you moderate your language in front of a woman.'

'Arrh, language!' The murmur rose in a dozen disapproving voices.

'Her wouldn't be hearing it if her weren't here!' the voice was raised again. 'A steel foundry don't be no place for a woman.'

Standing on the box Perry had found so she could be seen by all, Isabel sought out the man who had shouted.

Smiling deceptively she singled out a heavy-set figure, bare to the waist apart from a flat cap pulled well over a broad low brow and a muffler knotted at his throat. 'A steel foundry may be no place for a woman, but this particular foundry will be no place for you or for any other man who cannot accept the fact that I am mistress now. You have heard the facts: my brother is away in the armed forces and until this war is ended and he returns to Darlaston, the running of this and every other Kenton business is in my hands. If any of you find that too much to stomach then you can pick up your money now.' Breath caught in her throat, Isabel waited. Around her the men muttered to each other but when none moved she went on.

'We have been requested by the government to increase output in every one of our works. In order to do that changes will have to be made . . .'

'Changes?' Ernie Griffin laughed loudly. 'We might have known! First thing a woman does when her gets her hands on anything is make changes, whether they be bloody needed or not. I says we don't need changes at Bull Piece.'

'Fortunately, Mr Griffin, it does not matter what you say.' Isabel gave the man a cold stare before passing her glance over the rest of them, now listening avidly, fear of what that change might mean clearly stamped on every dust-streaked face. 'I have discussed the possibility of removing the process of making gun locks and rifle stocks . . .'

Immediately there was a murmur of dissent. Seeing his chance, Griffin called again: 'That be your way of removing a man's job, of taking the bread out of the mouths of his children. I always knew old Kenton was a bloody catchpenny – seems the females of his family be just as bad. Don't matter who they puts on the streets so long as they be adding to their own purse.'

'This move has nothing to do with saving money.' Isabel raised her hand as the murmurs of dissent mounted. 'And no man will lose his employment as a result of the change. It is my brother's decision to build a new factory for the purpose of making rifles and sidearms for the Army. A piece of land has been selected near Glovers Mound. This will provide easy access to the railway goods line that, thankfully, remains in operation. By locating the manufacture of gun locks and rifle stocks there, we will have more space here to expand our steel production.'

'Arrh, and add to the time a man spends walking to his work.'

'Glovers Mound ain't but three minutes up the road, Griffin,' Edward Perry answered him. 'Won't make no difference, you'll still be in the Widows long enough to drink yourself stupid.'

'Might make no difference to you, Perry,' Griffin spat, 'you be like to fall in with anything her says, but it makes a difference to we lot, don't it, lads?'

'There be a war on, Ernie,' a man beside him answered.

'Arrh, that's right!' a second man called. 'There be a war on. Won't 'urt you to walk a few yards extra, Griffin, get some of that lard off you.'

'Arrh, you be getting as fat as a pork pig, Ernie!'

This last comment caused a wave of laughter that deepened the scowl on the workman's round face.

'Won't none of we be fat against her be finished,' he growled. 'This be only the start. I told you her was a bloody catchpenny – like as not we'll all be out of a job afore her bloody change-making be done with! I tell you not to be putting up with 'em, we don't want no changes.'

'I promised that no one would lose his employment.' Isabel raised her voice, calling out strongly over the voices anxiously questioning that last comment. 'However, it would appear that the changes I have outlined are too much for you to cope with, Mr Griffin. Therefore in your case I withdraw my promise. You are dismissed. Collect your pay from the cashier. You are no longer an employee of Kenton's.' Her eyes flashed. 'Should any other man wish to query my plan he is free to go too!'

'You be the true bloody spawn of Luther Kenton!' Griffin pushed aside the men flanking him. 'But you won't get the better of Ernie Griffin. Kenton's don't be the only place can provide a man with a living.'

''Course not, Ernie,' a voice called from the group of men around him. 'A man with your brawn can get taken on anywhere. You might even try the Army!'

'He won't do that,' another answered. 'Griffin has the brawn all right, but he ain't got the bottle for the Army. Their fighting be too straight cut for him. A knife in a back alley be more his style, We've heard what you had to say, Miss Kenton, and it be all right with us. You build your factory and we'll make the

Army its guns. Who knows? Ernie might end up carrying one, whether he agrees to it or not.'

'They've heard what you said and you've heard what they said.' Griffin's look was murderous as he stepped closer to the box Isabel stood on. 'Now you hear what Ernie Griffin says. You watch yourself, daughter of Luther Kenton . . . you watch yourself real careful!'

True spawn of Luther Kenton . . . Isabel's hands trembled as she drove her carriage away from the foundry. His blood did not run in her veins. But which was the stronger: blood or a lifetime's influence?

Chapter Four

Standing in the crowd of people lining the Bull Stake, Isabel turned up the collar of her belted grey woollen jacket against the chill of the February wind. Mark had said the war would be finished and over by Christmas, but they were into a new year and as yet there was no sign of hostilities ending. His last letter refused to leave her mind:

> *A couple of our kites did not make it home. They bought it somewhere over Le Câteau. The news left everyone feeling very down. Losing two of our four pilots means Goosey and I will be doing extra flights until we can get more trained flyers.*
>
> *I miss you, Bel, and trust to God this war will end soon.*

More flying! Isabel felt a cold misery touch her soul. Much of the tomboy bravado had gone from Mark's letters, replaced by an air of seriousness that left her more afraid for him than before. What were the men suffering in France, and how much of the truth was being told here at home?

'Sign up, lads, and you could drive a tank like this one. Think how it would feel to have the power of this machine under you.' The loud voice of the recruiting sergeant floated over the crowd, driving away the thought of Mark's letter.

'Eh! It's grand, don't you think, miss? I wish I was old enough to join the Army, it would be grand to ride in one of them.'

And grand to die in one? Isabel looked at the boy who had spoken to her. Ten years old at the most, his face pinched with cold held a look of rapture. How like Mark's own look of six months ago. It had all seemed exciting to him too then. But now?

'Our Percy be goin' to join.' The lad stood on tiptoe, straining to get a clearer view of the massive machine. ''E be signing for the Staffords. Our dad were with them in South Africa. He reckons the South Staffordshire Regiment be the best fighters in the whole British Army.'

'I am sure they are very brave.' Isabel tried to smile, reluctant to dampen the boy's enthusiasm.

'They am, miss.' Beneath its flat cap the small face glowed with pride. 'My dad got a medal. 'E wanted to join up with the Staffords again but 'e ain't got but one leg – the other one were sliced off by a African. But our Percy be going and I bet 'e gets a medal an' all. Might be 'e will get two; our Percy ain't frightened of nobody. I bet 'e soon sees them Germans off.'

'C'mon, lads. Who will be the first to set his name to paper? Who will be first to enlist for King and Country? William Holden, landlord of the Castle Hotel here behind me, has set aside a room for the signing of recruits and will give a quart of his finest old ale to every man who pledges himself to fight for England.'

The recruiting officer's shout preventing the need to reply, Isabel watched the boy wriggle to the front of the listening crowd, then felt herself jostled as men from all sides began to move towards the beer house.

'Steady, miss!'

A hand fastened on her arm, steadying her as she was pushed from behind.

'It be men the officer called for. I don't think the Army be wanting women just yet so there be no need to go breaking your neck to join!'

'I . . . I'm sorry.' Isabel gasped as a fresh jolt sent her stumbling against the man who held her.

'I think it might be best if you were out of this.' Taller than her by several inches, he glanced about them. 'That sergeant already has the crowd whipped up to a fervour and when some of these men mix a few pints of beer with their heightened feelings, things could start to get rough.'

'I think you may be right.' She winced as a heavy boot caught her ankle. 'But how? We are wedged in quite solidly.'

'Hold on.' The man smiled as he threw an arm about her shoulders. Using his body like a battering ram, he forced a way through the crowd. Clinging to him, her face turned towards his chest to avoid jostling arms and elbows, Isabel allowed herself to be propelled along.

'I . . . I had no idea so many people would be here,' she panted when at last the man stopped and released her.

'I don't know if this be the way you wanted to be brought? If not, I suggest you let some of them folk get away home afore you go trying to force your way through them again, though when they will begin to break up be anybody's guess.'

'This is the way I wanted to come.' Isabel glanced back at the crowd blocking the length of Pinfold Street.

'You live here, on the Cross?'

Isabel answered while straightening the grey toque hat that had been pushed askew in the struggle to escape the crowd. 'Not actually on Catherine's Cross. My home is a little further on, along Woods Bank.'

'You have a position in one of the houses up there?'

Isabel smiled, letting a nod serve for answer.

'Pity I be off to join the regiment tomorrow, or maybe you would have let me call on you. That's if you don't be spoken for?'

'No.' She dropped her eyes. 'I am not spoken for.'

'In that case, allow me to see you home, Miss . . .'

'Isabel . . . Isabel Kenton.'

Embarrassment replacing his smile the man's grey eyes held hers for a moment before he looked down at his feet. 'Kenton? Be you Luther Kenton's daughter?'

She could have said no and it would have been the truth. Instead she nodded.

'Eh, miss, I didn't know!' A flush rose sharply to his cheeks. 'I beg your pardon for handling you like that.'

'It is as well you did, Mr . . .?

'Hawley.' He ran his hand through his thick dark hair, the movement tumbling it forward over his brow. 'James Hawley. Eh, had I known who you were, I would never have been so forward as to ask to call on you. I beg your pardon again, miss.'

'There is no need, Mr Hawley. I took no offence.' A smile touching the corners of her mouth, Isabel held out her hand. 'Thank you for coming to my assistance. Without your help I would never have broken away from the crowd. I wish you God speed and hope you return home safely.'

Away towards the Bull Stake, the roars of the crowd mounted.

'Seems like they have Julian on the move.'

'Julian?'

'The tank.'

'Is that what it is called, a Julian tank?'

'I don't think so.' He grinned, the flush fading from his cheeks. 'Each one that be built gets some bloke slapping a name to it, though I reckon that particular one be a mite fancy for a tank coming to boost recruitment in Darlaston. Might have been more suitable to send us an Eli or an Enoch. P'raps even a William, but never a Julian, not to the Black Country. They'll have to guard that thing well tonight, and even then I doubt it will still be a Julian when they come to move it on.'

'Do you hope to drive a tank, Mr Hawley?'

Without thinking he slid one arm protectively around her as a steam tram clanked noisily towards them, then dropped it as the vehicle trundled on its way. 'I don't have my sights set on a tank. I'll just get on with whatever it is they set me to. I don't see this war as a crusade, nor do I see it as a chance for fun and games like so many do. To my mind it will be better for everybody when it all be over.'

'I think that too, Mr Hawley. Good afternoon, and once again – God speed.'

'You never should have gone there at all, and 'specially not without you had somebody with you. Whatever would Mr Mark say if you was to have gone and got yourself 'urt?'

'But I did not get myself hurt, Mrs Bradshaw.' Isabel removed her hat. 'The crowd were all very friendly.'

'Arrh, I know,' the housekeeper replied sharply. 'I've seen the likes of that lot afore. They can be friendly one minute and the next – huh! They can go up like dry straw in a barn. I tell you, you best keep away. Feelings be runnin' high in the town; there's men has the blood fever in their veins with all this talk of rallying to King and Country. Don't be no telling what might happen, and you shouldn't be going along to such meetings, it don't be safe!'

'I'm sorry, Mrs Bradshaw.' Isabel assumed her most innocent look. 'I did not think.'

'That be the trouble with most young today!' Letty Bradshaw grumbled, taking advantage of her many years at Woodbank House. 'They never stop to think. I just be glad the old master ain't here. There would have been hell to pay if he had been! He would have given you a right old tongue lashing, miss, and you would have deserved it!'

Yes, Luther would have taken advantage of the situation. Isabel walked up to her room as the housekeeper returned to the kitchen. He would have delivered a tongue lashing but she doubted it would have arisen from any fear for her safety; more likely from another act of spite.

Why had her mother done it? In her room Isabel removed her coat, hanging it in the wardrobe. Why had she agreed to become that man's wife?

Catching sight of herself in the long mirror that stood between her wardrobe and dressing table, Isabel stared at a reflection that closely resembled her mother's. The same rich auburn hair, the same camellia-soft skin, the same high sculpted cheekbones and beautifully shaped mouth. Only the eyes were different. In place of the green ones that had held an eternal sadness, the pair that gazed back at Isabel were of hazel only lightly stippled with green – but it was a greenness that held a slumbering fire.

Smoothing her grey dress, she touched the band of black circling her left arm and lifted her head defiantly. She had all of her mother's soft beauty but she had something more besides and it had not been put there by Luther Kenton. Yes, it could be said that he had instilled determination in her, but it was a determination never again to follow in his footsteps, never to defeat others using hatred or spite. No, what she felt inside of her had not been a legacy of either of the two people she thought her parents. She felt a genuine interest in others – an interest her mother's sorrow had kept her from experiencing as she withdrew further and further behind her wall of misery, and one that had never developed in Luther.

'Why, Mother?' Isabel whispered to her reflection. 'Why did you marry him?'

I could not take you there. The words crept softly into her mind but with a clarity that held her attention, while the eyes in the mirror deepened to a sea green, the moisture of their silent tears reflecting the fading light. *I could not go to Victoria Road, I could not have my baby in that place, Forgive me, dearest child, forgive me . . .*

'Mother!' The illusion had been so strong that its fading tore at her heart. Isabel sank to the floor, rocking back and forth, sobbing out her hurt and loss as she had on that day ten years ago when her mother had finally given up the will to live. Victoria Road! Her mother had not been able to submit to the workhouse.

'Why did he leave you, Mother?' she sobbed. 'Why did he go away? Why . . . why?'

But in the silence of her room there came no answer.

*

'Excuse me, Miss Isabel, but Edward Perry be here. He says to tell you he wants to speak to you.'

Isabel looked up from the letter she was writing.

'Ask him to come back this evening. I have rather a lot of work . . .'

'He said as it was important.'

'Important?' Her glance dropped back to the letter.

'Something about the steel foundry. Said work was almost to a standstill.'

'What!' Dropping the pen, she ordered the manservant: 'Show him in here.'

'What has happened?' Isabel almost hurled the question at the charge hand, sparing no time for pleasantries.

'The men from the foundry at Bull Piece . . . most of 'em be jacking it in.'

'Leaving?' she asked, disbelief outweighing surprise. 'But why, for what reason?'

Edward Perry twisted his cap in his hands as he searched for gentle words, then finding none answered bluntly: 'The best reason of all in their eyes – money. It be money as be taking them. Timmins be offering thirty bob a week more than you be paying. That be where the men are going.'

One pound, ten shillings? Isabel did not need to calculate to know she could not top that offer, and even if she could reason told her Jago would then raise his own offer higher still. He had threatened she would be out business in three months. It seemed warfare had begun.

'How many of our workers say they are leaving?'

'About a dozen so far, miss, and most of them be furnace hands.'

The heaviest and most important work. Isabel's mind darted frantically in search of answers. Without the furnace, the steel foundry could not operate.

'On top of that there be a good couple of dozen as be off to the Army come the weekend. That recruiting drive as was held on the Bull Stake Saturday gone, together with Lord

Kitchener's posters, has the men of this town enlisting in droves.'

'But what of the munitions works? How can they keep going without men to operate them?'

'The government don't ask that!' The charge hand shook his head solemnly. 'They tells you what it is they want then takes the men. How you fulfil your delivery quota after that . . . well, seems they don't think as far as that.

It certainly seemed to be as he said. The government was lacking in foresight if it could not see that steel could not be made without the men to smelt and draw it. It needed strength to shovel pig iron into the furnace, strength to tip crucibles of molten metal and strength to draw ingots of steel through the rollers, teasing it into long bars. Take that strength away and the whole process would cease.

'I must write to my brother. Ask him what is to be done.'

'Begging your pardon, Miss Kenton, but there don't be time for that. It be my reckoning that by the time a letter comes back from France, or wherever Mr Kenton be, the foundry will be closed down.'

He was right. Isabel turned towards the window. Outside an overnight fall of snow covered the garden, turning it into a still, quiet scene. It would be so easy to give in, to let Kenton Engineering go, to do what she had so long promised herself to do: leave this house and everything it stood for behind her and to find a quiet place where she could live in peace.

Peace! From somewhere beyond the grave Luther's voice seemed to mock her. *Take it, take your peace.*

You win, Luther, she answered her own thoughts. You win, but only for a little while longer. Turning to face her charge hand, she said: 'Give me a moment to get a coat then we will go to Bull Piece together.'

'Can we replace the men who leave?'

Isabel drove her own small trap along Pinfold Street, calling softly to the mare who tossed her head nervously as trams rattled past.

'I wouldn't bet more than a brass farthing on that.' Edward Perry held tightly to the narrow polished brass rail that ran around the sides of the trap. He had nothing against a woman running a house or even a steel foundry, but driving a trap!

'There must be *some* men who are in need of employment?'

'Not in Darlaston there ain't.' Edward held his breath as they crossed the Bull Stake, busy with carts and wagons bound for the railway goods depot. 'Nor in Wednesbury if what I hears in the Frying Pan be anything to go by.'

'What of those men we have in the new factory at Glovers Mound?' Isabel caught her breath sharply as a heavily laden wagon turned across her path, causing the mare to shy.

'If we pull them out how do we continue the making of sidearms and rifles?' Perry asked, relief coursing through him when the trap did not overturn. 'That just be robbing Peter to pay Paul, there be little sense in it.'

Turning left in Avenue Road, Isabel realised the truth of his words. There could be no solution in bringing men from one place of work to another. Without steel there could be no guns and without guns she could not fulfil her commitment to the government. Jago must have known all of this when he made his offer. How he must be laughing!

'When have the man asked to leave?'

'Tonight. And they haven't asked, they've said. Come right flat out with it. They're finishing tonight and that be all there is to it. They were all for going right off to Jago Timmins's place there and then but I managed to talk them into seeing the day through, though it weren't easy. Money be a powerful weapon, miss. Most often it can beat the strongest of men, 'specially where there be families to be considered.'

'I understand, Mr Perry. Thank you for trying.'

'Sorry I weren't more successful, miss, but like I say, money be money and men will go where it be most plentiful every time.'

Drawing into the yard of the foundry, Isabel nodded to the timekeeper who shuffled out of the little office where the start and finish of every man's shift was recorded against his name.

'Assemble the men here in the yard,' she ordered.

'But it don't be wanting many minutes before the furnaces will be ready for opening.'

'The furnaces can wait!' she answered the objection abruptly. 'I want to speak to them, every single one. Do as I say and fetch them out here.'

Outside his little office the elderly timekeeper shivered in the raw February air, but sensing Isabel's anger he denied himself the pleasure of returning to his glowing coal fire. An argument was too entertaining to miss and judging by the look on the face of Kenton's daughter this one threatened to be a right bust up.

'I am informed there are those among you who wish to leave my brother's employ?' Isabel began, breath showing white on the cold air as she faced the group of men brought grumbling into the cold. 'I am told you wish to work for Jago Timmins. But does that not involve a longer walk to and from your place of work? Joynson Street is further away than Glovers Mound yet you objected to the walk there.'

'I'm willing to walk twice the distance for the money Timmins be offering,' a voice called from the group.

Climbing back into the trap the more easily to be seen, Isabel glanced along the line of faces until she found the one she was looking for. The months since taking Kenton's into her own hands had not been idly spent. She could, if called upon, put a name to every man now watching her.

'I see,' she called, her voice hard as the frost-gripped ground. 'You are willing to sacrifice your son's chance of having the best, are you, Elijah Price?'

'My son be in France fighting for this bloody country!'

'While his father quibbles over money!'

'What the hell do you mean by that?' The man's anger rose. 'A man has a right to the best in life and that be what I'm taking, the best offer.'

Isabel stood for several seconds, allowing a mocking smile to curve her mouth. 'Oh, you are doing that, Elijah. You are taking the best offer life is making. But what of your son? What offer are you making him – or does he not have that same right to the best . . . does his life not matter?'

'You ain't talking to me like that!' Furious now, the foundry man elbowed his way through the listening group, bounding towards the trap. 'Woman or no woman, I ain't taking that!'

'Eh up, Elijah!' Edward Perry stepped between the man and the trap, pushing a restraining hand against his chest. 'You'll strike no woman while I be standing here!'

'Then bloody well shift!' Anger blinding him, he struck out but the charge hand did not move.

'You want me to shift, Elijah, then you step away or else shift me yourself.'

'That I can bloody well do an' all!'

'No doubt you can,' Perry answered calmly. 'But they will carry the both of us away and Jago Timmins might not wait the length of time it will take your bones to mend. Think of that before you set to breaking mine.'

'There was no call for her to bring my lad into this.'

'He's right, miss.' Perry glanced up at Isabel. 'I reckon as you should apologise.'

'He was *not* right!' Isabel's eyes flashed defiance. 'I asked him, does his son not have the right to the best? And I ask again: does the life of his son, and every mother's son, not matter?'

'Of course it matters.' Elijah's hand closed over that set against his chest but did not move it. 'They all matter.'

'Then why deny them the best? You have said it yourself, you have all said it!' Isabel's voice rang out in the crisp air as she looked again at the assembled workmen. 'Kenton's make the finest guns anywhere in the country, and that means anywhere in the world. Yet by taking away your labour you would bring their production to an end. You would take away the finest protection our soldiers have. Is that what you want for your lad, Elijah . . . will any other rifle do for him so long as you are getting a higher wage? Is it thirty shillings you will be taking – or thirty pieces of silver?

'Consider, all of you, what higher price can the sons of England pay than to give their lives protecting their homes and loved ones? You cannot give a Kenton gun to every man in the Army but you can give them to some. I ask you now: give them to the ones you can.'

Isabel's voice softened and her eyes lost the gleam of anger as they rested on the man below her. 'I ask *you*, Elijah, give your son what chance you can of life, give him what you have always given him – the very best you can.'

'That be all well an' good for her to say.' Another voice rose in the silence that settled as Isabel finished speaking. 'It ain't her working her guts out in front of a furnace; it ain't her sweating her brains out for three pound a week! I say we take Timmins's offer!'

'An' I say her *do* be right!' Elijah Price knocked away Edward Perry's hand that still pressed against his chest, wheeling round to face his fellows. 'Kenton's *do* make the best, you all knows it, and I say we will give our men the best – as many guns as God provides us with the strength to make. Elijah Price will be stopping on here at Bull Piece, making the steel he has always made. Any man choosing to take Timmins's offer be free to do so, but he'd best not spend it in the Frying Pan, or any other place he might chance meeting me!'

'Or me.' Edward Perry stepped forward, one hand resting now on the shoulder of his workmate Elijah, a finger of the other touching the end of his flattened nose. 'I didn't box for the regiment for nothing. It might not bother you too much, just having Elijah to contend with. But he won't be on his own – I shall be with him.'

Watching the last man return to the foundry, Isabel sank down to the driving seat of the trap, every inch of her shaking.

'You did well, miss.' Edward Perry patted her hand. 'There ain't many young women would have stood up to that lot. It took some doing. But then I don't suppose there be many women the like of Luther Kenton's daughter.'

There it was again – Luther Kenton's daughter! Taking the reins in her hands, Isabel drove from the foundry yard.

Edward Perry was perhaps right in supposing not many women would face up to a group of men and challenge their loyalties. But he had not been even partly right to suppose there were not many the like of Luther Kenton's daughter. Luther Kenton had no daughter. But how many other women resembled the one who had been raised in his house, the bastard daughter of a broken-hearted woman and an unknown man?

Beneath the clatter of her horse's hooves Isabel could almost hear the soft sound of mocking laughter.

Chapter Five

Sealing the letter she had written to Mark, Isabel held it for a moment, the address turned up to her. Had that other letter once been in an envelope which bore an address? If so where was it now, and whose name had been written upon it?

'Maybe my idea did resemble a penny dreadful, Mark,' she whispered. 'But even penny dreadfuls can contain an element of truth, no matter how bizarre.'

Perhaps Luther had stolen her mother's letter? Laying her own aside, she reached her grey coat from the wardrobe.

Perhaps having read the letter he'd decided for whatever reason to keep it, but had destroyed the envelope so nothing would ever disclose the fact that he was not the true recipient. But in that case, why keep the letter?

She buttoned her coat, fingers blindly threading the line of jet buttons through the button holes as her mind dwelt on the events of long ago.

It could not have been in order to blackmail her mother; Victoria was already his wife and too much under his yoke for him to need that threat.

No, it was not his wife the letter had been intended to threaten. Her grey close-fitting hat lifted halfway to her head, Isabel stood stunned as realisation dawned. It was not her mother Luther Kenton intended to blackmail, it was her mother's children! That letter was kept for use as a weapon against them!

Lowering the hat, Isabel closed her eyes as a long breath shuddered through her. That was how he'd intended to keep them subject to his will. Luther had kept that letter as a form of insurance. Oh, perhaps he had not realised it at the time, but later, as their dislike of him showed, and as Mark became more rebellious at the thought of working under the direction of the man he thought to be his father, Luther must have come to see the letter as his way of holding them, guessing correctly they would not see their mother's name dragged through the mud.

Opening her eyes, Isabel set the hat on her head, thrusting a pearl-knobbed hat pin into the side and securing it to her hair.

But Luther was dead. He could no longer dominate her or Mark. He would never now use that letter to impose his will upon them. Mark was free, she was free. So why was it she still felt Luther's presence all around her? Why was her freedom no freedom at all?

Taking up her letter, Isabel walked slowly down the stairs of Woodbank House. Neither of them would be sacrificed to Kenton Engineering, that had been her promise to Mark. But wasn't she already sacrificed?

'There you be, miss.' Letty Bradshaw bustled from the kitchen, her plum-coloured coat stretched over her ample frame, an outdated bonnet covering her fading brown hair. 'I've left a pan of soup simmering on the hob for when you gets back. A cup of that will be right welcome then, I reckons. Bradshaw says it be too cold for the pawnshop's sign to be out today. Be you sure you should go, miss?'

'I don't wish to be the only woman in Darlaston who does not see those men off.'

'Then I'll come with you.'

'No, Mrs Bradshaw. You and your husband will go to your sister's as planned. She will need someone with her when her son goes.'

'Arrh, miss, 'er will.' Letty paused in pulling on the gloves she had knitted herself. 'He be her one lad. Ain't never had no other, nor no wench either. Seems we were not meant to have many kids, what with Bradshaw and me having none at all. But my sister's lad, young Billy, he were like a son to us.'

'Have you got those warm woollens you have made for him?'

Seeing the bloom of tears settle over the older woman's eyes, Isabel tried to sound matter-of-fact, though the pain of her own parting from her brother still smarted.

'I have, miss.' Letty sniffed loudly. 'A scarf, a couple of pairs of thick gloves, four pairs of socks and more on the needles. Our Billy won't go being cold, not if me and his mother have anything to do with it.'

. 'I am sure he won't. It is a pity I cannot knit or I could have helped.'

'It weren't for the want of trying.' A little smile edged along Letty's lips. 'I sat for hours with you as a child trying to teach you the skills of the knitting pins and the sewing needle but you never did pick it up. Somehow your fingers never could manage work of that sort.'

'They were all thumbs.' Isabel smiled, remembering the long sessions spent trying to master the intricacies of manipulating wool and thick wooden pins, only to fail dismally.

'Reckon they was. But we ain't all intended to do the same work. The Lord has His own uses for every one of us – and yours ain't for the knitting of socks.'

'Then for what? I cannot see the work that is intended for me.'

Letty reached for the basket she had set on the hall table. 'That be 'cos the Lord ain't showed you. He ain't ready for His work to be done yet. Mark my words, when time be ripe the apple will fall.'

'But what can I do? I can't take a gun and go to war.' Isabel reached for her grey chamois gloves.

'Bide your time. That's what you can do till you be shown otherwise!' Letty caught the fine leather gloves, replacing them with a pair of grey woollen ones taken from her basket. 'In the meantime wear gloves that will do more to keep your fingers from turning into icicles!'

This chiding bringing a smile to her lips, Isabel tucked her letter to Mark in the pocket of her coat and left the house. But as she walked down the gentle slope that formed Woods Bank she though of Letty's words. Was there a way she could help fight this war? She had hoped to train for nursing, but then who would run Kenton Engineering? She smiled grimly to herself. If the Lord had any sort of work in mind for her, He must first break Luther Kenton's hold.

King Street was thickly lined with people and Isabel found herself having to push her way through to the Post Office. Dropping her letter into the red-painted box set into the wall, she heard the sound of music drifting from Victoria Park around the corner.

'They're coming! I can hear them, Mother, the soldiers – they're coming!'

On the edge of the footpath a small boy jumped up and down with excitement but his mother ignored him, her head turned like every other in the direction of Victoria Road.

'Hooray! Hooray for the soldiers.'

Across the street another child joined his shout to the first, a shout that was taken up by the crowd as the bandsmen swung around the corner leading a procession of motor vehicles such as the town had never seen. Standing on tiptoe, Isabel stared at what seemed like motor carriages with driving seat and leather canopy mounted on a metal frame, but where the passenger seat should have been the body had been extended and now each had a long open box-like structure along which was painted the names of the owners or firms from which the army had requisitioned them: Garround's, Mason Aerated Water, Hudson's Quality Soap. Isabel noticed the names as the procession passed slowly by, but it was the men crammed into them that held her attention. Tall, short, young and maybe not so young, they stood packed together like fish in a barrel, every face wreathed in smiles. Then the face she had searched for was suddenly before her and Isabel raised a hand to her lips, a gesture of silent farewell to the young man who had rescued her from the crowds.

'I 'ope the war will be on when I be grown up, I want to get to ride in a cart without a horse!' Beside his mother, the small boy continued to jump up and down with enthusiasm. Only Isabel saw the shadow of fear cross the woman's face. A fear that was echoed in her own heart.

Trumpets blasting, drums beating, the vehicles passed by on their way to war; the shouts of other men's pride and the whispered blessings of the women seeing them out of sight.

What happens when the music fades and the cheers die? Isabel wondered as she turned away. Who would be there to whisper blessings when these men fell on the battle field?

Oh, Lord, let me help, she prayed silently. Show me what to do.

'Miss Kenton.'

The voice came softly from the dense shadow of the hedge abutting the gates of Woodbank House, startling Isabel so that she stepped sharply back. Mrs Bradshaw had warned her against walking out alone in these disturbed times, but surely she was safe enough in Darlaston?

But safe or not, her voice shook as she called: 'Who's there? Show yourself or I . . . I will call a constable!'

'Don't do that, miss. I mean no harm, truly. I . . . I only wants to speak with you.'

Hidden between the stone pillar of the gatepost and the thick yew hedge, a figure stepped forward. Isabel threw a quick glance back the way she had come but no one was about on the now silent Katherine's Cross. Night seemed to be rapidly approaching and the raw cold had dispersed the crowds quickly.

'I won't keep you but a minute, miss.'

By the last of the dying light Isabel looked at the thin figure of a woman, heavy boots showing beneath her ragged black skirts, head and face almost entirely hidden beneath a dark shawl clutched tightly around her breasts.

'What do you want?' Her initial nervousness fading, Isabel tried looking closer at the woman but she stepped back as if afraid of being recognised.

'I was 'oping . . .' The woman hesitated, glancing all around them with the quick nervous movements born of fear. 'I want to ask . . .'

'Look, don't be afraid. I did not mean it when I threatened to call for a constable.' Isabel took a step forward but stopped as the woman moved, keeping a distance between them.

'Whatever it is you wish to talk about, let us do so in the house. It is far too cold to stand here.'

'In the 'ouse!' The woman's voice was fearful. 'I . . . I can't. I mean . . . I don't want to be a trouble to you, miss.'

'The only trouble to me is standing here freezing! Come inside. A bowl of hot soup and a fire will make talking much easier.'

'No! No, I can't be going into a 'ouse like that.'

'That is your decision. But I am most certainly going indoors.' Isabel set off briskly for the house, and moments later heard the sound of boots scuffling along behind.

Thinking her visitor might be more relaxed in the kitchen than in the sitting room, Isabel made her way to the rear of the house.

'Come over to the fire.' Removing her own coat, she drew two chairs close to the shining black cast-iron range, a bed of coals glowing at its centre, the kettle on the hob and roasting spits gleaming in its light.

The woman's eyes darted about the neat kitchen, taking in the dresser which reached almost to the ceiling, rows of white plates and dishes of all sizes filling each of its five rows of shelves, the space beneath its flat table-like surface being given to a range of white jugs; on the opposite wall copper pans and moulds hung above a long wooden side table that also displayed kitchen implements.

Turning up the gas light Isabel felt thankful that Luther had introduced it into the house as the pale lemony glow pushed away the shadows; it was much more convenient than paraffin lamps, though Mrs Bradshaw vowed she would: ''ave nothing to do with that new fangled way. Food don't taste the same cooked in that there gas stove!'

Reaching two large cups from the dresser, Isabel filled them with soup left simmering on a bracket beside the fire, handing one to the woman who still stood hesitantly beside the door.

'I prefer to take my soup this way.' She smiled, holding her cup between both hands, relishing the heat on her cold fingers. 'I think it tastes better, don't you?'

The woman's eyes flickered from the soup cup to Isabel, then back to the cup. In the stronger light her face looked thin and drawn. 'I ain't come in search of charity.'

'And I am offering none.' Isabel placed the woman's cup on the table that occupied the centre of the kitchen, taking up her own and going to sit on one of the chairs she had drawn to the fire. 'I beg your pardon if I have offended you, I meant only to be polite. The evening is so cold, I thought something to warm us both would be a good idea. With your permission I will drink mine while you tell me what it is you wish to speak to me about.'

'It . . . it be about my husband.' The woman took a step forward, her heavy boots scraping on the stone-flagged floor. 'I want to ask . . . will you give him a job, miss?'

'A job?' Isabel's surprise showed. She had not known what to expect of this drab woman who looked half starved, but this was the very last thing she would have imagined.

'Yes, miss, a job.'

'He could apply at the foundry or any of the works for employment. Why send you . . . and why here?'

'Oh, he didn't send me!' the woman answered quickly. 'He don't know as I've come. There would be hell to pay if he did.'

67

Putting her cup aside, Isabel watched the woman tug at her shawl nervously. If it would cause her trouble to come here, then why had she come?

'Your husband,' she asked, 'has he already applied for employment?'

The woman nodded, glance dropping. 'Yes, miss. He asked at Kenton's foundry but they refused to set him on.'

Isabel felt her surprise returning. With the Army draining the town of manpower every man capable of work was assured of a job, so why had this woman's husband been refused?

'Your husband,' she asked again, 'does he have some disability that would prevent him from working in the steel foundry?'

'No, he ain't no cripple.' The woman shook her head. 'He's worked in the steel from being a lad.'

'If he has been employed in the process of steel-making for what I presume must be a number of years then I would have expected him to have been welcomed into the foundry with open arms. But as he was not there has to be a reason. Will you tell me that reason?'

Isabel heard a muffled sob as the woman lifted her hand, pressing it hard against her mouth.

'It . . . it be his temper, miss.' She managed to fight back the sobs. 'He never could hold his temper, especially when he's in drink. He would fight with the devil himself when he's been on the beer.'

'And that is often?'

Her sobs overwhelming her, the woman answered with a nod. Going to her, Isabel put an arm about her, gently ushering her to the chair before the fire. Then, when her tears had subsided, handed the woman the cup of soup and waited while she drank it.

'We've been to most parts of the country,' she continued her tale. 'A few months here, a few there. Always he got work and always he lost it through fighting or playing his mouth. Folk would put up with it for a time but always it finished up the

68

same way: draw your pay and don't come back. I thought that after the kids come he would alter but he never has.' She looked up, her eyes filled with worry. 'I just don't know what to do. He can't get work and yet he won't move on. Says there be something he has to do in Darlaston, though what it can be I have no idea. I do as much as I can, I've found a job washing in several of the houses round about, but as fast as I earn it, he spends it. It's getting so I can't feed my kids!'

'How many children do you have, Mrs . . .'

'Griffin.' The woman placed her empty cup on the table.

Griffin! The name was instantly familiar. Isabel had sacked a man named Griffin not long after assuming control of Kenton's. He too had been a loud, argumentative character. Was that man this woman's husband? If so it would explain why he had been refused employment at the foundry.

'I've got two children,' the woman answered. 'There would have been four but . . .'

'How old are they?' Isabel asked, seeing a twist of pain around the other woman's mouth.

'The lad be sixteen come spring and my girl will be fifteen come midsummer. They're two good kids, both find work wherever we go and be well liked by them as takes them on. But it always comes to the same thing in the end. Their father gets the sack and they has to move on.'

'Mrs Griffin, is your husband the same Ernie Griffin dismissed from my brother's employ some weeks ago?'

The woman's glance dropped to her lap, her only answer being a faint nod. Isabel looked at the skirts, too thin and worn to hold any more patches, the boots which were much too big and obviously made for a man, and felt a tug of sympathy. But if she gave the man back his job it could be construed as weakness; every other man in her employ could see it as a chance to defy her. And Jago Timmins? He had said she would fail; had already made one attempt to bring the Kenton foundry to a standstill. To be seen to back down in this matter would be a perfect invitation for him to try again.

'You say the children find work each time – have they found it in Darlaston?' Again a faint nod answered Isabel's question.

They should have been better off than the woman's ragged clothing indicated. It would not be a large wage two such young-sters brought home each week, but coupled with the woman's own earnings they would have enough to live on. But had she not said her man took what she had and spent it on drink? Doubtless the same happened to whatever the children earned.

Isabel stood up, knowing that what she had to say would be difficult.

'Mrs Griffin, I am sorry but Kenton's will not re-engage your husband. However, should your children or yourself at any time be in need of employment you will find it with me. My de-cision, I am certain, will be approved of by my brother.'

Her feet shuffling to find a grip inside the over-large boots, the woman got slowly to her feet. Drawing the shawl that despite the warmth of the kitchen had remained draped about her head even closer, she turned towards the door.

'I thank you for your time, miss, and for your kind offer on behalf of me and mine. I'll say goodnight to you.'

'Would you please take the soup?' Isabel asked, drawn between needing to stay firm yet wanting so much to help.

The woman turned and in the glow of the gas mantel Isabel saw the pride in her eyes. 'I did not come here to beg, and I'll take no charity.'

'I . . . I'm sorry,' Isabel apologised.

Recognising the distress in her face, the woman's eyes softened.

'But neither will I refuse an act of kindness. I will take the soup, and thank you, and with the Lord's help one day I might find a way to repay you.'

Taking a basin from a cupboard, Isabel strove to think of a way to put her next thought into words that would not wound. But was there a way of taking a woman's children from her and not causing pain? Ladling the hot contents of the pot into the basin, she at last made the attempt.

'Mrs Griffin, it is likely you will have to leave Darlaston if your husband is to find work.' She fetched a breakfast plate from the dresser, placing it over the basin for a lid. 'I have no doubt you will go with him then.'

'It be my place, miss, being his wife.'

'Of course.' Taking a clean cloth from the dresser drawer, Isabel brought it to the table. Spreading it, she stood the basin in its centre. 'I understand. But the children . . .' bringing two opposite corners of the cloth together she fastened them over the basin ' . . . do they also have to go? They are of an age where they could be left with someone you trust to care for them.' Tying the two remaining corners of the cloth, she felt the silence bear in on her.

'Leave my little 'uns!' The woman's voice carried a note of stunned horror that caught at Isabel's heart.

'I know how hard that would be for you,' she said softly, 'but isn't it hard for your children, moving every few months, finding work only to have to leave it again as quickly, to see . . .'

'To see their earnings splashed against a wall somewhere?' The woman finished the sentence albeit differently from the way Isabel would have. 'They works their guts out and their father drinks what they fetch in then piddles it up against a wall. Arrh, that be hard, it would be hard for any lad or wench, but what other course can I take? I've got no kin – none that would risk having Ernie Griffin banging at their door.'

'I would take that risk.'

'You miss?' Across the broad table the woman's face creased into a puzzled frown. 'You would take my kids?'

'If you would be willing to entrust them to me, I would find work for them both here at the house. They would have a room each to sleep in and their keep. My housekeeper would look after their meals.' Isabel smiled. 'Your daughter would be of help in the house while the boy would be found work in the stable and gardens. They would both be paid a wage of two pounds a month which could either be paid directly to them or kept until you yourself could come to collect it.'

'Two pounds!' It was barely a whisper. 'Two pounds a month and all found . . . and away from him an' all.'

'They would be very well looked after, I promise you, apart from being a little spoiled by Mrs Bradshaw.'

'I could come and see them, miss?'

'As often as you wished.' Isabel smiled reassurance. 'But the choice as to whether to come here or not must be theirs. I would not want to cause them any unhappiness by taking them into this house should they not wish to come.'

'I'll tell them, miss. I'll tell them what you say.'

Isabel picked up the basin, holding it while the woman slipped her thin fingers beneath the knots that formed a carrying handle.

'Let them think it over, and if they wish to they can come and have a word with the Bradshaws. That way they will have a better idea of what will be expected of them. Then if you and your husband do leave the town, the children can make their own decision as to whether to stay here or not.'

For several moments the woman stared at her, the silence of the kitchen disturbed only by the settling of the coals in the grate. Beneath the cowl-like shawl her tired eyes held those of the younger woman, and in their look was a search for understanding. Then, slowly, in the dance of flickering flame and dull gaslight the search ended, replaced by a glimmer of understanding that brought a soft breath from her parted lips. 'Women of this country have waited a long time.' She spoke softly, her mouth hardly moving, almost as though the words were not her own. 'But the wait be coming to a close. The finish of it be starting. Yours will be a different war and the fighting of it will be longer, but the ending will see a beginning. In you lies the shaping of the future, you hold tomorrow in your hands!'

'I don't understand?'

The woman started, Isabel's words seeming to break the trance-like state that had so suddenly descended on her. 'I'll be going now, miss, I have taken enough of your time.'

Boots scraping on the flags, she was gone before Isabel could say any more.

You hold tomorrow in your hands! The words echoing in her mind, Isabel stared into the settling fire. What on earth could the woman have meant? And: *Yours will be a different war . . .* what did that mean? *The fighting of it will be longer.* The words made no sense. They indicated a war that would outlast the one that was being fought against Germany. But she could not fight in any war, and who would be her enemy?

It was nonsense. The ramblings of a woman who had gone too long without food. But was it? Isabel stared at the flames, flickering from blue to gold to scarlet. None of what the woman had said before had been nonsense; she had not rambled then and all her words had made perfect sense. But then that look had not been in her eyes before, a look that seemed to be seeing what was not there, staring as though trying to penetrate a shadow. Tomorrow . . . Was the woman looking into the future?

'Pull yourself together!' Isabel murmured aloud. 'The whole thing is ridiculous, a few silly words!'

A few silly words. Yes, that was all they had been. But even as she felt the warmth of the fire against her face, Isabel shivered.

Chapter Six

'You say we will be unable to produce any steel at all?' Isabel looked at the man who over the weeks had helped her in so many ways, advising her in the buying of raw materials and in dealing with suppliers. Edward Perry had been invaluable to her; without him Jago Timmins would long since have seen his prophecy come true and Kenton's go out of business.

'I ain't saying the stuff won't make steel, miss. What I be saying is it won't make steel the like of which we be used to smelting. It won't be Kenton steel and as such the guns it be used for won't be Kenton guns, not to our usual quality anyway.'

'The ore is of low grade?'

'It be that all right.' Edward Perry removed his cloth cap only to resettle it at once over his greying hair. 'It be that low you could roll every piece under a snake's belly and leave room to spare!'

'Then it must be returned and exchanged for the usual grade.'

'I done that. I sent it back with instructions not to pass any sh . . . rubbish on to Kenton's.' He checked himself, fiddling shamefaced with his cap. 'I said to send a fresh load up right away but it seems there be no more ore to be had.'

'Is that the reply you got?'

'Yes, miss. Them be the very words.'

'How long can we continue in production?'

'Two days, no more.'

Two days? Isabel's thoughts turned circles in her mind. In two days' time the Bull Piece works would produce no more steel, consequently the works at Glovers Mound would soon be unable to produce gun parts and they would be forced to close. *Three months, I'll give you three months.* Jago's words returned to haunt her.

It had been much longer than that since Mark had put her in charge of his business and Jago's prophecy had not been fulfilled. But it had not been for want of trying. There had been many setbacks she'd felt were due to him though the man was shrewd enough never to let his hand show; but it did not take much of an imagination to see this latest incident as a carefully planned move against her or to guess who lay behind it. Who other than Jago Timmins?

Yours will be a different war. Isabel suddenly felt the presence of Luther Kenton, watching and waiting for her reply. Pushing away the papers she had been working on she stood up, her figure small and straight behind the heavy desk. While men like Mark were fighting the Germans, who fought men like Jago Timmins?

Giving instructions for Perry to return to the steel works, she went upstairs. *The finish of it be starting.* Reaching for her coat, Isabel's mouth tightened. The finish of Jago Timmins's underhand dealings against Kenton's was just about to start.

'I believe this is your doing?' Isabel stared coldly at the man whose lips were curled into a malicious sneer.

'Luther took ore from Bishop for many years and never once was he offered the rubbish that was sent today.'

'Luther were a man.' Pallid eyes assesed her. 'Who can tell what Bishop sees as fit for a woman?'

'Or what you will try in order to close my brother's business.'

Jago Timmins came around the desk, his lips losing their sneer, heat rising in his pale eyes as he stepped closer to Isabel. 'We could forget what you said when last we met.'

His hot gaze travelled hungrily over her body and Isabel had to force herself to remain still as it rested on her face.

'What reason would there be for my closing Kenton's down if you were my wife?'

With a speed Isabel was not prepared for, his arm flashed out, encircling her waist, pressing her close to him. 'You would have no thought of the steel business, I would keep you too busy for that.'

His breath was hot against her face. Isabel craned backward but Jago's free hand gripped the nape of her neck, his wet lips clamping over hers as she tried to cry out, tongue probing her mouth.

'Your only thought would be of me . . .' His voice was thick in his throat. The words fell rapidly from lips that barely left her own before pressing down again. 'Of this!' Pinning her against the wall, his body holding her there, his mouth preventing her from crying out, he snatched at her skirts, dragging them up to her waist, his hand sliding to her groin.

'You wouldn't want anything else.' His breathing, shallow and rapid, caught in his throat as his fingers slid beneath the cool silk of her cami-knickers, brushing the softness of her flesh. 'This be what a woman was meant for, not playing at business.'

An anger stronger than either fear or revulsion bubbling in her stomach, Isabel forced herself to stay calm. Screams would bring men running maybe, but they would be Jago Timmins's men, prepared to swear black was white if it meant keeping their jobs.

Allowing her body to relax and mould itself against his, she felt the thrust of his flesh against her thigh, the frenzied scrabbling of his fingers in her groin. Sickness surging in her, she touched her lips voluntarily to his, the offer he read into this jerking him like a puppet.

'Jago was right, wasn't he?' Groaning from the pleasure coursing through him, eager to increase it, he freed his arm from her waist, taking both hands to the fastening of his trousers. 'I said you would like it, you would enjoy it . . .'

'You were right, Jago.' Isabel kept her voice husky. 'I am going to enjoy doing this . . . very much.'

Raising her arms to his neck, she cupped one hand behind his head, drawing his face down to hers. Then, their mouths almost touching, she parted her lips. 'You will remember this afternoon, Jago,' she whispered, 'we both will.'

Lifting her mouth the remaining inch, she fastened her teeth in his flabby lips.

'You bitch!' Jago sprang away, blood pouring from his mouth as he staggered to the desk, dropping heavily into the padded chair behind it. 'You bloody bitch!'

'That is the second time you have assaulted me, Jago Timmins.' Isabel smoothed her skirts into place, surprised by her own calm. 'But it will be the last. I warn you – let this be the end not only to your so-called attempts at courtship but also to your threats against Kenton Engineering. Or I swear to you, you will regret it.'

'Will I?' Jago pressed a handkerchief to his bleeding mouth. 'There be only one of us going to regret this, and that one won't be Jago Timmins. You'll pay for this, by God you'll pay! By the time I be through you'll be lucky if you own so much as a pair of drawers to cover your arse. There'll be no bloody Kenton Engineering, not a stick nor a stone! No woman gets the better of Jago Timmins.'

'Maybe not in the business of producing steel.' Isabel regarded him steadily though every nerve in her body was taut. 'But what of attempted rape? Where would Jago Timmins stand in the eyes of his colleagues were he accused of twice attempting rape?'

Pressing the handkerchief against lips that were already swollen, Jago laughed despite the sting of it.

'They would most likely laugh, same as I be doing. Jago Timmins trying to rape one of your sort, Luther Kenton's daughter! Would he be such a fool when he could have a doxy from the town for a shilling? Bring your case before the magistrate! You'll be the one to suffer. After all, neither so-called attempt was made in a dark alley, there were people within calling distance!'

He glared at her across the desk, the bloodstained handkerchief held to his mouth.

'It's your reputation as will be ruined. Not to scream meant you wanted it to happen. You'll be seen as having led the proceedings, dangled the carrot, and who would blame a man for trying to take a bite?'

'I mean it, Jago.' Isabel knew he had won on that score but she would not let it show. 'You are deliberately trying to force Kenton's into closure. Marrying me is only one way of doing it, you know that and so do I. But I tell you again: let this be the end to your games or you will regret it.'

His pale eyes sparking with hatred, Jago's fingers twisted the bloodstained handkerchief. 'What will you do?' he ground out. 'Slap my hands with your fan? Pout your pretty lips and tell me what a bounder I am? Or maybe you'll get your brother to come and say boo to me! Now *that* really would frighten me. Promise not to do that to poor old Jago!'

Giving a final pat to her skirts, Isabel walked to the door. 'I promise not to have Mark deal with you, Mr Timmins. After all it does not take a man to deal with a worm, especially so insignificant a worm as Jago Timmins. That is something I can do for myself!'

'*You!*' Jago laughed again. 'What the bloody hell can you do!'

What could she do? Isabel had not the faintest notion, but something would turn up . . . it had to! Facing him across the walnut desk, empty except for a crystal ink stand, she forced a smile to her mouth. One she hoped would deceive him into believing she had a plan in hand when in truth she had none.

'You'll see.'

'Typical!' Jago roared as she turned to leave. 'How bloody typical of a woman. She stamps her foot and when a man don't give in to her, when he calls her bluff, she hides behind words.'

Glancing back at him, long side whiskers defining the line of his jaw, the thin mouth and long narrow nose, she felt she was looking at a fox waiting to pounce.

'I have not stamped my foot . . . not yet . . . and I do not hide behind words. You *will* see what I am capable of doing, that is my promise, unless you release to me the ore you know was destined for Kenton's steel works.'

'I know no such thing!' The sneer fading from his lips, Jago slammed a hand palm down on the desk. 'As for giving you anything, I give you what you gave me in answer to my offer of marriage – a refusal. I tell you to bugger off as no doubt you would have liked to tell me had it not been a bit too plain for a woman's tongue.'

'It was not too plain.' Isabel smiled and her heart warmed when she saw the answering anger stain his face with red. 'I appreciate plain words and I prefer to use them. I assure you that had you not accepted my second refusal I would indeed have told you to bugger off.'

Slowly pushing away his chair, eyes reflecting the bitterness that had burned in him since she had turned down his proposal, Jago rose to his feet. His gaze never once leaving her face, he came around the desk and planted his body firmly in front of hers.

'Listen to me.' The words came out softly, sibilant as a serpent's hiss. 'I will see you go under and laugh as I watch.'

Isabel felt his breath warm on her face and shuddered with revulsion. 'Do not let self-confidence blind you,' she said, amazed that the feeling inside her did not reveal itself in her voice. 'If you go on as you have since the death of Luther Kenton, if you continue to sabotage production in my brother's factories, then I will not only see you go under, I will see you go down the line. But I will not laugh Jago. I will applaud.'

'Nobody threatens Jago Timmins, especially not a bloody woman! That be the second time you have given me a warning. Now it be my turn. One more threat, one more accusation, and you will be made to prove your words in the Magistrates Court.'

His face had come even closer to hers but Isabel refused to step back. 'Should it come to that . . . so be it. Don't make the mistake of thinking me a woman to flutter tremulously before a man's anger or faint at his swearing. Men of your breed do not frighten me, Jago. If I have to fight you I will, and you may be sure I will not surrender lightly.'

'No!' Jago drew back his head but his eyes continued to hold hers. 'No,' he murmured, 'I don't expect you will. There be too much of Luther Kenton in you for that. We will have our own war, you and me. But there will be no surrender, only destruction. I will destroy all that Kenton ever gave birth to, and that goes for you especially!'

Yours will be a different war. The words leaped again to her mind and just as rapidly Isabel knew her enemy. *The fighting of it will be longer.* That too she knew would be true. Jago Timmins would use every trick he knew while she . . .? Isabel drew a determined breath. She would learn.

Aware of the stares that followed her as she walked from Jago's office and across the works yard to her pony trap, Isabel held her head high. About the yard pig iron lay raised in great heaps, silent witness to the fact that Jago was buying all he could, storing it away like a squirrel stores nuts – and all to prevent Kenton's from getting it.

That could be his mistake. Isabel climbed into the trap, an idea already forming in her mind. Driving back via Katherine's Cross she had to wrestle with Janey who made to turn off Woods Bank into the driveway as they approached the house. But Isabel was not going home, she had things to do and people to see. Urging the mare on past the house, she followed the road through Moxley. She had not wasted her time since becoming her brother's works manager. She had learned the location of smelting works farther afield than those in Darlaston, most of which were more likely to support Jago than to do business with a woman. But not all smelting works were in Darlaston.

Reaching Bilston's Loxdale Street, she stopped the trap to ask directions of a passing woman.

'Bradley Field smelting works?' The woman turned to face the way she had come, one hand creeping out from under a fringed woollen shawl, pointing as she spoke. 'Arrh, I knows the place. Carry you on down, keeping straight till you reaches Pothouse Bridge. Turn you left there and the works be but a little way further on. They be right beside the cut.'

Alongside the canal, Isabel thought, driving on after thanking the woman. That would be a better way of bringing pig iron to Bull Piece than using horse-drawn carts. The Birmingham Navigation Canal ran along the rear of Kenton's steel works. A path linking them would enable carts to transport the materials she bought the short distance to the works and provide her with a more convenient means of transport for her finished products.

That is all well and good, she thought as she took the turning that would lead her to the smelting works, but would this man do business with her or would he too laugh at the idea of a woman's attempting to run a steel works? Would he, like Jago Timmins, see that as a man's world and not accessible to women?

A man stepped forward as she entered the yard of the smelting works, one work-grimed hand catching at Janey's bridle. 'Afternoon, miss. You seems to have missed your way. Where was it you was making for?'

'This is Bradley Field smelting works?'

'Arrh, miss, it is.' He ran an eye over her smart grey coat and hat, pausing fractionally on the band of black Petersham ribbon that circled her left upper arm.

'Then this is where I was making for.' Isabel stepped from the pony cart. 'Kindly direct me to the works office.'

Surprise clear on his face, the man pointed towards a corner of the yard where a brick lean-to stood close to a larger building. 'It be there, miss, next to the foundry.'

'Could you please find a spot for Janey?' Isabel smiled,

touching a hand to the horse's shiny brown flank. 'I am afraid she is a bit of an old silly; loud noises frighten her.'

'I'll take her round the back to where the gaffer keeps his carriage, there be a man will take good care of her. If you will just wait a minute, miss, then I'll take you over to the office.'

She could quite easily have found her own way across the yard, but deciding it might be more appropriate to allow the man to escort her, she waited.

'It be this way, miss.' Heavy clogs thudding on the hard-packed earth, he strode ahead of her until Isabel was almost trotting to keep up with him.

'Gaffer has his office along of the corridor here.' He pushed open a door whose paint was lost beneath a generous coating of dust. 'Clerk be in there an' all, he'll see you right.'

Touching a finger to a cap that long ago had surrendered its pattern to the same all swallowing dust he turned about leaving her alone.

'I think we ought to go for him, old boy!' She had never met her brother's friend but his favourite phrase turned up regularly in Mark's letters. A hint of a smile touching her lips, she murmured: 'You know, Mr Gandere, I think you are right. Let's go for him!'

That went better than I dared hope! Returning home, Isabel congratulated herself on a success she had not really expected. Few of the men she had come up against in her business dealings believed she ran a steel works, and when they did they showed little interest in accommodating her. But this one had been different. Short and stocky, he had toffee-coloured hair and brown eyes that seemed capable of making an instant assessment of any situation.

She had carefully noted every aspect of the small room that was the works office; no speck of the dust that overlaid the exterior of the building had been evident on the neat polished desk or on the ledgers that stood tidily on shelves set against a green-painted wall. Everything had been orderly and clean, as was the manager in his dark suit and white shirt topped with disposable paper collar. "E were a bandbox!' Isabel smiled to herself as she thought of how her housekeeper would have described the neat little man.

He had listened politely, his eyes attentive, as she had enquired about the possibility of Bradley Field works supplying the pig iron she needed, a slight raising of one eyebrow his only sign of appreciation of her knowledge of the process of steel-making.

'And how much would you require per week?'

He had reached for a sheet of paper from the desk drawer and, pen in hand, glanced sharply across at her when she answered.

'None if you think to supply iron of inferior quality. Kenton produces only the very best and therefore uses none but the very best. I will require to see what it is you can supply and to have my own men work a sample.'

'I assure you there will be no dross in the iron we supply.'

'I did not think it.' Isabel had smiled then, letting it light her eyes. 'I have every confidence in Bradley Field otherwise I would not entertain the thought of conducting business with you; there are many iron ore smelters nearer home to which I could go were I satisfied with second best. But nevertheless I prefer we be perfectly frank with each other from the outset. That way we can avoid misunderstandings in the future.'

He had smiled then and Isabel felt he knew she had not spoken one hundred percent of the truth about her reasons for wanting to buy ore from his firm, but if he had guessed at her whitewashing of the true facts he politely refrained from comment, asking only the quantity he would be required to supply.

'A ton to begin with,' Isabel had answered, thinking only of the rifle barrels and locks. Those were her main concern. Better to be cautious in the choice of ore that would be used for the making of them. Then, as the man had written the amount beside her name, she had added: 'Should the iron be of the quality I need . . . and I fully expect it will be . . . then might I propose an exclusive contract between Kenton's and Bradley Field? I guarantee to buy all your produce provided you sell to no other steel manufacturer.'

He had put down his pen then, carefully replacing it in the crystal stand before folding his hands together, resting them on the desk and taking fully a minute before answering.

'I am not in a position to enter into any contract, Miss Kenton. Bradley Field smelting works does not belong to me, I be just the manager. The owner, Hewett Calcott, would have to decide on what you have suggested. I don't expect he will be coming along here today, it be getting a mite late.' As if to check his own suspicion he drew a pocket watch from his dark waist-coat, glanced at the dial, shook it then glanced at it again before slipping it back into his pocket. 'If you like, miss, I will tell him what you propose and let you have the answer, or I can give you his address and you can call on him?'

'No,' she had answered quickly, rising as a soft tap on the door of the office had heralded the entrance of the clerk who had proceeded to bring in an oil lamp, standing it on the desk. 'I will not call upon Mr Calcott. As you observed, it is getting a little late. I will wait to hear from you. In the meantime, I thank you and hope we will be able to do business together.'

Leaving the last of the huddle of houses and the occasional shop that grudgingly allowed a trickle of murky yellow light to escape its dust-covered windows, Isabel followed the Holyhead Road towards Moxley. So incensed had she been by what her charge hand had told her, and so intent upon turning the action of Jago Timmins – for the more she thought of what had happened, the more convinced she was that his was the hand behind it – back upon himself, that she had not noticed the time. Now, beyond the smoke-veiled town, the evening was already velvet dark and on both sides the heath sped away, wrapped in an eerie silence.

'Sorry to keep you so long from your supper, Janey,' she

called softly to the mare, feeling an almost overwhelming need to break the silence that somehow seemed to threaten her, to draw closer with every step, wanting to swallow her into itself.

Groundless as she knew her fears to be, Isabel nevertheless shivered, averting her eyes as the black silhouette of the Church of All Saints reared upward, its dark stones giving the impression of moving in the deceiving light.

Feeling a prickle of fear run over her skin, Isabel gripped the reins tightly. It would be a relief to get home. But there was a way yet to go, and every yard of it engulfed in darkness.

The church falling away behind, she knew there was no other building until Woodbank House. Calling again to Janey she felt the touch of the evening breeze against her face, but it was not the breeze that chilled her blood or brought the scream to her lips.

At the same instant as countless iron and steel smelting works opened their furnaces, flooding the sky with a brilliant crimson light, the figure of a man rose from the heath, catching hold of Janey's bridle.

Jago!

The thought flashed instantly through Isabel's mind: she should have known he would not give up so easily. Luther had always talked of him as a man who did not take kindly to being bettered, and this time he had chosen his ground more carefully. The heath was as dark as any alley and this time there were no people close at hand to hear her cries.

'Jago . . . let go!'

Reaching for the driving whip, Isabel's hand closed on thin air as the figure grabbed at her.

'I'll let you go when I be good and ready . . .'

The voice in the darkness was hoarse and rasping, the hands cruel as they bit into her arm, fastened on the collar of her jacket.

'. . . but first there is a lesson to be learned, and you have the learning of it. You won't be so high and mighty once I be finished with you. Kenton's stuck-up bitch of a daughter will be stuck up in a different way!'

'No . . . no!'

Isabel's cry was cut short by the pain of being dragged over the rail of the cart, bruising her ribs.

'Cry out as much as you want, there's none about these parts to hear you!'

Dragged free of the cart, Isabel hit the ground with a sickening thud but almost immediately was hauled to her feet, held by the neck of her jacket.

'Cry, you bloody smart-arsed bitch . . . you bloody Kenton bastard!'

Isabel gasped, her head snapping back as a stinging blow caught her in the mouth.

'Cry . . . it makes this all the more enjoyable for me.'

A second blow caught her across the temple, the force of it throwing her bodily backward and tearing away the front of her jacket.

Her senses reeling from the blow, lips already swollen to twice their size, Isabel instinctively rolled as her body hit the ground, but her attacker was on her before she had moved a yard.

'You can't leave yet!'

Fear cleaving her tongue to the roof of her mouth, Isabel tried to scream but no sound came. Jago must be out of his mind to treat her this way. He must know that this time she would prosecute him for assault, unless . . . terror clutched her, encasing her in ice, but the thought continued to beat its way into her brain . . . unless he intended to kill her!

Fear or self-preservation, Isabel did not know which, made her plead with him. All she knew was that she had to try. Talking to him might drive away the madness, calm him so he would listen to reason.

She looked up at him through bruised eyes. Against the darkness of the night sky his body was a column of blackness, face obscured by shadow.

'Please . . .' she sobbed, 'Think what you are doing. Think what will happen . . .'

87

'Like you did!' His foot lashed out, a heavy boot striking her thigh. 'Like you thought of what you were doing, you bloody bitch! Well, I *have* thought, thought long and hard of the lesson I would teach you!'

In the darkness she heard the laughter roll from low in his throat, the clink of his belt buckle as his fingers released it.

'Well, the punishment part be over. Now comes the pleasure . . .'

Above her in the darkness the same laughter rumbled in his throat and Isabel felt his hands about her skirts, dragging them up over her hips, above her waist.

'No . . .! Oh, God, please . . . No-o!'

But the cry was met only by a long low laugh as she realised her mistake.

'Do this mean Kenton's be closing?'

Edward Perry squinted through the haze of tobacco smoke that hung over the tap room of the Frying Pan. 'I don't rightly see it meaning any other. Her up at the house says Miss Isabel be pretty bad.'

'But what do that mean for we lot?'

'The bloody sack, that be what it means for we!' On the fringe of the group gathered in a corner against the fire, Elijah Price added his comment. 'An' I don't see it being any good asking for a place along of Joynson Street, not now I don't.'

''Lijah be right.' The first man nodded, threshing the air with his long-stemmed clay pipe. 'Jago Timmins won't be inclined to set any of we on, not after we turned him down.'

Delving into the pocket of moleskin trousers pitted with tiny scorch marks branded on them by the splattering of molten metal, Elijah drew out a number of coins. Selecting two half-pennies he placed them on the bar beside his empty tankard then turned back to the group. 'Jago Timmins would see every bloke who works for Kenton in the workhouse afore he would give them a job.'

'But we all got wives and kids!'

'Try telling that to Timmins,' Elijah said grimly. 'See 'ow far it gets you. It be my bet he'll throw you out on your arse!'

'Do anybody know who it was grabbed the wench?'

Edward Perry looked at the man nicknamed Dandylion thanks to his shock of yellow hair that obstinately refused to be hidden beneath his cloth cap, and his habit of wearing collar and tie every night after his shift at the steel works ended. 'Seems her seen the bloke.'

'Seen him?' Elijah Price retrieved his tankard from the bar, taking a mouthful of ale and wiping the line of froth from his mouth with the back of his hand. 'But I thought as it were dark when it happened.'

'So it was, 'cept the lifting of the furnaces lit the road up at just the very minute he jumped out on her. Her must have seen him clear as day.' Edward Perry took his pipe from his mouth. Blowing down the stem, he tapped the bowl against his palm before taking a packet of Nailrod tobacco from his pocket. Placing the pipe back between his teeth, he flicked open a small penknife and proceeded to shave thin flakes of tobacco, pressing them into the bowl of the pipe. This done, he returned the packet of Nailrod and the penknife to his pocket, then, the pipe still clenched between his teeth, went on: 'Them furnaces throw out enough light to thread a needle by. Kenton's wench would have seen him sure enough, but did her recognise him?'

'What did Bradshaw say happened afore he come for you?'

'Like I told you, Dandylion,' Edward Perry struck a match holding it to the tobacco-filled pipe drawing deeply on the stem. 'The hoss found its own way home and when it were clear the wench were not with it, Bradshaw went to look for her. Neither him nor his missis were sure where the wench had gone, they knowed only that her were in a right temper after I left. So after he walked to Katherine's Cross and found no sign of her, his missis said to come to my house in case I had knowledge of where her were going.'

'And did you have?' Elijah took the half-burned match with which Edward had lit his pipe, holding it to his own freshly filled one.

'Her said nowt to me other than her would deal with the matter herself. I went straight back to Bull Piece expecting to hear what was to be done about getting pig iron, but her didn't come. Next thing I knowed was Arthur Bradshaw banging on my door.'

'An now Luther Kenton's daughter be on her death bed and we lot be set for the workhouse.' Raising his tankard, Dandylion emptied it in one long swallow.

'What about that twin brother of hers?' Elijah asked as Dandylion rattled his empty tankard on the bar to call the attention of the landlord. 'Couldn't he come back and run the works? That be what he ought to be doing, not buggerin' off and leaving it to a wench. Steel works ain't a place for women.'

'The lad be away fightin'.' Edward frowned over his pipe. 'He be fightin' for his country.'

'Arrh, that be all well and good!' Elijah snorted. 'And while he be cavortin' across the bleedin' continent, who be going to fight his battles here, eh? That wench lying up in Woodbank House tried but her be no match for Jago Timmins and his like; it be a man's job and I reckon he should have thought of that before sodding off to join the Army.'

'You've said right there, 'Lijah.' Returning with a fresh tankard, Dandylion picked up the gist of the conversation.

Tapping the ash from his pipe against the fireplace, Edward Perry took a swallow of ale, eyes sweeping over the men filling the small room of the public house.

'I ain't saying you be wrong.' He placed the stem of the pipe in its accustomed place between his teeth. 'Nor am I saying that Kenton's lad be wrong. He joined up, believing it his duty to do so – a belief not shared by some in this town.'

'And some of 'em standing not far away.' Dandylion spat deprecatingly into the fire. 'Bloody conshies, my arse! They be bloody cowards! They won't go to the privy lessen their mother be there to hold their hands.'

'Well, their conscientious objecting to going to fight won't keep 'em safe much longer.' Elijah cast a disparaging glance in the direction of several young men, his hand curling into a tight fist. 'They'll be dealt with. Spite of what the law says, we have a way of dealing with bloody cowards, and I ain't too sure that don't be what Kenton's lad be. Was it too much of a job for him to stay here? Ain't he man enough to run a steel works?'

'He could have stayed at home. I guess every mother's lad could have stayed at home.' Edward Perry sucked on his pipe. 'That would have made the Germans' job much easier, and we would find ourselves working for a "*mein herr*" and bending the knee to the Kaiser.'

'Instead of which we be out of a job and set to bend the knee to the workhouse!' Following the other man's lead, Elijah too spat into the fire. 'I'd like to find the bloke who done for Kenton's wench, I'd pull his entrails out and stuff 'em up his arse!'

Dandylion nodded. 'Arrh, an' I would hold the bastard down while you done it!'

The three men stood silent for a while, the conversation of others in the tap room ebbing and flowing about them; the haze of tobacco smoke from a dozen clay pipes swirling as the street door opened on comings and goings. It was Elijah who spoke first.

'What do you reckon to that lad of Kenton's?' he asked, manoeuvring the words past his pipe. 'P'raps if we sent a letter he might come home?'

'It ain't the bloody Salvation Army he be with, he can't just up an' come home when he feels like it . . . have a bit of sense!'

'Hold on a bit!' Dandylion swallowed a mouthful of ale too fast, spluttering afterwards. 'Hold on, Edward. Could be 'Lijah be on to summat. P'raps a letter to the gaffer . . . you know, the boss over them soldiers . . .'

'The Commanding Officer.' Edward Perry supplied the term with a touch of pride. He was the only one of them who had served with the Army.

'Arrh, him,' Dandylion continued. If he had recognised his friend's pride it made no impression on him. 'Supposing a letter were sent to this gaffer – wouldn't he let young Kenton off, let him come out of the Army?'

'There be such a thing as compassionate leave.' Pride in his past shone in Edward's face. 'That be where a man is given a few days' leave if anything has gone wrong at home. Mind, it is only if it be summat serious.'

'Well, this be bloody serious!' Elijah's teeth clenched the stem of his pipe as he spoke vehemently. 'A bloody steel works be shutting down and men put out of a job . . . if that ain't serious then you tell me what is?'

'War!' Edward Perry removed his own pipe, knocking out the residue of smouldering tobacco against the inside of the fireplace. 'That's what be serious. We be fighting a war and I can't see the Army letting go of Kenton. It needs every man it can get.'

'And men need weapons! A bloke . . . any bloke . . . can only fight if he be given the weapons to fight with!' Elijah returned hotly. 'The Army needs men, we've been hearing that since this shindig started, but it also needs guns and ammo. Young Kenton be one man while he be in the Army; out of it and back here he can be a couple of 'undred and more. Think on it. Without him here not only will Bull Piece and Glovers Mound works shut down but gradually every holding of Kenton's will go the same way. But bring him back so he can see to things and the Army will have hundreds working for them.'

'What 'Lijah says be sound good sense,' Dandylion agreed, agitatedly fingering his blue necktie.

It could also be a quicker end to Kenton's, Edward thought. Isabel Kenton had said her brother was set to sell the place. Should he sell to Jago Timmins, not one of the Bull Piece men would have a job. But it seemed set to be that way, no matter what.

'What if the lad don't want to come back?'

'Don't talk so bloody pisspotical!' Elijah banged his tankard down on the wooden counter of the bar, drawing the eyes of several men. 'He has to bloody come! That officer bloke will make him come.'

'At least somebody should tell the lad what's gone on, give him a chance to choose for himself what he does.' Dandylion tried diplomacy as Elijah's voice grew louder. 'P'raps a letter should be sent.'

'Oh, arrh! A letter should be sent.' Edward's reply was caustic. 'An' Edward Perry be the one to write it, that be it, don't it? That be what you pair have in mind. An' what if Kenton's wench takes unkindly to me doing that? It'll be my arse as feels the bump when it hits the street.'

'You could ask her.'

'*You* bloody ask her!' Edward Perry's voice also rose. 'Take your dandy collar and tie up to Woodbank House and ask her. Then you can try asking Jago Timmins for a job.'

'You could always ask, but I know what his answer would be,' a voice called from the opposite corner followed immediately by a chorus of laughter.

'Arrh, so do we.' A stocky man in a greasy jacket, trousers tied at the knee with string, muffler tucked inside a collarless shirt, joined in, raising more laughter. 'Timmins will tell you to piss off!'

The smile dying suddenly on his face he stepped forward, tucking his thumbs into the sides of a waistcoat as grease-stained as his jacket. 'Timmins don't want you and neither do we,' he ground out between clenched teeth. 'You asking for work at any place held by Jago Timmins would be like banging your 'ead against a brick wall, and you don't want that, now do you?'

Taking his tankard from the bar, Elijah slowly drank the last of his ale. Replacing it on the counter, he put his white clay pipe alongside of it, catching Edward Perry's eye as he did so. Wiping the back of his hand across his mouth, dislodging a line of creamy froth, he turned to face the stocky man.

'No, I don't want to bang my head against a wall, but I bloody well be going to bang your'n!'

One hand flashed out like a striking snake, fingers twisting into the man's hair as his flat cap was sent flying. Elijah jerked him backwards at the same time passing his other arm across the man's throat, his heavy boots leaving twin lines on the sawdust-strewn floor as he was dragged through the door. Edward Perry followed, another of the men caught tight in one of his huge fists.

In the street, surrounded by a circle of men still holding tankards, Elijah dealt with his man. 'I be going to tell you summat your mother never did. First, it be rude to listen in where you ain't invited. Second, your mouth be too big. You needs a lesson, mate, and Elijah Price be going to teach you it.' Transferring his grip to the squirming man's jacket collar and trouser band, Elijah lifted him bodily, banging his head against the wall of the public house.

'Did you see that?' Edward Perry shook his captive like a terrier shaking a rat. 'You wanting the same?'

'I didn't mean nothing!' The man's frightened eyes bulged in their sockets. 'It were a joke.'

'Some bloody jokes I don't appreciate!' Edward shook him again. 'Next time you be in the Frying Pan make sure and drink your ale through a tight mouth, else it could be the last ale you be likely to drink for many a long month.'

Picking himself up from where Edward Perry had flung him against the wall, the man made to scurry away, pushing against the others standing around them in an almost solid circle.

'Hey!' At Elijah's shout the circle of men closed tighter, cutting off the man's escape. A fight was too entertaining to be missed, and this one they weren't going to have to pay to watch.

'Hey!' Elijah called again. 'Don't go buggering off and leaving your rubbish for somebody else to clear away. Take this shit with you!'

Hitting the stocky man's head twice more against the wall, Elijah released him. 'I'll just fetch me pipe,' he said quietly to Edward as the man slid to the floor. 'Then I'm going to find the bastard who set about Isabel Kenton and teach him the same lesson. Only his won't be over quite so quick!'

Chapter Seven

Isabel moaned softly, a wave of nausea sweeping over her, pain searing every part of her body as she opened her eyes.

'Miss Isabel. Oh, thank God, thank God!'

A vast timeless space away a voice hovered on the brink of the chasm that held her, a voice that came and went with the swirls of blackness that fastened upon her, dragging her back toward fathomless deeps.

'You be here with us, Miss Isabel.'

The voice lanced against her brain, every word a barb that made her want to cry out, but no sound carried from her mouth.

'Oh, my, you've had us that worried.'

'No more, Mrs Bradshaw.' Neat and efficient in her grey uniform topped with long white apron and small frilled bonnet, a nurse stepped quickly up to Isabel's bed. 'Miss Kenton must be kept very quiet. Please leave now.'

'Arrh, but . . .'

'No buts, Mrs Bradshaw.' The spare-framed woman spoke calmly but with a firmness that showed she would tolerate no denial. 'I will inform you of any change in the patient. Until that time you will please leave her to me.'

Through mists of pain Isabel heard the soft closing of a door as fingers closed about her wrist, holding it for a moment before placing her hand beneath a soft cover.

He had come from the darkness. Her eyes closed but did

not shut out the figure rising from the ground to take hold of Janey's halter. It had been so dark, the sky inky black and moonless. She had passed Moxley Church and taken the road to Darlaston. Isabel tried not to remember, tried to banish the pictures forming in her mind, but still they came. She had called out, her frightened cry losing itself in the deserted reaches of the heath. He had laughed then. She moaned again as the terrifying sound lived afresh in her memory. Laughed and called her a bitch – a bitch who wouldn't live to sack another man.

Beside the bed the nurse touched a hand to Isabel's brow only to withdraw it quickly as the half-conscious girl cried out in fear. Bending a little closer over the bed, she listened to the frightened mutterings.

'I did not want to take your children away . . .'

The nurse bent closer as the words were sobbed from Isabel's swollen lips.

'I only wanted to give them employment and a decent place to live . . . Listen, Mr Griffin . . . please . . .'

As a last frightened cry carried Isabel back into the silent, painless world of unconsciousness, the nurse straightened. After smoothing the sheet about the sleeping girl, she left the room.

'Kenton, you say?'

'Arrh Mr Calcott. Miss Isabel Kenton, that were the name her gave.'

'And you say she knew steel?' Hewett Calcott looked at the man who managed his Bradley Field iron works.

'Her certainly seemed to have a fair grasp. Told me she would accept nowt but the best, and that she would require a workable sample afore placing any definite order.'

'Which would be?'

'A ton to begin with.'

'A ton!' Hewett Calcott glanced at the paper his works manager had given him. Why would a well-known established firm like Kenton's come to him for pig iron . . . and why send a woman?

'Her said if the pig should be of the standard her wanted then would you consider an exclusive contract, dealing with none but her foundry?'

'And what did you say to that?' His head coming up sharply, Calcott's hazel eyes were as keen as his question.

Shorter than his employer by several inches, Thaddeus Upton touched one hand nervously to his stiffly starched white collar. He had a good position with Calcott, a position it would be almost impossible to better, and he had no desire to go back to puddling iron. But he could well find himself doing that should his next answer be the wrong one. Hewett Calcott always vetted new enquiries carefully but this vetting by Kenton's was no enquiry, it was more of an inquisition. Swallowing hard and praying even harder, he looked at the man awaiting his answer. Topping six foot in height, his shoulders broad and straight, rich brown hair showing no sign of grey, Hewett Calcott was an imposing figure of a man for all his forty-six years.

'I told her . . .' Thaddeus felt his throat tighten '. . . I told her I was in no position to make such a commitment.'

Hewett Calcott gave a brief nod that released his manager's throat from the stranglehold of tension, but he remained silent.

'I said as it was a bit late for you to be coming to Bradley Field but that I would tell you of her calling, then . . .' He paused as nervousness overcame him again. How would Calcott take the next part of what he had said to that young woman? His employer was a fair man but one who valued his privacy, as Upton had found out over the years of working for him. Feeling his mouth go dry he met those sharp hazel eyes; would he still be manager of Bradley Field in one minute from now?

'Well, man, out with it. What *did* you tell her?'

'I . . . I offered to give her your private address. I told her she could call on you there.'

'The devil you did!' Hewett Calcott slammed the paper he was holding down on to the tidy desk of the works office.

On the opposite side Thaddeus Upton mentally kissed his job goodbye. From the moment of that young woman's leaving this office he had known his move had been a wrong one. Not once in fifteen years had he made the mistake of directing a potential customer to Hewett Calcott's home, but there had been something about that girl, something he did not recognise but had instinctively liked and trusted. He almost smiled. Fifty years of age was a bit old to get himself sacked over a wench!

'So when am I to expect a visit from this female iron master?'

'Her wouldn't take your address, sir.' Once more Upton's hand strayed to his collar, one finger easing it against his neck. 'Her said as how her would make no call on you but wait to hear from me your reaction to her proposal.'

'That reaction being to her wanting an exclusive contract.'

It was not a question so the manager gave no reply, preferring to wait for his employer's instructions.

Why was it a woman was in charge of Kenton's? Hewett Calcott turned over what he had been told in his mind. It was obvious Isabel Kenton was in charge, she could not make such a proposition otherwise. He had read of Luther Kenton's death in the newspaper and of his business and home being left to his children. That was what Calcott found difficult to understand. Kenton had two children, a lad and a girl. So how come it was the girl who was running the steel works?

'You had a sample load sent over?'

Upton breathed more easily. He had expected a small explosion ending with his being thrown out of the door but Calcott seemed to have forgotten the business of his manager's offering to give the woman his home address.

'A ton, Mr Calcott. Sent it the next morning first thing.' The answer was given quickly. If his employer had overlooked his mistake, the manager wanted it to remain that way.

'Has there been any response?'

'No, sir.' Upton brushed a hand over his receding hair. He wanted this particular discussion over.

'They have had long enough to smelt that iron. It was of good quality?'

'The very best, Mr Calcott.' Upton's answer carried a note of pride. 'Ain't no better pig iron smelted anywhere in the Black Country than comes outta Bradley Field works, and that as went to Kenton's was the finest.'

'Then why no response, why no reply? The very fact of her enquiring about an exclusive contract would imply a certain difficulty in maintaining a supply of pig iron.'

It was said musingly but Upton knew that behind the softly spoken words a mind as sharp as a well-honed razor was mulling over the facts. 'The woman did specify quite strongly that Kenton's would take nowt but top quality pig. Could be as somebody has tried palming her off with a load of rubbish, 'er being a woman. Could be they thought as her wouldn't know A from a bull's foot about making steel.'

Hewett Calcott retrieved the paper he had slammed on to the desk, glancing once again over the figures his manager had written on it.

'Should that be the case, Tad,' he said, 'then someone was given quite a rude awakening, wouldn't you say?'

'The wench be no fool, sir, that be sure.' Thaddeus Upton breathed freely, feeling his own job to be safe once more. 'Whoever has had the teaching of her regarding steel has done a good job. Pity her wasn't born a lad.'

Hewett Calcott smiled as he handed back the sheet of paper to his manager. 'Should Miss Isabel Kenton ever visit Bradley Field again, Tad, I strongly advise you do not tell her that.'

'Braddy . . . please!' As she always had as a child wanting a special treat or simply her own way, Isabel used her pet name for Letty Bradshaw. Then she smiled, her still slightly swollen mouth holding its old baby pout. She had thought of trying it once or twice during the two weeks she had lain in bed but realised it would gain her nothing against the housekeeper's determination. Now, however, she was ready to try her hand.

'I don't know, Miss Isabel. Doctor says . . .'

'Doctor says that thanks to your very excellent care, I am completely myself again.' Beneath the crisp white sheet Isabel kept her fingers firmly crossed that such blatant flattery would work.

'Not completely you ain't, and well you knows it.' Letty Bradshaw crossed her arms over her ample bosom.

'Just a few minutes.'

'Oh, Miss Isabel, you'll get me shot, really you will. If that doctor finds out . . .'

'He won't.' Drawing her hand from beneath the covers, she held it towards the older woman who took it gently between her own plump ones. 'It will be our secret, Braddy.'

'Arrh, an' we have had a few of them in our time. Just a few minutes then,' Letty Bradshaw relented, beaten by a childlike smile she knew to be deliberate. 'And that is all you *will* get, miss, an' don't you go thinking you can get your own way all the time!'

Relaxing against the pillows, Isabel watched her housekeeper bustle out of the room. They had been so good to her, the Bradshaws. Each time, in those first long nights, as she had drifted in and out of the shadows she had heard the voice or seen through the mists of consciousness the face of one of the two people who had been closer to her than her own father. But then Luther Kenton had not been her father. Who had? Who was it who had once been Victoria Kenton's 'dearest love'?

Closing her eyes, she thought again of the words of that letter, words that had torn her apart a thousand times in the darkness of sleepless nights, words she could recite by heart.

I pray you come for me quickly. The words were printed on her mind with the power of branding, scorched into her brain. But he had not come, that mysterious lover. He had not come . . . for either of them!

'How bin you, miss?'

The softly spoken question startling her, Isabel's eyes flew open and for a minute a long-borne unhappiness lay stark in their depths.

'I am very much better, Mr Perry.'

'I hopes you don't think I be taking a liberty, calling at the 'ouse?' Edward Perry glanced at the housekeeper's face, then quickly back at the girl in the bed. He had known Letty Bradshaw all his life and would sooner take on the Tipton Slasher than pick an argument with her.

'I am glad you came, Mr Perry.' Isabel saw the glance and quickly assured her visitor of his welcome. Worry about the steel works had assailed her almost as often as thoughts of that man . . . 'I so much wanted to tell you how sorry I am that the works have closed.' She pushed the memory of that night as far away as it would allow, though she knew the reprieve was temporary. 'Would you please tell the men I tried? Tell them . . .'

Letty Bradshaw bent over Isabel as hot tears flooded her eyes. 'I think that be enough, Edward Perry!' she said sharply. 'You shouldn't ought to have come, it be too soon.'

'No,' Isabel sniffed, touching her eyes with a delicate lace-edged handkerchief. 'I want Mr Perry to stay. I wish to speak to him. I must have the facts so I can write to Mark. He will want to know what happened.'

Edward Perry dropped his glance to the Sunday best cap held in his hands. He had written a letter to Mark Kenton, urged on by Elijah and Dandylion – a letter asking him to come home and sort out the business of the steel works. He had not dared ask the Bradshaws to get him a proper address so had merely sent it 'care of the War Office'. But there had been no reply. Did young Kenton have no regard at all for men's livelihood? Was that the reason he had not taken compassionate leave – or was there some other cause, one that meant he might never come back?

'Five minutes then!' Letty said tartly. 'Five minutes, Edward Perry, then I'll be back and you will be leaving!'

'She isn't really as fierce as she pretends.' Isabel gestured towards a chair, smiling as Letty left them together.

'That be what you think, miss.' He drew the tall-backed chair to the bedside. 'I knows better. I went to school with Letty Bradshaw and a right bossy bloomers her was an' all.'

Isabel laughed, ignoring the sting of it against her ribs. 'I must remember that next time she orders me about.'

'Which will be the very next time her claps eyes on you.' Edward Perry grinned. 'Put Letty Bradshaw in the front line and I reckon we wouldn't need any soldiers, her would frighten the sh . . . life out of the Germans. By the way, miss,' he asked as Isabel laughed again, 'How is your brother? Have you heard from him lately?'

Her laughter dying away, Isabel's eyes clouded. 'Not for some time.'

'You will.' Immediately wishing he had not asked, Edward tried to sound reassuring. 'It takes time for letters to be delivered. I reckon the Army has thousands to sort out.'

'Yes, that is why I have not received one for a while. But as I began to say . . . please give the men my sincere apologies. I had no wish to see Kenton's go out of business, or for any of them to lose their job.' It was true, she had not wanted that, but Jago Timmins had. He at least must be pleased at the turn events had taken.

'Ain't no man lost his job.' Sitting down, Edward perched the cap on his knee. 'Nobody has gone from Bull Piece nor Glovers Mound neither, 'cept for them the Army has took. That be what I wanted to talk to you about, miss.'

'The works aren't closed?' Isabel cut in, a frown drawing the fine lines of her eyebrows together.

''Course they ain't, miss, they be going full strength, same as always.'

Pushing herself higher in the bed, the frown continuing to pull at her brows, Isabel stared at the smiling charge hand.

'But how? You said there was iron enough for only two days.'

'An' that were true enough, or at least it were till them supplies come from Bradley Field. That were a smart move on your part. Who would have thought you would go to Bilston to buy pig iron? Not me for one. I would never have thought a woman . . .' He paused awkwardly. 'Beg your pardon, miss, but you know what I means. We just ain't used to having a woman in the steel, but when it comes to a wench like yourself then we all be glad to have you there an' I ain't codding.'

No, he was not. Isabel felt a glow of pleasure. There was no trace of pretence on his face or in his eyes, the compliment had been genuinely meant. But she had made no agreement with Bradley Field; the manager there had told her he could sign no exclusive contract, nor had it been agreed for him to supply any pig iron other than a token amount. So how . . . ?

'We had a ton early on the morning after you went there,' Edward Perry continued. 'Fine stuff it were, produced some of the best steel I've ever handled. Been sending all we ask since then, regular as clockwork, and all of it the same top quality.'

'But I do not understand, who has signed payments?'

'Ain't bin no bills to be paid, not so far anyway.'

No request for payment? Isabel felt both confused and concerned. Why had Bradley Field sent no bill with the supplies? That was certainly the practice with smelters, with whom she had formerly had dealings. And just as worrying, would she have the money to pay when they did? The government paid for the guns they took, but not always as quickly as she would have liked.

'Like I told you, Miss Kenton . . .'

Her thoughts interrupted, she listened attentively. She would find out what Bradley Field was about later.

'. . . the pig be coming regular and we be turning out as much steel as ever. Certainly we be keeping each of Kenton's places working full tilt. But we be getting short-handed, what with so many lads joining up; now there be talk of the Army taking men whether they wants to go or not.'

'You mean men will be forced to join?'

'Reckon they will.' Edward fingered the cap draped over his knee. 'Them speeches Lord Derby be making don't leave much room for conjecture. I reckon come the autumn we will see them along of Westminster making one move or another, and if they do make it compulsory for men to join up then we . . . that is Kenton's . . . could well find ourselves facing a new threat of closure for I cannot see there being enough hands to keep things going.'

'But will the government not take that into consideration?' Isabel asked. 'They have to leave us the men if they want the guns and ammunition, surely?'

'Depends on how the fighting goes . . . how many of our lads has to be replaced.'

It will be over by Christmas, Mark had said. But that had not happened and according to what Edward Perry was now saying it was not likely to happen soon.

'I think we can be sure the government will take the question of workers into consideration.' Isabel tried to sound confident, but knew the charge hand would not have come unless he was worried. 'In the meantime . . .'

'In the meantime, miss, there have been several more attempts at 'ticing our blokes away.'

'Jago Timmins?' Isabel's mouth hardened.

'Not openly, though I don't harbour any doubts as he be the one at the back of it. There's been a lot of bragging about the town of late. Men with money in their pockets, money they be chucking about like water, crowing about the wage they be earning over at Bentley Mill and Wilcox Steel and more names I could be saying. Point is, miss, whoever be at back of 'em has every intention of putting you under, and they will keep on trying lessen you do something, and quick.

'Some of our men have the sense to put two and two together. They know that should anything come of the rumours of being took into the Army whether they wants or they don't want, they be the first ones who will be marched off, seeing they be mostly in their twenties or thirties; they all have families and know that once they be gone then their wives and kids will have a rough time. The King's shilling won't go a long way towards keeping them. So you see, miss, they can hardly be blamed for wanting to earn what they can afore the Army drops its clog!'

'No, they cannot be blamed.' Isabel's reply was slow in coming. What she was about to say could well bring the whole of Kenton's Engineering down about her ears. But if the walls of Jericho had to fall then it would be her, not Jago Timmins, who would blow the trumpet. Taking a determined breath, she looked square into the eyes of her charge hand, hoping the worry she felt did not show in her own.

'Mr Perry,' she said evenly. 'Please see to it that the furnace hands and the core makers are paid an extra thirty shillings a week, the steel drawers an extra twenty-five shillings a week, and the apprentices ten shillings.'

Yours will be a different war. Not for the first time did those words return to her. Leaning wearily on the pillow as Edward Perry left, Isabel breathed deeply. 'You will not win, Jago,' she whispered. 'And neither will you, Luther Kenton!'

'Have they got the man did that to you?'

Isabel looked at her visitor. Side whiskers masked the sides of his face, giving the centre an even longer, narrower look, wary grey eyes completing the fox-like illusion.

'Man, Mr Timmins? I have not said my injuries were caused by a man. I wonder why you should think it?'

Jago Timmins's hand strayed to the thick red-gold chain looped across his waistcoat, fingers toying with the Albert strung from it. 'It stands to reason, bruises don't come from no other source. Certainly no dab with a powder puff!'

Isabel eyed the man she had thought to be her attacker. Why had he called upon her, what deviousness did he have in mind? He knew he was not welcome at Woodbank House since the death of Luther so this could hardly be a social call. 'As you say, bruises do not come from a dab with a powder puff.' She spoke coldly, that coldness echoed in her eyes. 'But what reason do you have to think they were given by a man?'

A forefinger beneath the Albert, Jago Timmins tapped his nail against the metal, the sound matching the tick of the ormolu clock above the fireplace.

'Must have heard it said someplace,' he blustered, 'there's been talk in the town.'

'How strange.' Isabel affected a small puzzled frown. '*I* have spoken to no one regarding what happened.'

'Well, you knows how rumours start . . .' The gold medal bounced rapidly against his fingernail. 'An' Darlaston be a small place.'

Her voice losing none of its coldness, Isabel nodded. 'Of course, local gossip.' Her lovely eyes stone hard as they locked with his, she added, 'Darlaston is indeed a small town, Mr Timmins, and people will talk.'

'Arrh, well!' He coughed to clear his throat, her words doing nothing to ease his sudden discomfiture. 'Enquiring after your health be only part of my reason for calling on you, though of course that be my prime concern.'

Oh, I am sure it is, Isabel thought, watching the shifty movements of his grey eyes over her face. My welfare is of paramount importance to you . . . next to Kenton Engineering. But she kept her thoughts to herself, saying instead, 'I thank you for your concern but perhaps if I might hear the rest of the reason for this visit?'

'Arrh!' The hand that fiddled with the Albert transferring itself to his face, Jago pulled absently at his long side whiskers. 'I hear you're still having a bit of difficulty getting supplies of pig iron?'

'More rumours!' Isabel allowed a suspicion of a smile to curve her mouth. 'Really, you surprise me. I would not have thought you a man to take note of rumours.'

'Rumour or not,' the hand fell away from his whiskers, hitting the arm of his chair with a thud, 'pig iron be getting harder to come by and prices be going up. Prices Kenton's won't be able to meet if it goes on raising men's wages the way it has!'

Her fingers curling together in her lap the only sign that his words carried anything to discompose her, Isabel continued to regard him steadily. 'Rumours might have you well informed, Mr Timmins, but only an illicit enquiry into Kenton's finances can give you information on what we can and cannot afford. Do I take it you have made such enquiries?'

'It be common knowledge . . .'

'Really? You mean there are others who have enquired into Kenton's affairs? Or is that a rumour you yourself have spread?'

'I don't have to spread no rumour!' Jago's face reddened. 'All Darlaston knows a woman can't run a steel works, you don't have the knowledge.'

'No.' Isabel allowed her smile to widen though her eyes remained icy. 'I admit I do not. But I can go on learning from you, the way I learned to hold the men by raising their wages as you offered to do. But rumour does not only reach you. I hear that those men who did leave Kenton's to join you are now on the streets. They didn't enjoy your beneficence for long, did they?'

'A man earns according to his worth!' spat Jago. 'My foundry ain't run as a place for women. A man can't pull his weight then out he goes, I ain't no bloody charity!'

'Indeed you are not.' Her reply acid-sweet, Isabel reached for the pull cord hanging alongside her chair. 'If that is all you came to tell me, then please do not let me detain you any longer.'

'I ain't said all I came to say!' Jago Timmins glared at the woman who continually defied his every effort to best her. She should have been his wife by now. There would have been no besting him then, and her bruises would have come from his hand. He would have knocked this waywardness out of her. Damn bloody Luther Kenton! Damn his bawling his way into hell!

The false smile abandoned, Isabel glared. 'Then please say it and leave, I have business to attend to!'

'You'd best leave that cord till you've heard me out. The difficulty you have had securing supplies of iron be only the start. There be other ways a works can be forced to close. Things are going to get rough in Darlaston, what with the war causing a shortage of manpower. It'll take more than money to hold them as is left, and I intends to hold them all. You won't get any from Bilston and you won't be getting any more pig from there neither, not after I've paid a visit to Bradley Field. You think you be right bloody smart, another Luther Kenton. But I tell you this: you have to be a lot smarter yet to put one over on Jago Timmins. I warned you I would shut you down, I warned you . . .'

'And now I am warning you . . .'

They had not heard the door open and now both turned towards the tall uniformed figure watching them from the doorway.

'Mark!' Isabel was on her feet and across the room, her arms about her brother before Jago Timmins got to his feet. 'Mark! Oh, thank heaven you are home!'

One arm sliding protectively about his twin, Mark Kenton glared at the grey-haired figure of Jago and the threat in his voice was plain as he continued. '*I* am warning you, Timmins, you make any move against my sister or Kenton's and it is me you will have to deal with.'

'You don't bloody scare me, Kenton!' Jago ground out, his mouth thinning almost to obscurity, eyes brilliant with derision. 'What the hell can you do?'

'Do not think to hide behind the war,' Mark answered calmly. 'It will not last forever, and neither will I be away from home indefinitely. If, on my return, I find you have lifted your hand in any way against my sister, I will feed your furnace with every bone in your pathetic body!'

'I don't take threats from no man, 'specially not from Luther Kenton's pup!' Jago Timmins's face became a mask of hatred. 'I told your sister I would close you down and that is what I will do. Now I give you advice you will only pay for in the disregarding of it. Sell out to me while you have the option. Refuse and could be that sister of yours might meet up with more than a scuffle on a dark road.'

'Why you . . . !' Pushing Isabel aside, Mark leaped across the sitting room, his hand fastening on Jago Timmins's neat collar as Bradshaw spoke from the doorway.

'Mrs Bradshaw would like to know if you be requiring tea, Miss Isabel?'

'No!' It was Mark who answered, his grip still tight on the other man's collar. 'We will not be wanting tea. Neither do we want this scum at Woodbank House!' Almost lifting Jago Timmins off his feet, he half threw him towards the manservant. 'See to it this man is not allowed in here again.'

'This ain't the finish, Kenton!' snarled Jago as Bradshaw held the door open, standing pointedly aside for him to leave. 'Now you have two wars to fight, and Jago Timmins be a bad enemy.'

Chapter Eight

'Good evening, Mr Calcott, thank you for coming.' Mark stepped forward, his hand extended to greet the man Bradshaw was showing into the sitting room. 'May I present my sister Isabel?'

'How do you do?' Hewett Calcott took the hand of the girl who had occupied a prominent place in his thoughts since his first being told of her visit to the smelting works at Bradley Field.

'It was kind of you to agree to come at such short notice.' Isabel smiled. 'I did not know my brother was being given leave or I would have written to you beforehand.'

'Not leave exactly,' Mark answered as Isabel asked their guest to be seated. 'Goosey's uncle needed a chap to fly him home.'

'Goosey?' Hewett Calcott raised an enquiring eyebrow.

'That is exactly what I said!' Isabel remarked with a light laugh.

'John Gandere,' Mark explained as the older man nodded acceptance of the decanter he offered. 'The name, I think, is self-explanatory. His uncle, Field Marshal Sir William Gandere, is the top brass in the Flying Corps. He was in France visiting an HQ over there when word came the Prime Minister wanted to see him, and a bit sharpish.' Handing out a glass of dry sherry to Calcott, he took one for himself before sitting down. 'It seemed the pilot who had brought him over chose that moment to fall into a trench and bust his leg, which posed more of a problem for Goosey's uncle than it did for the pilot.'

'In what way?' Hewett Calcott swallowed a little of the sherry.

'No tin-winged angel to bring him back!'

'Tin-winged angel? Mark, do talk sensibly!' Isabel reprimanded him though her eyes smiled. 'What on earth is a tin-winged angel?'

'Tin wings is the way the Corps refers to the new metal aeroplanes, and the pilots are the angels.' Mark took a sip of his own drink, his face suddenly becoming serious. 'There's quite a shortage of trained pilots over there which means each man is doing more sorties than he should. When the signal came through for the Field Marshal to return, I was the only angel with his wings furled . . . er, not in the air.' He threw an apologetic look at his sister. 'So it fell to me to ferry Sir William back to England. Once here I was granted a forty-eight-hour pass after which I report back for duty. So you see, sir, I had no choice but to ask if you would meet us now even though, like Isabel, I know it's a hell of an imposition.'

'It is no imposition, I assure you.' Hewett Calcott laid aside his glass. 'It is a real pleasure to meet both of you.'

'Perry tells me that your works have supplied Kenton Steel with pig iron these last weeks, but that no bill has accompanied any delivery.'

'Mr Perry allowed it to slip to my delivery man that Miss Kenton had not been to your foundry at Bull Piece owing to a slight illness, therefore I decided the bills could wait until she was well again. There is no rush for payment.'

It had been more than a slip of the tongue. Calcott glanced at Isabel, seeing the last tinge of bruising on her temple. Perry had given a graphic, if imaginary, account of what had happened the evening she had been returning from Bradley Field, and had mentioned the name of her assailant learned from the manservant here at this house. But that bastard had paid, Perry and his friends had seen to it. He had dragged himself out of Darlaston with a broken arm and ribs, but could count himself lucky. Had Hewett Calcott been dishing out punishment, the man would have had a broken neck.

'That is more than generous.' Emptying his glass, Mark laid it aside. 'However, I would like to set our affairs in order before returning to France. If you could let me have your accounts, sir?'

'If you insist.' Calcott rose to his feet. 'You will have them by hand first thing in the morning.'

She was beautiful. Hewett Calcott leaned back in the carriage he still preferred to use. Motor carriages might be the more modern means of transport but for him there was real pleasure in riding behind a horse, and a certain soothing quality in the sound of the steady rhythm of its hooves.

He had questioned his own manager closely concerning Isabel Kenton's visit to the smelting works, but when it came to asking for her physical description he had held his peace. But she was all he might have imagined, and more. In the closed darkness of the carriage he pictured again the slim-figured girl whose smile had caught at his heart. The rich burnished auburn hair caught elegantly high on her head with just a few tiny curls touching the sides of her brow and the nape of her long neck . . . the finely boned face whose hazel eyes glinted with flecks of green-gold. Yes, Isabel Kenton was a beautiful woman, one any man would find desirable. And she had a fine mind, too. He smiled as the memory returned of what he had been told of her references to the quality of pig iron. A mind of her own, and one she was not afraid to use. He liked that, and he liked Isabel Kenton. He would be seeing more of her.

And of her twin brother? He glanced through the carriage window as a lighted tram rattled past. Mark's language was a little slangy but that was probably to be expected; *he* must have used the particular youthful argot of *his* day, though now he could not remember what that may have been. But beneath Mark Kenton's peculiar phraseology he sensed a mind sobered by war, and one torn between the duty of staying home and caring for his sister and his duty to his country. And he will do both to the utmost of his ability, Hewett Calcott told himself as the tram rattled away out of hearing. Mark Kenton was not the sort to shirk either. They would have the exclusive contract the girl had proposed. From tomorrow Bradley Field would produce pig iron for none but Kenton's.

Mark looked at his sister. The last of the marks had all but disappeared from her face, though memories of them still lay deep in her eyes and he could guess what she had suffered. God help that swine who had attacked her if ever Mark came across him. Isabel had said nothing of what had occurred but the nurse brought in to look after her had caught the name Griffin and passed it on to Mrs Bradshaw whence eventually it had reached the ears of Edward Perry.

'We sorted the bugger, Mr Mark,' Perry had told him when he had called at the works. 'We guessed it might be Griffin, what with your sister giving him the sack, but we give him what he never bargained for. It won't happen again, Mr Mark, you can rest easy on that score. Griffin knows next time we'll put his lights out. No, we've seen the last of that bugger!'

But supposing Griffin did come back? Mark felt his stomach twist. *He* should be here with Bel, *he* was the one who should be looking out for her. But the way things were shaping at the Front, the Army needed every man it could get. He would put it to Goosey's uncle when he got back to the War Office. Until then . . . Pushing the problem to the back of his mind, he said gently: 'Bel, I want you to tell me what happened the evening of your visit to Bilston?'

Isabel's hand flew automatically to her temple then came swiftly down into her lap as she realised what she had done. 'I told you of my meeting with Mr Calcott's manager.'

'Yes, but that is all you told me.' Going down on to his

haunches before her, he took her hands in his. 'Bel, I need to know the rest of it.'

'It . . . it was a tram. It sounded its bell as it passed. The lights and the noise startled Janey and she backed into the trap. I . . . I fell out.'

'That is not true, Bel. This is me . . . your twin. We have always known whether or not the other was even thinking something that was not quite true. Please, Sis, I have to know, did someone attack you?'

Isabel closed her eyes as the terrible pictures rose in her mind. The darkness, the silence stretching away on all sides yet somehow closing in on her with a suffocating, frightening thickness. Then the darkness retreating before a crimson brilliance that turned the sky to flame, irradiating the heath and the road with a gentle glow, and rising from the roadside that figure . . .

'Bel.' Mark's hands pressed hers in gentle reassurance. 'I'm sorry. It was brutish of me to ask, to bring it all flooding back to you. You don't have to tell me.'

But she did. She had to tell someone if the nightmares were ever to be banished for good. Keeping the horror of that night locked inside her would only cause more mental suffering. Yet by telling Mark, would she not cause *him* mental suffering? Didn't he have enough to worry over without her adding to it?

Torn both ways, Isabel took a long shuddering breath.

'I'm sorry, Sis.' Pulling her into his arms, Mark cradled her as he had so often when they were children and she had been frightened by something. Holding her against his chest, his chin resting on her head, he murmured, 'Remember when you insisted on climbing the old willow tree over by the wall at the far end of the garden, and then got so scared you turned rigid? We got it in the neck from Mrs Bradshaw, but I got you down. And the times you cried in the night wanting Mother to hold you but knowing she had died. I held you then till you went back to sleep. I held you as I'm holding you now, as I always want to when things go wrong for you. I can't leave you here, afraid. I'll ask for my release from the Flying Corps just as soon . . .'

'No!' Isabel pushed herself away from him, her eyes wide. She knew what it would cost him in his heart to turn his back on his country and fellow flyers, and no matter how strenuously it was presented as being essential for the smooth running of the steel works, she knew he would always consider it a dereliction of duty. 'No, Mark. There's no need for that. What happened that evening gave me a scare, I don't deny that, but I'm over it now.'

'Over it enough to talk about it?' He eased himself into a chair then reached across to take her hand. He had said she did not have to tell him, yet now as so long ago he felt that by getting her to talk of what had frightened her, he could somehow take it upon himself, take the fear away.

Isabel nodded, but her throat tightened as in her mind the figure rose stark and black, its shape etched against a glowing background.

Holding his silence, squeezing her hand gently when she paused, understanding the fear blocking the words in her throat, Mark listened as the story poured out.

'So it was Griffin!' he said as she finished.

'Yes. But I had no intention of trying to take his children from him, though heaven knows he deserved it. I just wanted them to have a decent home and a job.'

'But they never came?'

'No,' Isabel answered thoughtfully. 'I wonder why?'

'They probably went with him when Perry . . .'

'Perry?' Isabel looked sharply at her brother. 'Edward Perry . . . what has he to do with all of this?'

Releasing her hand, Mark sat back in his chair. 'He wrote to me care of the War Office. I got his letter just as I was about to ferry Sir William Gandere back to London.'

A sudden sharp anger surged through Isabel. How dare the man write and tell Mark of her ordeal? How dare he worry her brother? 'He had no right to tell you about Griffin. I shall . . .'

'He did not tell me about Griffin.' Mark smiled at the sudden blaze of indignation that stained her cheeks pink. That too had always happened in their childhood. Bel would go off like a ginger beer bottle being uncorked whenever something annoyed her, and he would be the one to calm her down. Perhaps that was the reason her hair was a deeper auburn than his: because her temper was more fiery. 'He told me about Jago Timmins trying to lure our workers away. He also told me how you stood up to the men at the foundry. Battling Bel.' His smile deepened. 'That really was an apt name I gave you.'

'Yes, well, don't use it any more.' The pink in her cheeks deepening a shade, Isabel fought away a smile. 'It's not very lady-like.'

'I promise not to if you promise not to refer to me as baby brother any more.'

Hazel eyes glinting with mischief Isabel allowed her smile to break through. 'Of course – after I have used the name just once when I eventually meet Goosey.'

'Isabel Kenton, you are asking for a spanking!' Mark said, laughter ringing out.

'And Edward Perry is asking for a piece of my tongue.' Quick as a flash she returned the conversation to its original subject. 'If you thought to make me forget what he has done then, baby brother, you have made a mistake.'

'There never was much point in trying to hoodwink you, Bel. Perry's letter went on to say our supplies of pig iron had been cut off and if Kenton Engineering were to survive, I should leave the Army and return home to run the business. There was no word in it of the attack made upon you, though I have no doubt he knew of it and of the man who made it.'

'But how could Perry know? How could anyone know? I have told no one until now.'

'Not when you were conscious, but when you lapsed into unconsciousness, and later in your dreams, the whole lot came out. The nurse and Mrs Bradshaw both heard it. And Braddy being Braddy, she told her husband and it filtered down from there to Perry. The way it was told they thought you were dying so he and a couple of others decided to administer a little justice of their own, and consequently the odious Mr Griffin has left Darlaston. So you see, Bel, you need have no fear of his attacking you again.'

'But his wife and the children!'

'They left with him. At least the woman and the girl did, the lad had already gone. His mother told Perry he had run away. It seems he had come home to find Griffin beating his wife; the lad grabbed the poker and struck his father with it before running from the house.'

'He would do well to stay away,' Isabel said softly. 'I only wish Griffin's wife and daughter had left him too.'

'There's no accounting for a person's sense of duty.'

'No, there is not,' she answered quietly. 'That is why we must both do ours, Mark. We must serve our country as best we can. You by returning to the Flying Corps and me by taking your place here until you return.'

'Bel!' Sliding from his chair, he took her once again in his arms, cradling her head against his chest. 'Bel, are you sure . . . you're not scared of Timmins or the others?'

'No, I'm not scared, not of Jago or anyone else.' She pressed her cheek close against his. 'But it's still nice to be held by my brother.'

She had told him what he wanted to hear. But even as his arms held her, pictures returned to haunt her from the shadows.

'What you did was no more than any man would, seeing his business suffer.' Hewett Calcott smiled at the young woman, her eau-de-nil gown a perfect complement to her rich auburn hair and creamy skin. He had invented more and more reasons for meeting her since that first time, and on each occasion was struck anew by the sheer beauty of her face. But Isabel Kenton possessed not only a physical beauty, she had a beauty of character that shone through in everything she did.

'Perhaps,' Isabel agreed. 'But I still feel pangs of guilt. I acted no better than Jago Timmins.'

'The man who attempted to take away your workforce?'

'The same.' Isabel nodded, the glow from the gasolier touching off a hundred points of ruby light in her hair.

The urge to take her hand and hold it in his own becoming almost too strong to control, he picked up his wineglass, taking a gulp of claret.

'There comes a time, Miss Kenton, when a man must fight fire with fire.'

'And a woman?' Isabel reminded him.

'A woman also.' Hewett Calcott's fingers tightened about the stem of the crystal glass as he caught the soft hazel gleam of her eyes. It had been almost a year since they had first met, a year in which his feelings for her had deepened with every passing day.

'That does not make what I did any more acceptable, at least not in my own eyes.' She pushed away her plate, her food virtually untouched. 'I accused Jago Timmins of using dirty tactics, of trying to shut down Kenton Engineering by securing all the best pig iron from local smelting works and leaving only dross for me to buy.' She glanced across the table, the twinkle gone from her eyes and replaced by a look of regret. 'But by insisting upon an exclusive contract with Bradley Field, I was doing the very same thing. I took the best and gave no thought to the next man; I gave no thought to how many Bilston people might be put out of work because of my selfish action. No, I behaved no better than Jago Timmins.'

He wanted to take her in his arms. To kiss that look of unhappiness and regret from her lovely eyes, to tell her . . . But he forced himself to lean back in his chair though he kept the wineglass in his hand, fingers pressing against the cool hard glass. 'Have you read any reports of people being put out of work in Bilston?' he asked, feeling every word squeeze past the barrier in his throat as he looked at her. 'Have you heard of anyone coming to Darlaston to find employment? Has any man come to you with tales of closures in his home town?'

'No.' Isabel's glance fell away. 'But surely there must have been? If Bradley Field supplies none but Kenton's then it stands to reason other firms who previously bought from you no longer have the iron they need. I am not nearly so well versed in the ways of industry as a man might be but I am not a fool, Mr Calcott. Somewhere along the line my selfishness must have caused others a deal of worry, if nothing else.'

In the softly lit dining room Hewett Calcott stared at his hostess, her head bent slightly over her discarded plate, partly concealing her lovely face. He had made it his business to do more than monitor supplies of pig iron to Bull Piece; he had followed closely this woman's every action – her dealings with the men who worked for her, her encounters with Jago Timmins.

'Your selfishness, as you call it, kept your head above water.' He spoke softly, his glance never leaving her. 'It also saved your workers, some of them possibly from the workhouse, for once Timmins had drawn them away from you and Kenton was safely closed down, all they would have got from him would have been the sack; nor would they have found employment anywhere else in this town. It is my opinion that the rest of Darlaston's iron masters are hand in glove with him.'

'It is kind of you to try to reassure me that what I did was right in the circumstances.' Isabel lifted her glance but uncertainty still clouded her eyes. 'Yet I cannot help the way I feel, I cannot just dismiss something I know to be wrong, and my taking everything you produce, leaving none for the next man, *is* wrong.' She lifted a hand to the table, leaning forward as she added: 'Mr Calcott, I feel it is time I redressed the wrong I did. I . . . I would like to draw up a new contract with Bradley Field.'

Replacing his glass on the table, Hewett Calcott stared at it for several seconds before answering. 'If that is what you wish then of course we will come to some new arrangement. Perhaps we could discuss it tomorrow, say at eleven?'

Rising from the table, Isabel led the way into the drawing room. Seeing his glance take in the overstuffed ponderous chairs and stoutly padded sofa, the overpowering fireplace with its ornate mirrored overmantel and assortment of porcelain figurines repeated on the heavy occasional tables, Isabel smiled.

'My father had a taste for the ornate,' she said as he took a chair. 'It is a taste that frankly I do not share. I had intended to clear some of the furniture out but . . .' she shrugged, '. . . somehow I still have not managed to get around to doing so.'

'Perhaps you are not ready to part with the reminders of your father just yet?' Hewett Calcott watched her closely, seeing her face cloud over as he spoke. 'It could be you wish to hold on to your memories of him and that is why you hold on to his furnishings?'

'It is purely a matter of time.' Isabel waited while Bradshaw placed the coffee tray on a table beside her then left. 'This house holds no memories I wish to preserve.'

'Not even of your mother?'

The question was asked gently but it struck Isabel to the heart as her eyes flew to the framed photograph she had brought to stand on a table close to the chair she always used. This house was filled with the shade of Luther Kenton, of his harshness and the cruelty two young children had found hard to bear and even harder to understand. But her mother had lived here too, and though very little of the house reflected her gentleness there was, beneath the aura that soured it, a trace of the love Victoria had given them, a love that had surmounted the hurt and fear inflicted by Luther Kenton; but then that love had been taken away, killed by the neverending torment of a husband's bitterness.

'My memories of my mother are not in this house, Mr Calcott, they are in my heart.' She glanced up as she offered him the cup of coffee she had poured, but his eyes were still on the photograph.

'You are very like her.' He seemed reluctant to take his glance from the face smiling back from the silver frame.

'My mother was beautiful.' Isabel glanced again at the photograph, fading a little with age.

'No more so than her daughter,' he answered softly, watching the colour suffuse her cheeks.

'You flatter me, Mr Calcott, and that makes me embarrassed.'

Hewett Calcott took the cup she held out to him. How he would love to touch the cheeks blushing from his compliment; how he wanted to hold her in his arms, to touch his mouth to that shining auburn hair, tell her of his feelings.

'Never be embarrassed by the truth,' he said, submerging the longing inside himself. 'And never mistake the truth for flattery. I am not a man who would impress a woman with lies. And that brings me back to our earlier discussion: your worry about an exclusive contract between Kenton and Calcott resulting in workers being deprived of their living. May I point out one more thing to you?'

'Of course,' Isabel agreed, relieved to have the conversation steered along fresh channels. It was not that she disliked Hewett Calcott or resented his compliment, the reverse was nearer the truth. She liked the man, maybe more than a little. He was considerate and thoughtful, charming without being sycophantic, a fair-dealing man in business – or at least he had been so with her. But that was all she knew of him. He had told her nothing of himself.

'It is this.' He laid aside the coffee cup and with one last swift glance at the photograph went on: 'Far from selling all of the Bradley Field production to you, causing unemployment or closures of other works, it has given rise to a great many more people being in jobs and a higher amount of iron being produced.'

'But how?' Isabel's slightly puzzled frown displayed her lack of understanding.

'Simple.' He smiled then, the corners of his eyes crinkling into a web of fine lines, his handsome features softening. 'I opened more smelting works and hired more workers. You have my assurance that your contract has in no way affected my workers or those of any firm I supply. Now, reluctantly, I must leave.'

At the door he took the gloves and tall black hat Isabel handed him.

'You also?' She touched the armband circling his coat sleeve. 'You too have attested?'

He glanced down at the ribbon. 'Lord Derby's scheme! It is a fine idea in theory, having every able man sign to say they will join the Army when called upon, though I fear it is having little practical effect. I think it will take more definite action if our forces are to be maintained.'

'But what else *can* be done? Men can no longer be press ganged.'

'I am not so sure. There are other ways to tie a man to the colours. Legal ways, yes, but not so different from the press gangs.'

'How do you mean?'

Glancing down at her, he experienced the same surge of emotion that gripped him whenever he looked at her, the same longing to take her in his arms.

'Conscription!' He flicked one finger against his tall hat, an empty gesture but one that served to take his eyes from her. 'Compulsory service in the armed forces for all able-bodied men – and not just the young. I think we will see those of middle age and more called to fight, and very soon.'

Watching him drive away, Isabel felt a weight of dread settle over her. Not him too. She prayed silently, not knowing why she prayed, knowing only that she did not want Hewett Calcott to leave.

Chapter Nine

Isabel glanced at the list of names written on the piece of paper Edward Perry had brought into the office at Bull Piece.

'This is three-quarters of the work force!'

'Arrh, miss, I knows it is.' The charge hand slipped off his cap, running fingers through hair that was growing greyer by the day. 'And most of them skilled men. We be down to operating with apprentices; we don't have enough who know the steel to oversee these lads. What furnace men we have left be overstretched.' He replaced the cap, his eyes showing the concern that had caused him to ask her to come to the foundry. 'They be doing their best by the young 'uns, trying to see they does things right, but they can't be everywhere at once. I'm feared there will be an accident. It has to happen sooner or later, stands to reason!'

'The Army takes the men and yet the government asks for more and more guns and ammunition.' Isabel looked up at Perry. 'Don't they realise what they are doing? Or don't they care!'

'I reckon they knows it be 'ard,' he said, the worry in her hazel eyes striking the same chord in him. 'But I don't see what more they could do. The grand scheme of Lord Derby never worked so they had to bring in conscription.'

'Meanwhile we are left to produce more and more steel with less than a handful of skilled men. Well, it cannot go on!' Leaving the list on the desk, she stood up. 'I will not have the lives of young lads put into jeopardy by having them to do a job for which they are not trained. I shall write to my brother and ask him to put the matter to . . . to . . . to the Prime Minister himself if need be!'

Edward Perry hid a smile that was more of sympathy than amusement. 'Begging your pardon, Miss, but that could take time, and like as not be fruitless at the end of it.'

'So what *do* I do?' she strode about the small room in frustration. 'There are no men in Darlaston to be hired, there are . . .' She stopped suddenly, the frown clearing from her forehead. 'I will be in touch later, Mr Perry.'

Saying no more than that, she swept from the office, leaving a puzzled charge hand scratching his head and muttering, 'Now what?'

Urging Janey into a trot, Isabel's mind worked quickly as the small trap made its way back along Station Street. Making a sharp right turn into Slater Street, she brought the mare to a halt outside the tall railings that ringed the Central School.

'Wish me luck, Janey,' she murmured, patting the horse's shoulder. 'If this does not work then I reckon Kenton's will be finished.'

Returning the greeting of the prim, tight-faced bespectacled little headmaster as he waved her towards a chair, Isabel felt her stomach clench nervously. Was this the right thing to do? Would this man who looked as if it pained him whenever a word escaped his lips, have anything to do with her request?

'Mr Thompson . . .' Isabel began, but was immediately halted as he took a silver watch from his pocket, flipped open the case, made a careful study of the time then replaced it in his pocket. Without a word he turned to a cupboard that stood to one side of his heavy oak desk, taking out a large shining brass bell. Still without a word, he opened the door of his study and stepped into a corridor, the bottom half of its walls painted dark chocolate brown, the upper half a dismal shade of green. Lifting his arm high, he brought it down with the finality of an avenging angel, clanging the bell loudly. With the third stroke he caught the clapper with his free hand, then stood with it as doors somewhere along the corridor opened and a stream of silent children filed past, their eyes directed straight ahead, carefully avoiding contact with his stony glance.

He returned to his seat finally, the bell neatly placed on top of the head-high cupboard. Isabel gave him a slight smile, disguising it immediately as the clipped moustache adorning the headmaster's tight mouth twitched fiercely. Telling herself she was not one of his staff to be dominated by him, and certainly not a pupil to be obviously fearful of him, Isabel began again.

'Mr Thompson, I am here to ask your help.' Isabel saw the gleam of satisfaction leap to his small black button eyes. She had struck the right note. This man clearly liked to think himself essential to the smooth running of things. 'As you will probably know, my father owned several works in Darlaston, but with his death, and with my brother serving in the Army, it has been left to me to keep the works in production. I fear this is not easy; industry, I think you will agree, is no place for a woman.' So far so good, she thought as his pomaded head bobbed rapidly in agreement. 'I need the advice of a man, Mr Thompson, a man who has the welfare of his town and his country at heart.'

Her glance suitably lowered, Isabel cursed herself for being a hypocrite. She did not need this man's assistance in administering the work of the foundry, but unless she boosted his self-importance by pretending . . .

A tap against the glass panel of the door drew his attention away from her and Isabel drew in a quick breath, raising her eyes as a woman entered the room. She had to keep up this charade of the helpless little woman if she wanted her plan to go through quickly.

Dressed in a navy skirt cut straight and a long-sleeved white cotton blouse picked out with navy pin stripe, mousy hair snatched back from cheeks and brow to form a bun at the nape of the neck, a woman entered the room. Timidly she laid a perfectly set tray before the man whose mouth was once more sucked into a prim hard line.

Wraith-like, every movement silent as a shadow, the woman departed, not once looking into the face of her superior or at his visitor.

'No man has the welfare of his country more at heart than I do, Miss Kenton. If I can help you in the absence of your brother, then be assured I shall do so.'

Accepting the coffee he poured from a graceful china pot, Isabel hoped her smile showed the proper amount of gratitude.

Taking his own cup, he leaned back in his chair, small button eyes scrutinising her.

'I find the boys who come to Kenton's from your school make the most conscientious of workers,' said Isabel, sipping her coffee. While this particular piece of flattery was no lie, the boys did work hard, she felt the words stick in her throat. 'They are also polite and attentive to what they are taught.'

'We tolerate no other way at Central School.'

Neither did their parents! Isabel sipped again at her coffee. He could take the glory if it meant getting what she wanted.

Replacing his own cup on the tray he dabbed at his lips with a pristine white napkin then drew out the pocket watch glancing at the time before proceeding to carry out the same ritual as before. Isabel watched through windows that reached from the ceiling down to waist level, giving a clear view of the long ordered lines of silent children returning to their classrooms.

The brass bell safely ensconced once more in its sanctuary, the headmaster returned his attention to Isabel.

'The problem is that while the boys are all I say they are, quick and responsive, they are not able to receive the instruction they need in order to become fully conversant with the processes involved in steel making. We simply do not have enough skilled men to teach them.'

'My dear Miss Kenton.' The neat moustache twitched. 'I understand the problem, as I do the probable cause. However,

I can see no way in which I can assist you. My staff are all female . . .'

'I was not thinking of asking for your staff, Mr Thompson.' Isabel placed her cup on the tray. 'But of whether you think it advisable to seek the help of the women, the mothers and sisters of the boys who work at Kenton's?'

'Women working in the steel foundries!'

His moustache twitched like a demented black beetle.

'Really, Miss Kenton! I find the suggestion altogether ridiculous. Why, you said yourself only moments ago that industry was no place for women.'

'And war is no occupation for men!' She looked coolly now at the man facing her across the desk. If he took offence at her reply and refused her request then so be it. She would just have to find some other way; but find one she would. 'But that is what we find ourselves in and we women must support our men in whatever way we can. I believe I can enlist the help of mothers and sisters . . .' Letting her lips droop a little and her eyes take on a helpless gleam, she looked full at him. 'If only I could get to see them, but it will take weeks for me to visit every home . . .'

'My dear Miss Kenton, there is no need for that . . . no need at all.'

Biting her lip to hold back her sense of triumph, Isabel watched the smile spread expansively across the headmaster's face, squeezing the clipped moustache until it resembled an insect even more closely.

'There is no call for you to go visiting people's homes, no call whatsoever. Just you leave this to me. My staff will have every child copy out a letter to be taken to their mother when they leave this building. I shall say it is my requirement they present themselves here at Central School . . . when?' He paused. 'When would you prefer they come?'

'Would they come this evening . . . perhaps at seven o'clock?' Isabel primed her voice to just the right pitch of uncertainty.

His smile disappeared, easing the strain on the little moustache, and he drew in a breath that puffed out his chest. 'They will not refuse, not when they see my name on the letter. We will say seven o'clock this evening then.'

'Mr Thompson.' Isabel fluttered her long lashes. 'How very clever of you to think of asking the mothers to come here. I would never have arrived at such a solution.'

Chest swelling even further, he rose from his desk to escort her to the door.

'A man's brain, my dear.' He smiled fatuously. 'A man's brain. It is superior to a woman's. Nature's design, my dear, nature's design.'

'A man's brain, Janey.' Isabel laughed softly to herself, climbing into the trap a few minutes later. 'A man's brain . . . it is superior to a woman's, nature's design . . . but only when the woman's design intends it to be!'

Still smiling, she shook the reins, guiding the horse to take the turning left into Walsall Street. Crossing Dale End she went over the scene in her mind. It had worked perfectly.

Calling Janey to a halt, she erased the smile from her face. Running a hand over the skirt of her grey coat she walked into All Saints Church School. What had worked once would work again.

Isabel looked at the crowd of women standing in the hall of Central School. She had smiled to herself at the headmaster's tone of confident authority when he had said they would come, implying they would not dare do otherwise when *he* summoned them. But she knew the women of Darlaston feared very little apart from any threat to their families. They had come because they were curious to learn what the daughter of Luther Kenton wanted with them.

The headmaster's patronising introduction over, Isabel got

to her feet. *There be nothing inside a woman's head . . . just do what a woman be meant to do, keep your mouth closed.* Luther Kenton's words seemed almost to burn in her brain and his laughter mocked her until her knees trembled and she half turned to walk away, off the raised platform and out of the building. But that would have delighted Luther; even now, from beyond the grave, she could sense his pleasure at her failure. But she would not fail, Luther Kenton would take no more pleasure from her.

'Ladies, I . . . I am Isabel Kenton.'

'We know who you be.' The heckler's voice was already tinged with irritation at the long drawn out speech of the starchy man sitting behind the table draped with its amber-coloured chenille cloth. 'Just get on with it, I've got babbies at home waiting on their supper.'

'And how long will you have those children should our troops fail to defeat Germany?' Isabel's head went up as she stepped closer to the edge of the platform. 'You have all heard the stories told by the Belgian refugees, of the horrors people were subjected to . . .'

'That were in their country!'

'Yes, it was in their country.' Isabel turned her eyes in the direction of the new voice. 'And without help from us it might be England next. We all have loved ones at the Front: husbands, brothers, fathers. Men who are fighting for everything they hold dear and will go on fighting, giving their lives if need be, so we may be kept from living through what those refugees lived through. Now we women must do everything we can to help our men.'

'The government has already taken the names of every woman and child over the age of fifteen. We have all been made to sign the national register. What will it be next, conscription for women?'

'If that be what it takes to kick the Kaiser's arse,' a second louder voice answered the first, bringing a rustle of approval from the rest.

'Shut up!' A woman in a feathered hat, her coat threatening

to give up the struggle to remain buttoned across her ample breasts, clambered on to the platform, one shove sending the dapper little headmaster stumbling back to his chair as he moved to prevent her. 'Shut up, the lot of you, give the wench a chance.' She glanced at Isabel. 'Go on, miss, say what you come to say.'

With a quick smile at her plump supporter, Isabel began again, and this time her voice was strong, ringing out to the back of the room. 'I came to say this. Our men can only fight with the weapons we give them. Take them away and we hold their lives cheap. We will make a sacrifice of hundreds, maybe thousands, of troops.'

'Ain't nobody takin' weapons away from our soldiers.'

'Perhaps not directly,' she replied. 'But every steel foundry and every ammunitions works that closes down takes away guns and shells and bullets, the very things that could keep our men alive; and those works *are* closing from a lack of skilled men to run them.'

'What you say might well be true, I don't odds it!' Again a voice called out from somewhere among the crowd. 'But there don't be anything can be done about that. Men be called up and they have to go, that be all there is to it!'

The plump woman stepped forward, coming to stand beside Isabel on the edge of the dais. 'You don't odds it, Maudie Crump, you don't question what this wench has said 'cos you knows it be the truth.' She threw out a bold glance, encompassing the faces turned up towards her. 'The men *have* to go,' 'tis true enough, and common sense tells all 'cept them smart-arsed buggers at Westminster that the more that goes, the fewer be left to work the foundries.'

'Well, it don't take no smart-arsed bugger to tell you that women can't work the furnaces or tip the crucibles!' the voice returned swiftly. '*I* can tell you that and my arse don't be smart, just sore from where my old man kicks it when his meal ain't ready.'

'I too am no smart-arsed bugger.' Isabel felt the wave of

amused appreciation flow back to her from the women. Her earthy answer had warmed them towards her, now was the moment. 'But I have what every woman in this room has got: common sense. Of course we cannot forge steel or tip molten metal but we can do the next best thing. We can take over the jobs of men not employed in the foundries. We can make guns, we can make shells, we can make bullets! It is not beyond our physical capacity to take over as conductors on trams or trains; despite what we have so often been told, we *do* have a brain, and that equal to any man's . . .'

Behind her she heard the indignant cough of the headmaster, but Isabel paid no attention. Many men would have their feelings ruffled and their smug beliefs overturned before this fight was over.

'. . . I say *we* can do these jobs and many more we can all think of, and by taking them on we can release men to work the steel.'

'You keep saying "we".' Towards the rear of the hall a woman was speaking. '*We* can do this and *we* can do the other, but what part be you takin' apart from standin' on a stage and spouting?'

'I will tell you what part I am taking,' Isabel returned hotly. 'I am trying to keep a steel foundry and its component works in production. I am trying to keep up the supply of ammunition we all know is so badly needed; and more than that, I am trying to keep open those jobs your men are going to need once they come home. How many of you have husbands or sons who worked for Kenton Engineering? That is the number of men who will have no job to return to.' Isabel paused, allowing her words to sink in.

'We all know what that could mean.' The plum coloured coat stretched to its full as the stout woman shouted her own warning. 'We all of us remembers what it was to be without food to eat or a fire to warm ourselves by, we have all been beholden to the Parish at one time or another, and I for one don't want to see them times again. What this wench be sayin' makes sense. Men *will* be needin' jobs when they gets back an' it be up to we women to see they be here waitin' on them!'

'You can do it,' Isabel said as a silence fell on the hall. 'It will feel strange at first and I am not saying it will not be hard . . .'

'Not nearly as hard as my man's old whatsit on a Saturday night!'

The chair behind the table shuffled again but the head-master's indignant snort was lost among the laughter erupting from the women.

'. . . but with your help,' Isabel went on calmly, though she could not prevent the blush rising to her cheeks, 'I can take the men from Glovers Mound and from other works and place them in the foundry where they can help teach the apprentices, take on the jobs the lads are not yet skilled enough to tackle alone. You whose men are still at home, talk to them, tell them what I have said here tonight. And you . . . any of you who are willing to work for the victory of our country, Kenton's has a job for you. Together we will win.'

Thanking the headmaster whose moustache fairly danced with anger as the women walked out on his well-rehearsed closing speech, Isabel stepped into the night with no sound of deprecating laughter filling her mind, no mocking presence walking beside her. Luther Kenton's baleful presence was absent . . . but for how long?

The evening had gone well yet beneath the elation Isabel felt the tingle of apprehension. She glanced about her, seeing the last straggle of women fast disappearing along the various streets and alleyways that led off in the direction of Butcroft and the Leys. She had told Mark she was not afraid of a further attack being made upon her, and she had Perry's avowed assurance they had seen the last of the man responsible, yet despite it all she felt nervous as she urged Janey into a trot.

Nearing the Bull Stake her apprehension calmed. Tiny shops

spilled pools of sallow light into the darkness, dispelling the shadows with the anaemic gleam of gas mantles, lighting the way of late shoppers and men finishing the evening shift in the foundries.

It was after a tram rattled past, taking the route to Walsall, that Isabel heard it: a sound she had not heard before, a dull pulsating throb accompanied by a low distinctive hum.

Janey had heard it too and pulled restlessly against the reins, almost as she had pulled that night when the figure . . . Isabel pushed the thought away, calling softly to the mare.

The sound steadily mounted, its rhythm from no particular direction yet at the same time everywhere, filling the night with an all-enveloping intensity. Then from behind her came the sound of an explosion, the force of it rocking the small trap, throwing her sideways to strike her shoulder against its side. Suddenly it seemed hell had opened its doors as buildings burst into flames and crashed down.

'Oh, dear God Almighty, it be an earthquake . . . we be having an earthquake!' A woman's scream rang out as a second explosion rent the air, shaking the ground and bringing more buildings toppling, lighting the remnants in great gushes of flame.

Fighting to hold the terrified horse, Isabel was dimly aware of women spilling from the narrow-fronted shops, of men running from the several public houses, all of them shouting to know what was happening.

'My babbies!' a woman screamed hysterically. 'My babbies, they be by theirselves!'

Rushing across in front of Janey, the woman's flapping shawl caught the animal's face, making her shy in panic, while another dropped her basket, her pitiful calls ringing out behind her as she ran into a sheet of golden flame.

Trying desperately to cling on to the reins as a third explosion added to the pandemonium, Isabel had not seen the man step from the gloom of a shadowed doorway. Whipping away the muffler from his neck, he threw it across the mare's eyes, hanging on to her head as the earth danced with the force that ripped through it once more.

'Get out!'

The order was not shouted but for all the noise Isabel heard it clearly, and the sound turned her heart to ice.

'I said, get out!'

Around her leaping flames drove back the night, lifting the shadows to scarlet and gold. Silhouetted against them, the dark figure left the horse's head, one arm reaching out to her as he stepped towards the trap.

Paralysed with fear, Isabel felt the hand close over her arm, pulling her sideways; felt the hardness of the low brass rail bite into her hip as she was hauled over it: the sharp thud to her spine as she was dragged from the trap, falling to the ground. Through it all her screams were silent.

Closer now in the smoke-filled roar of the burning night a further explosion ripped the roof from the Green Dragon public house, scattering tiles and shards of broken glass half the length of King Street.

The after blast of wind snatched the muffler from the horse's head, causing her to scream in fear, but Isabel was drowning in her own terror. He must have followed her, must have been watching her, but for how long . . . how long had this man trailed her?

'Let me go . . . let me go!'

Lost in fear Isabel did not register the face of the man who caught her flailing hands, did not hear the voice that shouted above the roaring hell that surrounded them, but her mind shouted the names: Jago . . . Ernie Griffin!

Both arms fastening about her, holding her own trapped, he pulled her close to him.

'Let me go . . . please.

Beside her ear his voice was hoarse and tight. 'You are coming with me. Now let's get out of here!'

'No . . . !' Her scream lost in the bedlam that was raging all around them, Isabel struggled to free herself.

A jerk as his arms lifted her half off her feet. Isabel felt the strength of him. She would stand no chance against him.

'I said, you are coming with me.' He set her roughly on her feet. 'Now either you move or you get it here.'

History was repeating itself and what people were around would be too busy saving themselves from whatever was shaking the town apart to bother about what was happening to her.

'I said, move!'

He pushed her forward but when she screamed he released one arm from about her and pointed.

'Look', he shouted close to her ear, 'look up there. Either we go now or we both die right here!'

Another explosion terrifying the horse, it screamed in fear, the sound breaking the trance of terror that held Isabel helpless. Her mind suddenly wiped free of the nightmare that had so quickly swallowed her, she reached for the bridle, calling the animal's name as it bolted.

'Let it go!'

Quick as Isabel was, the figure standing over her had been quicker, one hand grasping her wrist, one arm circling her waist and drawing her back against him.

'But Janey is . . .'

'The horse will find its way.' Close against her ear, his voice was tight. 'Now let's get out of here.'

'No!' Isabel struggled to free herself. 'We have to help. The earthquake . . .'

'This is no earthquake, look!' The man released her wrist to point to the sky.

Her breath coming in a long disbelieving gasp, Isabel stared at the huge shape, the light of the burning buildings throwing it into sharp silhouette. Moving slowly, like a great whale, it hung against the sky, its rhythmic throb beating like a giant heart.

'What . . . what is it?' Her fear of the man who held her lost before a greater fear, Isabel stared at the long cylindrical shape hovering above the town.

'Zeppelin!' He grasped her wrist again, holding her against his body as he pushed her forward. 'German airship, and it's dropping bombs! Now, move. I don't intend to go the same way of those buildings.'

Half dragging, half carrying her, darting for cover as fresh explosions rocked the earth and the sound of falling bricks and glass died against the crackle of flames, he forced her on. Isabel screamed as he dragged her further and further into the darkness.

Chapter Ten

'You be sure of what you heard?' Edward Perry looked at the man sitting opposite him.

'Sure as I'm sitting here, Mr Perry. He said as Jago Timmins was willing to pay to have Kenton's done over'

Edward glanced at the cheap tin clock that stood on the shelf above the fireplace of his tiny living room. 'He wants it done afore morning, you say, Kenton Steel works burned out?'

'He didn't say burned out, Mr Perry.' The younger man twisted the cap he held in his hands. 'In fact, no mention was made of how it were to be done, just that it needed to be done quick.'

'Was anybody else there?'

'Oh, arrh. The Frying Pan were full, it bein' Saturday night.'

Of course the public houses were usually at their most busy on Saturday, pay day. Edward thought rapidly. The Saturday shift worked the full twelve hours the same as every day except Sunday. If any of Jago's paid men showed up at the foundry during that time they wouldn't have the chance of spending their ill-gotten gains, Kenton men would see to that. But Saturday evening the furnaces were banked down, kept going on a low heat 'til Monday morning. So it would be Saturday night or Sunday when they made a move. Question was, which?

'Who was it Jackson were talking to?'

The younger man hesitated, running a hand through his fair

hair. 'That be it, Mr Perry, that be why I took it on meself to come to your house. The man Jackson were talking to . . . he . . . he were me father. If they be caught it could be ten years or more!' The man rushed on. 'I know what Jago Timmins has asked be wrong, but that ain't what be worryin' me. It be my mother. What will happen to her and the little 'uns if my father gets copped? I have to report to the Army tomorrow, my conscription has come through, but I can't go with this lot on me mind!'

'You have to go, lad, ain't no other way. You don't go, then they sends their own bobbies to get you, and unless you be a conshie . . .' Edward shrugged his shoulders expressively.

'I ain't no conscientious objector, Mr Perry. Any bloke raises his hand against my family or my country then I don't turn the other cheek. And I ain't no coward neither. It . . . it's just the thought of my mother bein' left to cope on her own. P'raps you think I should talk to my father, but I learned long ago to keep my mouth shut. He still be pretty handy with a belt.'

His wife bustling in from the scullery, Edward Perry clapped a hand to the young man's shoulder, walking with him to the door that gave immediately on to the footpath edging the road like a narrow grey ribbon.

'You get yourself off tomorrow, lad, and give them Germans what for.' Then, beyond the door, he added quietly: 'You did the right thing coming to me. I'll see to it your father don't go doing Jago Timmins's dirty work. He won't do time for smashing up Kenton's foundry.'

'Ain't just the foundry.' The young man settled his grease-stained cloth cap back on his head, pulling the peak well down over his forehead. 'The way I heard it Jago said to do all of Kenton's works: Glovers Mound, Butcroft, the Leys and the rest. That be why the money was so high, and half of the hundred pounds they was offered would be more than my dad could turn his back on.'

After reassuring the young man yet again, Edward watched him walk down the street, turning the corner at the end. The lad had no lack of courage for it certainly took that for him to shop his own father; Edward would keep his word. He would make sure the lad's father paid no price for aiding Jago Timmins.

Turning back into the house, he reached for his cap and jacket hanging on the back of the door. Two men could not hope to do for all Kenton's works, not in one night, and no way would they risk a second offensive. Easing into his jacket, he passed his muffler about his neck, crossing it over his chest and pushing the ends beneath his jacket. Taking his pipe from the mantel shelf, he called goodbye to his wife then left the house. Jago Timmins's men were going to need help . . . and so was he.

'Eh, Miss Isabel! I thought it were Gabriel ablowing of his horn, I did truly. I thought the end of the world had come. Me and Bradshaw, we heard the bangs from the kitchen here and when we went outside we could see the glow in the sky and knew it were no furnaces being opened, it were past time for that. Then we saw that huge great thing! It seemed to be hanging there in the sky like some great black monster. It 'ad to be a demon from 'ell, it couldn't be no other floating over our 'eads spitting fire and brimstone, its great eyes glowing . . . eh, I tell you, I've never been as feared as when I seen that horrible thing waiting to devour us!'

'What you saw was no demon, Mrs Bradshaw, though it could be said to be a product of hell.'

Owen Farr caught the woman's still frightened eyes, his own as reassuring as he could make them. Of slim build but not slight, his shoulders hinted at a concealed strength and muscles rippled beneath his dove grey coat with each movement. Fair hair free from the restriction of the popular brilliantine curled naturally over his brow beneath which eyes of river green regarded the terrified housekeeper with sympathy, his full mouth touched with a smile.

'Then what was it if it were no demon?' Letty Bradshaw

demanded, the reassurance in those striking eyes disregarded. 'Could be no other to my way of looking at it. Great long black body and fiery eyes . . . what else could it 'ave been up there in the sky 'cept a thing of the devil?'

'The use to which it has been put could be labelled the devil's work, but it was created by men, Mrs Bradshaw, men who see it as an instrument whereby they might win this war. What you saw passing over Darlaston was not a fire-and-brimstone-spitting demon, it was a flying machine, a Zeppelin.'

'A machine!' Letty looked at Isabel, standing beside her, a comforting arm about her shoulders. 'A machine that can fly in the sky?'

'That is what Mr Farr tells me,' Isabel replied.

'You mean, they 'ave them there horseless carriages up in the sky?' Letty made no attempt to disguise her disgust. 'Be you saying we 'ave to 'ave them machines over our heads as well as on the streets? Great hulking brutes of things! They be appearing everywhere. The only way a body can be safe on the roads today is to be off 'em, but where do you be safe from a machine that flies over your 'ead? You tell me that, Miss Isabel, you tell me that!'

'I don't know.' It was only a murmur but her voice carried all of Isabel's fear. For almost the first time in her life she felt she had come up against something for which she had no answer.

'I hears what you say, Mr Farr.' Letty transferred her gaze to the handsome man seated in the kitchen of Woodbank House. 'But if it were not fire and brimstone that . . . that Zepper plane was spitting down on the town, then what were it? The sound of it nigh split your ear drums and the flames lit the night.'

'It was bombs.' Owen Farr glanced at Isabel before returning his attention to the older woman, sitting in a large wooden chair drawn up to the gleaming black range.

'Bombs!' Letty frowned. 'What be bombs?'

'They are containers filled with explosives. When they strike or hit the ground they explode, shattering everything for many yards around, bringing down buildings and setting fire to anything that will burn.'

'Eh, who would ever think of such a thing . . . dropping bombs on innocent folk? What be the world coming to? It must 'ave been one of them come down in Great Croft Street – that be just the back of where my sister and her husband lives. Bradshaw went to see if they was all right after the Zepper plane floated away. He went down into the town after I got you put to bed. That were another shock, I can tell you, when we saw you being half carried up to the house. It fair turned my stomach.'

'Were your relatives safe?'

'Oh, arrh.' Letty nodded. 'Thanks be to God for His grace, they was safe and sound, Mr Farr, not like Jessy Carter. Her house was just a jumble of bricks, like an earthquake had hit it so Bradshaw told me though it must 'ave been one of them bomb things; whatever it was, it took the lot of them, and six of them no more than babbies at school. It don't be human doing such things . . . it don't be human!'

'I know, Braddy.' Isabel pressed her arm tighter about the woman's shoulders as Letty threw her apron over her face and wept.

'How could they, Miss Isabel?' Her sobs, muffled by the apron, filled the quiet kitchen. 'How could they do things like that to little children?'

'War is a brutal thing,' Owen Farr said softly. 'It is no respecter of persons, and neither does it select whom it will kill. It knows no compassion. I am afraid more than a few people lost homes and loved ones last night.'

'Like we would 'ave lost Miss Isabel had you not come along when you did.' Letty Bradshaw lowered the apron, displaying eyes red and puffy from weeping, but held it against her mouth, peering over it at the man who had half carried her mistress into the house the night before. 'I thought when I first saw you with Miss Isabel in your grasp that you were the same man . . .'

'The same man?' Owen Farr raised one well-shaped

eyebrow as his liquid green eyes switched to Isabel, still standing with an arm about her housekeeper's shoulder.

'I . . . I was approached by a man on my way home one evening.' She averted her eyes.

'Approached!' Letty dropped her apron. 'You was attacked, damn' near half killed and all by that swine!'

'A man attacked you?' The expressive eyes of the stranger had suddenly become hard and cold as glaciers. 'Was he caught? The police . . .'

'I did not inform the police.' Isabel felt the slight tensing of Letty's shoulder. She had long since guessed that her housekeeper had told a constable what had occurred that night, but without an official complaint from herself nothing could be done.

'But in Heaven's name, why not?'

'Because, Mr Farr, I thought the man's wife had gone through enough because of him. To be left to fend totally for herself whilst he served a term of imprisonment would only have caused her further hardship.'

'You thought his wife had gone through enough because of him?' Owen Farr's eyes narrowed. 'That would imply you knew the man who attacked you.'

'Oh, she knowed him all right.' Letty stood up, then grabbing the poker from the hearth, stabbed brutally at the coals smouldering behind the bars of the grate. 'Everybody in Darlaston knowed that one. A drunken, loud-mouthed wife beater . . .'

'Braddy, please, not now,' Isabel said, embarrassed for the subject to be discussed with someone who was virtually a stranger.

The smile that had earlier enhanced the sensual line of Owen Farr's full mouth and warmed his eyes was now a thing dead and gone forever. His lips clamped hard together, he kept his glance on Isabel. 'I would like to hear what happened?'

Feeling the trembling begin inside her as it always did whenever she allowed herself to think of Ernie Griffin and his hands hauling her to the ground, Isabel dropped the mental curtain that shut off her thoughts, veiling the terrors they still held for her. 'I have no doubt you would, Mr Farr,' she said, her back stiffening and her head lifting dismissively, 'but I have no wish to discuss it or to have any member of my household discuss it.'

'No more you would!' Letty returned the poker noisily to its stand in the hearth, a familiarity bred by long years of caring for the young woman making her immune to her mistress's unusual sharpness. 'But you should have discussed it with the constable soon as you was able.'

'If you will forgive my saying so, Miss Kenton, I agree with what Mrs Bradshaw says. You should have called in the police if only as a safeguard against the man repeating his action.'

'Oh, he won't come back again, he got a right good lampin' for what he done to Miss Isabel!' Letty rushed in then hesitated, realising she had said more than she intended.

'Ernie Griffin was given a beating?' Forgetting her words of a moment before, Isabel turned to Letty. Deciding that retreat was impossible, Letty folded her arms defiantly across her heavy breasts.

'He was,' she said, the look on her face defying Isabel to argue with her, 'and it were one he won't go forgetting in a hurry. And don't you go asking me who give it to him – he got what he deserved and that be all there be to it!'

'Well, if ever I discover who meted out justice to the man then I will shake him, or them, by the hand.' Standing up, Owen winked at the woman who stood before the fire, her arms still folded. 'Perhaps, should you ever get to learn who it was, you would tell them so, Mrs Bradshaw?'

'Should I ever find out,' the older woman's face broke into a smile, 'I'll pass the message on, Mr Farr.'

'And now I must go.'

Deciding to ignore that wink and to question Mrs Bradshaw later on the subject of her attacker's punishment, Isabel turned to the man who had brought her away from the chaos of the town the previous evening.

'Will you not take some tea, Mr Farr?'

The words came out awkwardly and Isabel blushed, realising they sounded like an excuse to keep him with her a little longer; then, the flush on her face deepening, she knew she did want to keep him longer. It was ridiculous that she felt that way, wanting to hold on to a man she had met for the first time only a few hours before. But ridiculous or not, she tried again.

'Braddy will not forgive my rudeness in failing to offer you tea when you first arrived, but at least she will not be so hard on me if you take some now.'

He smiled then and to Isabel it seemed the day had taken on a new brightness.

'Then it seems I must come to your rescue yet again, Miss Kenton.'

'Arrh, well, she can thank you in the sitting room, that be the place for tea to be served to visitors, not here in my kitchen.'

'I had hoped to become a very regular visitor, Braddy, but if your kitchen is to be barred to me then I must seriously rethink my plans.'

'Get along with you, Mr Farr.' Letty unfolded her arms, eyes twinkling as she swung the bracket with its kettle to hang above the gleaming coals, his use of Isabel's pet name for her going unchallenged.

'I refuse to get along unless you promise I can sit in your comfortable kitchen whenever I visit?'

Letty's laughter bubbled up. 'Kitchens don't be the proper place for a young man to come visiting.'

'I love doing what is not considered proper.'

His smile widened into a grin and for a moment Isabel was back in her childhood with Mark, confessing to taking one of Braddy's fresh-baked scones and grinning as she tried hopelessly to scold him.

'Off you go.' Letty laughed again as she reached for a tray kept on a long side table opposite the cooking range she had refused to change for a new fangled gas stove. 'Get you out from under my feet.'

Switching his glance to Isabel, Owen shed the grin though the twinkle in his green eyes said it was only just beneath the surface. His voice assumed a mock seriousness as he asked: 'Miss Kenton, do I have your permission to come into this kitchen and drink tea?'

'Of course, Mr Farr.' She felt the delicious stir of memory as a smile tugged at her mouth. 'But only when Braddy says you may. I would not dare go against her wishes.'

'Eh! If only that were true my days in this house would 'ave been a lot easier. Now take your little white lies out of my kitchen or there'll be no tea.'

The gleam in Owen's eyes deepened into roguishness as he moved quickly to the housekeeper's side, planting a swift kiss on her cheek. Isabel felt the stir of memory turn to pain. Mark had always kissed the motherly housekeeper like that, melting her to him as now she was melting towards an almost complete stranger; as they were both melting to him.

'Say I can come to sit with you, Braddy?' he said, his tone that of a little boy. 'The pleasure of my visits will be spoiled if I can't see you.'

Pleasure and embarrassment staining her cheeks, Letty fumbled with the china she was setting on the tray. 'Spoiled my eye!' A smile splitting her round face, she looked up at the handsome man, his river-green eyes threatening to transport her to worlds she had no business to be in. 'Eh, Mr Farr, if codswallop were music, I reckon you would have a full orchestra.'

'But I would play only for you, Braddy.'

Letty Bradshaw's rumbling belly laugh followed them from the kitchen as Isabel led the way into the sitting room.

'You have made a conquest there, Mr Farr.' She smiled as they each settled into a heavy ornate chair. 'Mrs Bradshaw will be your friend for life.'

'I hope to have more than one friend in this house.' His reply was soft and this time there was no trace of the rogue or the child in his voice. 'I hope we can be friends, Miss Kenton, very good friends?'

Isabel felt excitement stir within her. She knew nothing about this man whose tone implied he wished to know a great deal more about her. She should be polite but distant, make it plain to him she did not give her friendship lightly. But as he looked at her, as those marvellous eyes held her own, she knew she would do none of those things.

'It was so terrible, Mark. The screams of women and the shouts of men, buildings shaking as the bombs exploded . . .'

No! Putting down her pen, Isabel screwed the letter into a ball, throwing it into a basket beside the desk. What on earth was she doing writing such a letter to Mark? Even though she wrote that neither the house nor anyone in it had suffered from the Zeppelin raids, he would still worry, and that was the very thing she should prevent. Time enough to tell him of such things when he was back home. And he *must* come home. She stared across the desk into the garden beyond the windows of the study, heavy with the frosts of winter now. Was it frosty in France, was Mark looking out on gardens painted white, was he thinking of home? 'You *must* come home,' she whispered, tears blurring the whiteness beyond the window. 'Oh, Lord, keep him safe, keep my brother safe.'

The prayer was soft, a mere breath on the still air, but softer still was the whisper in her mind: *Let the Army find him a place for good . . .*

Luther Kenton's words. Despite the fire burning in the grate she shivered, her glance swivelling to the bookcase. However her so-called father had meant those words they would not come true, the Army would not keep Mark. He would return and then she could leave this house, leave behind the unhappiness that had been her childhood. She could forego the inheritance that had been left to her only as a means of keeping that misery alive.

He had fed on their unhappiness, her mother's especially. Isabel rose from the desk, crossing the thickly carpeted room to the bookcase, her eyes coming to rest on one particular volume. Luther had used that letter to destroy her mother. How often had he read it, how many times had he gloated over it?

Opening the glass doors, she touched the spine of the book, reaching for the sheet of yellowed paper as the hard cover swung back.

. . . I carry our child within me . . .

Isabel stared at the words. He could not have gloated over that. Luther had not been a man to take kindly to his wife bearing another man's child. But what had her mother brought to their marriage beside bastard twins?

. . . I pray God my letter reaches you before you sail for America . . .

Her fingers tightened as her eyes flicked back to the beginning. But the letter had never reached her mother's nameless lover, Luther had seen to that. Or had he? She stared at the letter, not seeing the lovely copperplate writing as her mind whirled in a new direction. What if the letter *had* been delivered to its rightful recipient – what if he had read it then returned it unanswered? What if he had deliberately turned his back on the girl who carried his child? What if . . . ?

'I know I shouldn't ought to disturb you, miss . . .'

Isabel turned hastily, the sudden start bringing a flush to her face. Letty Bradshaw stood inside the doorway and as she saw the letter in Isabel's hand the blood drained slowly from her face.

Chapter Eleven

'I wouldn't 'ave come, miss, truly I wouldn't, but I could find no place in Darlaston. Even Joe Baker's lodging house wouldn't give me a corner to sit in without first being given the twopence it takes, and I haven't a farthing, much less twopence.'

Isabel had followed Letty Bradshaw into the kitchen after pushing the letter back into its hiding place – one that was obviously no secret to the housekeeper, judging by her change of colour.

'But what brings you to this house?' Letty asked sharply. 'Miss Isabel don't be running no charity.'

'And we be asking none.' The thin figure that answered was dressed in a ragged brown skirt, toe caps cut away from worn boots allowing her feet to fit into them, what was left of a burgundy chequered shawl pulled tightly about her head and shoulders almost hiding a face pale as morning milk. Putting an arm about her companion's shoulders, she faced Letty Bradshaw, the armour of pride heavy about her. 'We came here seeking no charity but the employment once promised by the mistress of this house. It is clear that though that offer might have been made in good faith, the promise is now withdrawn. You have my apologies for having disturbed you. We would not have done so had we known we were not welcome here. Come, Mother, we will find a place somewhere else.'

Her voice softening on the last few words, the thin girl led her equally ragged mother towards the door.

'One moment!' Isabel called. 'You said the mistress of this house made you an offer of employment?'

'So my mother told me.' Turning about, the girl stood just within the circle of sallow light spilling from the gas lamp which lit the kitchen. 'And I have no reason to doubt the truth of it. We are among the destitute of the earth but we do not number among its liars. Good evening to you both.'

'Wait, please.' Isabel stepped forward her glance on the older woman. 'Are you . . .' She peered harder, trying to see more clearly the face swathed in a ragged shawl. 'Are you the woman I met at the gate one night, the woman who drank soup with me in this kitchen?'

'I am, miss.' The woman leaned heavily against the girl, using all her strength to remain standing. 'You were very kind to me that night. You said . . . you said should me and my children need employment, I was to come to you . . . but I see them words were said only in passing.'

'They were not said only in passing.' Isabel skirted the table as the two of them turned once more to leave. 'I said nothing then that I did not mean and is not meant now.'

Pulling a chair from beside the table, she helped the older of the two women into it. Indicating for the younger one too to take a chair, she turned to the dresser, reaching down cups and saucers.

'I said we want no charity.' Her pale face drawn with hunger, the girl stared at Isabel.

'Offering tea is not considered an act of charity in this town.' Isabel returned the girl's stare, understanding the pride but seeing the need. 'It is an act of friendship; the act will be made, refuse it if you wish.'

'My wench meant no offence, miss. It be only that we have been snaped so many times, 'er don't be ready to trust nobody.'

'You will not be snubbed in this house.' Isabel glanced

quickly at her housekeeper, still standing apprehensively beside the range.

'I'll see to the tea.' Catching the glance, Letty Bradshaw swung the kettle over the fire then went to fetch milk from the cool jar kept in the scullery.

'You are Ernie Griffin's wife?' Isabel asked, reaching a bowl of sugar from a cupboard and setting it alongside the cups and saucers.

'Arrh, miss.' The older woman nodded still holding her shawl tight about her head. 'I be Ernie Griffin's wife and this be my daughter.'

'I am pleased to meet you.' Isabel smiled at the girl.

''Er be Mary.'

The girl nodded but the stubborn line of her mouth did not relax.

'And your son, Mrs Griffin, is he here with you?'

'No, miss, he ain't.' The woman pressed a hand against her mouth but that did not hold back the slow tears that slid beneath her closed lids.

'Me brother . . . he ran off,' the girl said, leaning towards her mother and touching her hand with her own.

'And your father?' Letty poured boiling water into the large brown ironstone teapot.

'He . . . he . . .'

'My husband be in the Army,' Sarah Griffin answered as her daughter's voice faltered. Then, glancing at Isabel: 'I will have no misunderstandings atween we. You were kind enough to offer tea but I'll not drink it knowing there be an untruth, whether spoken or silent. 'Twere no more than a three month after leaving this town that he set about a man, knocked him about summat bad, breaking his arm and caving in some of his ribs. Drunk he were, drunk as a fiddler's bitch on money I had earned scrubbing floors. The constables come and took him and the Magistrate give 'im a choice. He could take the Army or go down the line for five years. Ernie took the Army.'

Isabel watched the thin woman, her fingers nervously

twisting together. What sort of torment was it to have to live with a man like that? She didn't know the half of Ernie Griffin's evil ways.

'Well, the folk along of Rugeley, they didn't take kindly to me and my wench after that. Reckoned we was every bit as bad as he was. We could get no work, not even cleaning a pig sty, it were a case of move on once more. It were after leaving Rugeley I remembered what you said and . . . well, here we be, but if you have changed your mind we will . . .'

'I have not changed my mind,' Isabel put in quickly. 'I will find employment for both of you.'

With Isabel's words the last of the woman's strength seemed to leave her and she sagged against the back of her chair.

'Mum!' The girl was on her knees in an instant, her arms about her mother. 'Oh, Mum, please don't go givin' up now. The lady said we can have work and . . . and I'll find somewhere the two of we can live. Please, Mum . . . please!'

'Your mother ain't givin' up, wench.' Letty Bradshaw bustled around the table, coming over to where the frightened girl held her mother in her arms. 'Her be tired, that's all. A bowl of broth, some good fresh bread and a night's sleep will have her perky again by morning. Come on now, Sarah Griffin,' she bent over the other woman, 'this don't be like you, passing out no sooner a body mentions work.'

Sallow skin stretched over sunken cheeks, dark circles curving about her eyes, the woman looked nearer collapse than Letty cared to consider. Looking at Isabel, she said softly, 'There be rooms in the attic. They ain't been used since your mother passed, but they be dry and there be beds in 'em.'

Isabel nodded. Sarah Griffin could not spend another night on the road, yet with no money that was where the two of them had obviously been sleeping. The girl had said they asked no charity and that was just as well, for charity did not lie thick on the streets of Darlaston.

'It did be the mention of work that took the go out of me.' The tired mouth stretched in a ghost of a smile as Sarah pulled

herself upright in her chair. 'But it were not the thought of doin'
it but the promise of having some to do as near put me lights
out.'

'There'll be nobody's light put out in my kitchen,' Letty said
brusquely, seeing fear still stark on the younger girl's face. 'I 'ave
quite enough cleaning to do in this house wi'out carryin' your
carcass into the yard, Sarah Griffin.'

Patting her daughter's hand, Sarah smiled again and Isabel
thought the skin of her face, taut as a drum, must surely split.
Mrs Bradshaw had mentioned rooms in the upper part of the
house, servants' rooms that had lain unused since her mother's
death. 'Unwarranted', that had been Luther's verdict. The house
had no need of a bevy of servants. 'Eat me out of house and
harbour, takin' my money and givin' nothing in return, just
sitting on their idle arses from morn' to bedtime . . .' The words
of her supposed father ringing in her mind, Isabel passed the cups
Mrs Bradshaw had filled, leaving one in front of the girl. She had
reacted strongly earlier when thinking the offer of tea was an
impulse of charity, how would she react to the offer of a bed?

'You can drink that tea down, wench,' Mrs Bradshaw said,
relieving Isabel of the need to voice her proposal and receive
back a possible snub, for the moment at least. 'It be sweetened
with naught but sugar. You'll find tea leaves at the bottom of it
but you'll not find charity.'

The girl's eyes, their beauty dimmed by weariness, were
fixed on Isabel who was afraid to smile lest it be misinterpreted.

'Drink it down, Mary wench.' Sarah Griffin's own weak
smile reflected her gratitude. 'It were offered in friendship and
it will be accepted the same.' Lifting her own cup, she hesitated,
holding it inches from her mouth as her gaze met Isabel's. 'I
thank you kindly, miss, as much for your words as for your 'ospi-
tality. I ask the Lord to look gently on you.'

Her throat tightening, Isabel looked away. Her own life had
been far from ideal but compared to what this woman and her
daughter had known . . .

'There be a pot of good barley broth won't take but a five

minute to warm over the fire. Would you and your daughter like to take a bowl while you be sitting?' Letty asked.

'We will missis.' Sarah nodded, the shawl losing its anchorage on her faded hair and slipping to her shoulders where it rested unheeded as she sipped the hot tea.

Fetching the pot from the pantry, Letty swung the kettle from the fire, replacing it with the soup pan. Then, crossing to the well-stocked dresser, she selected two bowls and a spotless cloth, laying them on the table.

'Mrs Griffin, your daughter said earlier that your son ran away. Will he know where to find you now you have left Rugeley, did you leave word for him?'

'Weren't nobody to leave word with.' Sarah left off watching the quick efficient movements of the housekeeper and looked at Isabel.

'Then how will he find you?'

'Be my guess he won't want to find we, not so long as he thinks his father dead and him the murderer.'

At her side the girl touched a hand to her mother's as the woman's voice broke on a stifled sob.

'But surely . . .'

'You don't understand, miss.' Sarah pressed the shawl against her mouth. 'How could you, how could anybody lessen they had lived with Ernie Griffin? He would pale the living daylights out of my children, and me as well, for no reason other than he felt like it; but that night, the night he bosted that man's ribs, he would like as not have finished the three of we off altogether, me and my two kids. He could be bad enough perfectly sober but when he had the drink on him . . .'

She paused, holding her shawl tight against her lips, fighting back the sobs that rattled in her thin chest. 'Well, that night he had drunk away what bit of sanity might have been left in him. He stormed in, his language fouler than a midden, his fists flying everywhere. He catched hold of Mary here and knocked her senseless, then when I tried to stop him laid into me with the buckle end of his belt.'

Drawing a long shuddering breath, her eyes now watching a scene being replayed in the theatre of memory, she went on, her voice as hollow as her cheeks. 'That were when my lad came in, my Peter. He tried pulling his father away, to stop the beating he was giving me, but Ernie threw him off, lashing the buckle again and again over his head till he tumbled agen the fire. Then he turned back to me, adding his boot to the lash of his belt. That were when Peter hit him. My lad could see I was near the finish of what I could take, he could also see his father would take heed of no word; he got up from the fireplace where he had fallen and taking the iron poker, struck out. The blow caught his father on the temple and as he half turned my Peter struck him another, this time across the top of his skull. He fell then, miss, fell as though life itself had been took from him, and God forgive me for wishing it had! That were when my lad run and I have had no sight of him since.' Sobs came through the shawl, mixing with her words. 'That be the worst of it, not knowin' where he be, not knowin' if my lad be dead or alive.'

'Of course the lad be alive.' Businesslike, Letty Bradshaw topped the bowls with broth, the appetising smells of barley and onion filling the warm kitchen. 'Ain't no reason why he shouldn't be . . . which is more than I can say for that 'usband of your'n.'

'Please God you be right.' Sarah Griffin dabbed her eyes with a corner of her threadbare shawl.

'Oh, I be right.' Letty's confidence was superficial, showing only on the surface. Times were bad all over the country, and now with these Zepper planes dropping bombs on the heads of innocent folk! 'Mark what I says, that lad will be turnin' up here any day now and the last thing he will want to see be two mawking women. Now, the pair of you, get that broth inside you and listen to what Miss Isabel has to say about employing · you both.'

Taking a chunk of the bread the housekeeper had sliced from a fat crusty loaf, Sarah broke it into her bowl. 'Eat up, Mary wench.' She smiled, waiting for her daughter to take up a spoon.

'The employment I had in mind the evening we spoke last,' Isabel said as mother and daughter began to eat and Mrs Bradshaw reseated herself in the chair set alongside the shining black range, 'I had thought to offer you both a position in the house. Braddy . . . Mrs Bradshaw . . . does a wonderful job but I would be happier if she would agree to take on some help. This is a large house and keeping it up to a standard she is happy with is no easy task. Therefore, if she is agreeable, I would like you, Mrs Griffin, to be her assistant.'

From her seat, Letty Bradshaw caught sight of the faded eyes, lit now with a spark of hope. 'I been thinking some time now as how I could do with another pair of hands about the place. Seems like this be the answer,' she put in.

'Is the work of assistant housekeeper agreeable to you, Mrs Griffin? It would carry a wage of two pounds ten shillings a week plus bed and board.'

'Suitable!' Sarah Griffin choked. 'Oh, miss, it be more than suitable, and you'll have no cause to complain about my work, I promise you that.'

'Then that is settled,' Isabel answered, turning to the house-keeper. 'I think the room that went with that position before my . . . my father decided the post was superfluous to the needs of the house should be perfect for Mrs Griffin. Would you please see to sheets and blankets?'

'I'll do it right this minute.' Letty Bradshaw pushed her ample frame up out of her chair. 'Should I make one ready for the girl?'

'That must be her choice.' Isabel looked at the face lifted to her across the kitchen table, pretty despite its thinness, golden-brown eyes lovely behind the veil of fear, the tilt of her head proud regardless of her poverty. 'I had thought to offer you the position of parlour maid, one that will carry a salary of two pounds a month, and as that of your mother it will also include bed, board and uniform.'

'Eh, our Mary! You couldn't wish for more than that, it be more than fair.'

Seeing her mother's words bring an even prouder tilt to the girl's head, Isabel spoke quickly. 'Fair, yes, but no act of charity. Mrs Bradshaw will settle for nothing but the best. You will earn every penny of that wage, Mary, should you accept.'

'Oh, I accept, miss.' Mary Griffin was proud but she was no fool. Chances like this did not come often in a lifetime. Meeting the gaze of the woman who was just a few years older than herself, she smiled at last. 'And like my mother, I promise you will have no cause to complain of my work. And neither will Mrs Bradshaw.'

Finishing the letter she had tried to write earlier, Isabel sealed the envelope. When would this terrible war be over, when would she see Mark again?

Turning off the gasolier, she made her way across the study to the window. In the two years she had been left to run the business she had got to know this room very well. Luther's study. Drawing back the heavy figured velvet curtains she gazed out over the garden, the only truly lovely part of Woodbank House; now its summer prettiness was turned to austere beauty by the touch of hoar frost. Isabel listened to the silence holding the gentle ticking of the clock over the fireplace. Outside everything looked so pure, so virginal. Like a bride dressed in white, the ticking the sound of her beating heart as she waited for her husband.

Would Isabel ever wait, gowned in white, heart beating out a rhythm of love with just a hint of apprehension? She leaned her forehead against the glass, feeling the bite of its coldness on her warm skin. In just a few weeks she would be twenty-four, an age when most girls of the town were married with children. Was that what *she* wanted?

Pulling away from the window, she stared out across whiteness silvered by the high moon. Her mother must have looked out on this same scene so many times, but her heart had not beaten with the rhythm of love as she waited for her husband.

In the beams of moonlight filtering into the room, Isabel glanced over to where the bookcase stood, its panes of glass reflecting the silver light like so many demon eyes. Why had Luther married a woman already with child . . . what had been in it for him . . . and why had he kept that letter? Isabel felt her hands clench at her sides. He had not kept it to torment himself, Luther Kenton was no masochist. No, he had kept it to use against her mother, the threat of exposure being enough to ensure her docile acceptance of his cruelty to her and his treatment of her children.

But why had he kept those children? She turned back to the window, letting her gaze travel out into the white silence. Once he was married to her mother it would have been so easy for him . . . his wife needed the peace and quiet of the country . . . a difficult labour, her child born dead . . . No one would have questioned the truth of that and Luther would have been freed from the sight of another man's children living in his house, calling him father. Isabel gave a soft humourless laugh. She had thought Luther no masochist, but surely there must have been self-inflicted pain in that? Or was his own pain overridden, submerged beneath the pleasure afforded him by hurting her mother?

And he *had* hurt her mother. Isabel's fingers tightened again at the thought. Not once or twice but many times. Often as a child she had asked her mother the reason for her tears only to be given some empty answer. It was not until long after her mother's death that she had guessed at the truth, but it had only been half the truth. Experiencing Luther's spite against Mark and herself, she had come to realise how much of it had already been directed against her mother, how many of her tears had been down to Luther. So many of them. Isabel's fingers curled deeply into her palms, the warmth of her breath forming a tiny lake of mist on the cold pane. Yes, many of her mother's tears were caused by Luther Kenton, but not all. Some were caused by a man she, Isabel, would never know, a man she loathed and despised. Her father!

What sort of a man would do that to a young girl? Seduce her, take his pleasure of her, then go off to another country, leaving her to pay the piper and dance to his tune for the rest of her life? What sort of man was it who had never come back; whether or not he had ever set eyes on that letter, surely the smallest spark of decency would have brought him back to the girl to whom he must have made promises?

What sort of a man, what nameless, uncaring swine, had fathered Victoria Kenton's children? Isabel felt the bile of hatred rise in her throat. He was one she was glad she would never know.

Outside the night sky stirred, sending a cloud fluttering across the moon, and from the deep shadows that engulfed the room seemed to come the sound of mocking laughter.

Chapter Twelve

'I was not in Darlaston when the air raid took place or I would have called sooner. I thank heaven you were not caught up in it.'

Isabel smiled at her visitor. Hewett Calcott made a strikingly handsome picture. Thick mahogany-coloured hair brushed back from his wide forehead, unhampered by pomade, showed no sign of grey though he must be in his mid-forties; the small beard was trimmed neat and close to a well-defined jaw; his shoulders were broad and strong-looking beneath his expertly tailored coat. But it was his eyes that held the most attraction for Isabel – attraction and something else. A feeling she had looked into those eyes a thousand times before.

'That is not quite the way it was, Mr Calcott. I was in the town centre when that Zeppelin . . . or Zepper plane as Mrs Bradshaw calls it . . . made its raid.'

'You were there when those bombs were dropped!' He did not return Isabel's smile at the housekeeper's mispronunciation of the word. 'What in heaven's name took you there?'

'Business, Mr Calcott, business and Janey.'

'Janey?'

Hazel eyes tinged with gold looked at her across the sitting room.

'Janey is my horse, Mr Calcott.'

'According to my information that air raid took place in

the evening. Is it usual for you to conduct business in the evening?'

'No more than it is for you to do so, Mr Calcott!' A thread of irritation running through her as she thought she detected a note of censure in what he said, Isabel answered sharply.

'Forgive me,' Hewett Calcott apologised, his gold-flecked eyes holding hers. 'It was the thought of you being in danger, I fear it made me forget myself.'

Why should he fear her being in danger? Isabel watched him realign the fine leather gloves draped over one knee. Why should he care what happened to her? She was nothing to him.

'It all happened so very quickly.' She could not keep a conciliatory note from entering her voice, nor did she want to. She had a liking for this man sitting opposite her, a strong liking, one she did not want marred. 'And it was more than a little frightening, I do admit.'

More than a little frightening! That was an understatement if ever she had made one. It had been absolutely terrifying: the explosions, the terrible screams of frightened women, the shouts of men; and then those hands reaching for her, dragging her from the trap . . .

'I imagine so, judging by the state of some of the buildings I have seen, or rather what is left of them. I would never have expected Zeppelins to reach so far inland. Neither, it seems, would the Royal Flying Corps.'

'Could they have prevented that air raid taking place?'

'Most certainly they could. The Zeppelin is a much slower, more ponderous machine than a fighter aircraft. It could easily have been brought down . . . a bullet in the gas-filled body would have turned it instantly into an inferno.'

Isabel shuddered at the thought. Those machines had to be manned by men, just as Mark and a co-pilot manned his aeroplane. To speak of them being enveloped in a burning inferno turned her blood to ice.

'Would . . . would the Royal Air Corps really have done that?'

'They would had they been able, but to be fair to them, they probably had no planes left in this country, and especially not in the heart of the Midlands. They would never expect the Kaiser to deploy a bomber this far over England. No, it is my bet that each and every aircraft we have is in France.'

'Do we drop bombs too, Mr Calcott?' Isabel asked softly, remembering the cry of the woman who had run into a blazing building, screaming that her children were inside it. Was that what her brother was doing . . . was Mark dropping bombs on women and children who had no part in the war? Whose voices would count for nothing towards the ending of it?

'I cannot say what course our armies are taking,' he answered, 'but I think Germany is not alone in this form of warfare.'

'If only it would end soon, why has the world gone mad?'

'Why indeed?' Following her glance, Hewett Calcott felt his stomach lurch. The photograph she was staring at showed a young man, his handsome face smiling back at her.

'Have you had word from your brother?' he asked, keeping his eyes on the framed picture, taking in the uniform of the Royal Flying Corps.

Reaching out a hand, Isabel took the photograph from the table her mother had so often used and held it, looking down into the laughing eyes. 'Not for some time,' she said softly. 'I know how pressed the Corps must be, but not hearing for so long worries me.'

'Mark!' Hewett Calcott seemed to roll the name around his tongue as if savouring the sound and feel of it. 'Your brother will write soon, I am sure of it.'

'Mark and I are twins.' Isabel smiled at the face in the photograph. 'I tease him about being the youngest . . . my baby brother; it used to make him so angry when we were children.'

'You are very alike, Miss Kenton. I remember from meeting your brother, you have very similar colouring.'

Returning the photograph to the table, Isabel turned her glance to Calcott, a tingle of pleasure stirring in her as she looked at the handsome face now smiling at her.

'Mark's hair is redder than mine.' She swallowed hard as the pleasure inside her intensified. 'I used to call him Carrot Top whenever he annoyed me. I could always be sure of that turning the tables.'

'It sounds as if you were quite a pair.'

'You should talk to Mrs Bradshaw on that subject!' Isabel laughed.

'Who knows?' He leaned forward slightly, the warmth in his eyes intensifying. 'Maybe one day I will.'

Trapped in his glance, Isabel felt as though she were being pulled forward, drawn down a gold-flecked tunnel, unable to resist the allure of those eyes, not really wanting to break the feeling of warmth and comfort they had so easily evoked in her. It was only when a tap sounded at the door and Hewett Calcott leaned back in his chair that she felt the bond between them break, leaving her almost breathless.

''Scuse me, Miss Isabel, but Mrs Bradshaw sent me to ask if you be requiring tea?'

'What!' Isabel's senses still had not fully recovered. 'Tea? Oh, yes . . . yes, of course.'

'If you will once again forgive me, Miss Kenton?' Hewett Calcott lifted the gloves from his knee and stood up, 'I will not take tea. I have an appointment at eleven.'

'Thank you, Mary. Tell Mrs Bradshaw we will not be requiring tea after all. And, Mary . . . I will see Mr Calcott out myself.' Isabel got to her feet as her visitor checked the time on his pocket watch.

'Very good, miss.' Her hair shining beneath a trim lace-edged cap, pretty face already reflecting the benefits of a comfortable bed and nourishing food, Mary Griffin bobbed a brief curtsey before leaving.

'I thank you for receiving me.'

Hewett Calcott's smile revived the connection she had felt between them, sending it tingling along her nerves. Isabel returned the smile but broke quickly away from his eyes, not wanting to be trapped yet again. There was a sort of magnetism about him, a certain quality she found more than pleasing. It would be very easy to fall in love with Hewett Calcott.

The open door giving a view of the carriage he had travelled in, he hesitated. 'Miss Kenton, the prime reason for my calling was of course to satisfy myself you had suffered no hurt from the air raid . . .'

'No, no hurt. A little indignity perhaps, being dragged from the trap . . .'

'Dragged?' His movement towards her was swift as his words, his face darkening. 'By whom . . . not Griffin again?'

'No.' Isabel's laugh was light but the anger that had sprung so rapidly to his face disturbed her. There was more than friendly concern in it, it was fierce, almost passionate, and yet beneath it she sensed an anxiety she did not understand? 'I was pulled from the trap but I was not attacked.'

The darkness did not leave his eyes nor did the white line of anger fade from about his mouth as he looked at her. 'Then what?'

It was almost barked, it was so abrupt. She could say it was no concern of his, tell him though his concern for her welfare had been kindly meant it did not give him the right to speak so sharply or to pry into her affairs. But as she saw the pain that was revealed by the darkness in his eyes, Isabel realised she could say none of those things.

'The noise and the smell of burning had terrified Janey,' she explained. 'I was trying desperately to hold on to her when Owen Farr appeared from nowhere. He scared me at first. I . . . I thought that it was Ernie Griffin attacking me a second time. I tried to fight him off. That was when he pulled me from the trap. He very kindly brought me home.'

'Then Owen Farr has my gratitude as well as yours.'

Reaching out a gloved hand, he touched her arm, the anger dissolving from his face. But no smile took its place. Instead it seemed to fill with a new emotion, one that made the hand resting on her arm tremble before, withdrawing it, he turned towards the carriage.

Watching him walk away, his figure tall and straight, Isabel felt a sharp stab, a thrust of an emotion that was almost tenderness.

'Mr Calcott.' She half ran to catch up with him. 'You said the main reason for your calling on me was to ensure I had come to no harm in that air raid.' She smiled up at him. 'That implies you had a second reason . . . what was it?'

'I did have a second reason, Miss Kenton.' His eyes swept her face, drinking in every detail with an intensity that brought colour flooding into Isabel's cheeks. For a moment she felt he might sweep her into his arms.

'But I fear that to voice it would be to impose upon you.'

'Women are not as weak as they sometimes appear, Mr Calcott.' Isabel folded one hand over the other, resting them against her skirts as she fought against the tide of colour staining her cheeks. 'An imposition does not terrify all of us, a challenge can be a welcome diversion, and I am not a woman who is afraid to say no.'

'I can see that, Miss Kenton.' He did smile then, and again that strong pull of emotion stirred in Isabel.

'In that case, would you deny me a welcome diversion?'

For a long moment he stared down at her, his eyes becoming gold-flecked velvet that seemed to engulf her, enfolding her in warm softness, an embrace that left her with no wish to escape. When at last he spoke it was with a huskiness that caught at her heart. 'No,' he murmured as the liquid softness of his eyes enveloped her, 'I would not deny you a welcome diversion. I would deny you nothing.'

'I tell you, summat needs to be done afore one of we finds ourselves out of business!' Jago Timmins brought his fist down hard on the oval mahogany table, his irate glance sweeping the men sitting around it.

'Now, now, Jago. That be a bit strong. Ain't none of us likely to go under, not while the country be cryin' out for steel.'

'That be what Paxton thought, an' you all knows what 'appened there!' Jago glared.

'That was a one off.' A second voice spoke up.

'Was it?' Jago was on his feet, thin mouth tight with frustration. 'You be sure of that, be you?'

Leaning back in his chair, the man tucked his thumbs into his waistcoat. ''Course I be sure, Paxton let his works run down, he was bound to go under sooner or later.'

'Oh, arrh, he let his place run down!' Jago rounded on the man, his face suffused with rage, his tone laced with sarcasm. 'And why was that? Go on, tell 'em . . . you seem to be so sure, p'raps you knows the reason for it?'

'Paxton didn't say.'

'Paxton didn't say!' Jago mimicked. 'I bet he bloody well didn't. Well, I didn't need Paxton to say, I know why he sold out and I know who he sold to.'

Around the table the assembled iron masters exchanged glances. They all knew of Jago Timmins's feelings, and the reason for them.

'It were nowt more than a lack of men brought Paxton to close his doors.'

'So what the bloody hell you reckon will close your'n?' Jago darted a look at his colleague. 'This war has two sides to it so far as we be concerned. The one has brought we money with its increased demand for steel and ammunition, but the other will bring the same as it's brought Paxton . . . that be the selling up of the foundry of each and every man 'ere lessen we do summat about it now.'

'That be hoss shit you be talking, Timmins, and you knows it.'

His narrow nose twitching with anger, his pallid grey eyes sharp as broken glass, Jago leaned both hands on the table, bringing his face closer to the man who had defied him.

'Hoss shit, is it?' he ground out between clenched teeth.

'Well, it might just come about you will wish you had shovelled some of it up! Might be as your place be the next to go the way of Paxton.'

'That will never happen, I will never sell Conley Iron.' Withdrawing his thumbs from his waistcoat, the other steel man consulted his pocket watch.

'I seem to recall Paxton saying the same nobbut a twelve month gone, here in this very room.' Jago straightened up as a murmur of conversation broke out around the table.

'That can't be argued with,' a third man said, his comment quietening the others. 'Paxton did say that, right here in this chamber.'

Confident now of their closer attention, Jago pressed home his advantage. 'I said there be two sides to this war – t'other being it's draining the works of men, and wi'out manpower we can't go on producin', and wi'out production we go down the Swannee!'

'I am sure we all see the point in that, Timmins,' the chairman of the Chamber of Commerce intervened. 'But with the Army taking every man capable of walking, I see little we can do to preserve the numbers of workers in our factories and foundries.'

'An' it be 'cos you can't see that that you'll lose 'em!' Jago snapped. 'The same one as took Paxton's will take your'n.'

'Come now, Timmins,' the chairman said, condescension clear in both tone and glance. 'Kenton bought the Paxton place but that don't mean . . .'

'Don't mean 'er won't buy your'n, or your'n, or your'n.' Jago angrily jabbed a finger towards several of the men seated at the table. 'Old Caleb Paxton thought the same, 'e thought his business were safe and he would hand it over to that son of his. But he reckoned wrong, and you lot be doing the same.'

'But a woman, Timmins! You can't seriously believe a woman could drive any one of us out of business?'

Jago's narrow nostrils flared, his colourless eyes receding

further into the dark circles that stood sentinel about them as a ripple of mocking laughter spread throughout the room.

'Oh, I believe it, Horton, and you better had an' all.' Jago glanced slowly at each face turned towards him. 'There don't be a man in this room as don't know how wily a woman can be or how grasping. Give her a bob and her wants half-a-crown, give her half-a-crown and her asks for a sovereign, and on it goes till her bleeds you of every penny you've got. And I tell you that Kenton bitch be no different!'

'So the Kenton girl bought out Caleb Paxton?' The chairman lifted his glass, sipping at his brandy. 'But we are all in a healthy position financially, besides which this war will be over soon and her brother will be back to take over . . .'

'Can you guarantee that?' The question whipped across the table as Jago's fist thumped against the surface. 'As I recall it were said this war wouldn't last six month and that were almost three year gone. Three year and we be no nearer kicking the Kaiser's arse than we was in 1914, and judging by the numbers of wounded coming into the 'ospitals week on week we don't be likely to do it. Them Germans must be chopping down our men like chaff in the wind.'

'And *that* is your answer, Timmins . . .'

Swinging his head around, Jago fastened his watery eyes on a new speaker.

'. . . it will be shortage of manpower that will jeopardise our works, not a woman!'

Shaking his head slowly, mouth curling derisively, Jago surveyed the young man who had interrupted, his natty mauve-coloured coat jarring against the black worn by every other man. When Jago replied it was slowly and deliberately. 'We spoke of hoss shit a minute ago. That must be what your father has for brains, putting *you* in charge of his foundry!'

'Now see here, Timmins . . .'

'No!' Jago's fist hit the table hard, jarring the fragile brandy goblets. 'I've done all the seeing I intends to. I've said my piece.

173

Ignore it if you will, but I won't be among you when you regret it. I've warned you. Don't none of you ever say as Jago Timmins didn't warn you. That Kenton bitch be every bit as sly as her father was.'

'Hold up, Jago.' From the farther end of the table another of the group spoke up. 'Given Kenton's wench be all you say her is, it still don't follow her could go buying up half the town. Her wouldn't have that kind of money.'

Jago stared into each face like a schoolmaster and when he spoke it was with an air of controlled calm. 'I ain't saying her would have that kind of money – then again I ain't saying her *don't* have it. There be no way of telling what Luther Kenton salted away in his lifetime. But this much I do know. The Kenton woman be like the rest of her gender: make sheep's eyes at a man and she can spend his money while keeping her own.'

'I believe you are deliberately maligning the Kenton girl!' interrupted the young man in the mauve coat, his face still pink from Jago's scathing words. Nevertheless he entered the fray once more. 'My father says you have had bitter aloes on your tongue ever since she refused your offer of marriage!'

'Your father has a headful of shit, same as the nancy boy he calls a son . . .'

'Timmins, we will have no more of that talk!' The chairman was on his feet as indignant voices were raised all around them.

'We won't have any more talk at all!' Jago kicked a foot backward, sending his chair over. 'It be no use trying to sow sense where none will take root. But afore I takes my leave think on this. Who is it will sell pig iron to none but Kenton's from his Bradley Field smelting works? Who is it has just set up an ammunition works down past the Green? Who is it Kenton's wench be setting her cap at? Could be he's got the money if her don't have it – money that could put you on the same work-house bench Caleb Paxton be sitting on now. Get them two joined and it could be that all Darlaston will be her wedding gift.'

Hesitating only to draw breath, he added vehemently, 'Well,

I ain't waiting for no celebration and I ain't waiting while that bitch gets her hands on what I've worked long and hard for. I've told you what I think, now I tell you summat else: Jago Timmins will look out for hisself!'

Tucking the ends of his muffler beneath his jacket, Edward Perry made his way towards the Frying Pan public house. He had given the Paget lad his word and that word would be kept if he broke the father's legs in the keeping of it. It would be tonight, Saturday. Any time after dark an attack on Kenton's was probable. Timmins would take no action before then, would not risk his henchmen being caught by men still on shift.

Reaching the beer house he paused, eyes on the bull's eye panes of glass, their frames bellying out less than a yard from the ground. Then he glanced towards the door which leaned drunkenly at an angle. The whole place would disappear one of these days, he thought, drop down into the coal shaft it was built across. You took your life in your hands every time you walked into the place. But where was there in Darlaston you could walk and not risk being swallowed by a pit shaft opening beneath your feet? The town had more disused shafts than currants in a Christmas pudding.

Removing the clay pipe clenched between his teeth, he glanced across to the opposite side of the street where a second beer house displayed its sign: a fire wagon drawn by two horses, beside which a fireman with a double row of brass buttons, a shining buckle on his wide black leather belt and a gleaming helmet on his head, stood with his hand on their halter.

The Fireman! Shoving his pipe into the pocket of his jacket, Edward Perry stepped into the first of the public houses. If the men he wanted to speak to were not in the Frying Pan they would be in the Fire.

Though it was yet early in the evening tobacco smoke hung like a thick fog in the bar of the Frying Pan. Placing a sixpenny piece on the counter Edward nodded to the landlord, waiting until he placed a foaming tankard on the counter. Picking up the four pennies that were his change, Edward raised the tankard, taking a long drink. While he exchanged greetings with those of the men he knew, he nevertheless avoided being drawn into their company. Taking a penknife from the pocket that held his pipe and plug of tobacco, he proceeded to shave hair thin slices from a threepenny stick of Nailrod. Packing the shavings into the bowl of the pipe, he placed it between his teeth before walking over to the fireplace, taking up his position at the corner where the bar curved around to join the opposite wall. From this vantage point he could see the whole room: who came in by the street door and who went out; which man went to the privy across the backyard and who was his piddling partner.

Reaching for a taper standing in a pewter pot in the hearth, he thrust it into the heart of the fire then held the lighted tip to his pipe, drawing heavily on the long stem. At the other side of the room the street door opened, the inrush of frost-sharpened air swirling the fog of tobacco smoke, which as the door swung shut settled sulkily back into place.

Elijah Price walked to the bar, his hand already signalling to the landlord. From his corner Edward watched the landlord serve up a pint of Old Best but made no move as Elijah turned, leaning back against the bar, squinting through the lavender haze that enveloped the room. It would suit his purpose better to draw no other man's attention. Taking another swallow from his tankard, Edward waited. Elijah would spot him soon enough.

'I 'ad Edgar Paget's lad round at my house a while ago,' Edward said a while later, once Elijah had joined him in the corner beside the fireplace.

Elijah nodded. 'I hear he got his call up papers. His mother will take that bad, him being the only lad.'

'Every mother in the town takes it bad when her lad has to go, whether her has but one or a dozen.'

'You'm right.' Elijah nodded. 'It be a bad business that don't be gettin' any better!'

'Arrh.' Edward swallowed more of his ale, wiping the back of his hand across his mouth before resetting his pipe between his teeth. 'An' it don't be the only bad business.'

'Oh! Summat up then, Edward?'

Edward Perry watched his friend shave tobacco from a stick of black shag. 'There will be if we don't do summat to stop it.'

'Young Paget don't be thinking of doin' a moonlight?'

'No, he ain't thinking of running from the Army.'

'So why come to your house?'

'Your question sounds like you think I might help him to flit?'

'I don't mean that at all, it just seems strange the lad coming to you. You ain't never been what you'd call pally with Edgar Paget, so what *did* he want if it wasn't to learn how to dodge the Army?'

'He wanted me to keep his father from doing time.'

'Time!' Elijah spluttered, sending a trickle of Best running down his chin. 'Edgar Paget be frightened to call his dick his own. He ain't got the guts to do anythin' as would send him down the line.'

'I reckon that be what a lot of folk think,' Edward replied as Elijah wiped his chin with his hand. 'Jago Timmins bein' one of 'em.'

'Jago Timmins!' Elijah wiped the back of his hand down one leg of his moleskins. 'Where does he fit in?'

Casting another glance at the men crowding the bar, satisfying himself they were not being overheard, Edward replied, taking care to keep his voice low: 'Seems Jago Timmins be offering a tidy sum to see Kenton's ain't in no shape to make steel come Monday mornin'.'

Elijah tapped the bowl of his pipe gently against the inside of the fireplace, the familiar movement drawing no unsolicited attention while giving him time to mask the anger that had appeared on his face. Stirring the smouldering shag with a spent match he glanced at Edward. 'Which one of Kenton's places does he want doing?'

'All of 'em.' Edward reached casually for his tankard. 'Timmins wants the lot bosted.'

'Timmins said to smash 'em all . . . every one?'

'So Paget's lad told me. Said he heard Harry Jackson talking to his father here in the Frying Pan. The lad said as how 'alf a hundred pounds be more than his father could turn his back on.'

'Phew! A hundred pounds atween two of 'em!' Pushing back his cap, Elijah scratched his head. 'A bloke would need to slave his guts out to make as much in under a year! It even be enough to wipe the yellow streak from Edgar Paget's back.'

'That be what his lad feared. He was worried what would become of his mother and the rest of her kids should his father get copped by the Bobbies.'

'Do you think the police would find out it were them?'

'I think the bloody man in the moon would find out it were them! Jackson wouldn't think twice afore flashing his money around. As for Paget, he would tremble so much you'd think he had the palsy.'

'So what can we do?' Elijah asked. 'We can't be in half a dozen places at once. Lessen you know which they will go for first, then I reckon Kenton's will soon be like a hog on a spit.'

'Not quite.' Edward picked up his tankard. 'Kenton's ain't gonna be the hog that'll roast. I reckon Jago Timmins's arse will feel the flames afore this night be over!'

Chapter Thirteen

'Thank you, Owen, but I shall not be celebrating Christmas. I would not have the heart, not with my brother away at war.'

'I'm sorry,' Owen Farr apologised quickly, seeing the shadow cross the face of the young woman seated opposite him at the dinner table. Isabel Kenton was beautiful and especially so at this moment, the gasolier sprinkling her auburn hair with pinpricks of diamond lights, pale yellow silk dress luminous in the soft lamplight. Only her lovely eyes, shadowed with worry, marred the picture. 'I did not think. Forgive me please, Isabel.'

'There is nothing to forgive.' She smiled, but she shadow in her face remained.

'I should have known, nevertheless.'

'Don't be too hard on yourself. You are not the only one to make the same mistake; but then I do not see your offer as a mistake, I see it as well-intentioned.'

'Well-intentioned or otherwise, I should have given it more thought. But you say someone else made you the same invitation?'

Asking Bradshaw to have coffee and brandy served in the sitting room, Isabel led the way, seating herself beside the small table her mother had so often used while Owen Farr chose the couch set at an angle a little to the side of the large open fireplace.

'Hewett Calcott called this morning.' She settled the soft folds of her dress about her knees.

'Calcott!' Owen's eyebrows drew a little closer together.

'Yes. You remember, he has given me an exclusive contract for pig iron from his smelting works in Bilston . . . Now what is there in that for you to laugh at?'

Leaning back against the couch, Owen crossed one foot over his knee, eyes green as river water still glinting with amusement. 'The thought of you running a foundry. Who could think of a girl as beautiful as you are, and of pig iron, at the same time?'

'Without laughing? Not you, obviously.'

'You are not offended?' He pulled a wry face pretending to dab tears from eyes that were slightly almond-shaped. 'Say you are not offended?'

Feeling a smile tugging at her mouth, Isabel gave the benefit of it to Mary as she set the coffee tray on the table but the remnants of it remained in her eyes as she poured a cup for Owen, asking that he help himself to brandy.

'Will I need it to drown the sorrows of chastisement?' Once again he adopted a hang dog expression, holding it until Isabel dissolved into laughter.

'No,' she told him. 'There will be no chastisement . . . not this time.' Then laughed again at his outrageous show of relief.

Lowering his foot to the floor he leaned forward, taking the cup from her while refusing the brandy. 'So, your partner in steel issued an invitation to celebrate Christmas with him?'

'Hardly my partner. We have a contract, nothing more.'

'An *exclusive* contract. One it seemed he granted at the drop of a hat.'

'I was most grateful for it. Mr Calcott has been more than kind.'

'True!' Owen sipped the coffee, eyes never leaving her face. 'But why should he be? Why drop his other customers to sell exclusively to a young woman he had never set eyes on, and to a firm with whom he had no previous dealings?'

'You make it sound as though he had some ulterior motive?'

Isabel felt the beginnings of anger. His words did have an underlying note of accusation, one she found disturbing. She liked Hewett Calcott, a liking that came nearer to affection than perhaps it ought, and it pained her to think his actions toward her should be misconstrued; especially by Owen Farr who had also found a place in her affections – a place dangerously close to her heart.

Laying his cup aside, he stretched out one hand to touch hers. 'If I sound apprehensive of the man, it is because I am concerned for you. A young woman – a very beautiful young woman – taking on the rigours of an industry she can know very little about. It would be very easy for a man who had spent the greater part of his life in business to take advantage.'

'And you think Hewett Calcott might do that?'

For a moment he did not answer, only a very slight tightening of his mouth and a faint crinkling at the corners of his eyes bearing witness to the seriousness of his thoughts; and when at last he answered it was with a slow shake of the head.

'No, I do not think that. To be perfectly truthful, Isabel, I think Hewett Calcott makes a very good friend and I . . . I was a little envious.'

The annoyance of moments before fading completely, Isabel's eyes widened. 'Envious of what?'

'Envious that Calcott got in first.'

'If you mean the invitation to join his party at Christmas, I have already told you I prefer not to celebrate with my brother still in France. I would hardly say that had I already accepted Hewett Calcott's invitation.'

Lifting her hand, he held it in both of his, eyes suddenly deep and magnetic as he leaned further towards her. 'I was not thinking of his invitation, Isabel. I envy the fact that he met you before I did; that he may already have taken the place in your heart that might otherwise have been mine.'

Her hand still between his, Isabel felt the stirring of an emotion she could not name. The place in her heart that might otherwise have been his . . . Was he saying he wished to become special to her? Was he saying she had become special to him?

'Hewett Calcott is a friend.' She tried holding his gaze with her own but the intensity with which he seemed to study her caused her to glance away, fearful of betraying herself. 'He is no more than that, Owen, just a friend.'

'And I?' His voice was suddenly husky, soft and vibrant with something she had not heard before; something she was afraid to name.

'You too are my friend.' She kept her eyes lowered, trying to keep the tremor from her voice but certain he must feel the racing of her pulse in the hand he still held.

'And for that I am grateful, but . . .' His voice dropped lower, becoming an intimate murmur to be shared with her alone. 'I hope that in time I may become more than that? Tell me it is not wrong of me to carry such a hope, tell me you feel something too?'

Her heart racing, Isabel tried to remove her hand but he held it tight between his own. She wanted to tell him, wanted to say how in the few weeks she had known him he had become dear to her, he and Hewett Calcott both. Hewett! The thought of him slowed her impetuous response to Owen's question. Hewett too was special to her. True her heart did not trip when she saw him, or pound at the touch of his hand, yet at the same time there came a surge of emotion, a deep swelling of something she could only describe as joy, a flood of happiness that bathed her in its warmth, bringing with it a sense of security she had never known before. But was that security born of love? The feelings she had for Hewett Calcott might be different from the ones coursing through her at this moment, yet they were as strong as those she held for Owen Farr. But were those feelings love? Was that which she felt for either of these men really love?

'Owen, I . . . I . . .'

Isabel broke off as a tap sounded on the door. Pulling her hand free, she glanced up, cheeks reddening as she caught the smile in the depths of Owen's green eyes – a glance that said her words were not needed, a glance that said Owen Farr knew his hopes would be realised.

'Beg pardon, miss.' Mary Griffin bobbed a curtsey, her cheeks turning pink as the glance she shot towards Owen was rewarded with a smile. 'But you did say as Mr Bradshaw could take the evening to visit Mrs Bradshaw's sister.'

Struggling to pull her thoughts together, Isabel looked at the girl. She had settled well into her duties, taking more than care in what she did, taking pride.

Isabel smiled, understanding the reason for the colour in the girl's cheeks, knowing the self-conscious, almost embarrassed feeling that was the cause of it. A feeling she herself had known often since the coming of Owen Farr into her life.

'Yes, Mary. I said they could both take the rest of the evening off. Why, is something wrong?'

'I don't know, miss, not exactly. Me mother said not to bother you, but the man be that agitated . . .'

'Man?' Suddenly Isabel was painfully alert, the intimacy of her exchange with Owen forgotten.

'Arrh, Miss.' Mary nodded. 'Me mother told him to sling his hook. What with Mr Bradshaw not being in the house her thought . . .' The girl broke off, a shadow of guilt crossing her face. 'Her didn't want you . . . Any road up, me mother told him to sling his hook and to come back when Mr Bradshaw be in, but he said he wouldn't go. Not till he had seen you. What shall I do, miss? Shall I tell him to go?'

Isabel had seen the guilt in the girl's expression and knew what it was she had found impossible to say. Her mother was afraid – afraid of the danger to Isabel from the man waiting in the kitchen.

'You . . . you have not told me who it is wishes to see me.' Isabel felt a stinging pain in the palms of her hands as her nails dug into the soft flesh. Drawing a long breath, she forced herself to ask calmly: 'Did he give a name?'

'No, miss.' Mary's chin bobbed as she swallowed hard. 'He didn't have to. Me mother and me, we knows him well.'

In her bedroom, Isabel slipped out of the silk dinner gown, exchanging it for a warm grey cashmere two-piece trimmed with darker grey astrakhan collar and cuffs. She had been so frightened when Mary had announced that a man wished to see her; frightened at the prospect of coming face to face once more with the one who had attacked her and yet too afraid to refuse, knowing he would get to her one way or another. Better it should be sooner rather than later, and where there were others on hand to help her.

Owen had seen her fear and at once declared his determination not to leave her, however private the business this man had with her. He had stated flatly it must be discussed in his presence or wait until some other time when a person of Isabel's choosing could be present.

Reaching a matching astrakhan hat from the shelf of her wardrobe, she settled it on her head, securing it with a jet bead hat pin.

If only she had known!

Changing her mind, she discarded the hand-knitted gloves Mrs Bradshaw insisted were the warmest for her to wear during the cold weather and took out the fine grey leather pair from her drawer. They would be warm enough inside the muff that matched her suit.

If only she had known!

The thought bringing a smile to her face, she remembered the relief that had flooded through her when Mary had shown her visitor into the drawing room, and the struggle between amusement and puzzlement in Owen's eyes as they had asked their silent question. Can this really be the man who terrified you so much?

The man Edward Perry only ever referred to as Dandylion had been more nervous than Isabel herself, shifting his weight from one foot to the other, first fingering the bright blue tie knotted at his throat then twisting his flat cap in his hands.

Seeing her relief, understanding this man was not the same one who had attacked her, Owen Farr had made to leave, but stayed at Isabel's request.

'Perry, miss, 'e wouldn't let me go back 'ome and change into me Sunday trousers. Said I had to come straight away and bug— without me Sunday trousers.'

'It is just as well you were wearing those then,' Owen said, seeing the laughter bubbling inside Isabel.

'You look very presentable, Mr . . . ?' Avoiding Owen's eyes, Isabel reassured the man nervously wiping the toes of his boots on the back of each trouser leg.

'Just call me Dandylion, miss. Everybody else does. It be that long since I were called anything else, I've forgot the name me father give me.'

It was then he had told them of Edward Perry and Elijah Price fetching him out of the Fireman, barely giving him time enough to finish his ale. Then together with a couple more of the foundry furnace hands they had visited first the Jacksons' house and then the Pagets'; now they had the two conspirators 'holed up in a shed at back of the old mine shaft along the Lodge Holes colliery'.

They had planned to destroy Kenton's! Isabel's hands tightened on the muff she took from its box. And Jago Timmins was behind it!

It had been Owen who had taken charge then, asking the dapper little man to get the others to bring Jackson and Pagets to the White Lion Hotel next to the Fold. 'That is where Magistrate Garret will be at this time.' He had consulted the watch kept in his waistcoat pocket. 'Have those two there in one hour.' He turned to Isabel as Dandylion scurried out, and taking both of her hands in his, told her not to worry, that he would see to this matter.

But that had not been acceptable to Isabel. Kenton works were threatened, it would be a Kenton who would address the problem. 'Except you aren't a Kenton,' she whispered, catching sight of herself in the long dressing mirror. But right now she knew that fact made no difference. Luther and she had never been close, never felt for each other as father and daughter should, but it was his name which had shielded her mother from the shame of giving birth without the blessing of a wedding ring, and her children from the stigma of bastardy. Now Isabel would protect that which Luther had striven a lifetime to build.

'I shall appreciate any help you can give me, Owen,' she had said quietly, 'but I must confront Jago Timmins myself. I must hear from his own lips if what I have learned is the truth.'

And if it did prove true?

. . . *I will not see you merely go under, I will watch you go down . . . and laugh while I am doing so.*

Turning towards the door, Isabel remembered the words she had flung at Jago Timmins. She might well watch him go to prison for this night's work. But would she laugh?

It would be some time tonight. Jago Timmins looped the tie about his neck, stumpy fingers fumbling it into place beneath a collar starched stiff as wood. Those men would not risk letting a hundred pounds go by; they would do for Kenton's before Jago Timmins changed his mind or got some other men to do it.

The tie in place, he reached for his jacket, tapping the bundle of notes in the pocket as he shrugged into it. Tonight would see the end of Kenton's foundry and all of Luther's ventures if the men he had hired hoped ever to hold that money in their hands; the end of Luther Kenton's works, and the end of that bitch who was his daughter. She had refused Jago Timmins's offer of marriage, made him a laughing stock among all who knew him. But he had sworn to see her go under, and tonight that vow would be fulfilled. After tonight, Isabel Kenton's choice of husband would have to be made from among the penniless, for who else would wed a woman with nothing?

How would they do it? Crossing to the window of his large bedroom, he looked out across the darkening sky. Tonight it would not glow with the scarlet of opened furnaces thrown like a brilliant shawl across the darkness; tonight it would burn with crimson slashed with gold and blue, the colours of living flame – the flames of burning steel works, for such a fire was the quickest, the hungriest. Fire would devour everything Luther Kenton had striven for and leave nothing but ashes in its place. His eyes on the brick chimney stacks standing tall and straight against the shadowed sky, Jago's thin mouth curved into a smile. Yes, those men would choose the way of fire, one that would warm his heart.

But he must be seen as having nothing to do with it. He must be free from any possible suspicion, and in a week or so he would be. There were many disused pit shafts in Darlaston, deep enough to hide the body of a man, especially one who could pose a threat to Jago Timmins. Turning away from the window, he touched again the pocket that held a wad of neatly folded white five-pound notes. It was a pity Jackson and any partner he chose to help him would not live long enough to enjoy the fruits of this night's work. The smile widened, becoming thin and evil. But then, as they sowed so should they reap.

And he too would reap. But his harvest would not be the bitter fruits of death, but the warm, sweet-tasting delights of revenge.

'Such a dreadful thing, this war. I swear not a day goes by when my dear Charles does not declare a wish that he could fight for his country – but I should be absolutely terrified to think of him out there among all those horrid Germans.'

Not half as terrified as your dear Charles would be should the government raise the compulsory recruitment age. *I* swear he would need no dose of Glaubers Salts to ease his trip to the privy then!

Jago hid his thoughts as he accompanied his dinner guests to the drawing room. From the hall the long case clock struck ten. Two hours! It had been two hours since his guests had arrived, two hours of putting up with the stupid small talk of gossiping women when all he wanted . . . but he could wait, and it was more sensible to wait surrounded by witnesses.

'My dear Mrs Horton, I know how you feel.' Bessie Hayden reached one hand to the corpulent man who took up his stance behind her chair. 'My Joseph too hankers after joining up. I have to remind him constantly that though it is his dearest wish to serve in the Army, should he give in to that wish who would run Imperial Steel? Our son is not yet fourteen so could hardly be expected to stand in his father's place.' She patted the thick-fingered hand now resting on her shoulder. 'Though I know how it pains him to hear it, I tell him he must stay here in Darlaston. That it is his duty to do so, and go on producing steel for his country.'

Glancing at his fellow industrialists, seeing the waistcoats stretched across well-filled stomachs, the brandy goblets cradled in their hands, Jago hid his thoughts once more. There wasn't one among this lot hadn't made a dash to collect his Derby armband – then dashed off some place out of the way when the call for volunteers went up. Nor almost done it in his trousers last May when the conscription age limit had been raised to thirty-five. They didn't want the white feather, but neither did they want the Army.

The feathers perched on Violet Conley's head fluttered in the breeze from the fan she waved rapidly beneath her triple chin. She had no intention of being outdone by either of the other women. 'We must all put our own wishes aside. We cannot think of ourselves whilst our country is in such dire need. I declare, almost every day I become quite fatigued from begging Mr Conley to forego his own desire to join the forces and remain here to produce the goods our men in France sorely need. A man cannot always follow the path of his own choosing, do you not agree, Mr Timmins?'

Hiding contempt behind a thin smile, Jago gave a slow, judicious nod. 'Indeed I do, Mrs Conley, indeed I do. But there is nothing my friends want more, and I know they will be well pleased should the government institute a third Military Service Act and raise the compulsory service age to include them.'

There had been hints at just such a third Act being passed, all the papers had carried talk of it for days, and as he refilled brandy glasses and passed them round his smile widened as he saw the white-knuckled hands that grasped them.

'We ladies have to bear the burden, too.' Violet Conley's feathers jigged precariously. 'We have to do what we can; it seems I am forever telling my cook and maids to work harder at knitting comforts for the troops. I tell them two hours less in bed will do them no harm. Why, in two hours they can knit a sock!'

'Do you knit comforts, Violet?'

Jago knew it was a snide question, but it gave him pleasure to see the tide of confusion swiftly flood her dumpling face.

'I . . . I would of course . . .' Her fan beat the still air in short staccato movements, feathers dancing to its rhythm '. . . but with my visiting the hospital almost every week, I am afraid time does not allow. We all bring comfort where we can and visiting the wounded here is every bit as valuable as knitting socks and scarves to send abroad.'

'Oh, every bit.'

'Our wounded men need to know we think of them.'

The other two women fell over themselves to agree as Violet's eyes swept over them.

'And think of them you do.' Richard Conley's glass swept a wide arc as he smiled at his audience. His wife would take a deal of soothing now if he were not to have to listen to her carping all the way home. 'Why, only last week Violet took two of the men for a drive in the motor carriage, would you believe!'

I believe the sour-faced bitch capable of anything she thinks will put her one better than anyone else. The thought rose immediately to Jago's mind but he allowed it no expression.

'I *can* believe it, 'cos my wife has asked can her take the carriage out this Thursday afternoon. Be that why you want the carriage instead of the governess cart, me dear? Be you taking a couple of soldiers for a drive?'

'I had thought of it.' Charles Horton's wife glanced timidly up at him. 'But of course, like Violet, I would take only officers.'

How like Violet Conley to admit only an officer into her motor carriage! Jago resisted a sardonic smile. But how long would he resist that deeper urge? The urge to remind her of the times they could both remember, the times when Violet Conley owned no bloomers to her arse!

From the hall the chimes of the clock stole softly into the drawing room. Half-past ten. Jago gripped his glass with fingers taut with the tension of waiting. How much longer would Jackson wait, how long before the sky turned to flame, how long before that brilliant glow announced the end of Kenton's?

'I beg your pardon, sir . . .'

Jago's glance jerked to the door, his pulse pounding as his butler entered the room.

'. . . but there are two men at the door. They claim they have business with you.'

Chapter Fourteen

'I have to admit it, Calcott, some of the things he said made sense. The way the government is draining the land of men to fight this war leaves very few to work the foundries. Keep it up at this rate and Timmins's words will prove true, we will all be out of business.'

'I understand what you mean, of course, but what else can the government do? You can't have women at the Front.'

'Neither can you have them work a furnace or tip a crucible full of molten steel – though they be doing many jobs we thought only men could do just a year or so gone. But there still be work only a man can do, and like Timmins said, able-bodied men be getting like diamonds: hard to find and heavy on the pocket.'

'Jago Timmins's pocket was ever his first concern.' Hewett Calcott offered his guest a cigar from a silver humidor, taking one for himself and trimming its end.

'Arrh, he holds his hand on his halfpenny in more ways than one.' The chairman of the Chamber of Commerce trimmed his own cigar, lighting it with a match from the box of England's Glory Hewett Calcott pushed across the table towards him.

'Such as the way he offered men a higher wage to go and work for him then dropped them two minutes later?'

'They *were* mostly in the call-up age range, he would have lost them soon anyway.'

'That doesn't make his action any the more acceptable.' Hewett Calcott squinted through the smoke of his cigar. 'The man is nothing but a get on!'

'I agree he would sell his own soul if it meant another penny in his pocket, but in all fairness to him these are difficult times. We all have to do what we feel we must if we are to survive.'

'And that includes standing on the shoulders of any man so long as your head be above the water . . . or woman perhaps?' Through the haze of tobacco smoke, Hewett Calcott's face hardened. 'Well, in my book those tactics are unacceptable.'

Removing the cigar from his mouth, John Bradford surveyed the man with whom he had eaten dinner. Hewett Calcott was a powerful figure in Bilston; smelting works, steel foundries and engineering factories all bore the Calcott name. He had already brought that name to Darlaston, was thinking of adding to his list of assets. Was that the reason behind his interest in the business that had gone on last week in the Chamber, and his interest in Jago Timmins?

'As they are in mine, Calcott,' Bradford soothed his host. 'I tried to tell him it was no fault of the girl that Paxton had gone out of business . . .'

Hewett felt his nerves tauten. Timmins had obviously directed his ire towards a woman, and as far as his knowledge went there was only one in Darlaston who was directly involved in the running of steel works, and that woman was Isabel Kenton. Was Jago Timmins gunning for her?

'. . . but he was beyond reason. He seems to think everything that goes amiss in the steel works round here is due to that young woman. In his view it was she brought about Paxton's sell off, and given time she will do the same for every steel man in Darlaston; then he left, saying if the rest of us did not look to our welfare, Jago Timmins would look to his own.'

Forcing his hand to remain steady, Hewett handed the decanter of port to his guest, but beneath the surface his emotions ran like a mill race. Jago Timmins blamed Isabel for the pressure each of the town's manufacturers was under. Even though he must know that was not justified, he was using it as a stick to beat her with. For what reason? And more importantly, to what end?

'Did Timmins say what it was he intended to do, how he meant to look out for himself?' Hewett watched the other man fill his glass, the ruby liquid glinting like a sleeping fire.

Running a mouthful of the wine around his tongue, John Bradford swallowed appreciatively before answering: 'No, but there again he was merely letting his sails flap in the wind. He was all worked up. A man gets like that when a woman refuses his offer of marriage.'

'Jago Timmins offered marriage to the Kenton girl?' This was something Hewett had not known; now, every sense heightened, he listened to the answer.

Sampling his port once more, the chairman of the Chamber of Commerce refilled his glass. 'Just after Luther Kenton dropped dead of a heart attack, so it seems. Don't ask how these things get to be known outside of a house – servants' ears flap and their tongues wag. I suppose that were how it came to be talked of. It appears the girl's father and Jago Timmins had already decided on the marriage, and it would have gone through had Luther not been called away, so to speak.'

Isabel married to Jago Timmins! Hewett Calcott felt every part of himself rebel at the thought. That man with his hands on her, taking her into his bed . . . Snatching up his own glass, he threw the contents into his mouth, swallowing them down at a gulp.

'Now, according to Jago, Luther's daughter has her cap set at a different angle. He claims she be aiming to marry a man who will give her this town as a marriage gift . . .' John Bradford broke off, suddenly aware that his own tongue, loosened by the effects of a good meal and fine wine, had run away with him.

'Oh!' Hewett recharged both glasses, taking his time in the doing of it. 'And just who does Jago see as having so much money he can buy up a town?'

'It were just bluster.' The chairman's eyes remained on his glass. 'Timmins would grab any straw to try to make his point.'

'Nevertheless he must have a point to make. What was that point?'

Realising he could not withdraw what had already been said, Bradford moved uneasily in his chair. He had acted as unwisely as Timmins, saying more than he should, but he knew his host would not leave it there. In fact he would not leave it until the last word had been said.

'It all blew up from nothing.' He glanced up, his unease reflected in the look he directed at Hewett. 'Jago was going on about the Kenton girl, saying she was like the rest of her kind . . .'

'That being?' Hewett asked as the other man stopped speaking.

'Really, Calcott, I don't see as how going over what was said is going to do us any good now!'

'I should like to hear the rest of it, nevertheless.' Hewett Calcott countered the protest with practised calm, his eyes on the other man's face showing none of the cold fear beginning to build in him – a fear that detracted from the heat of anger, a fear that Jago Timmins might already have struck at Isabel.

'He said . . .' Bradford grabbed at his glass, swallowing a substantial amount of port as if the drinking of it would bolster his will to speak. '. . . he said that she was sly and grasping, a self-interested bitch who was determined Kenton's would be the only engineering concern to survive this war. That what she couldn't buy now, she would once she was married to . . .'

'To whom, Bradford?' Hewett coolly regarded the man opposite him. 'Whose money will she use to buy what she wants?'

'Really, Calcott, I would rather not say.' Pushing himself away from the table, Bradford rose to his feet.

'I cannot compel you to tell me what you have no wish to.' Hewett Calcott too rose from the table, but where his guest's movements had been jerky, almost nervous, his own were smooth and perfectly controlled, no visible sign of the turmoil within him breaking the surface calm. 'But then neither will I forget that you felt unable to comply with my request when next you order a load of pig iron!'

The quiet words stopping him dead in his tracks, Bradford half turned, the handle of the door underneath his hand. He did not need to query the threat hidden beneath those words; Hewett Calcott would do all that they implied and in so doing would take Bradford Steel out of business. But if Bradford repeated to Hewett Calcott the claims Jago had made? Would the anger they roused be directed at him, bringing with it the same reprisal?

Bradford swallowed the nervous bile suddenly scalding his throat. 'As I remember, the words Jago used were, "Who is it will sell pig iron to none but Kenton's from his Bradley Field smelting works. Who is it has just set up an ammunition works down past the Green? Who is it Kenton's wench be setting her cap at? Could be he's got the money . . . money that could put you on the same bench Caleb Paxton be sitting on. Get the two joined and it could be Darlaston will be her wedding gift!"'

So that was what Jago Timmins thought. In his bedroom, Hewett went over in his mind what John Bradford had reluctantly told him. Did the rest of them think the same, were the steel magnates of Darlaston afraid of that happening? Did Isabel Kenton know of the rumour, had she too heard it? Taking a small box from a drawer set in a table next to his bed, he held it in his hand, staring down at it.

She had refused his invitation to attend the small dinner party he had planned to hold on Boxing Day. His fingers closed a little tighter about the box as he recalled the tremor of her lips as she'd spoken of her brother. His disappointment had been keen during the return drive to Bilston and time had not dulled its edge. He had intended to ask her to assist him by acting as hostess for the evening, then to do him the honour of accepting this.

He stared at the box nestled in his hand, its blue leather picked out with decorative gilding. He had intended to offer her what this box held, treasuring the thought of her smile as she accepted, savouring the thought of helping her to slip it on. But now Isabel Kenton would not be coming to this house. The dream he had nurtured for weeks would remain a dream, at least for the time being.

And perhaps it would be better if he left it to remain a dream, a silent wish locked away forever in the deepest reaches of his heart. Should he even have considered asking her to accept it? By doing so he might have caused her embarrassment, or she might have felt obliged to accept out of pity.

The thought painful to him, he glanced across the room, catching sight of his reflection in a long oval mahogany-framed dressing mirror. The face that stared back at him showed no lines, the skin still clear and firm. The hair that complimented it was still thick, its deep auburn colour showing no touch of grey; only the eyes, their hazel depths highlighted by hints of gold, held the sadness that was a part of him. There were those who would call him handsome still.

But handsome was not enough! He returned his glance to the box, closing his fingers tight about it. His face may not show them but the years were there, weighing heavy on his shoulders, too many years dividing him from Isabel Kenton. The thought of her married to Jago Timmins had all but revolted him. Why? Because of the man's character . . . or because of his age?

Calcott suddenly felt every one of his own years. Placing the box back in the drawer from which he had taken it, he stood staring down at it.

He had no right to offer what it held, no right to ask her to share her life with him.

Slowly closing the drawer, he turned away. He had no right! Isabel Kenton would never see what it was that the box held, never know it held his heart.

★

'Business, Jago, at this time of night?' Charles Horton snorted. People have no consideration these days.'

'No, none at all.' Violet Conley's feathers danced a jig. 'They need to be put in their place. You must tell whoever it is that this hour of the evening is no time to be calling, no matter what the business. I know my husband would do so, and sharply.'

I should think he would welcome visitors at any time as a distraction from you, Jago thought to himself, but replied instead, 'I am afraid I have allowed business to come first in my life. It is an inevitable consequence of not having a wife to keep me company of an evening. Please accept my apology for this disturbance, I will see to it the visitors leave at once.'

It had to be Jackson and his accomplice, which meant the job was done. Glancing at his guests, Jago muttered a further excuse then made for the hall. He had told Jackson to come to the house after dark but had expected him to come tomorrow night, after first making sure the whole of Kenton's was destroyed.

Standing where the manservant had indicated, the door still open behind them, the two foundrymen snatched off their flat caps as Jago hurried over to them.

'Is it done?' he hissed after dismissing the servant hovering a little to the rear.

'We was . . .'

'I don't have time now.' Jago glanced over his shoulder towards the door of the drawing room. 'Just tell me, did you do Kenton's?'

As both men nodded, he took the neatly folded bundle of notes from his pocket, pressing them into Jackson's hand.

'It be there,' he muttered, 'all of it. Count it outside, well away from here.'

'I have no doubt it is all there, Mr Timmins, the full one hundred pounds you promised these men in payment for wrecking Kenton Engineering!'

'You!' Jago's voice was almost a squeak. 'But how . . .?'

'Did I find out your intention to ruin my brother's business?'

Her face pale, Isabel stepped into the well-lit hall. 'There will be time enough for explanations in the Magistrates Court. For now, suffice it to say I know.'

'Magistrates Court!' The surprise had gone from his voice, leaving it harsh with anger. 'Arrh, there'll be time for explanation and condemnation. I will see you and your . . . your accomplices go down for slander!' He glared at the two men still standing, cap in hand, the blood drained from each face, eyes glued to the toe caps of their boots. 'And you two be set for a long stay. The law takes unkind . . . very unkind . . . to a man's good name being slandered.' Turning back to Isabel, his mouth curved in a vicious smile. 'If what I hear be true, them women's prisons be worse than men's. I shall enjoy thinking of you locked away in one of them. I only hope it be the worst of all!'

'That is where we differ, Mr Timmins.' Inside her muff, Isabel's fingers were tightly clenched. 'You see, I have no preference for your place of confinement. Any prison will do so long as it holds you for a very long time.'

'Get out! Get out now afore I forget you be a woman and knock your teeth down your throat!' Seeing his smile turn to a snarl, the two men took a step back but Isabel held her ground.

'Surely not?' she said, her glance going over his shoulder. 'Not in front of your guests.'

'Be there trouble, Timmins?'

Jago whirled round as Charles Horton stepped out of the drawing room. 'No . . . No. It was just a little matter, it be finished now.'

'Just a little matter?' Isabel's tone was icy. 'Just a little matter . . . destroying a man's property! And now it is finished, you have paid your henchmen their dirty money.'

'Why, Miss Kenton!' Charles Horton came across the hall. 'We were not told you were among Jago's callers.'

'That is because I came in a little after Mr Timmins's business associates.'

'But you must come in, my dear. The cold has taken the roses from your cheeks. That be right, don't it, Timmins?'

'It is not the coldness of the evening that has taken the colour from my face,' she replied, eyes still on Jago, 'but the perfidy of a man's actions. I doubt Mr Timmins would want me in his drawing room, after just paying one hundred pounds to have Kenton's put out of business!'

'What's that?' Charles Horton looked astounded. 'What's that you say? Destroy your works!'

'My brother's works,' Isabel corrected him. 'Jago Timmins paid these men one hundred pounds to destroy all my brother owns.'

'That be a bloody lie!' Jago's voice rose, carrying beyond the hall. 'It be a bloody lie, and I'll see you pay for it!'

'Should it prove to be a lie then I will pay, but I have grounds . . .'

'Grounds!' Jago's guests were forgotten as fury got the better of judgement, carrying his words to almost every part of the house. 'Be these your grounds?' He jabbed a finger in the direction of the men now almost cowering behind Isabel. 'The word of two bloody foundry rats? You'll have a job on getting any Magistrate to believe their word afore mine.'

'Are you saying these men have lied?' From the corner of her eye Isabel saw the cluster of people standing at the open door of the drawing room.

Glancing again at the men almost shielding themselves behind her, Jago's face twisted with contempt. 'If you say they claim I asked them to do for Kenton's, then I be saying they be liars.'

Feeling the eyes of Jago's guests fixed on her, Isabel refused to let their obvious interest deter her. The matter would soon no doubt be in the *Express* and *Star*, and from there become common gossip all over the town. Besides which she had no intention of backing down before the man who so much wanted to see her fall.

Keeping her voice calm and polite and her gaze on Jago, she asked: 'Mr Timmins, knowing the penalty for lying under oath, why should they risk paying that penalty? Why should they lie? Is it for this, do you think?'

Turning to Jackson, she summoned him forward, pointing to the money he held up.

'What be that supposed to be?' said Jago, laughing derisively.

'It is the one hundred pounds you have just paid to these men for . . .'

'For what?' Unaware of the interest behind him, Jago laughed again. 'They won't say! And as for lying under oath, you won't even get them near a Magistrates Court. So you see, you smart-arsed bitch, you won't never prove what you claim, nor prove that money were paid by me.'

Seeing the fans flutter and the way delicate handkerchiefs were pressed to the mouths of the watching women at Jago's choice of language, Isabel resisted a smile. They would hear worse condemnations of Jago Timmins than the use of improper language before they returned to their homes.

'But that is where you are wrong, Mr Timmins . . .'

From the shadowed doorway Owen Farr stepped into the hall, closely followed by a uniformed constable.

'Both of these men have signed a sworn affidavit, authorised by Magistrate Connor and witnessed by the clerk to the Court. It is their sworn testimony that you promised to pay them one hundred pounds to so damage Kenton's works that they would be unable to continue in production; furthermore you have, as was witnessed by myself and the constable, handed over the promised sum to these men: your precise words being: 'Just tell me, did you do Kenton's?' I think, Mr Timmins, that Miss Kenton has evidence enough to prove her claim.'

'Is this true, Timmins?' Richard Conley came to stand beside Jago, a grave expression on his face. 'Did you hire these men to damage Kenton Engineering?'

Guessing there was no alley down which he could dive, Jago set his shoulders.

'Arrh, I did. I done what needed doing, what none of you mealy-mouthed buggars *would* do. I put the Kenton foundries out of business, stopped that bitch from taking the rest of Darlaston. It be me the lot of *you* have to thank for saving your arses, though truth to tell I wouldn't have cared tuppence if you'd lost everything.'

'My God, Timmins!' Charles Horton breathed. 'Do you know what you are saying?'

'O' course I bloody well knows.'

'Yes, I am sure he knows.' Owen came to Isabel's side 'Just as the two men beside me knew the penalty their actions would have incurred had they succeeded in carrying out Mr Timmins's orders.'

'*Had* they succeeded!' Jago's narrow eyes seemed to start from his head. 'Had they succeeded? You mean . . .'

'That is correct,' Owen answered. 'Kenton works have suffered no damage. These men were apprehended before they could carry out their task.'

'Then you got no case against me.' Jago's eyes receded behind their fleshy lids, his smile one of triumph now.

'Oh, I think Miss Kenton does have a case against you,' Owen continued, his audience hanging on his every word. 'But hers may have to wait, for the Crown takes precedence.'

'The Crown!' Richard Conley frowned as he fiddled with his side whiskers. 'I'm afraid I don't follow?'

Owen glanced at the assembled company. 'Then allow me to explain. As the constable will no doubt attest, and as I, a practising solicitor, know to be the law: attempting to destroy a means of supply to the nation's armaments in time of war is seen as an act against the Crown, whether said act be successful or otherwise. And, as we all know, an act against Crown and country is viewed as treason, and treason carries the most severe of penalties. Mr Timmins could well be looking at a death sentence for tonight's work.'

Going to their wives' assistance as the women gasped with horror, Jago's visitors stared at Owen until finally

Richard Conley spoke. 'A death sentence! Surely that can't be possible?'

'I assure you it is, sir.' Owen's face was grave 'Were it any other time the offence would be looked at in a different light, but we are at war, sir, and war is a very serious business. This affair will not be taken lightly. It is my opinion that should the ultimate sentence not be given, then a very long term of imprisonment is the most for which Mr Timmins can hope.'

'Prison!' Violet Conley spat, setting the feathers waving on her head. 'Then the longer the better. What that man has done *is* treason and he must be made to pay. And if you do get off with a prison sentence, Jago Timmins, don't think as you can come back to Darlaston. Don't think you can carry on as though nothing ever happened. My husband will never trade with you again, nor any other industrialist whose wife I know. You be finished in this town, Jago Timmins . . . finished!'

'That be right, Timmins.' Picking up his wife's coat and draping it over her ample shoulders, Richard Conley led her to the still open door. 'We want none of your sort. 'You've done your last deal with Conley Iron.'

'What you tried to do was unforgivable, Timmins.' Joseph Hayden put an arm before his timid wife as they passed Jago, as if shielding her from contagion. 'You and I have no business from tonight!'

'Count me in on that.' Charles Horton, his wife clinging to his arm, averting her eyes from Jago as if to look at him would strike her dead, strode after his friends. 'It be deeds such as that could win this war . . . for the Germans!'

'I said as you was sly!' Jago snarled, pallid eyes seeking Isabel. 'Sly as that fox you called Father. Luther Kenton done a fine job in rearing you, you should be grateful to him. You were both cast in the same mould!'

Receiving a nod of permission from the constable to collect a coat from his bedroom, he turned towards the stairs.

'It is over Isabel,' Owen murmured as she slumped against him. 'Jago Timmins will worry you no longer.'

Her hand pressed against her mouth, she did not hear his words, only those of Jago echoing and re-echoing in her mind. *Luther Kenton done a fine job in rearing you, you should be grateful to him. You were both cast in the same mould!*

Faster and faster the words revolved like a whirligig in her brain: . . . be grateful to him . . . cast in the same mould . . . Again and again they taunted her, followed each time by a mocking, spiteful laugh. The sound of it filled her ears until it was banished by the sharp retort of a gun shot.

Chapter Fifteen

'Oh, Braddy, it was awful. He . . . he said he would need his coat against the night air. The constable agreed and we waited but he did not come down. Instead there was the sound of a shot and . . .' Covering her face with her hands, Isabel gave way to the tears that had threatened throughout that terrible journey home, a journey filled with nightmare pictures of a man lying dead in his bedroom, and her own guilt at the part she had played in bringing him to suicide. 'It was my fault!' she sobbed through her fingers. 'Oh, Braddy, it was my fault. I killed Jago Timmins!'

'Now don't you be talking like that!' Anxiety sharpening her voice, Letty Bradshaw dropped the clothes she had been folding and went quickly to the bed, taking the crying girl into her arms, rocking her back and forth, comforting her as she had done countless times in the past. 'What happened in that house were none of your doing. Jago Timmins brought it on hisself with his scheming. Then, when he knowed it was all up with him, he couldn't face the consequences. Like many another he had danced to the tune but couldn't pay the piper, so he finished it the quickest way he could.'

'But if I had not confronted him . . . if those people had not been dining with him . . .'

Touching a hand to the head resting against her breast, Letty Bradshaw smiled grimly. If. How often in a lifetime was that word used? Were it a gold sovereign everybody in the world would be a millionaire. Aloud she soothed: 'Your confronting him or not would have made no difference. He would have had to face the law, be it tonight or tomorrow, and Jago Timmins, call it pride or call it cowardice, couldn't be doing with facing a prison sentence; he done what was best for him and we shouldn't blame him for that.'

'I didn't really want him to go to prison.' Isabel broke away from her friend's arms, looking at her with drowned eyes. 'I . . . I admit I once said I did, but I was angry then. I . . . I only wanted to warn him off, make him stop trying to close Kenton's. I would have told the Magistrate it . . . it had all been a mistake, then he would not have been sent to prison.'

From where she sat on the side of the bed, the housekeeper looked at the pale, tear-stained face of the girl she had loved from a child. There was no harm in Isabel Kenton, no spite or envy, so why had her life been turned upside down, why was she being put through this hell? If only Luther Kenton had not written that will, if only that letter had never been found. Letty almost smiled. Two more 'gold sovereigns' to add to her pile!

Getting up, she crossed to a mahogany tallboy. Taking a handkerchief from the top drawer, she handed it to Isabel. 'We all says things we don't mean when we be angry, same as we hopes for things we know we can't have when we be sad. There could have been no getting off for Jago Timmins, say what you would to the Magistrate. Like Mr Farr told him, things be seen in a different light in wartime. This country be in a bad way, truth of it being we be fightin' for our life, and Jago Timmins tried to interfere with the supply of weapons. I don't know whether that be treason, I have to take Mr Farr's word for that, but I do know as there ain't a Magistrate anywhere in the land as would have taken it lightly; not one as wouldn't have sent Jago Timmins so far down the line you would have had to fasten another one to it. It be my opinion as Jago knowed that an' all, and that be why he brought his life to a swifter end than p'raps it might have had. He probably said to himself: "Ain't no use in scraping the pot when it be empty." I just thank the Almighty that Mr Farr was here when that man they calls Dandylion come to tell you what was going on.'

'So do I.' Isabel wiped the last of her tears. 'Owen was so kind, Braddy. I don't think I could have done it without him.' She leaned against the pillows, the last of her energy deserting her, content for the moment to be fussed over by the motherly Mrs Bradshaw.

'Arrh, well, that Mr Owen be a good man, one you can depend on. A wench could go a long way and not find one the like of him.'

Sipping the hot cocoa the housekeeper had insisted she have, Isabel smiled to herself. She knew what lay behind those words. Braddy was saying Owen would make a fine husband; that she, Isabel, should encourage his attentions. But she did not *discourage* them. In fact, she felt a strong liking for Owen Farr, liked his looks, his manner, everything about him.

Holding the delicate china cup between both hands, she let the warmth of it seep into fingers chilled more by the events of the evening than the cold night air.

Yes, everything about Owen was pleasing to her. She had liked him from the beginning. Well, maybe not when he'd dragged her from the trap, but certainly *after* that. She had very quickly come to like him and that liking could well become love.

Her eyes following the plump figure of the housekeeper, putting away the clothes she had hurried her out of, Isabel thought over the months since Owen Farr had entered her life.

They had spent many evenings together, in the parlour of Woodbank House or sometimes taking a walk in Victoria Park. But wherever they were, he was always solicitous of her comfort, so attuned to her feelings he seemed intuitively to know those times when she felt guilty at enjoying herself while Mark was away at war. Those were the times he would ask if they could just sit and talk, making it appear to be his choice not to seek any further distraction. Braddy was right in what she had said, he would make a good husband, but a girl had to be asked before becoming a man's wife, and Isabel had not been asked. She liked Owen Farr a great deal, but how strong was his liking for her? They had talked of many things in the hours they had spent in each other's company, but the word 'love' had never once been mentioned.

'There you be.' Mrs Bradshaw smoothed both hands the length of her apron, a movement Isabel had come to recognise, one that indicated a job well done. 'Everything put away and tidy, just like my old mother taught me, God love her. Now you finish your cocoa, then take my advice and have yourself a nice long lie in tomorrow. There be nothing as can't wait an hour or two, and the rest will do you good. You takes too much on yourself. All that to-ing and fro-ing to them works . . . it were hard on your father so I know it be too hard for you.'

Her father! A picture of the housekeeper with the blood draining from her face in shock flashed into Isabel's mind. Braddy had come into the study and seen the letter in Isabel's hand. She must have known what it was, could not have thought it had arrived in the morning post, or her face would not have paled so drastically. Letty Bradshaw had seen that letter before. The question was, when? She must also have read what was in it, in which case she knew that though Luther Kenton had reared both Isabel and Mark, he had not fathered them. Yet not once in all these years had the woman so much as breathed a word of it. Why? Isabel placed the cup on her night table. Was it because *her* hand had been the one to place the letter in that book? Was it she who prevented its being delivered to the rightful recipient? Isabel felt the sudden touch of ice against her spine. Could she and Luther have been in on the whole thing together?

'Braddy,' Isabel spoke quietly though the blood was pounding through her veins, 'You know Luther Kenton was not my father, don't you? You also know what was in that letter I found.'

Standing at the foot of the bed, Letty Bradshaw's shoulders slumped and her plump face seemed to crumple. When she spoke her voice trembled. 'Arrh, me wench, I know. I've known for a long time.'

'But you said nothing!' Isabel's voice was reproachful. 'You never told me. Why, Braddy? Why let me think . . .'

'It were for your mother I held my peace. 'Twas her wish I say nothing, God rest her poor soul.'

Isabel's eyes filled with tears, reflecting the light of the lamp beside her bed until they gleamed like liquid bronze. 'My mother knew . . . she knew that letter was in the study?'

'Her knowed. All them years, her knowed.' Letty flung her apron up to her face, sobbing the rest of her words through it. 'It were her found it, your mother, and the finding nigh on killed her. May the Lord hear my prayers and let Luther Kenton rot in hell! May he burn for all eternity for what he done to that woman!'

For what Luther had done . . . Isabel felt a touch of remorse at her next question, but the words had to be said, she had to know. Fingers digging into the soft satin-covered eiderdown, she asked, 'Braddy, who put that letter in the spine of that book? Who else knew of it?'

'Oh, Miss Isabel.' Behind the apron, Letty Bradshaw drew a long shuddering breath. 'Don't make me say, it will break your heart to hear. They both be dead now so let it lie with them in the grave. You can rake the ashes of the past but it won't make the future burn any the brighter.'

Her breathing none too steady, Isabel curled her fingers tighter, feeling her nails bite through the bed cover and into her palms. 'Braddy,' she said, determination making her voice hard, 'I have to know. Who was it hid that letter, and what happened to the envelope?'

'I ain't never seen no envelope.' Letty lowered her apron until it covered only her mouth. 'As God be my witness, I never did see no envelope, just the letter, the way you seen it for your-self.'

Believing her housekeeper, Isabel shook off the icy feeling that had her in its grip. Whoever had hidden that letter, it had not been Letty Bradshaw. Throwing off the covers, she climbed from the bed, going over to where the housekeeper stood, still quietly sobbing.

'Oh, Miss Isabel!' Letty's tear-filled eyes turned to her. 'You didn't think as I 'ad put it there? You didn't think I could take from your mother . . .'

'No, Braddy. No, of course I didn't.' But she had. Just for a moment she had considered the possibility. Guilt and remorse filling her, Isabel put her arms about Letty. How could she ever have doubted, how could she have thought such an awful thing of the woman who had been more like a mother than a house-keeper to her? Leading the still tearful woman across to the fire, she pressed her into the deep, comfortable chair there then sank to her heels beside her. 'Please understand,' she said softly, 'I had to ask. Ever since finding that letter the question of who put it there has plagued me. Who stole it? For it had to have been stolen. Surely the man to whom it was written would not have been so callous as to return it? And even had it been returned to my mother, having arrived too late to reach him, why keep it? Would she not have destroyed it in view of its contents? I cannot believe it was she who hid it.'

'It wasn't!' Letty let the apron fall. 'It wasn't your mother put the letter in that hidey hole, that much I would stake my life on. It were as much of a shock to her, finding it there, as it was to me. And as it must have been for yourself.' Staring into the heart of the glowing coals, she seemed to be watching something more than the flickering flames. 'I was in the hall when I heard it, the cry your mother made. It were like the 'eart was being dragged from her body. I run into the study to find her standing afore the opened bookcase, a paper lying on the floor by her and her looking like to die on the spot. It were then I shouted for Bradshaw to carry her to bed and as he took her from me, I scooped up the paper from the floor and shoved it in my pinny pocket!' She paused, hand straying to the pocket of her apron as if to find the letter still inside. 'I think that were the day your mother started to die.'

Tears burning in her throat, Isabel rested her head against the housekeeper's knee. 'Did he know? Did my mother tell Luther she had found the letter?'

'No.' Letty Bradshaw continued to stare into the fire, watching a drama she had relived many times before. 'Her never told him, an' Bradshaw an' I kept quiet about putting that paper back where she'd found it. It were your mother showed me what it held, what she herself had written, then asked me to put it back after making me swear I would never tell you or your brother what I'd seen. Her said there were nothing could be done about it and it were no good passing on her 'eartache to you. That were the reason I never spoke of this afore now.'

'Thank you, Braddy.' Looking up into the older woman's face, Isabel tried to smile despite the tears. 'Thank you for telling me, though I'm sorry I made you break your promise.'

'I think her would understand,' Letty said softly. 'It p'raps be all for the best, 'specially after you heard what was written in that will.'

'You mean, about Luther's not being my father? I am glad he could not resist that final dig, glad he told us. If only he knew how little it hurt Mark or myself, how happy it made us to find we had nothing of him in either of us!'

'That thought give me a secret happiness an' all.' Letty answered. 'All the years I watched your mother fading, I thanked God there were none of Luther Kenton's blood in her children. Whoever it was brought her to the birthing bed did wrong, we all knows that, but I thank every power that be for his doing of it, for at least it means you two do not carry the evil that were in Luther Kenton.'

Her eyes still moist, Isabel held the other woman's gaze. 'You say the letter had no envelope? Did . . . did my mother ever say to whom she had written it?'

Letty Bradshaw looked into eyes soft and trusting as a fawn's, then touched a hand to the face she could not have loved more had it been the face of her own child. 'No, wench, your mother never named the man whose blood you carry. But . . .'

Catching at the hand that caressed her cheek, Isabel held it as her heart leaped in her chest. 'But what, Braddy . . . please, if you know who he is, then tell me!'

'I vowed as never so long as there was breath in me would I tell you this. Now, God forgive me, I be going to break that vow. It were no more than a six month afore your mother passed away that she told me.'

'My father's name?'

Letty Bradshaw's insides twisted at the hope and longing in that one question. A hope and longing she could not satisfy. Laying her hand over Isabel's, she stroked it as she continued.

'No, it were not your father's name, her never did speak that, not even when her felt the touch of the angels come to carry her to her rest. But her did tell as how the man who left her did so not knowing her was carrying his child. Her told me he had come back, come here to Darlaston, when you and your brother was scarce two years old. Her told me of his despair at finding her married, and that no letter had ever reached him. That after almost two years of never hearing from her, of his letters being returned unopened, he sold the business he had begun in America and sailed home. But it was too late. She was Luther Kenton's wife.'

Isabel shifted her glance to the fire, feeling the pain of her next words almost too much to bear, and when she spoke it was in a whisper. 'Did my mother tell him about us?'

'No.' Letty felt the shudder that ran through the girl seated at her feet. What cruel fate had ordained a young woman should go through life not knowing the man who had fathered her? And what special kind of devil had prompted Luther Kenton to tell her of her bastardy?

Bending forward, she pressed a kiss to the shining auburn hair, then straightened herself and took a slow deliberate breath. 'Like I said a minute gone, her never did speak his name, but her last words were of him. "Don't ever blame him," her said. "He did not know my children were also his. I told him never to visit me or contact me again, that Luther Kenton was my husband and nothing could alter that.

"But I never stopped loving him, and I could not die without telling him the children Luther had reared were his. This I wrote in a letter. I put it in among those set out for the morning post after Luther had left for the foundry. In it I begged that what I had written be kept secret by him, as it must be by you . . . promise me.'" Leaning her head against the back of the chair, Letty closed her eyes. 'I kept my promise, until tonight. But now it be better out. You and your brother have a right to know your father didn't abandon you or your mother.'

'Thank you for telling me.' For a second time Isabel murmured her gratitude. It had not been easy for Braddy to break the promise given to her mistress. But for all that the housekeeper had told her it still did not explain the letter, or how it came to be hidden in the study.

Years of caring for the girl, of knowing her every mood, helped Letty Bradshaw guess the thoughts that must now be going through her mind. 'You be wondering about that letter, why it was it finished up in this house rather than with the man it were sent to? Well, I can answer that. One evening Luther was in a particularly black mood. I don't be knowing what it was had gone wrong but as usual he brought his vile temper home. They were in the small sitting room – your mother preferred it to the drawing room, said her always felt more comfortable there than any other room in the house – and that room being closer to the kitchen, Luther's shouting could be heard plain. He was ranting on about a letter, one your mother had written to a man. It seems Luther had stolen the letter from a table in the hall of her parents' house while calling on her. He had kept the letter, he said, kept it where her would never find it. Kept it to show the world what a slut she was, to prove to the world she had borne bastard twins.'

So Isabel had been correct in thinking Luther was the one who had taken that letter. She stared hard into the fire. He had held it over her mother's head for years and she had never destroyed it. Why? could she have seen keeping it as an act of repentance for what she had done? And the man it had been meant for, did he know of the death of Luther and her mother? Was he himself still living? If so, would he still feel his promise binding upon him, or would he now reveal his identity to his children?

The coals in the small grate settled, sending up a shower of sparks that equalled her myriad thoughts, but of them all one burned longer and brighter than the rest, just as one thought burned the longest in her mind. Should he still be alive, would her mother's lover wish to recognise his children or would he prefer to remain unknown? Would he too prefer to leave the ashes of the past undisturbed . . . would she go through life a bastard who had never known her real father?

Her letter to Mark in her pocket, Isabel walked along Pinfold Street, her breath making a white cloud on the frosty air. Braddy had not wanted her to walk to the Post Office in King Street, but Isabel had insisted. She did not get about the town as much as she once had since taking over the works, and this brisk walk would do her good.

Taking the left turn that would take her into King Street, wondering when the new road the Town Council was talking of constructing opposite the Town Hall would be built, Isabel was unaware of a figure draped in a faded shawl, head bent over the coins she was counting in her hand, coming from Durnton's butcher shop.

Apologising as they bumped against each other, the other woman glanced up. 'I be sorry, Miss. I . . . I weren't looking where I was going.'

'Neither was I really.' Isabel looked at the package that had fallen from the woman's basket, strewing its contents on the ground.

'Don't you be bothering, miss.' The woman bent quickly,

picking up the small pieces that were more fat than meat, wrapping them once more in their paper.

'You must allow me to replace that. You cannot eat it now.'

Pulling the shawl tighter about her head as she straightened up, the woman glanced at the package in her hand. 'Ain't done it no 'arm, miss, it'll wash.'

'Please.' Isabel smiled into a face that tiredness had aged beyond its years. 'I would feel better.'

Taking the package from the woman, she walked with it into the butcher's shop, leaving its owner no alternative but to follow. 'Will you replace this with whatever Mrs . . . ?'

'Tait.' Pale-faced, eyes wide with worry, she glanced from the butcher to Isabel. 'Daisy Tait. But there be no need . . .'

'C'mon, Daisy. The lady be good enough to offer to replace what her knocked out of your basket, but her can't be standing here all day while you be dithering.'

Isabel glanced about the shop, its floor covered in a fresh layer of sawdust, the air filled with the smell of raw meat. Behind the huge wooden chopping block the wall was festooned with hooks from which hung poultry and game. Long curled loops of sausages together with fat black rings of pig's pudding were festooned like Christmas decorations, while to the farthest end near the door that gave on to a back room hung great haunch ends of beef clothed in thin layers of yellow fat; legs and shoulders of pork brushed against carcasses of mutton, while the small bottle glass window displayed every cut of meat, surrounding the centre piece of a huge pink pig's head, holding an apple in its mouth.

'I think a chine of best beef.' Isabel smiled at the butcher who could not hide his surprise that someone of her apparent class would know of such a cut. Silently thanking Mrs Bradshaw for teaching her, Isabel watched as he cleaved the meat, chopping cleanly through the bone. Returning the hind quarter to its hook, he first weighed the chine then wrapped it.

'Your Bert will enjoy that, Daisy,' he said, long side whiskers jiggling as he smiled. 'And you can take him these from me – put a fresh egg and a knob of butter in with them after you've boiled them, then chop them and put them with a slice of bread and it'll make a meal fit for a king.'

'Thank you, Mr Durnton.' her gratitude showing in a thin smile, the woman watched the scoop of pig's brains being wrapped in a separate package. 'And thank you, miss.'

Bobbing a curtsey, she grabbed her parcels and hurried from the shop. Taking her purse from her pocket, Isabel pretended not to notice that among the packages hurried into her basket was the one she had carried into the shop and placed on the counter to be thrown away.

'Poor wench!' Taking the money Isabel held out to him, the butcher carried it to the drawer set in a table on the surface of which were set out his knives. 'You can't help but feel sorry for her, what with five little 'uns to feed and care for, and her man as helpless.'

'Has her husband no work?'

'Her husband be flat on his back. He were sent home from the Army – some sort of marsh fever so the doctors reckoned, caused from lying in trenches half filled with water. Dumped the lad back home they did, and that being so, Daisy had to give up her job.'

'Daisy . . . Mrs Tait was working as well as caring for five children?'

Counting the change into Isabel's hand one coin at a time, the butcher looked at her as he pressed the last penny into her gloved palm. 'Daisy Tait be like many another woman in Darlaston. Her couldn't manage on what the Army paid her man. 'Sides, kids have a way of looking after theirselves.'

Slipping the coins into her purse, Isabel frowned. 'But why is her husband at home? If he so ill, why is he not in hospital?'

'Same reason as many another who got a blighty from the Germans,' the man answered, running his hands over the blue-and-white-striped apron tied about his middle. 'Ain't no room in the hospital. I hear that the Sister Dora has blankets set along the corridors, and so has the Dudley Guest. Even the temporary places they set up in church halls and such be overflowing, and not enough nurses or doctors to look to them!'

Blighty. Isabel recognised the word. Mark had written in one of his letters how it was used to describe a wound serious enough for the patient to be returned to England. And now those men were lying on floors in their home towns without proper medical care. Thanking the butcher who had already begun to serve another customer, she walked from the shop.

Her mind once again a thousand miles from the street she was walking along, Isabel stepped from the narrow footpath.

'Get out of the bloody hoss road!'

The irate shout came from a waggoner, the wheels of his heavily laden cart missing her by a hair's breadth as she was pulled back to safety.

'Really, Miss Kenton. Do I have to spend my life dragging you away from danger?'

Straightening her hat as she was set once more on her feet, Isabel stared up into a pair of laughing eyes and felt her face suffused with warmth. She had seen those eyes before. Twice when awake, but many times in her dreams.

Chapter Sixteen

Isabel glanced at the circle of faces, each turned to her and each with hostility in their eyes. Maybe Braddy had been right, maybe she should not have come. Maybe had Luther not stolen that letter . . . maybe had Mark not joined the Forces . . . maybe had she not bumped into that woman coming from the butcher's shop . . . Her whole life had been built on 'maybe', perhaps this evening would prove to be another.

'Gentlemen.' The chairman of the Chamber of Commerce rose to his feet. 'We all of us know Luther Kenton's daughter.' He half turned towards Isabel but did not look at her.

'Arrh, we all knows her, and we knows this be no place for her.'

A series of nods and grunts followed the sharp retort and Isabel inwardly quailed. Braddy had warned her that the death of Jago Timmins would be too fresh in the minds of these men, that she might be thought of as responsible for it, but still she had come.

'Since when did we allow women into the Chamber? Since when did a woman know anything about business!'

The remark too much for her stretched nerves, Isabel was on her feet, her open palm slamming down on the polished surface of the table as the first ripples of laughter rose.

'Since my brother went to fight for his country instead of sitting home on his arse as you are doing! while others buy him the privilege of being able to do so with their lives; As for my being in this Chamber, I am the legal representative of Luther Kenton's son . . .'

'Arrh, you be that, and you be old Luther's wench, there be no disputing that neither. You can turn a phrase the way he did.'

'I make no apology for my language!' She snapped at the speaker. 'I find men listen better when you speak to them in their own way. Kenton's is running as well as the business of any one of you, and that under the supervision of a woman.'

'That don't stand arguing with.' A voice from the further end of the table rose over the murmurs of assent. 'But that be with the backing of a man, and we all knows which one. Question be . . . what's he getting for it?'

The room became suddenly silent, every eye on Isabel's face; only her eyes, flashing cold contempt, betrayed her emotions.

'There is no man backing me other than my brother.' She spoke slowly, icily, making sure her words reached every corner of the room, making sure they missed no man's ears. 'Unlike yourself, Mr Hayden, I have not reached the point where I have to buy my 'business services', but should it come to that, I would not buy where you do – in the bawdy houses of Birmingham. I would hope to have sense enough to spend my money more wisely. For, you see, the prostitutes *you* buy are women – and since when did a woman know anything about business!'

'Jago Timmins were right when he called you a bitch! I'll have the law . . .'

'Oh, sit down, Hayden!' another man said amid the laughter. 'The wench got you fair and square. I vote we listen to what her's got to say, her deserves that much for having the backbone to come here.'

Their cries of assent fading into silence, the men looked expectantly at Isabel. She had won their approval, but would she win their help? This was the second time she had run the gauntlet, the second time she had faced these men in a domain they saw as strictly their own, a place no woman had ever entered until today. She had once before set her ideas in front of them but could not truly claim they were accepted because of what she'd said; it was wartime circumstances which had forced these men to employ women. And didn't those same circumstances apply now when she had something else to propose?

Taking a long breath, she forced herself to appear calm. These men had seen what she was made of, they had seen she was not easily frightened off. She would put her request in a businesslike manner and trust them to receive it in the same way.

'Gentlemen,' she began, 'yesterday I visited the Sister Dora hospital in Walsall. Every inch of available space was filled with wounded men sent back from France. Soldiers – some of them dying – were lying on makeshift beds or laid out on the floors of corridors. There simply isn't room to treat them any better than this, especially since one wing was destroyed in an air raid. While I was there I spoke to the matron and to the military medical personnel. They both told me that Hallam hospital at West Bromwich, Dudley Guest and Wordsley hospitals were in the same predicament, and that every train arriving brings further wounded men whom they cannot accommodate anywhere within the building. Even outhouses are being used as wards apparently. The only alternative now is tents set out on heathland. But I say that is no place for men who are sick and in pain, men who have risked their lives for us and yet may lose them.'

'What about the fever hospital along of Bull Lane?'

'That too is filled.' She glanced in the direction of a younger man, his mauve coat a colourful contrast to the sober black of his colleagues. 'Most cases of what is called marsh or trench fever are directed there, though those who have homes in the area are sent for nursing by their family.'

'Then if everywhere is filled, the army must send its wounded elsewhere.'

Isabel drew in her breath sharply, eyes turning to green-flecked glaciers as anger overtook her like an avalanche. '*It's* wounded!' She glared at the man, a green silk cravat clashing loudly with his jaunty mauve coat. '*It's* wounded! Surely these men are the responsibility of all of us, each and every one they fought to protect . . . including you!'

'Of course, I . . .' the man stammered, the icy rebuke in Isabel's voice bringing a dull flush to his cheeks. 'I did not mean . . . I . . . I just did not think.'

'Oh!' Isabel's words cracked like a whip. 'How very strange for a man. You must take care, sir, such a condition brings you dangerously close to the world of women!'

'I told you her were Luther Kenton's wench,' another man called as the roar of laughter subsided. 'Her's got his bite to prove it.'

Luther Kenton's wench! Isabel felt a moment of distaste beneath her anger. She had no love for her so-called father but it was he to whom her thanks must go if these men listened to her, for it was Luther's teaching that had made her strong enough to stand up to them.

'Gentlemen.' She returned doggedly once more to the task she had set herself. 'There is a way in which at least some of these men can be cared for other than in tents. I intend to turn over Woodbank House to be used as a military hospital.'

'What!' The chairman turned to her, incredulous. 'Turn Luther's house into a hospital?'

'Not Luther's house, Mr Chairman. *My* house. It was left to me in my . . . my father's will.'

Halfway along the table, Joseph Hayden leaned forward. 'Is that what you suggest we should all do – give up our homes to be turned into military hospitals?'

'No, Mr Hayden. I would not have the temerity to suggest anything of the sort.'

'Then what are you here for?' asked the young man in the mauve coat, his blushes subsiding.

'To ask for help.' The words were blunt and to the point, and Isabel could see her answer had taken them by surprise. Before they could recover she pressed on. 'I am willing to give my house to be used as I have said, but I need help in getting it ready. I have only one manservant and three women at Woodbank. Unaided they cannot cope with the moving of heavy furniture and the clearing of outhouses.'

'So how do you expect us to help? Do you want we should send our wives to do the shifting?'

Realising the crucial moment had been reached, the point where a sharp tone or acid rebuke would alienate them completely, Isabel smiled. 'No, that is not the help I am asking.'

'Why not?' Joseph Hayden erupted into laughter once more. 'It were you behind the employing of women in our works, you had the temerity to suggest that!'

'Arrh, you did,' the chairman said with a nod, wiping away tears of mirth with a large white handkerchief. 'So out with it, young woman, what is it you really want?'

Glancing along the table, seeing smiles soften faces that had been tightly set upon her arrival in the Chamber, Isabel felt some of the tension ease from her, but she could not yet afford to relax, the day was not quite won. Mentally crossing her fingers, she plunged in. 'What I really want, really need, gentlemen, is for each of you to give me a few of your men to do the heavier work. It should take no more than a week or two at the most – depending, of course, on the number of men you can spare.'

'That is the trouble, Miss Kenton.' Completely reconciled to the beautiful young woman brave enough to face them in this way, the chairman answered her regretfully. 'Every man capable of heavy work is already engaged in the foundries and factories. Take them out even for a few hours a day and production will fall, which in turn will lead to a reduction in supplies of arma-ments. I do not have to tell you the effect that would have on our forces in France and Belgium. It could, in effect, increase the number of Tommies wounded, or worse.'

'What the chairman says be right enough.' Joseph Hayden got to his feet, his glance encompassing every man at the table. 'And my works can spare no man, same as yours. But I be willing to pay any of my workmen as will give an hour or two of their evening time, and of their Sunday rest, to help turn Woodbank House into a hospital.'

'Work on the Lord's day?'

'Arrh, on the Lord's day!' Joseph Hayden turned a scornful glance on the long, mournful face of the church warden of St Lawrence's. 'If you read the Book near as much as you press others to do, you would remember the Lord's words: 'Comfort the poor, succour the needy'. Well, I reckons them wounded men be needy. And as for the Lord's day, it be my opinion He would help out Himself were He here, and be buggered to what day it was!'

'Seems Mr Hayden has the right idea.' The chairman rose as Joseph Hayden resumed his seat. 'I think there will be more than one man willing to earn an extra shilling or two, and I shall certainly make the same offer. What do you say, gentlemen?'

'Darlaston is a small place, Miss Kenton. Gossip travels around it fast. I've called to offer any service I might be allowed to render. That is, supposing what I hear is true?'

'It is true, Mr Calcott, I do intend to turn this house into a temporary hospital.' She smiled at Mary as she laid the tray, neatly set with tea and home-baked cakes, on the low table between Isabel and her guest.

'I admire your courage and tenacity.' Hewett Calcott's gold-flecked eyes were warm with feeling. 'And not only for your plan to sacrifice your home. Word of what you said to Darlaston's men of steel is also going the rounds.'

Did that gossip include the reference made to his being the man backing her? she wondered. Bending to the task of pouring tea into delicate china cups, Isabel tried to conceal her blushes.

Taking the cup from her hands, Hewett Calcott smiled again, looking deep into her eyes. 'It seems they met their match in a woman of steel.'

'I said only what I felt.' She lifted her own cup and gazed modestly into it.

'Feelings that are most laudable, and which you seem determined to act upon.' Seeing the tinge of pink deepen on her fine skin, Hewett Calcott smiled to himself. He had called Isabel Kenton a woman of steel, but it took the peeling away of many layers of velvet to expose the strength at the core of her. 'May I be allowed to help?'

Isabel felt instinctively that the offer had not been given out of empty courtesy, but was born of a genuine desire to help.

Looking at his handsome face, unsmiling now within the confines of its neatly trimmed beard, she felt that familiar tug at her emotions. It was not a leap of the heart she felt whenever they met, or the swift jolt to her senses that a meeting with Owen Farr brought about, but a warm feeling of happiness, a wanting to keep him here with her, a feeling as close to love as any she knew.

'My mother taught me never to turn away an offer kindly meant,' she said, voice softer than she had intended.

Hewett Calcott's eyes turned to a photograph standing in a silver frame beside one of Mark. Faded a little with age, it nevertheless showed the beauty of the woman whose eyes held only sadness and whose mouth was unsmiling. 'Your mother had wisdom and consideration,' he said quietly, the slight tremor in his voice surprising Isabel. 'That is the true mark of beauty in any woman, and one she has given to her daughter.'

In the brief silence that followed, Isabel felt her heart reach out to him. Hewett Calcott seemed to nurse a deep hurt, one ever present in his eyes, one she suddenly wanted to kiss away.

'I have the promise of men to do the heavier work.' Conscious of the fact that her own inner emotion was betrayed in her eyes, Isabel took her time returning her cup to the tray then offering him a plate of cakes.

'But will they do the cleaning, to say nothing of the nursing?'

Hewett Calcott smiled as he spoke, but the sadness remained behind his eyes, enhancing Isabel's desire to wrap her arms around him.

'I would not ask it of them,' she answered, fighting the urge that both embarrassed and confused her. 'What has been offered to the men, I myself shall offer to the women. I will pay any who are willing to devote their free time to cleaning and to assisting with the running of the hospital. But the medical side of it . . .' She faltered, not yet knowing herself how this obstacle was to be overcome. What she had not told those men in the Chamber of Commerce, or anyone else, was the fact that while delighted with her offer of Woodbank, the matron of the Sister Dora had said the staff there were fully stretched, that no doctor could be spared even if she released a few nurses, which in any case would only increase the load falling upon the others.

'Am I correct in presuming that trained medical help is the overriding problem?'

Isabel nodded. The pale winter sunshine falling through the window gilded her head with auburn fire, kindling a response that pulled at his heart – a response he had to fight hard against as it threatened to disrupt his previous determination and have him on his knees beside her. But that would be wrong. He thought again of the small blue leather box finely tooled with gilt. No, the moment was not right. He must wait.

'What of the local Voluntary Aid Detachment?' he asked, continuing the conversation.

Isabel shook her head. 'I mentioned that to the matron but she held out little hope. That avenue too has been exhausted, apparently. The only help I have recruited is that of William Langton who was once the Parish doctor for Darlaston. He has offered to come daily but is rather old now, so how long he can keep on coming is anyone's guess.'

'Miss Kenton, will you allow me to try to find you a doctor, and if possible, some trained nurses?'

'It would be marvellous if you could.' She rose with him as he got to his feet.

'Then leave it with me.' At the door he turned, eyes warm on her face. 'Give me a week or so. One way or another, Miss Kenton, you will get your medical staff.'

She could not help herself. She stepped close and, raising herself on tiptoe, kissed him gently on the cheek.

'Thank you,' she murmured as she stepped back, eyes soft as velvet. 'And my name is Isabel.'

'But you can't go turning the place into a military hospital! Or any other kind of hospital for that matter.'

'Why not?' Isabel went on peeling potatoes, glancing side-long at Mary who was busy shelling peas at the opposite side of the kitchen table. They both enjoyed Mrs Bradshaw's periodic outbursts.

'Why not!' Letty Bradshaw slapped a lump of pastry noisily on to a floured board. "'Cos . . . 'cos you can't, that be why not. I mean . . .' she attacked the pastry with a wooden rolling pin '. . . the house don't be big enough for one thing!'

'It will not make a very large hospital, I agree. But it will help, and you yourself often say: "Even a little be a big help when you've got nowt.'"

'Well, I still says as this place don't be big enough.'

Resting her hands on the sides of the big enamel bowl that held the potatoes, Isabel looked across at her housekeeper. 'The pastry will be hard if you continue to beat it like that, Braddy.'

Plunging one hand into the flour jar, Letty deluged the pastry, her frown deepening as she set aside the rolling pin to brush most of the flour to one side of the board. 'Well, if it be hard then it be suitable for a hard-headed wench, and that be you! I never knowed one so stubborn. Get summat in that brain of your'n and there be no peace till it be done. And as for this latest hare-brained scheme . . . well! It be the daftest I've heard yet!'

Isabel's glance stole again to Mary, who sucked her cheeks hard against her teeth to stifle a giggle.

'Hospital, indeed!' Letty took up the rolling pin, passing it in swift light strokes across the pastry, teasing it into a wide creamy circle. 'And who be going to run it, eh? Answer me that, Miss Noggyhead!'

Not daring to smile at the housekeeper's reference to her stubbornness, Isabel kept her eyes wide and innocent. 'The medical side must of course be the responsibility of the doctors and nurses, but for what I see as the housekeeping part, then there would be no one better suited to it than you, Braddy.'

It was calculated flattery, yet with a strong underlay of truth. Letty Bradshaw had proved herself over the years to be competent and efficient, but in those years she had not looked after the numbers who would shortly be living at Woodbank House.

'Hmmph!' Laying the pastry in a greased enamel dish, Letty trimmed the edges with a knife, mouth pursed as she fetched a pan from the hob. Tipping the cubes of meat from it on to the pastry bed, she returned the pan to the hob, all the time holding her peace.

Resuming her own task, Isabel peeled the last potato then carried the bowl to the scullery.

'Give that to me, miss.' Sarah Griffin smiled as she took the bowl from Isabel. 'You should be getting yourself some rest. You be running around the whole time, and what with them foundries and one thing and another, you be looking peaky.'

'I am quite well, Mrs Griffin, please don't worry. We will all take a rest once this war is over.'

'Arrh, one day it will be over and with the Lord's help your brother and all the other brave souls who be fighting will return to their homes. It's been hard for every mother but at least they 'ave known where their sons be.' Sarah paused then added: 'I ain't got that knowledge. I know only that my son ran away.'

Seeing tears spill down the woman's cheeks, Isabel put her arms about her, holding her while stifled sobs wracked her thin body. 'Oh, miss! If only I knowed. He could be dead . . .'

'No, Sarah.' Isabel used the woman's Christian name for the first time since employing her. 'Your son is not dead. He will come back to Darlaston soon, and when he does you will be here waiting for him.' Holding her at arm's length, Isabel smiled reassuringly. 'And when that happens he must not find you crying or he might think we beat you.'

Sarah Griffin lifted her apron, wiping her eyes with it. 'No, miss, my Peter mustn't see my crying. He seen enough of that in the past, same as he seen enough beatings from his father.' Eyes dark with the memories she held the apron against her mouth. 'That be the one man in all of creation I wish to see dead! The only one to whose body I would give no burial. Ernie Griffin be the spawn of the devil and I hope the devil claims his own! That I never again set eyes on him again.'

'You won't.' Isabel knew what she said offered cold comfort, but cold comfort was better than none. 'Your husband will not return to this town. He would not risk the vengeance of the foundry men should they find him here.'

'I pray God what you say be true.' Sarah dropped her apron, turning back to the shallow brownstone sink. 'And I pray Ernie Griffin no longer walks this earth.'

Putting the potatoes Sarah rinsed in a fresh bowl, Isabel tried to look confident though in reality she knew it was a sham. Ernest Griffin would no more be afraid to return to Darlaston than he would fear a fly in the air. And if he did . . .

'We have both seen the last of your husband but we still have to face Letty Bradshaw, and she will give us both what for if we keep her waiting for these potatoes much longer.'

'You take 'em into the kitchen, miss,' Sarah sniffed, 'while I takes these peelings to the heap.'

'I thought as you was waiting for next year's crop to grow!' Letty said tartly, lining a second tin with pastry. 'Get them 'tatoes sliced. Nice and thin, mind. Keep a body waiting all day! Canting, I've no doubt.'

'Sarah and I *were* gossiping.' Catching Mary's worried glance, Isabel gave her the tiniest of nods, her quick smile saying that nothing was wrong. 'Sorry Braddy, I'll have these sliced in two ticks.'

Busy trimming the second baking dish and making no comment on Isabel's use of the woman's first name, Letty returned to the large range, its black iron silvered by years of polishing. Her back turned to the two young women, she said over her shoulder: 'Go find your mother, Mary, there's a good wench. Ask her to come and make a cup of tea. I couldn't spit a tanner, my mouth be that dry.'

Watching Mary dart for the scullery, Isabel stepped up behind the housekeeper, putting her arms about the woman's comfortable waist, hugging her from behind, her own voice soft and filled with love. 'Mrs Bradshaw, you are no more dry-mouthed than you are truthful. You deliberately sent Mary out so she could see if her mother was all right, didn't you? You are a fraud, Letty Bradshaw, but I love you.'

Pressing her own hand over the two clasped at her waist, Letty felt a surge of love also and when she answered her voice was gruff with emotion. 'Arrh, well, it takes more than love to bake the pies – as you be going to find out when this kitchen be feeding half the British Army!'

'Oh, Braddy!' Squeezing her tighter, Isabel touched her face against the plump shoulder, pressing a kiss to it. 'Oh, Braddy, then you will do it?'

'Arrh, wench, you knows I will. We all 'ave to pull together, and Letty Bradshaw ain't one to sit down when a job needs doing. There be more than them in uniform be fighting in this war.'

An hour later, the pies wafting a delicious smell from the oven, the four women sat nursing the second pot of tea Sarah had brewed.

'What I be wanting to know,' Letty said, resting her cup heavily on its saucer, 'is what part Bradshaw be expected to play in all this? Ain't hardly much call for butlering in a hospital.'

'I shall need him more than ever.' Isabel felt the first pin prick of doubt since setting her mind to transforming the house into a temporary hospital. Was Bradshaw thinking of leaving . . . if so would he insist that his wife go too? 'I have depended upon Mr Bradshaw to see to the smooth running of Woodbank since the death of my father. I . . . I don't think I can see this through without his help.' This time there was no undercurrent of flattery in what she said, but the plain truth. She *did* depend on Bradshaw, but only now, with the prospect of his leaving, did she realise how great that dependence had been.

'You won't have to, don't you go fretting on that score.' Letty smiled broadly. 'It be just that he will want to be knowing what his new duties be.'

'What they have always been.' Isabel's relief showed in her eyes. 'To keep our part of the house running as smoothly as our new circumstances will allow. I shall expect no more.'

'Mebbe not.' Letty's smile became a chuckle. 'But it be my bet Bradshaw won't see things in that light. The whole of Woodbank House be his concern and he won't have that alter, hospital or no hospital. It'll all be run like clockwork or he'll know the reason why.'

'Braddy, this is a lot to ask, and if it is unreasonable then tell me so before I ask it, but do you think Mr Bradshaw would take on the job of Superintendent?'

'Take it on?' Letty picked up her cup, smiling proudly over its rim. 'Why, bless you, wench! Bradshaw would have resigned had you asked anybody else. He'll do it and glad to, and there'll be nowt to be grumbled at. Bradshaw has a lot more in his head than it takes to be a butler.'

They all had a lot more than they showed: the Bradshaws, Mary, Sarah. They would not let Isabel down. But what of herself? Had she let enthusiasm run away with her? Was she capable of achieving all she had set out to do.

Isabel asked herself the same questions again when later she lay in bed, watching silver shafts of moonlight play over the walls of her room. Bradshaw had assured her he could handle the running of things, and the women were adamant they too could manage. But could she? The constant worry of the foundries, of keeping up with requisitions from the War Office for ever more armaments, often left her weary to the bone. How could she cope with more? But she must. She could not ask others to do what she herself was not prepared to tackle.

And Hewett Calcott had promised to find medical staff. He had been so kind, so reassuring. Hewett Calcott . . . Isabel's eyes followed the cloud-chased moonlight. Just saying the name to herself brought a warmth to her heart, a sense of love and security. Yes, she could depend on Hewett. Then, of course, there was Owen. He too had promised assistance; with the permission of the military, he had said, he would attend to the papers of the wounded and keep the authorities informed of their subsequent progress or intended release from the hospital.

Owen . . . The name slipped silently from her lips but Owen Farr's were not the eyes that laughed back at her from the dark reaches of sleep; instead she was thinking of the pearl grey eyes of the man who had snatched her from under the wheels of a waggoner's cart.

Chapter Seventeen

Slipping on her grey woollen suit, Isabel stared at her reflection in the long mirror as she did up the tiny pearl buttons of the jacket. They were almost the same colour as *his* eyes and she had worn this same suit the first time they had met, the afternoon he had led her away from the crowd assembled at the Bull Stake. It was at almost the same spot that she had watched him drive past on his way to war.

Had it really been three years since Mark and so many others had left to fight? Like Owen, her rescuer had returned wounded, a leg wound that had left him with a limp. But at least he and Owen were home! If it was a wound it took to bring Mark back . . . no! It was wrong to wish that. Turning from the mirror, Isabel collected a handkerchief from the drawer of the tallboy. How would Mark react to being invalided out? He had always been so athletic, how would he cope with any disability? But as she left her room, Isabel could not help but wish.

'You shouldn't be going out there, you've done enough for one day. You go making yourself poorly and that'll be one more problem.' Letty Bradshaw cast a disparaging glance at Isabel as she walked into the kitchen.

'You worry too much, Braddy.' Skipping across to her, Isabel placed a kiss on her cheek.

'And you don't worry enough!' the housekeeper returned, her hands deep in flour and lard. 'You seem to think nothing can happen to you but it can, my girl, just like it happened to Mary. A cold summat awful that wench has gone and catched.'

'Mary is much better, I looked in on her on my way down.'

'Arrh, her is better!' Letty's retort was sharpened by concern for Isabel. 'But that one had the sense to do as her was told and stay in bed!'

'Yes, well, so will I if I get a cold.' Isabel almost ran for the door that gave on to the yard separating the main house from the outbuildings.

'There be no "if" about it. Going outside at this time of night and with no thought for a coat . . .'

Letty's voice following her, Isabel walked into the yard, her feet sounding loud on the cobblestones, her breath white on the cold air. Stopping halfway to the outbuilding, she stood looking at a sky strewn with stars, like a meadow sprinkled with white daisies.

Hidden by the hedge that enclosed the rear gardens, a figure silently watched the slim girl, her breath tiny white veils on the crisp air. This was the one! This was the woman he had followed for days and nights; always near her, always watching, yet never seen. This was the woman he had come for, the one he wanted to feel in his arms, to watch as she lay beneath him. Yes, he would finally do to her all he had dreamed of, taste her mouth, her body, do each of the things he had promised to himself and been thwarted of last time, do them slowly, savour every second . . . and then he would kill her!

For a few moments longer he watched, the blood stirring in his veins. She was beautiful. The face lifted to the night sky was like carved alabaster; pale moonlight etched the lines of a body that was soft and shapely. This one he would enjoy, this would be so different from last time. Anticipation filling him, the man smiled as he moved from the hedge.

'First it was a crowded street, then it was the wheels of a cart, now it's the cold of night . . . just what will I be called upon to rescue you from next!'

At these words the figure pressed himself back against the hedge, an oath falling silently into the shadows.

Startled, Isabel swung around, a smile coming instantly to her lips as she recognised the tall form limping towards her.

'I thought you enjoyed rescuing a maiden in distress? Don't tell me I was wrong, that I've got myself half frozen for nothing?'

'Oh, you haven't stood there freezing for nothing.' A smile that matched her own spread across James Hawley's face. 'It will have earned you quite a decent cold.'

'That's what Braddy told me.'

'A sensible woman is Mrs Bradshaw. Why is it you can't be as sensible?'

Slipping off his jacket, he placed it around Isabel's shoulders and she shivered at the delicious warmth of it.

'I could plead to having no common sense.' She snuggled into the jacket. 'Most men would readily agree with me.'

'Not this one!' Taking her arm, his other hand holding a stout walking stick, James directed her towards the outbuildings. 'I might not have known you very long, Miss Kenton, but I feel I know you very well. Too well to make that mistake!'

Turning into what a few days before had been the carriage house, she glanced at the freshly whitewashed walls and clean-swept floor. There was space here for at least a dozen of the narrow iron-framed beds Hewett Calcott had made her a gift of.

'It is extraordinary how much work the men have managed to get through,' she said as they walked in. 'The rooms in the house have been emptied and the furniture stacked in a couple of the old barns. It should not be long now before we can take in patients.'

'The women have worked just as hard from what I hear.' James Hawley looked at the young woman standing beside him. How often had he remembered her: how many times had her eyes smiled at him in the darkness of the trenches, how many times had he seen her smile and heard her soft words blocking out the sound of guns – words that had kept him from going mad in the carnage that was life at the Front, kept him alive in that field hospital. Words she had never in fact spoken to him.

'The women *have* been marvellous.' Isabel walked partway down the room. 'Coming here as soon as they've finished work in the factories. It seems everyone wants to help in some way.' Turning to face him again, she laughed. 'Why, even the schools have joined in, bringing the older girls here to take their cookery and housekeeping lessons. They have baked, cooked meals, washed dishes and scrubbed floors. Even Braddy was impressed, only don't tell her I told you. The boys school also brought lads in their final year. They helped with clearing furniture and emptying outhouses. I thought they were wonderful.'

'I think *you* are wonderful.'

He had spoken the words softly, meaning them only for his own hearing, but in the emptiness of the huge room they carried to Isabel, bringing a swift surge of colour to her cheeks. Seeing it, and the confusion in the swift glance she shot him, he laughed. But the sound was hollow, an attempt to bolster the disclaimer he rapidly made.

'I think all women are wonderful, the way they always seem to work things out for the best. I only wish I had the knack.'

Those first words had taken her by surprise, bringing a flush of embarrassment to her face; his qualifying of them brought only a cold stab of disappointment.

She glanced once more at the freshly painted walls, using the inspection as a means of avoiding his eyes. His first softly spoken words had shaken her, but pleased her too. If only he had not continued! Striving for a flippancy she did not feel, she answered: 'That knack you speak of, Mr Hawley, I am afraid it is the prerogative solely of women, so you see, you can never acquire it.' I could add that it belongs to women because they are made to earn it, that most of them learn early in life that they have to fight hard to be listened to. Isabel pushed the thought away as he laughed again, the sound echoing against the bare walls.

'It is a trait you utilise well.'

She liked his laugh, it sounded so happy, so filled with the love of life it made you want to respond to it, but she resisted. Instead she pulled a wry face as she returned her glance to him.

'Not well enough, it seems. I prayed I would find a way to get some form of heating put into this place. The men are not going to find it very warm in here.'

James Hawley's smile died and his grey eyes darkened as he seemed to look into the far distance. 'Believe me, this carriage house will be heaven after what they have been through. You will receive no complaints.'

Isabel's heart twisted again, but this time for a different reason. What sort of hell had *he* been through? What was it brought such utter despair and sorrow to a man's face?

'But, you woman of little faith, come with me, I have something to show you.'

His face clearing, James clamped her wrist with his free hand, pulling her along as he limped from the carriage house, going in the direction of a disused stable Isabel had earmarked for cleaning so it could be used as a store by the medical staff.

He had something to show her! In the lee of the carriage house where he had sidled from the hedge, the watching man grinned, his gap teeth yellow in the moonlight. Whatever it was that gimpy fool had to show, it would be nothing compared to what he himself had in store for the bitch. He would teach her. He would show her that nobody messed with Ernie Griffin; nobody gave him the push without paying for it, especially a bloody woman!

Keeping to the shadow of the wall, he moved nearer the house. Luther Kenton's brat wouldn't stay out here long, her would soon turn back to the house; only her would never go inside it again. He would see to that.

Overhead the frosty moon sailed clear of a bank of cloud, bathing the house and gardens in its cold brilliance.

'Shit!' Ernie Griffin spat the word. That bloody moon! If

anybody came by now they would be certain to spot him. He stood out like a bluebottle on a cream cake and they would squash him the same way. He eased along the wall, courting the treacherous shadows. Where was the bloody woman, what was keeping her so long? A chill wind swept suddenly from the garden and he pulled his jacket tighter about him, turning up its ragged collar. Why couldn't that bloke bugger off so the woman would come back?

'They are perfect, and so unexpected. It was a lovely surprise.'

Whatever it was that bloke had shown her, it would be nothing compared to Ernie Griffin's surprise. Anticipation stirring between his legs, he allowed his smile to become a grin.

'It will be no surprise to me to hear that you have taken a chill. Now no more arguments, Miss Kenton, I am taking you back to the house and shall watch you go in. I'm used to women's tricks, I have three sisters of my own.'

Pressed tight against the wall, knowing the thin shadow was no real camouflage, Ernie Griffin's grin became a snarl. That bloody gimp was bringing her back, seeing her into the house! On his own, crippled as he was, he would present no problem; a swift chop to the back of the neck, a knee on his back as he fell, a sharp tug of the head backward and his neck would be broken. It would be over in a minute, Ernie knew. Hadn't he showed that Army sergeant who had tried to order him about? But in that minute the bitch could scream, raise the alarm. He couldn't risk that. Once they heard he was in Darlaston, Perry and Elijah Price would come looking for him and then he would stand no chance of getting his hands on the Kenton woman.

He would wait, but he would not be denied! Glancing up as the moon slipped on a fresh veil of cloud, he grasped the lapels of the jacket he had stolen on absconding from his regiment, holding them together at the base of his throat. While he waited he would think of the pleasures to come: how he would strip her naked except for the gag that closed her mouth, shutting off her screams; how he would take those small breasts, oh he would be gentle with them . . . at first! How he would slide a hand over her body, down and down, all the time watching the fear in her eyes, down to the cleft between her legs. She would struggle and he would enjoy that too, enjoy holding her down, feeling her move and twist. But not when he was ready to take her, to thrust himself deep inside her. He would want no struggling then. That was when he would tie her hands together and spread her legs wide apart, fastening her ankles so she could not close them.

Aroused by his thoughts he drew in a breath, feeling desire quicken his flesh. Yes, he might keep her like that for a few days. Throbbing with lust, he snatched another breath, a sharp intake that hissed on the cold air. Oh, he would take his time with this one, all right.

'You will give him my thanks?'

They were almost around the corner of the carriage house. Another minute and they would be bound to see him, especially if the moon chose to throw off the clouds once more. Moving only his eyes, Ernie glanced about him. To return to his previous vantage point would mean crossing too close to them. He caught his breath, holding it as if the sound might carry to them. It was move or be caught. Either way that Kenton bitch wouldn't escape. He'd go for her first. Perhaps he wouldn't have time enough to kill her outright, not with that bloke her was with having a stick, but he would have long enough to spoil that pretty face. By the time they dragged him off her the scars would be deep, scars her would carry for life: Kenton's daughter would no longer parade around the town throwing her weight about, there would be no more coming 'the great I am', them days would be finished for her. He'd mark her that bad her wouldn't have a face fit to show in the streets ever again . . .

From the corner of his eye he caught a movement just beyond the door to the kitchen, a quick flurry of skirts that disappeared around the side of a small brick building set some distance from the house.

A woman, or maybe even a girl! His grasp on his lapels tightened. Maybe he hadn't stood here for nothing. One woman was as good as another, in some respects. He could wait for Isabel Kenton. Her wouldn't spend every minute of her time in that house or in the company of that man, and when that minute arrived then Ernie Griffin would be waiting!

His steps making barely a sound on the cobbled yard, he moved in the way he had learned early on in life: quickly, silently, hugging the shadows.

He was at the door when the woman came back from the privy. Attacking from behind, he threw one arm across her shoulder, hand covering her mouth, his other arm fastening about her waist and pinioning her close against his body.

'Scream and I'll snap your neck!'

He felt the thin body tremble beneath its layers of clothes. That was good, that was the way he liked them. He passed a tongue over lips already wet with spittle.

'You don't call out and you don't run, you 'ear me, bitch?'

The fingers of the hand covering her mouth crooked and nails bit into the tender flesh of her cheek. The woman whimpered with fear.

'I says, don't scream!'

The arm across her shoulder tauntened, snatching back her head until the breath could no longer pass her throat.

Slowly, the hands clawing at his sleeve fell away and the slight body slumped against his. Easing his grip but never for a moment releasing his hold, Ernie Griffin turned the half-conscious woman to face him, the prospect of what was to come within the next few minutes raising his excitement to fever pitch.

One hand already tearing at her skirts while the other fastened itself in her hair, he dragged her towards the row of bushes that screened the privy from the kitchen garden.

Once shielded by the bushes he threw her heavily to the ground, knocking what little breath she had left from her lungs.

'One sound!' His voice harsh and ominous, he glared down at the face, white against the shadowed ground. 'One sound!' he repeated, opening his trousers. 'Just one, and you won't get yourself fucked – you'll get yourself killed!'

Lust thickening in him, he fell on to the woman who fought to hold back the screams she knew would end her life. Fastening his hand in the waistband of her drawers, he snatched them away, at the same time using one knee to force her legs apart. Then he drove himself into her, each thrust biting deeper and deeper, until with a gasp he rolled away.

But lust and the satisfying of it had not dulled his wits altogether and he was on his feet in an instant. He had gratified one need but he had others. Grasping the woman's bodice, he hauled her upright.

'No! No more, Ernie, please!'

His hand still grasping the front of her dress, he held her at arm's length, staring into her chalk white face.

'Sarah?' He drew her closer, peering through the shadows, then smirked. Fate was playing tricks on him this evening. 'I knowed it was you!' he lied. 'I thought to give you a little remembrance of the way things used to be, of the way they can be again. Just a taste of what Ernie Griffin can do.' He shook her hard, adding the memory of his many beatings to his words. 'I bet you be set up a bit of all right here, you and them two brats of kids. Warm beds, plenty of food and money, eh! Her will be paying the three of you well.' Still holding her, he brought his face closer to hers, rancid breath fanning her mouth as it had moments before. 'That be the way of it, don't it? The Kenton bitch pays you to skivvy for her?'

Lips pressed close to hold back the sobs of fear and pain, Sarah nodded.

'That be what I thought.' He shook her again, throwing her head sharp back on her neck. 'Well, if you wants to keep things as they am, you will fetch that money to me, 'cos if I don't take it with me then I takes you – and your brats – and that will put an end to your warm beds and fancy dinners! You 'ear me, Sarah? You 'ear what I says?'

His fingers pressing against her throat, she could only nod.

'Then you listen to the next bit too,' he snarled. 'You bring that money here and be quick about it, or I'll fire this whole place. I'll burn this bloody house about the ears of everybody in it, and you know I be telling the truth. You know I mean what I says, don't you, Sarah?'

Coughing and trying to catch her breath as he pushed her away, she forced her answer through the burning rawness of her throat.

'There don't be much of it, Ernie, just a few shillings the girl and me be paid. Peter . . . he ain't here. He never come back after . . .'

'After he hit me over the 'ead with a poker.' Ernie Griffin touched his head. 'Well, that be all the better for him, the little shit! But I'll catch up with him one day, and when I do it'll be more than a broken head he'll suffer. Now fetch that money. And remember, Sarah, one word to anybody and one dark night you'll all fry!'

James was so easy to talk to. Back in her bedroom, Isabel stepped out of the grey suit, slipping it on its hanger then placing it in the wardrobe. She felt comfortable with him, as if they had been friends for a long time, as if they had met many times instead of just once before he'd left to fight in the war and a couple of times since then.

Taking out a brown linen dress, she stepped into it, drawing it up over her hips then easing her arms into the long tapered sleeves.

He had been wounded in the field as Owen had, but they were the lucky ones. She stared into the small mirror hanging on the wall over the marble washstand. That, apart from her narrow bed and the table-topped three-drawer chest beside it, was all the small room would hold.

Yes, Owen Farr and James Hawley were two of the lucky ones, two who had lived. Out of how many? The eyes that regarded her from the oval of mirrored glass darkened with pity. How many had not lived? How many men had lost their lives on the battlefields of France and Belgium, and how many more would be called upon to die before the authorities called a halt to the madness?

And Mark, her brother? Would he be one of the doomed, one upon whom the brand of death had already been set? Would the payment fate exacted from him be more than a wound?

But she must not think like that. Breaking away from her trancelike state, she began to fasten the small bone buttons that ran in a line from waist to throat of her dress. Mark would be home soon, maybe he would come in time for Christmas.

Taking her hairbrush from beside the wide pottery bowl on the washstand, she tidied the strands of hair loosened from their coil by the breeze that had sharpened as James Hawley had walked her to the rear door of the house.

He had been fortunate, he'd told her as they had walked together to the empty stable. He could not hope to be given back his job in the steel works until his hip had completely healed, and every other enquiry after employment had met with the same answer. Then he had met Hewett Calcott. James had called at the foundry that had been sold by Jago Timmins's sister, and had already been turned away when Calcott emerged from the works office, stopped and questioned him. The result, he had told Isabel, surprise still registering in his voice, had been his appointment as manager. Calcott had asked how much experience he had of working in the steel; on being told James had done nothing but work in the foundry from thirteen years old to thirty-one, and that he had been made sergeant twelve months before being repatriated due to wounds received, Calcott had said the job was his if he wanted it.

Replacing the brush, Isabel remembered the way he had laughed when telling her this story. Wanted it? How badly could a man want heaven? he'd asked her.

Managing a steel works, was that James Hawley's idea of heaven? At least he knew what it meant to him, while she . . . what constituted heaven for her? The return of Mark would be a large part of it, but was it all, the whole of her hopes and desires? Or would there be a part left unfulfilled, a part that marriage alone would answer? Marriage? But to whom, Hewett Calcott or Owen Farr? Isabel glanced into the mirror then turned quickly away. In her mind's eye she could see neither of those men.

'Who was that I heard you talking with as you came in?' Letty Bradshaw threw a keen glance at Isabel, who was reaching for an apron from a drawer in the huge kitchen dresser.

'James Hawley.' She lowered the huge white apron over her head, crossing the straps around behind her waist and bringing them to a knot at the front.

'Oh, yes? Been here a time or two these past few days. Nice lad he is. Bradshaw and me have known his mother and father for years. Got three wenches too, but he be their only lad. 'Twere heart-breaking to see the worry on his mother's face when she heard he had been wounded, but at least her worry ended happy. Not like others I could name. Arrh, there be many a mother in this town cries herself to sleep at night, my own sister among 'em.'

'Has there been no word yet?'

'None.' Letty wiped her eyes with the back of a flour-covered hand. 'Bradshaw, he goes to the house every day, and I go whenever I can. We try to cheer her up but I admit I don't do much good. My sister's lad be to me what a son would have been and my heart aches as much for him as his own mother's do.'

Crossing the kitchen, Isabel flung her arms about the tearful woman. 'Oh, Braddy, don't cry. He will come home. Missing in action doesn't mean he is dead. They will find him soon, I am sure of it, and then you and his mother will have him here with you.'

'If only we could be sure,' Letty sobbed, throwing her apron up over her face. 'If only we could be sure.'

Burying her face against her friend's neck, Isabel's own eyes smarted from the sting of tears. 'We *have* to believe, Braddy,' she said softly. 'We have to make ourselves believe and hold on to that belief because that is all we have.'

Clinging to each other, lost in their shared uncertainty and fear, neither of the two women was aware of the figure, moving silently as a wraith, picking up a sharp knife from the table.

Chapter Eighteen

Owen Farr pushed away the papers he had been reading. Leaning back in the leather chair in which his father used to sit at this same desk, he closed his eyes, but the words of that last page still danced before them.

He'd thought to be finished with the Army when he was given his discharge papers, finished with it all, and now . . . Running a hand through his hair, he let out a long breath. He'd known the time would come, believed through it all that it would come again. Now it seemed it had!

Opening his eyes, he straightened in the chair. Fishing a packet of Balkan Sobranie from his pocket, he took out one of the slim brown cigarettes, lighting it with a gold lighter taken from the same pocket.

He ought never to have offered Isabel Kenton his help. He blew out a long stream of pale smoke, the hand holding the cigarette shaking visibly. He never should have offered to undertake to see to the paperwork, never become involved. But the fact remained that he had and the military, hard pressed on every front, had accepted. A qualified lawyer, a respectable practice that still carried his father's name and at no cost to them . . . of course they had accepted. Now he was stuck with it.

He drew again on the cigarette, taking the perfumed smoke deep into his lungs, holding it for long seconds before exhaling through dilated nostrils. He could always plead his health was not yet sufficiently restored, that sadly he was forced to with-draw his services. That excuse would be accepted by the Army but where would it leave him with Isabel Kenton? He held the cigarette between his fingers, watching the pale smoke curl towards the ceiling. He could hardly expect her to believe a story such as that or be quite as friendly towards him should he ever tell it. Lifting the half-smoked cigarette to his lips, he took another long pull then stabbed the remainder into a heavy crystal ash tray on the desk. No, he must see the thing through or risk seeing Isabel walk out of his life!

He had a chance with her. She liked him, he knew. Give her a little more time, a few more months, and he would ask her to marry him. The past need not concern her, she need never know; what purpose would it serve to tell her? She would be in love with him by then, deeply in love, he was certain of that, her every smile when they were together indicated as much, so why risk spoiling it all by telling her of something already buried in the past? There was no one else in Darlaston who knew of it, no one to tell her, and he certainly would not.

Drawing the papers back across the desk, he shuffled them neatly together. That did not mean he would not need to go on being careful – careful as he had been during his time in the Army. Owen Farr's smile became ever more grim. He had held no particular wish to become a soldier but had seen the armed forces as a gateway to freedom, a way of breaking loose from the restrictions placed on him by a town so small everyone knew a man's thoughts, let alone what he did. But that freedom had not been gained. In fact his particular prison had closed more firmly about him, in bonds he could not break.

He had thought none of the others knew, his fellow officers. He had thought his tracks well covered, the secret his own. Then had come that day, that one terrible day out of the hundreds of terrible days that had gone before; days when eating, sleeping and dying had become inextricably merged into one. That day had been no different from the others. Each was spent dug into trenches filled knee-deep with water, slimy and threatening to suck down anyone who moved carelessly; there was a constant stink of death, of rotting bodies, of corpses half eaten by rats.

That battle should have been no different from the many battles they had already fought, except it was one to which the enemy would offer no resistance, the Thiepval ridge having been wiped out by British shells. That was what they had been told by the General Staff. All that was left for them to do was walk across no man's land and occupy the deserted enemy trenches. But it had been a walk with death for almost all the men the whistle blast had sent over the top, men who had no choice but to run towards the enemy line. But they did not run far!

Clutching the sheaf of papers, Owen Farr closed his eyes against the horror filling his mind. They had run, hundreds and hundreds of men, and as quickly as they ran they fell, cut down like corn before the reaper! And the machine guns never stopped; the hunger of the Angel of Death seemed insatiable, taking even those pitiable few who crossed that space between the lines. He shuddered as he saw again the picture of a young man of no more than twenty, his body caught against the barbed wire, head lolling to one side, both arms spread wide, blood oozing down his face over closed eyes, spilling neatly from the hole in his forehead. The crucifixion of war!

He had prayed for nightfall, the coming of the all-enveloping darkness that would still the guns. But when at last it had come the torment had not stopped for the air had been filled with the cries of the wounded and dying still lying in no man's land, their screams of pain and fear mixing with calls for help no one could give.

Owen swallowed hard, pressing back the assault of memory. The first day of the Battle of the Somme was already in the past, but the horror of it would never be forgotten by the few men who lived through it. Fifty-seven thousand had not.

But nothing could come of those memories but sorrow, and this evening Owen Farr was not in the mood for melancholy. Tonight he wanted pleasure.

After depositing the papers in a black Gladstone bag, he walked out of his office.

Hyde Cottage stood alone on heathland that stretched away to both sides of Hyde's Road. Built by a colliery owner who had wished to be near his mines, it had stood empty since the coal deposits had run out.

Owen turned his automobile in between tall iron gates. It was the isolation of this house that had recommended it to him. Glancing up at the red brick walls and high rectangular windows, he smiled. 'Cottage' was hardly the name for a house with six bedrooms, nor perhaps entirely suitable for a bachelor living alone with just one servant, but Hyde Cottage suited him. Taking the Gladstone bag from the passenger seat, he climbed from his automobile.

It suited him very well.

'I thought perhaps the private dining room, sir?'

Owen's ex-batman held the tray with its glass of brandy, waiting beside the bed on which his master sprawled.

Owen turned his head, a slow luxurious movement, his eyes holding an almost hedonistic gleam. 'Thank you, Simms. The right choice as always.'

'I took the liberty of choosing a light supper, sir.' Holding the tray while Owen hitched himself into a sitting position and took the glass, the batman then folded it beneath his arm.

'And what delights does that hold in store?' Owen sipped the brandy, holding the warmth of it in his mouth.

'I thought mussels in a cream and saffron sauce, followed by a little pâté-de-campagne, and then veal with apricots.'

Owen let the brandy trickle slowly down his throat. 'Sounds perfect as always, Simms.'

'Thank you, sir. There is, of course, dessert to follow. Though you yourself do not normally take it, I prepared plum brûlée with a dish of tuiles d'amandes, should your guest desire.'

'Thoughtful as ever, Simms.' Owen smiled at the man who

stood almost to attention beside the bed. 'Whatever would I do without you?'

'I hope we never have to find that out, sir.'

'Me too, Simms.' Owen closed his eyes, his head falling back against the pillow. 'Me too. Don't you ever go getting married on me.'

'No, sir.' Simms turned away, his well-proportioned body making hardly a sound as he crossed to the door.

'Simms!' Owen called as he heard the door open. 'I will see to dressing myself tonight, no need for you to lay anything out.'

Not glancing back, the batman smiled. 'Yes, sir,' he replied quietly. 'Very good, sir.'

Owen glanced at the pocket watch lying on a small table in his dressing room. A quarter to nine. His guest was expected on the hour. Turning again to the long cheval mirror, he smiled at his reflection. This shade of grey shot with just a hint of eau-de-nil that picked up the colour of his eyes suited him admirably. His guest should find him more than satisfactory. Picking up a silk handkerchief, he looked again into the mirror, running a critical eye over the sculptured cheekbones, the straight well-shaped nose and slightly almond-shaped eyes. He had met with no complaint before; there would be none tonight.

'Beg pardon, sir.' Simms left a suitable margin between tapping on the door of Owen's room and entering. 'Your guest has arrived.'

'Thank you, Simms.' Casting one last glance over his impeccable appearance, Owen came out of the dressing room. 'Please say I will be there directly.'

Lifting a glass of wine, Owen held it to his lips, smiling over its rim. 'To a pleasant evening.'

Opposite him eyes like polished bronze glowed in the light

251

of candles set about the room. Owen preferred candles, they cast a softer, more intimate glow than a gasolier.

'There is more yet to come.' The answering glass rose to touch his own, the voice throaty, pulsing with promise. 'Much, much more.'

Swallowing just a little of the heady liquid, Owen laid his glass aside. He wanted to savour every moment of the rest of the evening, wanted no fumes of alcohol to cloud his mind, to dull the touch of those hands, that mouth.

'You are beautiful, Rowena, and that gown is perfect but I much prefer you without it.'

Owen stretched out his hands, smiling, as soft white ones were laid in them.

'Why don't I take it off?'

The loosening of every button, the untying of every ribbon accompanied by a kiss to a soft mouth, Owen groaned softly, the pleasure of it hardening the flesh between his legs.

'Not yet.' Bronze eyes laughed up at him. 'Not yet, you naughty boy. You must be patient. Gobble the goodies all at once and you have none left for later.'

'I will have plenty left for later – enough for the whole night.'

His mouth closing over lips lifted to his, Owen felt the blood surge hot through every vein. Flesh naked as his own moulding to him, fitting inch to inch, line to line, a tongue expertly exploring his mouth, drawing him into a world of exquisite pleasure, he groaned softly as clasped in each other's arms they moved towards the bed, discreetly curtained in an alcove of the room.

Later, drowsily opening his eyes, Owen glanced at the window. A slight parting of the drapes showed pale opalescent grey. It was dawn and time for the fun to end. Glancing at the figure sleeping beside him, he slipped from the bed. Gathering his clothes, he walked quietly to an adjoining room, prepared as always by the thoughtful Simms.

The water in the large pottery bowl was cold but Owen sponged it liberally over his body, washing every crevice. The years had taught him to be careful. Cleanliness is next to Godliness. He smiled at the thought. How often had his father used those words to him? How many times had he proved his father wrong!

Dressing quickly, he glanced at the reflection regarding him from the mirror, smiling as he picked up the five pound note Simms had placed ready. Below the auburn wig almost green eyes returned his look of approval.

'My amorous little friend was right,' he murmured, 'you are beautiful, Rowena!'

Parting his lips to kiss his own reflection, he turned and as quietly as he had left it, re-entered the private dining room.

The figure on the bed was still asleep but sprawled now, legs stretched wide apart as if eager for more of what they had shared during those long sensuous hours.

It was tempting. Owen stared down at the well-shaped limbs, but it was time to leave. There would be other nights.

Bending over the sleeping form, he lifted the limp penis between thumb and finger.

'Other nights,' he whispered.

Placing the note in the cleft of the groin, he laid the penis over it, brushing it gently with one finger.

Rowena had pleasures yet to come. Smiling softly, Owen returned to his bedroom.

The money she had earned since coming to Woodbank clutched tight in her hand, Sarah Griffin crossed the cobbled yard towards the privy. She could not see him but he would be there, hidden in the shadows like the evil creature he was. He would leave once he had the money. Please God he would leave! But deep inside Sarah felt her prayer was in vain. Ernie Griffin knew he had tapped a source he could draw on as long as she and Mary were in this house. The only chance of driving him away was for the two of them to leave. If she left on her own he would still stay, preying off Mary, draining her of every penny to spend it instantly in the beer houses and on prostitutes. Mary was young and strong but would stand no chance against her father, especially when he was the worse for drink.

Sarah's hand tightened on the two white five-pound notes neatly folded in half. She had not taken her daughter's money. Ernie would not know how much Isabel Kenton paid them and would not ask . . . not yet. He would just take what she had and go. But he would stay away only until the last shilling was gone!

Several yards from the brick building Sarah halted. Ernie Griffin would never be gone. He would return again and again, if not to her then to her daughter. He would cling like a leech, sucking them dry. But to defy him was to place them all in danger, for Ernie Griffin was a man of his word when that word was to his own advantage; and he had said he would burn this house to the ground. Sarah shivered but it was not the frosty night air that chilled her blood. She would not sleep another night easy in her bed. Who knew how long money would prove enough to stay Ernie Griffin's hand?

'Not there, you stupid bitch! Bring it over here in the shadows. If I have to fetch it, I'll break your back!'

Coming from the lee of the wall, the words were sharp and vicious. Clenching the money in her hand, Sarah moved forward. Hidden in the darkness, he watched her come. It would be hard lines on her if there were no money in her pocket! Waiting only until she came level with the small building, Ernie Griffin shot out a hand, fastening his fingers in her hair and snatching her under cover before slamming her hard against the privy wall.

'Did you bring it?' he snarled.

The breath knocked from her, Sarah tried to nod, feeling the cruel bite of his hand in her hair.

'Give!' he snapped. She placed the money in his hand.

'You told nobody?'

The fingers tightened yet more harshly in her hair, dragging it against her scalp, and Sarah whimpered.

'You know what will 'appen, if so don't you, Sarah?' He brought his face close to hers, the stench of his breath turning her stomach but he held her head too tight for her to twist away. 'You know what I will do if you 'ave opened that mouth of your'n. You'll be warm enough when Ernie Griffin sets his fire. They'll all be warm enough!' Throwing her hard against the wall as he released her, he glanced at the money in his hand, then unfolded the notes.

Not daring to move, she watched the way he fingered each note. Would it be enough? Would he believe that was all she had? What if he didn't, what would she do then? What would *he* do then?

'This be all of it?' His voice coarse and grating, he glanced at Sarah pressed against the wall. 'Your'n and the wench's?'

Fear holding her by the throat, she nodded.

'It'll do for now!' he grunted, shoving the notes into his pocket. Half turning from her, he hesitated, the moonlight touching his face. Sarah's heart somersaulted. She had seen that look before, a look that said Ernie Griffin had not yet taken all he wanted. Breath catching in her throat she watched him bend, pushing a hand into the bushes that screened the privy from the garden.

'Get your things!' he ordered as he straightened up. 'And bring the wench. You both be coming wi' me!'

She had guessed wrongly! Sarah tried to breathe but couldn't. She had thought he would leave them here, Mary and herself. That way he would have a regular supply of money.

'I said, get your things!'

The sting of his knuckles against her cheek catching her unawares, Sarah gasped: 'But . . . but we got jobs here.'

'There won't be a house to work in after tonight, nor no Kenton bitch to sack a man!' Ernie Griffin smiled at his wife. 'I can find you jobs, the pair of you. Mebbe blokes won't pay as much for the use of you as for the young 'un, but they'll pay, and you two will work 'ard enough.'

His tread silent as a cat's, his body at one with the shadows, he moved towards the house; only then, as he crossed the small yard behind it, did she see the large can he carried in his hand.

'I don't reckon on it taking more than two or three nights. We should 'ave the last of them stoves in by the weekend.'

Hands deep in their pockets, jacket collars turned up against the sharp-fingered touch of night, Edward Perry and Elijah Price came through the gate set into the wall enclosing the gardens of Woodbank House.

'You think Bradshaw will have lit the couple we fixed up last night? We could do with a fire. This frost be enough to freeze old man Butler's balls.'

'Bradshaw be gettin' a bit stuck up since he was told he was to be Superintendent of this here 'ospital,' Elijah sniffed, reluctant to withdraw a hand from the warmth of his pocket to wipe away the drip from his nose.

'Arrh!' Edward Perry laughed, sending a cloud of white vapour into the darkness. 'But he ain't the only snotty-nosed bugger in these parts!'

'No, he ain't.' Elijah ignored the reference to his own dripping nose. 'And he ain't got three brass balls neither. But I tell you this: if he keeps coming his old buck with me he'll 'ave no bloody balls at all, 'cos I'll squeeze the buggers off!'

'Pity you couldn't get to the Kaiser.' Edward Perry chuckled into the turned up lapels of his jacket. 'You would have made his eyes water!'

'Arrh.' Elijah sniffed his agreement. 'And his arse would 'ave worked overtime an' all! They would 'ave to cut up a few newspapers to keep it wiped!'

Sharing their coarse humour the two men walked on, then both stopped abruptly, holding their head to one side and listening.

'Did you hear that?' Elijah cocked an ear to the night breeze.

'I heard summat!' Edward too strained his ears.

'Sounded like a scream to me, sort of strangled like.'

'Probably a cat.' Edward began to move on, the cold already biting through his thin jacket.

'If that be a bloody cat then I reckon it just parted with all of its nine lives.' Elijah's head turned sharply as the muffled cry came again.

Taking their hands from their pockets, both men began to run towards the sound, clearly distinguishing the sobs of a woman by now.

'I told you not to do it, I told you . . . I told you!'

Rounding the corner of the privy both men saw the flash of silver, each flash accompanied by a groan, each groan followed by a woman's sob as the knife rose and fell again.

'Christ Almighty!' Edward Perry gasped as the blade buried itself in the back of the figure now sprawled on the ground, face resting against a large tin container. Grabbing the figure on its knees beside the one sprawled and still, he hauled it roughly away.

'Sarah?' He stared into the white upturned face, then as the woman fainted in his arms, looked at Elijah. 'It be Sarah Griffin!'

'And who be this?' Elijah bent to see more clearly the face lying against the container. 'God Almighty!' He glanced up at Edward. 'It be Griffin. Her's done for him.'

'You sure?'

Elijah nodded, glancing once more at the figure sprawled at their feet. 'Sure as I be standing here, and surer that Ernie Griffin be roasting in hell this very minute.'

'Wait here!' Edward hoisted the unconscious woman into his arms. 'Don't let anybody see you, and for Christ's sake, don't let 'em see that! I'll be back in two shakes.'

'Where you going?'

'To take Sarah into the house. We can't let her lie out here. When I get back, you and me will find a spot to bury that louse. Ain't nobody going to know what we two have seen. Won't nobody know as Ernie Griffin ever come back to Darlaston.'

'But Sarah . . .'

'Sarah nothing! One thing Sarah Griffin won't ever do, her

257

won't let anything harm that daughter of hers. And neither will we. We seen nothing except for Sarah lying spark out on the cobbles. I'll say as her must have slipped crossing the yard and bumped her head on the ground. It be nigh freezing so it'll be easy believed her lost her footing. The cobbles be slippery with frost.'

'Well, hurry up coming back!' Elijah hunched into his jacket. 'I had little enough liking for Ernie Griffin when he were living. I've got a damn' sight less now he be dead!'

Minutes later, the body of Ernie Griffin propped between them, their arms supporting him as though he were a man gone in drink, Elijah and Edward walked across the silent heath behind Woodbank House. Skirting the marl hole, its black waters reflecting silver moonlight, they made for the Lodge Holes. Their unused pit shafts would accept a body dead or alive, keeping it fast in the bowels of the earth, in a silence that was deep and binding.

'Eh, Miss Isabel, why do you reckon me mother went on like that?'

Isabel glanced at the girl propped up on the pillows, her bed separated from that of her mother by a narrow space filled with a chest of drawers.

'Your mother had a fall, Mary, she bumped her head.'

'I know that, miss, but why was her so moithered?'

'Now you heard what the doctor said, Mary Griffin!' Letty Bradshaw pressed the girl firmly down beneath the sheets. 'He told you: people often ramble on after a bump to the head, ain't nothing unusual. Her will be right as rain in a day or two – that's if you keeps that tongue of your'n still long enough for her to sleep.'

'But I heard her say . . .'

'No doubt you did!' Letty snapped. 'Now you best heed what I have to say. You get yourself off to sleep, my wench, 'cos cold or no cold, you will be up and in that kitchen by half-past six in the morning. I can't manage all them extra folk what with you and your mother laid up.'

'The doctor, he was telling the truth? Me mother was just having one of them allu . . . allu . . .'

'Hallucinations.' Isabel's smile was gentle. The girl had been terrified when Edward Perry had carried her mother into the bedroom, and even more frightened when Sarah had rambled on about stabbing a man. 'Of course he was telling the truth, Mary. The medicine he gave her will ensure a good night's sleep, then a few days of rest and Sarah will be well. Now you try to rest too, we don't want the influenza to strike you again.'

'It were lucky that Army doctor were here already. It would have taken old Doctor Langton a couple of hours at least to get here from Bescot.'

'It isn't *that* far.'

'I know that, miss.' Mary grinned cheekily. 'But knowing Doctor Langton it would take him an hour to find his trousers, and half the other one to get them on.'

'Mary Griffin, you are a cheeky young madam.' Letty tried to hide her own smiles. 'In my mother's day you would have had your backside tanned for saying such a thing.'

'It will still be smacked if your mother wakes and hears you!' Isabel followed Letty to the door, quietly whispering a final goodnight as she closed it behind them.

'It all seems more than a bit strange, though,' Letty said as they reached the kitchen. 'It don't be like Sarah to say such wild things.'

'Normally I would agree with you, but after a bump on the head . . .'

Fetching a fillet of roast pork from the pantry, Letty set it down on the table where she set to slicing it. 'I know about the bump to the back of her head, I felt it meself and big as a duck egg it is, but I still say her wild talk were caused by no bump. I've dealt with enough accidents such as that woman had tonight and never once heard no ramblings; that doctor can say what he likes but I still maintains there be more to it than we knows.'

Breaking off, she glanced about the kitchen. 'I could swear I put my sharp knife on this table. I used it to dice meat for tomorrow's pies, yet I've searched everywhere and I just *can't* find it. Tcha! This one be useless for slicing cooked meat . . . a body gets used to her own tools.'

Crossing the kitchen, Isabel checked the long side table set along one wall. 'Perhaps Mr Bradshaw has borrowed it?' she said.

Bradshaw wouldn't take my knives,' Letty said emphatically. 'Wherever it has got itself to, it won't be with his help!' Irritation plain on her homely face, she stomped back to the pantry, this time bringing out a large crusty loaf from that morning's baking. 'Ain't no use you looking. Be it in this kitchen, I'd find it.' Pulling open the wide drawer set in the table, she selected a long-bladed knife, its serrated edge gleaming in the gaslight. 'Strange folk in the house no more than days and things start to go missing!'

Cups from the dresser still in her hand, Isabel turned. 'Braddy, you're not saying one of the nurses has taken your carving knife?'

Letty touched the knife to the bread, sawing savagely. 'I ain't saying they did, but then again I ain't saying they didn't. But I ain't never lost one afore!'

Setting the cups on a tray, Isabel returned to the dresser, reaching down several more and placing them beside the first batch. 'It will turn up sooner or later, I expect.'

Letty began to spread the slices of bread with dripping saved from the meat, little blobs of rich brown jelly shining like tiny gems. 'Arrh, well, I hope it be sooner. I miss it already, and only a few extra folk to make sandwiches for. Lord knows how I will get on when them wounded gets here!'

Swiftly counting the number of cups laid out, Isabel gave an impish smile. 'I tell you what, Braddy. Tomorrow I'll organise a search of the whole house. I'll even ask for a loan of Hayden's bloodhound.'

Looking up from her task, Letty Bradshaw's mouth was firm

but her eyes betrayed the laughter bubbling inside her. Raising the knife coated in dripping, she pointed at the neat line of cups. 'You just organise the making of the cocoa, there be folk waiting of a hot drink. The men out there working on them outhouses will be nigh on perished.'

The sandwiches finished and piled on several plates, Letty fetched jars of her home-made chutney for people to help themselves to. Then while Isabel poured boiling water into jugs, each of which she had prepared with cocoa powder, she brought over another tray from the shelf beneath the long side table. Covering it with a sparkling white tray cloth, she set sandwiches and chutney beside the cups and jug of steaming cocoa. After adding spoons, sugar bowl and a smaller jug of milk covered with a square of linen weighted with tiny pink glass beads, she nodded her approval.

'I'll take this through to the nurses.' Taking charge of the heavy tray, Letty indicated the rear door with a backward toss of her head. 'You give the men a call to come for their cocoa. They'll think we have forgotten them else, and them giving of their free time to help!'

Doing as the housekeeper asked, Isabel smiled as she handed cups of hot cocoa and a sandwich to each man, thanking them as she always did for what they had done. Coming to Edward Perry, she glanced at the half dozen men standing bunched near the door, awkward at being in 'the master's' house. Satisfied they would not overhear, she whispered, 'Mr Perry, would you stay behind a moment, please?'

The last of the workmen having left the kitchen, Edward Perry placed his empty cup on the table. 'You wanted me, Miss Kenton?'

Isabel fiddled with a corner of the apron she had donned on first coming to help in the kitchen. It seemed like weeks since James Hawley had shown her the stoves stored in the stable, then insisted on watching her enter the house.

'Yes, Mr Perry. I . . . I wanted to ask you . . . did you see Mrs Griffin fall?'

Lifting a hand to his head, he ran his fingers through his greying hair, darting a glance to where Letty Bradshaw sat next to the fire. He must take care the way he answered if Sarah Griffin were not to hang.

'No, miss.' Drawing his flat cap from his pocket, he fidgeted with it, folding and unfolding it. 'Her were lying there in the yard when 'Lijah and me come up through the garden.'

'Elijah Price, he was with you?'

Edward nodded, his eyes on his cap. 'We come up together, miss. That young James Hawley called in at Bull Piece and said there was some more stoves as needed fitting, so me and 'Lijah come up here straight after our meal.'

'You saw no one leaving?'

'No, miss.' He shot another glance at the woman watching from her chair. 'Why, you ain't had anything took, have you, Letty?'

'Not unless you count my best carving knife,' she replied, her mouth a tight line.

'I'll ask around.' Edward opened the cap, lifting it to his head then lowering it as he remembered he was in his employer's house. 'If any one of them has . . .'

'Forget the knife!' Isabel lowered the corner of her apron, smoothing it with a rapid unsettled gesture, her eyes anxious as they met his. 'Mr Perry, Sarah said some disturbing things after we got her to bed. She claims to have killed her husband.'

From her chair Letty Bradshaw watched Edward closely; the way he averted his gaze, the twitch of a muscle beside his mouth, the constant fiddling with his cap – all the movements of a man not quite comfortable with himself.

'I shouldn't take any notice of that, miss,' he laughed, though the sound was unconvincing. 'Like I said when I brought her into the house, her must have bumped her head. People can say all sorts after a knock like that.'

'We thought so too, Mr Perry,' Isabel answered. 'But she was truly terrified and so insistent. Over and over she kept on saying she had killed her husband, that she had . . .' Isabel paused.

262

Sarah had insisted she had stabbed a man out there in the yard, and Letty's carving knife was missing . . .

Edward noted the pause, and the fear suddenly filling his young employer's eyes. This wench could put two and two together and come up with the right answer.

'Well, miss.' He looked at her, all innocence, the lie rising readily to his tongue. 'Seems to me that if Sarah Griffin has gone and killed her husband then there should rightly be a dead body out there in your yard, and there ain't. Least not as I've seen, and I've been knocking about for the last couple of hours. Not to mention your husband, Letty.' He glanced again at the house-keeper. 'There ain't a lot escapes his eye, as well you know. Seems to me if there had been murder done, then Bradshaw would have seen it.'

'What you say be right enough.' She nodded. 'Bradshaw don't miss a thing.'

He missed that bugger all right! Edward Perry fiddled with his cap. Seemed they'd all missed Griffin except for Sarah. Aloud he said, 'If Sarah had killed anybody then there should be a body out there to prove it, and there ain't no body, dead folk don't get up and walk away, so if her killed Ernie Griffin then where is he? No, you take it from me, Miss Kenton, there's been no killing. Sarah Griffin knocked herself senseless and woke up imagining things.'

'Given the sort of life that toe rag Griffin led her, then we needn't be surprised the woman woke up with her mind all of a lather. Like Edward tells you, if there be no corpse then there be no death.' Letty gave her support to the man she instinctively felt was lying, but that lie would meet no challenge from her. Should it be that Sarah *had* killed her husband then it was no more than he'd deserved! That was her idea of any man who could beat a woman and kids while taking every penny they made and drink it away.

Of course it made perfect sense, Isabel told herself, but Sarah had been so sure . . .

Watching the indecision chase shadows across her face,

Edward Perry spoke quickly. 'Elijah be waiting for me outside. If it makes you feel any better, miss, we could take a good look around the place afore we go home?'

It was hard to believe Sarah could have done so awful a thing. But the missing knife and then her garbled 'confession' . . . To have the grounds searched would put an end to any lingering suspicion. 'Thank you, Mr Perry,' Isabel sighed with relief. 'That would be most reassuring for everyone.'

Outside, the moon lighting his grim smile, Edward Perry pulled his cap on to his head and turned up the collar of his jacket. They would search but they would find nothing. Nobody ever would. Lodge Holes would keep their secret.

Chapter Nineteen

'She was delighted, Mr Calcott. Said she had prayed for a way of heating the carriage house and the big stables that had been cleared to house more beds.'

'To think men should come to being nursed in buildings that once housed animals!' Hewett Calcott kicked savagely at the floor.

'Mr Calcott . . .' James Hawley stared at the ledgers set out in the office that once had been Jago Timmins's, seeing only bodies, faces twisted with pain as they writhed in grey sucking mud. 'Believe me, they will have no complaint,' he said quietly.

'No, perhaps not. But it is a sorry thing nonetheless.'

'Would to God they were all home in England, sir, no matter what place they found to lie here.'

'Amen to that, James,' Hewett Calcott answered. 'Amen to that. But until it can be brought about we must do all we can to help those who are home as well as those who are not – and we can best do *that* by keeping up production. So tell me, what are the figures for this month?'

Listening as James gave him the latest output from the steel works, Hewett concealed his real reason for visiting the foundry. There was no need for him to be here. James Hawley ran the place as well probably better than he could himself, and a run-down of the production figures reached him at Bilston as regular as clockwork on the last day of every month. No, he had no real need to see this man, but then it was not him he came to see – it was Isabel Kenton. But he could not face being with her, seeing her yet not asking the one question he burned to ask, being close to her yet not telling her . . .

'So you see, Mr Calcott, the month has been a good one all round.'

'Yes . . . er, yes.' answered Hewett, his inner eye not yet free of a vision of a beautiful face, hazel eyes smiling at him. 'That's good, James.'

'Were you wanting to make changes, sir?' James Hawley looked at the older man, reading something in his eyes yet unable to comprehend the unhappiness that suddenly crossed his face.

'Changes?' The expression vanished as Hewett brought his glance to bear on his works manager. 'Not unless you have any to suggest, James?'

'There are none at the moment.'

'Good.'

It was said as absent-mindedly as the last time he had spoken the word, and again James wondered just what it was his employer felt so strongly about. Hewett Calcott, he knew, was not a man to balk at telling another what he thought, unpleasant though that might be; this man did not prevaricate, so what was it he was hiding? What was it took his mind whenever he allowed himself a moment's lapse, the merest break in his concentration? What had broken the man's heart and was still twisting the pieces?

Taking up his tall black hat, Hewett walked from the stuffy little room into the crisp December air. One gloved hand on the carriage door, he hesitated, glancing over his shoulder to the man who had followed him into the foundry yard. 'You say Miss Kenton was happy with the stoves I sent to Woodbank?'

James ran a hand along the smooth flank of the chestnut mare. 'More than happy, and more than surprised when I took her into the stable and showed them to her.'

'You put them in a stable?'

'It was about the one place left.' He soothed the horse with long slow strokes. 'The whole place has been turned inside out – house, barns, stables, the lot. Miss Kenton hasn't gone about the thing half hearted. I was talking to Mr Bradshaw while the stoves were being taken down from the wagon. He said every room downstairs, apart from the study and the kitchen, had been turned into wards and each held as many beds as it was possible to cram in. The bedrooms have all been given over to medical staff, Miss Kenton's included. She said they would need them as they would then be closer to the wards should an emergency arise.'

'Isabel's own room!'

James Hawley gave a measured glance at the man stood with his hand on the carriage. His voice had been sharp, almost angry. Could Isabel Kenton mean more to him than he showed, was he interested in her as something other than a friend? Hewett Calcott had to be at least twenty-five years her senior, he couldn't be in love with her . . . But why not? James felt a cold ache in the pit of his stomach. Why else would Calcott do the things he had done: giving her an exclusive contract with Bradley Field ironworks, helping to fit up Woodbank House as a temporary hospital, the sharp concern he had shown a moment ago on hearing about her bedroom? These were not the actions of a man who had little interest in a woman other than as a mere acquaintance. No, Hewett Calcott had more than a little interest in Luther Kenton's daughter, and it was not unknown for a man to marry a woman less than half his age.

'That was what Mr Bradshaw said.' James gave the horse a final pat then stepped back. 'Miss Kenton insisted her room be given over to the nurses.'

The ache inside him intensified. The razor edge was still there, honed to a new sharpness in the question that snapped out. James was not mistaken, he was sure. Hewett Calcott had more than a routine interest in Isabel Kenton. His own voice even, displaying none of the trepidation he felt, James continued: 'He said Sarah Griffin and her daughter had decided to share a bedroom so the servants' landing could accommodate all of the medical staff. That left a tiny room right at the end, and Miss Kenton took that one.'

'She is sleeping in the servants' quarters? Good Lord, what does the girl think she is doing!'

'I don't reckon Miss Kenton *thinks* what she is doing.' James Hawley looked squarely into the face of his employer. 'I reckon she *knows* what she is doing, and a very good job she is making of it. I for one applaud her.'

Pulling himself into the driving seat of his small carriage, Hewett Calcott took up the reins. Eyes cold, he turned to his works manager. 'So that is what *you* think, is it? Isabel Kenton is doing a good job of pulling that house to pieces?'

James's chin came up, his own stare calm and unwavering. 'Yes, Mr Calcott, that is what I think.'

Within the confines of his neatly clipped beard, Hewett Calcott's jaw twitched, the muscles moving spasmodically as he stared down at the younger man standing back a little way from the carriage. Then his lips moved, parting slowly as a wide smile overtook him. 'You know something, James, so do I. A bloody good job.' Then, sobering, he added quietly: 'That house has wanted pulling apart for years . . . I would to God it were mine, I would set a match to it!'

'Eh, I only hope we be going to manage, there be more of 'em than I thought! Cooking for that lot will take some doing even if the Army do be providing the food. We never could have managed on our rations. But provisions or no provisions, it's still going to be a job.'

'You'll manage, Braddy, you always have. But I'm sure I can get you more help somewhere . . .'

'Be no need of that!' Letty Bradshaw cut in quickly. There would be more than enough bodies in and out of her kitchen without bringing in more. 'Sarah and young Mary be well now, and with the young women coming up from the works after their shift to do the cleaning and the laundry, I reckon we can manage.'

'Sarah is still very quiet, it must have been a worse bump to the head than we first thought to cause her such awful nightmares.' Isabel paused in the task of tying cloths about the suet puddings the housekeeper had made. 'She was convinced she had killed her husband. Each time she spoke of it she was so sure she had stabbed him to death. Braddy, you don't think . . .'

'No, I don't! And neither should you!' Letty snapped. 'Least said, the less to cry over.'

Taking the cloth-covered puddings, Isabel lowered them into a large saucepan suspended from a bracket swung across the fire, glancing as she did so at the gas stove which Braddy had so far stolidly refused to use; with so many to cook for it would have to be used soon, and probably a couple more like it. Covering the large pan with a lid, she turned back to the table, wiping her hands on a square of white cloth before tipping flour into a huge cream-coloured earthenware bowl.

'It does seem strange though,' she said, cubing fat into the flour, 'Sarah being so convinced she stabbed a man who was about to burn down the house, and that after your knife had gone missing.'

'You say nothing about that knife!' Letty hissed, throwing a glance past Isabel's shoulder towards the door that led from the kitchen to the living quarters of the house. 'You forget this house ever held such a thing, and you forget Ernie Griffin. He was never here, you understand me? He was never here and we never lost no knife!'

Glancing up from the mixing bowl, Isabel's brow creased into a perplexed frown. Braddy was not usually so sharp nor so reluctant to hold a discussion. 'But . . .'

'No, Miss Isabel, no buts!' Letty's voice was gentler but it held the same note of finality. 'Sarah has been through enough without having seeds of doubt sown by us. Her has been feared of Griffin coming back ever since he were taken by the Army, feared of him coming and taking her and Mary away, and when you be so feared of a man your nerves be on edge every minute of the day and you get to have all sorts of imaginings. That be all it was, imaginings, but there be folk who would make more of it if talk got out, regardless of the fact that no dead body were ever found. So let there be no more said, not in this house or out of it. Gossip can do more hurt than enough and Sarah has suffered more than her share of pain.'

Turning back to the shank end of pork she was preparing, Letty scored the skin with a sharp knife then rubbed it with salt. There were things about that night that were best left unsaid, things none but Edward Perry, Elijah Price and Bradshaw knew. He had told her later, alone in their room. They had smelled paraffin, finding it splashed over the rear of the kitchen wall, the smell acrid on the clear frosty air; a little further on they'd discovered the tin beside the garden privy. But the body of Ernie Griffin was gone, carted off by the two steel men who had thrown it down an old mine shaft, while the knife was sunk deep below the dark waters of the marl hole. It was over, finished, and Letty Bradshaw for one would shed no tears.

Placing the meat into a roasting tin, she spread it with a thick layer of dripping before setting it round with a layer of potatoes. Then, carrying it across to the range, she placed it in the side oven. Ernie Griffin would cause no more women to cry.

Straightening, she glanced warningly at Isabel as Sarah entered the kitchen.

'I dusted the study like you said to do.' The woman looked to Letty still stood by the gleaming black leaded range. 'Then I did the nurses' sitting room.'

'Did you build up the fires?'

'Yes, they be drawing nicely.' She turned to Isabel. 'I went up to your room next, miss, but I didn't set light to your fire. Should I do it now?'

'No.' Isabel shook her head. 'I won't be going upstairs yet for a while, it can wait until teatime.'

'It will wait until no such time!' Letty said quickly. 'The weather be too parky to leave a room without heat. Come

270

teatime it will be right cold up there. Why you had to give up your own room beats me! But you had your own way same as you always do. Well, you won't get your own way this time 'cos Sarah be going right back upstairs to set that fire going, and from now on it will be kept burning. Will you make sure of that, Sarah?' She glanced at the other woman then back to Isabel. 'And if Miss Isabel here tells you other, then you come and see me. There has been plenty given up in this house to help the fighting of this war, and I don't grudge none of it, but I won't have Miss Isabel going without a fire.' Coming back to the table, she tipped sprouts into an enamelled bowl. 'Daft idea! Whoever heard the like!'

The last potato peeled, Isabel stretched her aching back. She had not really thought the business of turning her home into a temporary hospital through as thoroughly as she might. Desperate to help in any way she could, she had jumped in at the deep end, giving too little thought to the heavy burden that would fall on Braddy and the others. Those women with no family commitments who had come to prepare the rooms after the furnishings had been removed had promised to come each evening to scrub the makeshift wards and do the hospital laundry, but that still left the preparation of all these meals. Of course Sarah was a godsend and Mary too worked as hard as any of them, but Braddy was the one who had the responsibility of feeding all those men.

'Get yourself away to your room and rest yourself, you look just about all in.' Letty glanced about the kitchen. 'There be nothing more you can do here. Sarah and meself will tidy the bowls away, then the pair of us be going to take five minutes afore serving the evening meal.'

'I'm not tired,' Isabel lied. Every bone in her body was screaming out to her to rest, but how could she when she had placed so much extra work on the others? 'I'm just cramped, we must have peeled half a mountain of potatoes.'

'Not to mention sprouts.' Mary smiled, flexing her fingers. 'We must have peeled half a field.'

'Arrh, and you've got the other half to peel tomorrow!' Letty turned to the kettle, hiding her smile. That daughter of Sarah Griffin's was a real little worker. There was never any swinging the lead with that one; her never shirked anything, no matter what job her were asked to do. Swinging away the bracket that held the pot of steaming puddings, she settled the kettle over the coals then turned again, her smile hidden but not gone. 'Meantime, young woman, go swill your 'ands and then reach down the cups from the dresser, I reckon we 'ave all four earned ourselves a cup of tea.'

'What about the doctor and the nurses? I imagine they might be grateful for a drink.'

'I daresay you be right, Miss Isabel.' Letty watched as Sarah spooned tea into the large brown pot. 'I'll 'ave a tray sent through, Mary can . . .'

'I'll take it,' Isabel said, quickly following Mary to the scullery to wash her hands. The girl too was entitled to a rest.

'I met the Mistress of All Saints School yesterday evening when I was visiting my sister,' Letty said as Isabel returned to the kitchen and removed her apron, putting it aside for washing. 'Her said if we needed a bit of afternoon help then her would bring the older girls along, provided they was not sent along to the wards. Her said they could help with the preparing of meals and the like, it would be good practice for when they had to run a place of their own.'

'What did you say?' Isabel smoothed her skirts, then turned to help Mary who was adding milk and sugar to several cups. She knew Letty's feelings on 'folk running in and out of my kitchen'!

Taking a fresh white tray cloth from a drawer of the dresser, Letty handed it to Isabel who draped it over a tray before rescuing five cups from Mary's liberal pouring of milk. 'I said as how that would be very helpful. Them young wenches be well behaved and knows their manners.'

Covering the small milk jug with a linen square edged with glass beads, Isabel set to filling a matching bowl with sugar, placing both on the tray with the cups. The schoolgirls *were* well behaved and good mannered, she thought, but then which of them would dare be otherwise in the presence of a schoolmistress renowned for her disciplinary measures? She and Mark used to listen, terrified, to accounts of her strictness and the severe punishments that followed any misdemeanour. She smiled secretly. Letty did not take kindly to any invasion of her kitchen, but it seemed even *she* thought twice before saying no to the formidable Miss Patrick.

Reaching a smaller teapot from the dresser, Isabel warmed it with boiling water from the kettle before making another pot of tea.

'I am glad you said yes, Braddy.' She glanced over the tray, mentally checking that all was there. 'Not only will it give the girls the satisfaction of knowing they are helping, but it will ease the burden of the cooking for you and Sarah.'

Fetching a large fruit cake from the food safe at the farther end of the kitchen, Letty sliced it into generous wedges, setting five pieces on the tray. When she looked at Isabel, her eyes were starry with unshed tears. 'It be wonderful the way everybody, even the children, has turned to helping in some way. Darlaston has done you proud.'

Knowing that to say more would set Letty's tears flowing, Isabel took up the tray, carrying it through to the small sitting room her mother had preferred and which now served as a day room for the nurses and doctor.

They had arrived a few days after Hewett Calcott had sent over all those beds. Isabel remembered his quiet confidence, that warm smile that tugged at her heart. He had kept his word, but why had he not come himself? Was he purposely staying away, and if so was it because of something she had said or done? But they had parted on good terms.

Isabel balanced the tray precariously as she turned the handle of the sitting-room door. Using her hip to push it open, she carried the tray inside. Hewett Calcott's smile had been more than warm, she thought, setting her burden on a mahogany pie crust table. In fact, she had thought . . . bending over the table, she felt a quick rush of heat swirl in her stomach. They way he had smiled, so deep into her eyes, the way his hand had moved, she had almost felt he was reaching out for her, to take her into his arms. And would she have taken exception? Isabel straightened. No, she would not have done.

'Now that is how a man should be welcomed from his work . . .'

The words taking her by surprise, Isabel spun round. She saw a man whom she guessed to be in his early-thirties. He had brown hair brushed straight back from his brow, eyes of the same shade beneath straight brows, a strong acquiline nose above a full mouth that sported no moustache. He stepped towards her, stride long and easy.

'. . . and such a pretty serving maid. I swear I would stay in the Army forever were I assured of such treatment with each posting.'

'Good afternoon, Doctor Seaton.' Isabel returned the smile. 'Brad . . . Mrs Bradshaw thought tea might be welcome.'

He sank into the pretty armchair her mother had favoured, his eyes closing as he sighed with the luxury of rest. 'Oh, that is heaven! I don't think I will ever open my eyes again.'

'Not even for a cup of tea?' The senior nurse bustled into the room, starched apron crackling with every step. 'And cake too! Now *that* is what *I* call heaven.'

'Mrs Bradshaw's special,' Isabel said. 'Her eyes fairly lit up when she saw all the provisions the Army brought over. There was no holding her then. She had her sleeves rolled up and flour in the bowl before we had time to breathe.'

The nurse poured tea into two of the cups. 'You have given your entire house over for the duration of the war. The very least the Army can do is to be generous with provisions.' Cup in hand, the woman glanced up. 'I have no doubt the War Office has expressed its thanks, Miss Kenton, but it can be nothing compared to the feelings of the wounded. They would like nothing more than to thank you themselves. Please, if you have a few minutes, would you go into the wards and speak to them? Any of your staff too, if they will. These men are mostly too far from their families to receive visits and I know how they would appreciate someone to talk to. My nurses are very good, but the pressure of work leaves them little time for conversation.'

'We would have visited the men before now but we all thought it best not to in case we got under your feet.'

'The mornings are taken up with changing dressings.' The nurse handed tea to the doctor. 'But the afternoons and evenings would be suitable. We can afford to ignore the usual hospital rules on visitors. I think these men have earned that much.'

That was beyond dispute, Isabel thought, making her way back to the kitchen. The men had definitely earned that much, and as she had said the others were willing to go and chat to them. The only problem was, where would they find the time?

'I am afraid I did what I always do,' she told Mrs Bradshaw a few minutes later. 'I said something without thinking.'

'Arrh, well, it wouldn't be like you to do things any other way.' Letty sipped her second cup of tea. 'You jumps off the pier afore looking to see if the tide be in. But it makes no harm this time. I for one will be glad to go spend a minute or two with them lads, and it be my bet Sarah and Mary will an' all, to say nothing of Bradshaw. He'll enjoy a chin wag with 'em – and a pint of beer if them nurses don't keep a sharp eye out.'

'Their eyes be sharp enough, Letty, but I reckon there'll be times they'll be turned the other way.'

'And no more than right neither.' Letty's eyes twinkled. 'Bradshaw tells me a pint of Old Best sets a man on his feet quicker than any doctor. And he should know, he has tested his words often enough.'

'And Bradshaw speaks truly, though for the moment I will settle for a cup of your excellent tea, Braddy.'

'Eh, Mr Owen. I didn't expect to see you so soon in the day.' Juggling the cup and saucer in one hand, Letty used the other to ease her ample frame from her chair, smile wide and warm.

'But you be right welcome whatever the time of day. Mary, reach down a cup for Mr Owen.'

'I could not sit in my office another minute with the thought of you plaguing my mind, Braddy, not to mention the pretty girls you have in your kitchen.'

'That be nearer the truth,' she laughed, her several chins wobbling. 'Trust a man to have an eye for a pretty face.'

'Yes, and they don't come prettier than yours, Braddy.'

'Get away with you!' Letty's broad smile was stretched to breaking point. 'I only ever knowed one man tell an easier fib than you, Mr Owen, and that were me granddad. He was as Irish as Paddy's hat. He didn't just kiss the Blarney stone – he bit a piece off and chewed it!'

Owen Farr pulled his mouth down at the corners, pretending to feel offended, though the action did nothing to dilute the laughter in his eyes. 'Now would I ever fib to you? I ask you, Isabel, and you, Mary, would I ever lie to women as beautiful as you all are?'

'I shall follow diplomatic procedure,' Isabel answered as Mary blushed, 'and say I could not possibly comment without full and proper discussion with my colleagues.'

'What is a man to do when women team up against him?'

'Give in gracefully?'

'As you say, Miss Kenton.' Owen sat himself down at the table. 'I shall give in gracefully. Now get a move on and serve a man his tea before he collapses from thirst.

'I had intended to call this evening.' He smiled at Mary as she handed him a cup of tea, setting the girl blushing at once. 'But there was nothing stirring in the office, not even the dust, so I thought perhaps I could get the business of the military done. That is, if you have no objection, Isabel?'

'Of course not.' She glanced towards the Gladstone bag he had placed beside his chair.

'I thought to get these papers filed. Knowing the Army, there will be a fresh batch with every post.'

'I hope you have not taken on too much, Mr Owen,' Letty

said in concern. 'You still don't be fully recovered from that wound of your'n. You go overdoing things and you will make yourself poorly.'

He flashed a smile meant to devastate. 'It would be well worth it if I had you to nurse me, Braddy.'

'Lord alive!' Letty giggled like a schoolgirl. 'Would you listen to the man? Like my grandmother used to say, he would charm fish from the water and birds from the trees.'

'Ah!' Owen sighed dramatically. 'But all the time I want only to charm your lovely self – charm you straight into my arms.'

'It's a good thing I no longer be eighteen,' Letty laughed, jiggling her chins all over again. 'Listening to you would 'ave my head turned so I'd be looking down at my own backside! And before you say what a pretty backside it be, Mr Owen, remember all these fibs can be heard upstairs.'

Owen smiled as Letty turned her face upward. 'In that case I shall only think them. But whether heaven keeps score or not, you do have . . .'

'Now you stop right there, young man.' Letty beamed. 'Miss Isabel, take that scoundrel out of my kitchen.'

'I think perhaps it might be as well to do so, before he has the three of us looking down at . . .'

'Miss Isabel!' Letty's sharp exclamation had Mary scuttling for the scullery and Sarah gathering the cups.

'I was about to say, Braddy,' Isabel said, smiling innocently, 'Mr Farr will have us all looking down at our feet with embarrassment at his flattery.'

The expression on Mrs Bradshaw's face saying that was one more lie that would be heard in heaven, she pushed herself up from her chair. 'I know what you was about to say, I weren't born yesterday! Now get you off, the two of you, and leave a body in peace.'

'I have never known Braddy take so well to anyone as she has to you, Owen,' Isabel said a few minutes later as they entered the study. 'She allows you an awful lot of licence. I can't imagine her letting anyone else tease her as you do.'

'I like Mrs Bradshaw very much and am pleased she has taken to me.' Placing his Gladstone bag on the desk, he turned quickly, gathering her hands in his. 'But that liking is nothing compared to the feeling I have for you, Isabel.'

Releasing one hand, he gently tilted her chin, looking deep into her eyes. 'The crucial thing is,' he said softly, 'have *you* taken to me, my love?' Lowering his head very slowly, his eyes holding hers, he hesitated a hair's breadth from her lips. 'Could you love me, Isabel?'

Overcome with emotion, she closed her eyes.

'Yes, Owen! Oh, yes, I could love you.'

Chapter Twenty

James Hawley frowned, the movement drawing his dark well-shaped eyebrows together. Where had this man sustained an injury that caused him to limp, relying on his cane, and how long ago?

'Good afternoon, Mr Hawley.' Isabel Kenton's smile widened as she caught sight of his tall figure coming up the drive to Woodbank House.

'Miss Kenton!' His reply terse, James Hawley kept his gaze on the fair-haired man at her side. 'Forgive my intrusion. I should have asked permission to call, I am afraid I have forgotten my manners.' Diverting his glance from her companion's face, he looked at Isabel, seeing the smile dancing in her hazel eyes. 'Perhaps, with your permission, I may call tomorrow? There are some points Mr Calcott wishes me to go over with you concerning business.'

He had come here to save her from making the journey to the steel works, knowing she spent every possible moment of her time running this house and assisting the nursing staff wherever she could. At least that was the excuse he had made to himself. In fact he would gladly sieze any reason, however flimsy, for seeing Isabel Kenton, speaking to her if only for a moment; to hear her voice as he had so often imagined hearing it in the trenches, in the short moments when the gun fire had wavered on the brink of silence, and in the long dark reaches of the night when the desperate need for sleep had turned into a deeper, more hopeless need, a need he knew could never be answered.

He watched her now as she came towards him, the smile curving her lovely mouth matching that in the depths of her eyes. How many nights had he stood hip-deep in trench water or lain on damp bedding, the remembered sound of her voice the only thing keeping him sane; the words slipping, melting and tender, into his mind yet bruising his heart for he knew they were words which in reality she would never speak to him. He had wanted her so much then: to touch her hand, to see her smile at him, to hear her speak his name. Remembering, he almost laughed aloud. How badly could a man want heaven, and how many times see it just beyond his reach?

'Mr Hawley and I know one other.' Owen Farr held out his hand as Isabel made her introductions. 'We served in the same regiment. I am happy you are home, Mr Hawley, though not entirely unscathed, I see.'

'Not entirely.' Taking the hand held out to him, James shook it briefly. 'I took a bullet to the leg just after . . . just after you were ordered home.'

'Nothing too serious, I hope?' Owen returned quickly, glancing at Isabel to see if the pause in Hawley's reply had impressed itself upon her, relieved to see she appeared not to have noticed.

'No, not serious, just an inconvenience at times. I was one of the lucky ones.'

'Yes.' Owen's glance slanted back at him, uncertainty and something like fear swirling together in its green depths. 'Yes, we were both lucky.'

His own eyes hard as the slate they resembled, James Hawley stared for a moment at the man who now turned from him, taking Isabel Kenton's hand with the air of one who would soon have the right to take more. Had she promised him that right, had she consented to become the wife of Owen Farr? Anger, colder and more intense than any he had felt on the battlefields of France, welled in him like a tidal wave, closing his throat, gripping him with the intensity of steel. He had played Owen Farr's game once, he would not play it again.

Finding it an effort to speak through stiff lips, he turned again to Isabel, his anger only increasing at the smile she gave Farr. 'My apologies once more for intruding upon you, Miss Kenton. And good afternoon.'

'There is no need for you to leave on my account, Mr Hawley.' Owen flashed him a smile, the shadows gone from his eyes. 'I myself was just leaving. Isabel, my dear . . .' He gathered both her hands in his, pressing each to his lips before drawing her close enough to touch his mouth to her cheek. 'Until tomorrow, my love.'

My love! The words pounding in his brain, James Hawley made no reply to the other man's goodbye. My love! He watched the motor carriage roar away down the drive. No man other than a father or a fiancé would use such words to a woman in public; so Isabel Kenton *was* affianced, she had agreed to become Owen Farr's wife!

'I was unaware that Lieutenant Farr had returned to these parts.' Remembering little of the discussion relating to the business that had served as an excuse to bring him here, knowing only the anger and, yes, the bitterness that raged in him, James Hawley stood once more outside the front entrance of Woodbank House. He had refused all offers of hospitality, afraid that each moment in this woman's presence would be a moment longer than he could contain the chaos of his own feelings and emotions.

'Owen?' Isabel's eyes followed the line of the drive as if still seeing Farr's gleaming motor carriage. 'He returned to Wednesbury after being demobilised from the Army. He wished to stay with his comrades in France, to see the war through to the end, but his wound proved too serious for that; he had to accept the advice of his doctors and leave the fighting to others. Poor Owen, that hurt him more than the bullet wound.'

'Bullet wound?'

'Why, yes!' A tiny frown marred her smooth brow as she looked at him. 'But I thought you would have known, Owen said you served in the same regiment?'

Dropping his glance, he replied, 'There are many men in a regiment, Miss Kenton, you cannot always know what is happening to each and every one of them. Mr Farr must have been injured while I was away. Patrols sometimes take men some distance from their own lines.'

'Of course, how silly of me.'

'Not silly at all!' Anger contained behind a thin smile, he looked up. 'How could you possibly know?'

How could anyone know who had not been there? How could they know how it felt to stand beside a man, to be speaking to him, one minute only to see him blown into the air the next, his body landing in fragments at your feet? James swallowed hard. How could any of them know how that felt?

'Owen took over his father's solicitor's practice. He has an office in Wednesbury. He has agreed to be responsible for the paperwork the military insists on while Woodbank is run as a temporary medical unit, though I fear it might be a little too much for him, especially so soon after being wounded.'

'I think Mr Farr is a man with enough common sense to know when he has reached his limit . . . in anything.' The hand that held the walking cane tightened until James's knuckles showed white. If Owen Farr had any sense at all he would know – know that this time there would be no hiding the truth!

'I will inform Mr Calcott of our discussion.' Half an hour later James was leaving, having kept talk of business with Isabel brief and to the point. The pain of not being able to touch her as Farr had touched her, of not being able to speak to her as that man had spoken to her, was almost too much as he turned away.

'Mr Hawley!' Isabel's quick words halting him, James faced her once more, glad the gathering shadows hid the expression

282

in his eyes. 'I . . . I have not seen Mr Calcott in some weeks. He's not ill?'

James shook his head. 'No, Miss Kenton, he is not ill.'

'I see.' For a moment her mouth drooped. 'I thought perhaps . . . but then he must be very busy. It is selfish of me to expect him to call. Would you please convey my good wishes to him?'

Across the space separating them James could see the light of affection gleam in her eyes and almost feel the warmth of her voice, but this time no icy volcano exploded within him; there was no bitterness in knowing the feeling she held for Hewett Calcott.

Were it he who had called her 'my love', would there have been bitterness then, would the same cold fury have risen in him as it had when Owen Farr spoke those words? Pushing the thoughts away, reluctant to acknowledge the truth, he nodded. 'I will. Goodnight, Miss Kenton.'

So that was what he had told her? Coat collar turned up against the chilly evening air, James Hawley walked slowly down Woods Bank towards Katherine's Cross. Farr had told her he had been wounded in France. How many more had he told the same lie? Not that it mattered if everybody in England believed him – everybody except Isabel Kenton.

Waiting while a tram rattled past, he crossed the road, taking the turning that led into King Edward Street.

The months spent fighting in France had led him to the belief that each man's life was his own, to live as he wished with interference from no other. But what if the living of that life meant bringing heart-break to another? Could he in all honesty still hold to his belief then?

On the fringes of the town the foundries and iron works opened their furnaces in unison, turning the overhead sky a brilliant crimson, brushing away the purple shadows of night. James lifted his face to the awesome beauty, one born of toil and heavy labour yet one that for a few minutes wiped away the ugliness of foundry stacks and belching chimneys, caused a man to forget the fears of war. If only his own fears could be brushed aside so easily, but like the chimney stacks they would still be there long after the momentary beauty faded.

My love! The words returned to his mind, the beat of them matching his footsteps. But *was* Isabel Kenton the love of Owen Farr . . . the only love?

Head bent against the chill breeze, James Hawley felt a different coldness touch his heart.

Turning back into the house, Isabel heard the swift shrill of the telephone sounding in the larger of the sitting rooms now serving as hospital wards. If only it could be for her, to tell her Mark was on his way home. For a moment her heart lifted, held on the wings of hope. Perhaps . . . Then as she heard a crisp voice speaking in reply she turned towards the stairs. Maybe it was wrong to pray so hard, to ask every night for the return of her brother. But surely God would not think that? He would understand the fear that lived in her heart, understand the love that drove her continually to ask for Mark's safekeeping.

In her tiny room at the end of the servants' landing she slipped off the maroon mohair suit she had worn for visiting the foundry earlier in the day. Had James Hawley called there to see her? He had not said as much, but then he had said very little except to give her Hewett Calcott's message concerning business. Placing the suit on a hanger, she hung it in the cupboard that served as a wardrobe, taking out the serviceable brown serge she had bought for helping in the house. He had not been his usual self, she thought, shivering as she slipped the cold fabric over her shoulders. Even with a fire kept going day and night the room was never really warm. It was almost as cold as James Hawley's attitude today. But why? She fastened small buttons at her throat, her fingers clumsy with cold. Why had he acted that way?

She would have thought he'd be pleased to see a comrade safe from the war, but his manner had seemed to border on hostility. That was not like James. She did not know him well apart from his being Hewett Calcott's manager but from what she had seen of him, he was not a hostile person. Jealous then? Smoothing the dress over her petticoats, she took up the hair-brush from the tiny table wedged at the foot of the bed. Was that the reason he had been so cool with the other man? Was it because Owen had been an officer while he . . . Of course not! But there was surely nothing else of which to be jealous. She passed the brush lightly over her hair, smoothing back into place the few strands disturbed by her dressing. James would not let mere rank disturb him, he was not the jealous type. Holding the brush still, she stared at herself in the damp-speckled mirror hung on a nail above the table. But what type was he? She did not know, theirs was not such a deep relationship she could say, so why was she defending him so strongly? Colour seeping swiftly into her cheeks, she returned the brush to the table, turning away from the mirror. Owen was the one she should have been concerned for, his the feelings she should have defended. After all, he was the one she loved.

The one she loved! The thought brought her up sharply. It was the first time she had admitted it though the thought was by no means new. She did love Owen Farr but at the same time she loved Hewett Calcott. Arms hanging limply by her sides, she stared at the whitewashed wall. Was it possible to be in love with two men? Perhaps it was, but it was not possible to take both as a husband! So which would it be? The thought hummed in her mind like a bee searching for pollen, resting for a few seconds then launching off at a tangent. You love them both, but should each of them propose, whom do you love enough to marry?

'I don't know.' The words escaped in a soft whisper as she sank on to the narrow bed. 'I love them both . . . I love them both . . .'

'Miss Isabel . . . Miss Isabel!'

Mary's voice together with the soft tap on her door brought Isabel to her feet, driving thoughts of Owen and Hewett Calcott from her mind. Crossing to the door, she swung it open.

'The sister and the doctor, Miss,' Mary said, 'they asks if you could come and see them right away.'

Isabel felt the world lurch away from her. Mark! It must be Mark. They had heard something. They knew . . . they knew he was dead!

'Be you all right, Miss Isabel?'

Somewhere a million miles away a voice spoke but Isabel did not want to hear.

'Miss Isabel . . . Miss Isabel!'

The hand gripping her arm pulled her back, out of her floating empty world and into one full of pain.

'Mary!' She clung to the girl, leaning heavily against her as her own legs threatened to give way beneath her. 'Mary . . . is it my brother . . . is it Mark?'

'Mr Mark?' The girl sounded bewildered. 'I don't know nothing about Mr Mark. No, it be some more of our Tommies. Seems there be no room for them in the 'ospital over at Wordsley so the military be sending them here. Least, that be what I heard that doctor tell the sister.'

It was not Mark! The rush of gratitude sent her swaying, causing Mary to hold on to her.

'Eh, miss! I don't think you be well. Lay you down on your bed and I'll tell them downstairs you be resting. Perhaps the doctor will pop up here and take a look at you?'

'No.' Isabel smiled as her breathing slowed once more. 'No, I am quite well, it is just that I thought . . .'

'I know, miss. You thought it was bad news about your brother. Me mother is just the same. Every batch of soldiers that comes in, she trembles in case our Peter be among them. Though, truth to tell, I wish he was. It be better for them to be wounded and at home. At least that way you know they be alive.'

Yes, Isabel thought. At least that way you knew they were alive. The pain that had swallowed her a moment ago would be gone. But what of their pain? What lay behind the silent drawn faces of the men she had seen carried into this house? Men with arms and legs missing, men with eyes bandaged – eyes that would still see only darkness when their wrappings were removed. Who knew the pain such men felt?

'You say the sister and the doctor wish to see me?' Isabel drew herself upright, shutting out thoughts that brought nothing but sorrow and anger – anger that so-called civilised men could allow so terrible a thing as war.

'Yes, miss. Doctor Seaton said that if you could spare a couple of minutes . . .'

'Of course,' Isabel interrupted, her usual efficiency taking over. 'I will come at once.'

'But we have nowhere to put them!' In the small sitting room set apart for a rest room, Isabel shook her head. 'Every room in the house is already filled with wounded. We can't possibly place more. Didn't you tell them?'

Opposite her, Doctor Seaton pushed his fingers through his hair, eyes reflecting the tiredness of his body. 'Miss Kenton, you do not *tell* your Commanding Officers anything . . . they tell you. We can only follow orders.'

'But *what* orders? Who is so foolish as to issue such stupid ones! God knows I want to help as much as anyone but I can't just flick my fingers and make rooms and beds appear.'

'Miss Kenton.' The senior nurse spoke gently. 'We are all grateful for what you are doing, none more so than the men you have already taken in. We realise the burden that accepting yet more will place upon your staff, as it will upon ours, but there is no other place to put these men.'

'But there must be!' she protested. 'There are hospitals in other places, other towns.'

'The Sister Dora at Walsall is full to overflowing.' The doctor dropped his hand tiredly, leaving his normally smooth hair ruffled. 'As is the Dudley Guest. At Stourbridge, Studley Court, like your own home, has been given over as a military hospital and that too is overflowing. At Wordsley even the workhouse has been commandeered to serve the same purpose. Amblecote, Gornal, Kinver . . . whichever direction you turn, the entire area is the same.' He smiled but it was a thin attempt, devoid of any trace of humour. 'Have you heard the saying "no room at the inn" Miss Kenton? Well, this is the same, it is happening all over again, only this time it is not the birth of a child we expect, but the death of a multitude!'

Stepping to Isabel's side as the doctor turned away in his distress, the sister spoke again, her own voice controlled but tight with emotion. 'Miss Kenton, what I am about to say may be viewed as a breach of confidence by my superiors but at the moment I do not care. It is my opinion that you deserve to know why you are being asked to make so many sacrifices. No, Doctor!' she said as the tall figure turned quickly. 'I will speak. After I do, you must act as you think fit.' She fixed her eyes back on Isabel. 'The fact is that we thought the fighting on the Somme was over, or at least the worst of it was, but that turns out to be yet one more official white lie, a salve for the nation's breaking heart. In reality the War Office in its wisdom ordered another onslaught, a big push that would turn their lie into the truth. But all it has done is destroy the lives of thousands of men and injure thousands more – thousands who are being shipped home, longing only to be here, cared for in a dry bed under a warm roof. But there are no beds and no roofs! Many will lie out in the open here in England just as they did in France. Doctor Seaton was right, this is just one more inn with no room.'

'Then we must make room.' Isabel looked from one to the other of them, seeing the glint of tears in the eyes of the sister and feeling her own heart catch in sympathy. But saying she would find room was one thing. Doing it would be something else.

'I had hoped as much.' The doctor stepped forward, his strained expression giving way to one of relief. 'An outhouse or a stable, anything would do. There are patients . . . walking wounded . . . who can be relocated. That would leave room in the house for the sicker new arrivals.'

But there are no more outhouses, all of them have been put to use, Isabel thought. Aloud she asked: 'When do you expect these men?'

Seaton lifted a hand to his already tousled hair, his lips pursing as he considered. 'A few days, a week at most. It depends on how many men they can cram into the boats. That was all Area Command would say except that some are coming back in pretty bad shape.'

'Then we must do the best we can for them.' Isabel glanced over to where the nursing sister stood, tension in every line of her body. 'Tell me, apart from more room, is there anything else you will need?'

'Beds and bedding, of course, though the Army will provide that. The question being – when!'

'Then we will not wait for the Army.' Isabel lifted her head determinedly. 'We will find what is needed for ourselves.' But where? As always she had jumped in head first, spoken without using her brain! There was not so much as a spare blanket in the house, much less beds and mattresses, and she could not ask Hewett Calcott again, he had done enough already. She began to feel the hopelessness of her situation. She had promised the impossible, but how did she achieve it? Somewhere in the shades of memory words long forgotten rose to her mind: . . . *yours will be a different war* . . . Isabel drew a long slow breath. Hers was undoubtedly proving a different war, but the fighting of it was just as difficult. Showing none of the uncertainty she was feeling, she tried to smile. 'If you will both excuse me, I will set about finding you the room you need.'

'Miss Kenton.' The doctor's words halted her as she made to leave. 'There is one more thing we feel you should know. There is a man listed among the wounded, a man I think will probably be known to you . . .'

Chapter Twenty-One

Owen Farr threw the Gladstone bag on to the table that stood in the hall of Hyde Cottage then took the stairs two at a time, the supposed wound to his leg forgotten. Life would change once he was married to Isabel Kenton.

Married! Loosening the knot of his tie, he pulled it free from his neck. That would put everything right for him, he would be his own master then. And Isabel? He threw the tie aside, a smile curving his handsome mouth. She would prove no obstacle. She was already in love with him, that was easy to see. She would be too glad to be Mrs Owen Farr to raise any objections, and there was nobody else to whom she looked for marriage. Unless . . .

The buttons of his waistcoat half undone, he paused. She had spoken often of Hewett Calcott and always with a warmth in her voice that could be more than mere affection for a friend. Were they in love? The man was more than twice her age, but then what did that matter to a woman who had thought to find no further prospects?

Unfastening the last of the buttons, he tossed the waistcoat on to the bed beside his discarded tie. Isabel Kenton and Hewett Calcott . . . He had to admit there were possibilities there. The man was wealthy, that much Owen knew already. It was he who had bought Jago Timmins's place, lock, stock and the proverbial barrel; it was not unthinkable that he hoped to add a good percentage of Luther Kenton's assets to those he already held by taking the daughter. And if Kenton's son did not survive the war? The smile that had remained on Owen's mouth faded and his lips tightened. Yes, Hewett Calcott was a man with his eye very much to the main chance.

Going into the dressing room that adjoined his bedroom, he flicked through the jackets and trousers hanging neatly there, movements jerky with anger. He had been a fool. He should have proposed to Isabel Kenton long before this, should have been married to her by now! What if he had left it too late . . . what if Calcott had beaten him to it?

But surely she would have said? His hand resting on an indigo blue jacket, he forced himself to think calmly. Had Calcott asked her already to be his wife then she would have made some demur when Owen himself had asked if she could love him. When he had said those words to her, called her 'my love'. But she had not. She had said she could love him, Owen Farr.

He flicked along the rack that held a dozen pairs of trousers, selecting a pair of pale grey worsted. So Hewett Calcott had not yet made his move, and there was no other rival for Owen to fear. Whatever had brought Hawley to Woodbank House, he was most certainly not suitable material for Isabel Kenton's fiancé. She might want a husband, but not badly enough to take a foundry worker!

Easing the garments from their hangers, he carried them back into the bedroom. There was still time. And after that? Afterwards he would be in the clear. After all, he would have a beautiful young woman as his wife. Who could suspect him of wanting more?

But there was still Hawley . . . No matter what the reason for his calling on her, Isabel Kenton's smile made it obvious he was welcome. The confidence of a moment before fading a little, Owen dropped the jacket and trousers, leaving them in a heap at his feet as he sank on to the bed. Isabel Kenton had done many things since being given charge of Kenton Engineering, things never expected of a woman. It might not be out of character after all! It might just be that she would choose a man who possessed neither class nor money, a man from the rat-infested hovels of those who laboured for a weekly pittance. And if she did, where would that leave him? Without her money, it would be impossible to have Ruth . . . Swinging his feet on to the bed, Owen lay back, resting his hands beneath his head.

'Your brandy, sir.'

He had heard the tap on his door but did not open his eyes.

'You seem tired, sir?'

'Yes, Simms, I am. Tired of paperwork, tired of this whole bloody war!'

The batman held the tray in one hand. He had been assigned to Owen Farr from his first being commissioned, had been his batman on campaign in France. Not that Lieutenant Farr had done much campaigning other than in other men's tents, and the only battles he had ever engaged in were battles of the bed. But when Farr had been discharged Simms had been offered the chance to return to Blighty with him; miracles like that didn't happen twice and he hadn't been about to refuse.

'If I might make a suggestion, sir?'

Simms had learned quickly during those months in the Army; learned how to anticipate, when to suggest. That way Farr enjoyed the game while offloading the moral guilt.

Waiting while Owen took the glass, he slid the tray beneath one arm.

'Perhaps a quiet supper in the private dining room?'

'I had planned to work this evening.'

'All work and no play, sir . . . you know what they say!'

Owen sipped his brandy, swallowing it down, feeling the heat of it in his chest. 'And they are right, Simms, but . . .'

'Beg pardon, sir, but I really think one night . . . A little break, sir, it will do you good.'

'Yes, Simms.' Owen's eyes closed again. 'You are right. A break will be beneficial, it will help me work all the harder tomorrow.'

'Will nine o'clock be agreeable to you, sir?'

Owen took a longer pull at his drink. 'Nine o'clock will be fine, thank you, Simms.'

Easing himself from the bed as the door closed behind his manservant, Owen glanced at the jacket and trousers lying in a heap on the floor then walked past them and into the dressing room.

He had been lucky to get his batman discharged along with him. Perhaps his superiors had thought that once returned to his unit and assigned to some other officer, the man might talk a little too freely. But the Army's loss was Owen's gain and he was grateful for it. Simms knew how to arrange things discreetly and also which side his bread was buttered. A tight mouth meant a comfortable home and a well-paid job. Simms appreciated the benefits of that compared to the horrors of the Somme.

Bathed, his skin dusted and face carefully painted with the best of Helena Rubenstein's 'Valaze' range of cosmetics, Owen turned his attention to the gowns locked away in cupboards that stretched the length of the room.

Choosing the latest addition, he slipped into the beautifully draped maize-coloured chiffon overlaid with cream lace. Fastening the line of tiny mother-of-pearl buttons that led up from below the breast, he stared at his reflection. The colour suited his naturally fair hair, but against the carefully coiffured auburn wig it would be sensational.

In the bedroom beyond a discreet cough announced the presence of Simms. That meant his companion for the evening had arrived. Spraying a touch of Chanel perfume on to his neck, Owen smiled at the reflection nodding to him from the mirror.

'You *are* beautiful, Rowena.'

Closing the door of the private dining room behind him, he stared at the figure by the fireplace. They were no strangers to one other. Owen's glance travelled from the dark head, down over the broad shoulders and tight hips, the long, lithe muscular legs. It was a body that pleased him.

Beneath the dress his own masculinity quickened. It pleased

him when he was clothed but it pleased him even more when, as now, he was naked beneath his dress.

'Good evening, Rowena.'

The voice was dark as the hair, sultry and enticing like the naked body.

'I hope you like my welcome?'

'It is something of a surprise.' Owen smiled. 'But, yes, I like it.'

The figure remained with its back turned to Owen, the light of the fire mixing with the glow of candlelight flickering over the sleek limbs.

'This is not my only surprise, Rowena.' Smooth as black velvet the voice flowed over Owen, filling every inch of him with a living, pulsing excitement that had the breath tight in his lungs. 'I have a gift for you.'

Slowly, like a beautifully sculpted statue on a rotating pedestal, the figure turned. Smiling it raised one hand, the gold of the chain that dangled from it glinting in the room's soft light.

'This is for you.' The full lips parted in a smile. Lowering his hand, Owen's guest draped the chain about his erect penis. 'These are both for you, Rowena, but you have to come and get them.'

Crossing to the fireplace, Owen felt the nerves in his groin tighten. It would be a most pleasurable evening . . .

Afterwards, his sleeping bedfellow paid in the usual manner, he returned to his own room.

Standing before the long mirror, he gazed at the lovely silk of his gown, the necklace draped about his throat. If only it had been Ruth who had given him that gift! If only Ruth had been the one sharing the evening with him!

One day it *would* be Ruth. It was meant to be, they had to be together. With Ruth he would not need the likes of that man sleeping in the private room. One day Ruth would be his. Nothing must get in the way of that, nothing must part them again.

But to keep Ruth he must have more than a solicitor's

earnings. Drawing off the wig, he laid it aside but his glance stayed on it. He needed the Kenton money. He should not have left Woodbank without first making sure of Isabel. He should have made his proposal, got her consent to become his wife, everything depended on that. But it was still not too late. Getting up from the bed he ignored the clothes lying in a heap where he had dropped them.

Going again to the dressing room, he selected a suit of dark grey barathea, teaming it with a plain white shirt and grey tie. The sober lawyer's clothes would definitely stand him in better stead!

Once more in his bedroom he stood for a moment. James Hawley had made no reference to those last days in France but that did not mean he never would. Hawley knew it all, enough to wreck any idea of marriage with Isabel Kenton, but then, he worked in a steel foundry, and as everyone knew, steel foundries were dangerous places; a man could easily lose his life there . . . How easily a problem could be solved! Humming softly to himself, Owen left the house.

What if she were not at home? He turned the steering wheel of the motor carriage, guiding it into a right turn at the Bull Stake, ignoring the cry of a woman startled by the sudden deep-throated sound of the horn. If she were not home then his question would have to wait until tomorrow. In fact somehow he rather hoped she was not. The patients would be all settled for the night and the doctor would be free. They had come face to face several times since his coming to Woodbank but each time Isabel or one of the nurses had been present, preventing them from exchanging more than a few brief words.

He had been so surprised, Owen thought, remembering the look that had passed over the doctor's face as Isabel and himself had walked from the sitting room just as Seaton arrived at the house. The doctor's surprise had been quickly hidden. But it had been no surprise to Owen Farr. He had read that name on the official document sent by the War Office, he knew who it was who had come to Darlaston as Army Medical Officer.

Steering the vehicle between the stone pillars that flanked the gateway to Woodbank House he drove slowly up the drive, coming to a halt before the main entrance. Yes, he would rather Isabel were not at home.

Coming from the wards, Isabel paused as Mary opened the door.

'Owen, I did not expect to see you again tonight!'

Forcing back the disappointment that rose in him, he handed gloves and coat to Mary. There would be time enough to talk to Doctor Seaton, time to recall shared memories, time to renew old friendships.

'I am not unwelcome, I hope?'

'Of course not. We are always happy to see you.'

'Are you, Isabel?' Not waiting for Mary to disappear into the kitchen he caught Isabel by the hands, eyes displaying none of the thoughts of a moment ago. 'Are you truly pleased? I tried to stay away, to wait at least until tomorrow, but I could not. Isabel, come into the study.'

Bemused, she allowed herself to be drawn into the room set aside for use as his office.

'Owen, what on earth is wrong?'

Closing the door firmly behind them, he turned to her, once more taking both her hands in his. '*I* am wrong Isabel.' He said it softly, achieving just the right tone, the right level of emotion to his voice. 'Wrong for being such a coward.'

'A coward?' She gave a half laugh, brows drawing together in confusion. 'Owen, I don't understand. You are . . .'

'No, Isabel, let me finish. When I was here earlier there was something I meant to ask you, but when the time came I could not. My courage failed me and I left the words unsaid. But I regretted that immediately and once I was home I could not prevent myself from thinking of it. What I had *not* said preyed on my mind until I knew I must return. Until I had done that, and at least tried to speak, there could be no rest for me.'

Confusion still clouding her eyes, Isabel tried to free her

hands, wanting to touch his face, to hold him in her arms, to soothe away whatever it was that worried him. 'Owen,' she began again. 'We have been such good friends since you first came to this house . . .'

'That is it, Isabel!' The words rushed out as if she had tapped some hidden source. 'We are friends . . . just friends. But . . . but . . .'

'But?' She said it softly, eyes filled with tenderness.

Her hands still held between his, he raised them on a level with his mouth, touching his lips to them. 'Isabel.' His voice throbbed and he did not lift his eyes. 'Isabel, if what I say offends you then know now I did not mean it so. If your answer is not the one my heart craves then I will accept it, asking only that our friendship be allowed to continue. Isabel . . .' He touched her hands again to his lips then lifted his face, eyes like stormy river water in which his emotions swirled out of control. 'Isabel, could you . . . would you . . . will you do me the honour of becoming my wife?'

Owen had asked her to marry him.

Isabel stood in her bedroom which was lit only by the sharp glow of a frosty moon.

If your answer is not the one my heart craves . . .

The words returned to her from the shadows. He had twice touched her hands to his lips, had looked deep into her eyes, emotion darkening his own. He had asked her to be his wife – but he had not said he loved her. And she had listened, had felt an urge to hold him, to soothe him, but she too had not spoken those words.

But Owen *must* love her. Why otherwise should he ask her to marry him. And she must be in love with him, or why else would she have accepted?

Isabel glanced out at the scudding clouds. Why had she not spoken to Owen of love? Not happy with the questions crowding her mind, she crossed to the bed, sliding in between the sheets.

It had not been the thought of Owen's smile that had taken her to buy that new dress a week ago, nor was it of Mark's, even though she had pretended it would be the perfect dress in which to welcome him home.

But when might that be? And would there still be a home to which to welcome him?

Her whole body suddenly trembling, Isabel touched the bandages that still wrapped her arms, the scratches about her throat.

She had been alone in the fitting room at the rear of Marsden's gown shop when she had heard the screams. For a moment she had stood there, the delicate aquamarine silk poised ready to slip over her head. Then the explosion had come.

Isabel pressed her eyelids tight shut but the noise went on, wave upon wave of screams and the thuds of collapsing masonry, all surging together like a tide in her memory.

Then came the blackness. First it must have been loss of consciousness but then she had woken – woken to a stillness and silence broken only by the occasional creaking of a beam or falling of plaster.

She had tried to stand, only then realising she was trapped. Held by something that lay heavily across her chest and shoulders, she could not move.

Opening her eyes, Isabel turned her glance to the moonlight beyond the window. She had not drawn her curtains since that night, could not bear to close away light she'd once thought never to see again.

How long had she lain there in a darkness that could only be matched by that of the grave? How many times had she screamed until she was exhausted? Then she had heard the movement overhead, the falling masonry. Fear lent her the strength to scream then – fear of being buried deeper and deeper.

But even as she screamed a thin flicker of light had appeared and a voice called to her softly.

Isabel remembered the relief that had flooded through her then, a wild mixture of laughter and tears; the gratitude as someone pushed aside the rubble.

There had been another air raid. The man's voice had been quiet and reassuring as he'd explained. She was safe now. The upper rooms had collapsed but because of the way the beams had fallen, the room where she had been standing had not entirely caved in.

He had held a jar with a lighted candle inside, casting its light over her but leaving his face obscured by shadow. Then he'd bent over her twisting the heavy gold ring from her right hand, snatching the necklace from her neck. The tiny golden ball on it had been a gift from Mark.

She had cried out but he had quickly covered her mouth, warning her he could smash her head with one of the fallen bricks; the softness gone from his voice as he'd added that no one would view it as anything other than an injury caused by the bomb that had destroyed half the street.

Knowing it to be no empty threat, she had clenched her teeth against sobs of fear. The man was a looter robbing the dead and injured.

Unable to hold back her fear, she had cried out as he took up the candle jar and held it over her once more.

'I . . . I have no more jewellery!'

The pain of recollection searing through every part of her, Isabel tried to banish the rest of the memory but it refused to be ignored, just as it did every night when she tried to sleep.

'P'raps not . . .'

She had not seen the face obscured in shadow but she had heard the thickness in his voice.

'But jewellery is not the only thing that interests me. There are other rewards!'

Laying aside the jar, he had dropped to the ground, his knees shoving her legs roughly apart, hands sliding along her legs before snatching at her cami knickers.

Her screams had pierced the semi-blackness and as his hand smacked against her mouth there had come shouts from above.

Quick as a striking snake he had moved away, blowing out the candle, shouting to those above to strike no match for fear of gas leaks.

There was a woman trapped, Isabel heard him shout. He had tried but couldn't manage to free her. He couldn't do much more, he was exhausted.

'Right, mate.' The answer rung through the darkness. 'Let's have you out.'

She had heard the scuffle of feet on loose bricks, the grunt as he was hauled through a hole in the ceiling, then hearing women's voices she had dropped away into that blessed, all-enveloping blackness, knowing no more until the voices of Doctor Seaton and Braddy welcomed her back to the world.

Hewett Calcott replaced the earpiece of the tall black telephone. Isabel would be pleased to receive him at Woodbank House. It had taken him days to find the courage to telephone her, unwilling to face the hurt a refusal would bring. Lord, he had mooned about like a young lad with his first love! Smiling, he returned to his bedroom and then took the leather-covered box from the drawer in his bedside table.

He carried it to the window. He had taken this with him on his last visit to Isabel's house. Looking down, he watched the pale lemon-coloured December sun illuminate the box, glinting on the gold tooling. He had taken it to give to her but at the last minute his heart had failed him. He had lost that first love, a woman he had adored heart and soul: he could not take the risk of losing a second time, of pushing too hard or too soon, of alienating where he wished only to awaken love.

But would Isabel take offence? Twisting the box in his hands, he watched the light reflected from the tracery of gold. Would she think him an old man merely on the lookout for a young woman, not to love and cherish but to serve as a prop to his ego? Would Isabel Kenton think that of him? The fear of it had kept him once before from offering what this box held. Prising open the lid he glanced at the contents, light spearing from diamonds set in gold. It had kept him from speaking what was in his heart, saying what he longed to say. But silence had proved no solace, had brought no relief from the longing that had become a part of him. Snappping shut the lid, he slipped the box into his pocket. There could be no relief for him, no easing of the emptiness in his soul until those words had been said. Whatever else it brought him it would bring an answer, one final definite answer.

Two hours later he stood with Isabel, seeing the pleasure on her face as the packages were carried in from his carriage. One after another they were placed on the large circular table that still graced the hall of Woodbank House, though it now stood half hidden in an alcove that had once held a coat cupboard, leaving the way clear for orderlies carrying in stretchers.

'Mr Calcott, this is so kind,' Isabel acknowledged the last of the parcels. 'The men will be very grateful, I know.'

'That they enjoy what I have brought is gratitude enough for me, Miss Kenton. Though this,' he indicated the two large barrels of ale being rolled past the open door on their way to the cellar, 'must be given only on prescription, I fear.'

'Oh, undoubtedly.' Isabel smiled. 'Though I think Doctor Seaton will prescribe this medicine in fairly liberal doses!'

'A sensible man, I see. And these?' He pointed to the piled up packages. 'Should I rely upon the doctor and his staff to distribute them? They were good enough to agree to my supplying each patient with a small gift. I would not wish to repay that kindness by adding to their burden. They are over-worked enough already if I am any judge of the Army.'

'The medical staff would be only too happy to give out your gifts,' Isabel replied, 'but if you have no objection, perhaps I might perform the delightful task? That way no one will be overworked.'

'No one but yourself, Miss Kenton.' He raised a hand, almost touching her cheek, then let it fall. She looked pale and thinner than when last he had seen her. It was not just the medical staff who were working themselves too hard, it seemed.

'I shall enjoy it.' She led the way to the study, the one room that remained where a visitor could be taken. Though it was by no means suitable for entertaining they would be undisturbed there, for Owen was not working at present.

'I was correct in assuming there are four women . . . er . . . nurses? No more have joined the staff?'

'No, Mr Calcott.' Isabel's green-flecked eyes looked puzzled. 'There are only four nurses here. But why do you ask?'

Looking down at the hat and gloves balanced on his knee, he seemed reluctant to answer. Then, lifting his head to show the smile spreading across his face, he glanced across at her, sitting in a chair opposite his own.

'Because,' he spoke in a stage whisper, 'The only feminine gift I could think of, or anywhere near decently buy by myself, was perfume.' He leaned towards her, carrying on with the charade though his eyes were laughing. 'It was bad enough asking for four bottles of French perfume. I had to go to Birmingham before I could face doing so. I would not have dared ask for the like in Darlaston or Bilston.'

'You would not have been likely to find so expensive an item in either town,' Isabel whispered back.

'But the looks I got would have been the same.' Merriment overtook him. 'I swear the assistant in that shop thought me some kind of ageing Lothario. I tell you, I have not the courage to go back for more, I could not face that woman a second time.'

'You don't have to,' Isabel laughed. 'Though I doubt you lack courage, and you are definitely not old, though as for being a Lothario . . .'

'Why, Miss Isabel Kenton, are you implying that I . . .' He stopped as his own laughter joined Isabel's.

'Can I offer you tea?' Their laughter subsiding, she stood up. 'You will have to excuse my leaving you to get it but everyone is so busy here I cannot ask them to drop their work to make tea.'

'No. No tea, thank you,' he answered quickly. 'I have heard how busy this house is, and what little time you can spare I would rather spend talking to you than taking tea.'

Isabel raised her eyebrows. 'You have heard?'

'Yes.' He glanced again at the hat and gloves on his knee. 'The manager of my Darlaston foundry has spoken of it. He tells me you do not visit your own works so much as you did before this house became a temporary hospital.'

'Your manager?' A gleam of understanding lit her eyes. 'You mean James Hawley!'

'I believe you knew him before he became my works manager?'

He watched as she nodded, the light that had earlier played over the box now playing on her hair, gilding the rich auburn until it became a halo of red-gold fire. He watched the smile curve her lovely mouth, adding to its gentle softness, and felt his heart skip a beat.

'Yes,' Isabel answered softly, her mind already back to the moment of that first meeting with James Hawley. 'He helped me through a crowd. I had gone to watch a rally, a recruitment drive for the Army. I'm afraid people became rather too enthusiastic. Had it not been for Mr Hawley, I might not have broken through without mishap.'

'A recruitment drive was no place for a young woman, especially one on her own.'

'So Mr Hawley told me.' Pulling herself back from her reverie, Isabel smiled again. 'Quite forcefully, as I remember.'

'Good for him! Putting a woman in her place.'

Isabel caught his smile and her own became teasing. 'Is that what you would have done, put me in my place?'

Along the line of his neatly clipped beard, the muscles of his jaw tensed. His eyes darkened and his voice became husky with emotion. 'Had I been the one to rescue you, Miss Kenton, you would not have escaped me so easily.'

Tension clutching her throat, Isabel found it hard to breathe. She had not expected their conversation to take such a turn but it had and now she was at a loss as to how to answer.

'I was never one to enjoy being held prisoner.' She opted for flippancy, afraid her emotions would show if she chose any other response.

Hewett Calcott's eyes were velvet wreathed in smoke. 'You would never be a prisoner with me – unless one can be imprisoned by love, for those are the only chains I could ever set upon you.'

Love? Her breath caught afresh in her throat. Was Hewett Calcott telling her he loved her? Were these words a declaration? Isabel swallowed, trying to free her throat of the constriction in it. Did he, like Owen, love her? Again the question formed in her mind: which of the two did she love enough to marry?

But that question had no right in her mind any more, it should not be there. Had she not already given it an answer? Had she not consented to become the wife of Owen Farr!

'Miss Kenton, Isabel . . .' Hewett leaned forward as he had minutes before but this time there was no laughter in his gold-spangled eyes, only a deep earnestness and something more, something that caught at her heart as she read it. 'There is something I wish to ask you.'

'Oh, and what is it you wish to ask my future wife?'

Neither of them had heard the soft tread in the hall or been aware of the door opening. Now they glanced across the study to where Owen Farr stood smiling at them.

His future wife! Hewett Calcott straightened up, the gentleness leaving his eyes, a band of pain fastening tight about his chest. She had promised herself to Owen Farr! 'Forgive me.' His glance returned to Isabel as he rose to his feet. 'Had I known I would have offered my good wishes beforehand. As it is, may

I offer them now, Miss Kenton? And to you, Mr Farr, congratulations.'

'Thank you.' Moving to Isabel's side, Owen placed a hand on her shoulder. 'I count myself the luckiest man alive.'

'As do I.' Holding gloves and hat in one hand, Hewett held out the other to Isabel who placed her own in it. 'Thank you for receiving me, Miss Kenton.'

'But . . . but there was something you were about to ask me?'

'Isabel is right, Calcott.' Cat-like, Owen's eyes gleamed, bright and challenging, devoid of any trace of friendliness. 'I heard you say so myself. "There is something I wish to ask you." Those were your very words.'

'Of course.' Hewett met the challenge, his own eyes holding the temper of forged steel. 'Your news caused me to forget.' Shifting his glance to Isabel, his eyes softened. 'Now I have heard it, I fear my asking might meet with disapproval.'

'Disapproval?' Owen laughed but the challenge remained in his eyes. 'Surely not? I cannot see a gentleman asking anything of a woman if the request might give rise to discomfort. And if you mean *my* disapproval then you have no grounds for worry. Isabel has made me so happy I could not possibly feel animosity towards anyone.'

Isabel rose as Hewett released her hand. 'Yes, please say what it was you wished to say, Mr Calcott. You have been so kind to the patients in this house as well as to myself that if there is any way I can repay . . .'

'There will never be need of repayment between us!' he intervened quickly, not wanting to hear that she felt indebted to him. 'But with your fiance's permission, I would ask you to accept this.'

Taking a small box from his pocket he laid it on the desk, then with a brief nod to Owen Farr he walked from the house.

Chapter Twenty-Two

A man I think may be known to you. The words had hit Isabel like a blow to the stomach, sending the world spinning around her. She had heard the anxious voice of the nurse, felt the hands of the doctor supporting her, preventing her from falling, but had not had the strength to answer. Mark! her heart had screamed. It *was* Mark after all. He was one of the wounded, could be dying . . . or perhaps dead already! The fear had whirled in her brain, cutting off all thoughts of anything but the horror of losing her brother. It had taken a sharp slap to her cheek to pull her together, a slap she had readily forgiven the apologetic nurse for delivering when the relief had shortly followed, surging through her like a torrent as the doctor had said Mark's name was not on the list read to him over the telephone.

Looking at Braddy and her husband, Isabel felt almost guilty. She had been so heady with joy at hearing that Mark was not among the casualties that the rest of the news had gone over her head. It had not been until the third time that Doctor Seaton had asked if she knew of a man by that name that his question registered at all.

'Tolley,' he had said. 'He was conscripted from Darlaston and this being such a small town we thought there was a strong possibility of your recognising the name, perhaps knowing his family . . . or where we might contact them?' He had smiled apologetically, one hand ruffling his hair once more. 'The Army can sometimes be a little slow in these matters, and a visit from loved ones always proves better medicine than any a doctor can prescribe.'

'Tolley.' She had repeated the name, rolling it on her tongue, her brain still not fully functioning.

'Yes,' Seaton urged gently, recognising that the effects of shock had not yet fully left her. 'Tolley – William Tolley. Apparently his papers show him as coming from Darlaston.'

A frown puckering her brow Isabel had tried to pull her still whirling thoughts together, to apply her mind to what the doctor was saying when all she wanted to do was cry, let the tears of relief wash her mind clear.

'Don't worry if you cannot place the name.' Seaton glanced despondently at the nurse. 'But if we could ask you to enquire of your staff? Should someone recognise the name then at least one of our new patients might receive the Christmas gift he most wants this year: the presence of his family.'

She had turned away, Isabel remembered. She had almost reached the door to the sitting room, forcing herself to repeat over and over again the name the doctor had spoken, settling it in her mind lest by the time she reached the kitchen it was forgotten. 'William Tolley,' she had murmured softly. 'William Tolley.' Then, as memory returned, she had swung about, her eyes wide. 'Billy!' she had gasped. 'Billy Tolley! Of course . . . of course I know him! He is Mrs Bradshaw's nephew!'

Doctor Seaton had smiled then, his tired eyes creasing at the corners. 'Thank you, Miss Kenton,' he had said. 'But for now I must ask you to say nothing to your housekeeper. We must first ascertain the condition of the patient, to see whether or not a visit can be allowed within the next few days. But rest assured,' he had crossed the room to stand beside her, gentleness showing through the fatigue that left his face drawn and pale, 'we will inform his family of his return to England, and they will be allowed to see him at the very earliest opportunity.'

★

They had arrived five days later, ten more men with limbs bandaged and desolation in their eyes. Men who had tried to smile as they were helped into the house, but on several faces tears had glinted. Isabel swallowed hard, still finding it difficult to remember her emotion at the thanks of those men though some words had been barely audible through frost-swollen lips.

Thank heaven they had found room! It had been Bradshaw who had found the solution, reminding Isabel of the solidly built hot houses that had fallen into disuse after her mother's death, Luther Kenton having no great liking for orchids. 'They 'ave a glass roof,' Mr Bradshaw had told her, 'but the walls and floors be as good as the day they was laid, and the heating system should still work, after the woodburner be given a good clear out.' And so it had. As for beds and bedding, Braddy herself had taken care of that. A few words with her other housekeeper friends had brought in all they needed, provided from large houses as far afield as Brownhills and Willenhall, their mistresses 'glad to help', Braddy had said, a firm set about her mouth, 'without 'aving to open their own houses to the wounded'. But whatever had motivated them, conscience or kindness, Isabel had welcomed everything they sent.

And Billy had been among them. Now she watched his aunt, apron thrown over her face as she wept.

'I've told 'er, miss.' Over her shoulder Bradshaw looked at Isabel. 'I've told 'er the lad will be all right, given time. I seen men like this in the last scrap. They just couldn't face no more fightin' so they turned off like. I told 'er and 'er sister, it just takes time.'

'Mr Bradshaw is right.' Isabel knelt beside Letty's chair. 'Doctor Seaton said the same thing: Billy is suffering from shell shock. It is a condition of the mind. Although he has no wound that can be seen he has nevertheless been severely hurt; so much so that he has withdrawn into himself, closed himself off from everything. But with careful nursing and love, he will come back.' Putting her arms about the housekeeper, she laid her head against the woman's shoulder. 'Please believe that, Braddy,' she murmured, her own tears not far away. 'You must believe that. Billy needs your strength and that of his mother, don't fail him now.'

'I won't, Miss Isabel,' Letty sniffed as Isabel released her. 'I know what you says makes sense. It . . . it's just seeing him like that, eyes closed and lying so still, you would think him dead. Our Billy, who was always such a live wire, always on the go. He never gave a toss for anybody save that teacher along of the school. Oh, God, he was such a happy lad, always had a smile for everybody.'

'He will have that smile again, Braddy.' Isabel glanced up at Bradshaw, his hand still resting on his wife's shoulder. 'We just have to pray.'

'We have done that,' Letty mumbled through her apron. 'We done plenty of that and to spare. Me and his mother have spent hours on our knees asking the Almighty to bring him back to us in one piece.'

'And is that not just what He has done? Billy has lost no limb nor been wounded so he cannot walk or see. Your prayers have been answered. God has done his part, now we must do ours. We must not give Billy any hint that his condition has us worried. We must be cheerful whenever we are with him. Doctor Seaton tells me that is the quickest way to recovery for men like Billy.'

'And he be right. I've watched men . . .'

'Seems that's all you be doing now an' all, Arthur Bradshaw!' The apron whipped sharply away from her face, Braddy glared at her husband. 'Ain't you got no work to do, superintending and the like? I don't want you standing about my kitchen like a mawkin!'

His eye catching Isabel's, he smiled. 'Seems like one recovery be well on the way!'

Spooning tea into the large earthenware pot, Isabel set about the task of making tea as Bradshaw departed. God had answered the women's prayers, she thought, as Braddy wiped her eyes on her apron. He had brought the boy home, his body in one piece. But what of his mind, how many pieces was that in? She had said nothing to them of this part of the doctor's conversation with her. 'Who can say?' he had told her, shaking his head. 'Who can say if he will ever recover?'

'Billy Tolley will wake, but the time is not yet come.'

Stepping from the scullery, Sarah Griffin seemed to look beyond the two women who turned to face her. Her mouth tight, stare fixed and vacant, she stood just inside the kitchen.

'His body is awake but his mind be sleeping. Doctors will not bring him back nor nurses neither . . .'

'Sarah!' Isabel spoke quickly, afraid of Braddy's being hurt yet again, but the steady, almost hypnotic voice went on unbroken.

'. . . theirs are not the hands, nor theirs the voice . . .'

Laying the teapot aside, as Braddy gasped, Isabel placed an arm about the housekeeper's shoulder, once more calling the woman's name in sharp rebuke. But as before, it seemed Sarah did not hear her.

'. . . it be a love that speaks not of its own being,' she went on quietly. 'A love that is stronger than the lock that holds his mind. The same love that is felt for you, Isabel Kenton. You think to love two men, one as a friend only, but there is one who stands beside you as voices sing, one who hands you a slip of white paper . . .'

'Mam!' Her face taut, Mary Griffin came to stand beside her mother. 'There be pots in the scullery waiting to be washed.'

As if waking from a dream, Sarah's face took on a puzzled look, brows drawing together as though trying to recall a faded image already lost in the shadows of the past. Then, without a word, she turned back into the scullery.

'Beg your pardon, miss, but my mam, she meant no harm. I . . . I'm sorry, it won't happen again.' Mary told her.

Isabel felt her nerves tingle. Sarah had looked so strange, so withdrawn, and her words . . .

I hope you won't take exception, miss, nor you, Mrs Bradshaw? She never meant to upset you.'

The girl's obvious distress chasing away her thoughts, Isabel smiled though the chill in her blood remained.

'We know that, Mary.' Isabel spoke for both of them. 'Don't worry about it. Far from doing any harm, Sarah has given us fresh hope for Billy. We should be grateful to her.'

'Thank you, miss.' Mary's taut expression softened though her eyes still held their frightened look. 'Thank you both.'

'Eh! What do you reckon to that?' Letty Bradshaw stared at the door Mary Griffin carefully closed behind her. 'I've never seen the wench act that way afore. It seemed like her was in a trance. And Mary – her face were like thunder!'

'Mary thought Sarah had butted in where she was not wanted, that she had eavesdropped on our conversation.'

'Don't seem likely to me,' Letty answered as Isabel returned to brewing the tea. 'Had we wanted to talk private like, I would have told the pair of 'em. I don't think that be what set her hackles rising. It be more than that, it be summat that hasn't been spoken of.'

Handing Letty her tea, the thoughts that Isabel had dismissed returned. Mary had spoken as if the words came from outside her.

. . . you think to love two men . . .

The words, so surprisingly true, set her tingling with nervousness.

. . . but there is one stands beside you as voices sing . . .

Two men! Owen and Hewett. The tea forgotten in her hand, Isabel gazed over to where the kitchen fire glowed softly.

Voices singing. Could that mean a bridal choir? Would it be Owen or Hewett standing at her side then?

'I think that would be very nice, Miss Kenton, and I know the patients will love it. I will write a reply to the school at once.'

Miss Kenton. Isabel watched the nursing sister write. Soon

that name would be hers no longer, soon it would be changed and she would be Mrs Owen Farr. Strange. She'd thought impending marriage would bring more of a thrill, a constant longing for it to happen. But she felt no surge of passion when Owen took her in his arms. Oh, she loved him, she was sure of that, but where was the passion?

'There.' Folding the piece of paper, the nurse handed it to Isabel. 'If you would please give that to the child to return, I will make the necessary arrangements.'

'If it is agreeable and convenient to you, I will accompany a group of children who will sing carols for the patients.' The brief note had been signed 'Emma Patrick'. In the weeks since her older pupils had been helping in the kitchens their teacher had sometimes asked leave to visit the wards. Experiencing the welcome she received there and the gratitude of the men occupying them had caused her to change her mind. 'For this one night,' she had said, discussing her proposition with Isabel, 'and for this night only, I think the pupils may be allowed into the wards. But not those of the more serious cases, of course.'

Looking now at the smiling faces of men seated on an assortment of chairs and stools crammed between the beds on the larger ward, Isabel knew she had done the right thing in giving her home to the military. Her home! Fate certainly had a way of altering things. Only three years ago she had been determined to leave this house forever. *Hers for as long as she lives in it.* Luther's words returned to her. She had repeated them to Owen when he had urged an early wedding, telling him that to leave now, before the war was ended, would mean these men having no place where they could be properly nursed and cared for. He had tried several arguments, one being that they had both given enough already, must they give up time they could spend together? But in the end he had stopped his pleading, though for the first time she had seen anger on his face. *For as long as she lives in it.* The words haunted her mind and with them the sound of derisive laughter. Luther Kenton's laughter. But was that laughter his response to her being tied to this house, or

313

because she felt no real disappointment that her marriage was delayed?

'I think everything is ready.' The senior nurse walked along the narrow space which was all the massed chairs and stools allowed, the starched skirts of her uniform rustling even above the murmurs of the assembled patients. 'Did you ever see such a ward!' She turned to Isabel, tut-tutting several times, but a smile hovered at the corners of her mouth. 'Let us hope no one from headquarters decides to pay us a visit.'

'I wouldn't give them any more of a chance than I be willing to give the Kaiser.' The housekeeper's mouth set determinedly as she glanced at her mistress. 'It will take more than a General or two to deprive the men of this treat.'

'They certainly seem to be looking forward to it.' Isabel cast another glance about the crowded make-shift ward. 'It is a pity they could not all be here.'

The nurse smiled. 'Doctor Seaton agreed to the doors of the wards being left open so those who could not be moved would at least hear the children singing. They will not miss it altogether.'

'And what of our Billy?' Letty's voice trembled. 'His eyes have never opened since he arrived here. Will he be part of it? Will he hear it?'

'We have no way of knowing that, Mrs Bradshaw, until there is some movement or reaction from William, as we explained to you and to his parents. Doctor Seaton is convinced recovery is possible if only we can find the motivation, a trigger if you will that would shoot him . . .'

'It were triggers and shooting caused all this in the first place!' Letty's lashes shimmered with tears.

'It was an unfortunate simile to use, Mrs Bradshaw, I'm sorry.'

Touching a corner of her fresh white apron to her eyes, the older woman sniffed. 'There's no call for you to be sorry, wasn't you started this blessed war! If kings and governments want to fight, it should be them sent on to the battlefield with a gun in their 'ands, not lads that be little more than babbies! I tell you summat, nurse, if they did send out them big nobs there wouldn't never be another war, you can depend on that!'

'Would you like to sit with William? I think I might find another chair from somewhere.'

'Thank you kindly.' Lowering her apron, Letty Bradshaw nodded her gratitude. 'But his mother will be with him. I'd like her to be alone with him for half an hour or so. I will go join them later if that be all right with you. Or mebbe this be Doctor Seaton's chair I be sitting on?'

'Of course you may go to William. And as for the chair, it is not reserved for Doctor Seaton. He will not be present for the carol singing.' Sensing Isabel's glance, the nurse looked in her direction. 'The doctor has not been outside these four walls since we were first assigned here. I. . . ' She hesitated. 'I urged him to take a walk, thought a break from the wards and some fresh air would be good for him. He looks so drawn and peaky. I hope it was not too rude of me? There was no offence intended on either Doctor Seaton's part or my own.'

'And none has been taken,' Letty Bradshaw put in quickly. 'You cast such thoughts from your mind, me wench. You did the sensible thing in getting that young man to take a break. The way he works would put a Trojan to shame.'

At that moment the school mistress led the children into the space left for them and, excusing herself, the nurse went over to where they had grouped themselves in order, boys at the back, girls at the front. Watching them, their noses red from cold, Isabel was transported back to her own childhood when she and Mark had been taken to St Lawrence's church to sing carols before a manger containing wooden figures of Mary and the Christ child. And now Mark was gone, caught up in a war nobody wanted but everybody must endure. A war whose greed for blood and the continued sacrifice of men seemed to know no bounds. Had Mark become part of that sacrifice . . . was that why no letter had come from him for weeks?

'It came upon a midnight clear,
That glorious song of old . . .'

A movement on her left caught Isabel's eye as the clear voices of the children lifted in song. Mary's arm had gone about her mother's shoulders as the woman bent her head to hide her tears, and now as the girl's eyes met her own Isabel read the same fear as was in her own heart.

'. . . O hush the noise ye men of strife
and hear the angels sing . . .'

Hush the noise ye men of strife! Isabel repeated the words silently, each one a prayer, but even as she did so she knew the men of strife would not listen.

One after another the carols filled the room where each man sat silent, transported by children's voices to his own particular Bethlehem, a place where he was surrounded by his loved ones and peace surrounded them all. As the last carol ended they sat quiet and unmoving, unwilling to break the thread that linked them to their homes.

'Mary and I will take the children to the kitchen for a hot drink and a piece of pie.' Eyes still swimming with tears, Sarah Griffin got up from her chair.

'That be right good of you, Sarah. If you two can manage then I'll just pop in to see Billy.' Raising her apron, Letty Bradshaw dabbed it again to her eyes. 'Oh, if only the lad could 'ave heard them carols!'

'Which lad would that be?' Urging the children in the direction Mary and Sarah indicated, the school mistress directed a glance at the still weeping housekeeper.

'It be our Billy.' Letty's voice caught in her throat.

Standing to one side as the last of her charges passed into the kitchen, the school mistress made no move to follow. Then as the nurses began to shepherd their patients back to bed she asked, 'Why would he not hear?'

'He is suffering from shell shock,' Isabel explained as the housekeeper, apron still pressed to her mouth, walked towards the room that had formerly been the dining room but now housed the more seriously injured. 'Mrs Bradshaw's nephew has not spoken or opened his eyes for several weeks. He was brought back from France in that state. It was thought he might recover more quickly in England.'

'The Bradshaws' nephew!' For several seconds the woman thought hard. 'That would be the Tolley boy, am I correct?'

'Why, yes!' Isabel answered, amazed at her memory. 'But it must be nine years since he was at school, I am surprised you remember.'

'Some you *never* forget.' The answer was short but the smile that accompanied it was wide. 'The Tolley boy could be a rogue, but he was a lovable one. Do you think his mother would object to my seeing him while the children finish their refreshment?'

'I am sure she wouldn't, neither would the medical staff.' Isabel caught the look directed towards the disappearing nurses. 'They say visitors do a great deal to aid recovery. Their conversation might trigger Billy into consciousness, supposing he *can* hear.'

Sitting to either side of the bed the sisters looked up as Isabel and the school mistress came quietly into the room.

'Stay where you are.' She lifted a hand as the young man's mother made to stand up. 'Miss Kenton tells me this has been the situation for some weeks now?'

'Arrh, that be the way of it.' Sinking back on to her chair, the woman looked at her son, his face pale and sunken, eyes closed like as effigy carved from marble. 'We don't rightly know how long.'

'Wouldn't matter how long if we only knowed he was going to get well. Doctor says . . .'

'The doctor says he is getting well, Mrs Tolley.' Isabel said quickly, giving a warning shake of her head as the woman turned to her.

'Mrs Tolley, May I speak to you?' Making a beckoning movement the school mistress stepped several paces away from the foot of the bed, speaking quietly to the patient's mother who first stared, a frown creasing her forehead, then nodded and walked back to her chair.

Returning to where she had first stood, the teacher drew in a long breath then set her foot tapping against the floor, shaking her head as Letty Bradshaw's mouth opened.

Tap, tap, tap, tap. The small black boot drummed against the scrubbed floorboards, the sound magnified by the silence of the room. Tap, tap. For long seconds the sound continued, then as suddenly as it had begun it ceased.

'William Tolley!' Her voice quiet but full of authority, the teacher looked at the figure lying motionless, pale face almost one with the white pillows.

From either side of the bed, men with legs strapped to metal hoists watched with pity in their eyes.

'William Tolley!' Slightly lower, the voice took on an undertone of gathering displeasure. 'William Tolley, is that you I see skulking in that corner?'

Braddy's quick intake of breath was audible in the still room. She and her sister reached for each other's hand across the bed.

Her eyes never leaving the motionless form, the school mistress squared her shoulders, hands clasping together across the front of her skirts, mouth firming into a thin hard line, all the time staring at the man in the bed as though at some miscreant child. Taking a deliberately deep breath, she held it for endless seconds. Then, voice honed to razor sharpness, she rasped: 'I see you there, boy, hiding in the corner. Come out here at once!' Raising her hands she clapped twice, a sharp sound that shattered the silence. 'William Tolley, I will not tell you again. Come out here *NOW*!'

The hands clasped across the bed tightened and Isabel's own curled into fists which she thrust against her mouth, trying without success to stem a tide of tears.

At the foot of the bed, slowly and with measured beat, the boot began to tap its rhythm once more.

Against the pillows the young man's head moved. His eyelids flickered then were still. At his side his mother loosed a

318

suppressed sob, burying her face in the coverlet, but the eyes of the school mistress stayed on the pale face as she repeated: '*NOW*, William!'

Beneath the almost translucent lids the man's eyes moved, rolling from side to side as if looking for a way of escape. Then, with a long sigh, he opened them.

'Yes, miss,' he breathed. 'I be coming, miss.'

Chapter Twenty-Three

'I *saw* you!' James Hawley brought his fist down hard on the desk in the lawyer's office. 'Oh, your motor carriage was well hidden! But you – you hadn't got the sense to move away from the road. I saw you, you and that . . .'

'Don't!' Owen Farr's eyes flashed like the sun on water. 'Don't speak ill of Ruth!'

'No.' James Hawley straightened but the anger remained plain on his face. 'No, maybe I should not speak ill of Ruth. Maybe it is you alone at fault, you who are greedy. That is more likely. You want both of them, don't you, Farr? You want Ruth *and* Isabel Kenton. Or should that be you want Ruth and the Kenton money?'

'You go to hell!' Owen spat, shoving himself away from the desk and going to stand beside the window. But when he turned his face was wreathed in a mocking smile. 'Who will believe you, a gutter snipe who hoped to haul himself up by lifting a woman's skirts? You have no proof that you saw Ruth and me together.'

It was true, James thought. He had been alone last night when he had seen the two of them, Owen's hands reaching out as the light of a passing tram illuminated them. There was no one to corroborate what he said. But then, Owen Farr did not know that! His own mouth assuming a cold smile, he countered: 'You were not the only one walking with a companion last night.'

Despite the light from the window being at his back, casting his features in shadow, James saw the sudden paling of Owen Farr's face. The man was afraid. Engaged to Isabel Kenton he might be but that seemed to be of little comfort to him now.

'Isabel will see no harm in my meeting a friend.' Owen recovered quickly.

'Can you be sure of that? When she hears how you took that "friend" in your arms, how you kissed . . .'

'God damn you, Hawley!'

'He might well do that,' James answered calmly. 'But you will not marry Isabel Kenton.' Turning towards the door, he opened it before adding: 'Think over what I have said. Ruth you may have and with no interference from me, but you will not scar another woman's life. There will be no marriage between you and Isabel Kenton.'

Leaving the office, he breathed in crisp cold air, scouring the stench of Owen Farr from his nostrils. He had made it his policy not to interfere in other men's affairs, to live and let live, so why abandon that policy now? Following the road to Darlaston reasons and excuses flitted one upon another through his mind, but only one struck him as important. He was in love with Isabel Kenton! But that did not give him the right to prevent her marrying, to snatch away her happiness . . . But what happiness would there be for her once she found out about Farr's seedy carrying on? The breaking off of the engagement would hurt her for a while, but better that than suffer for a lifetime. Isabel Kenton would find another man to be her husband. Turning up his collar against the cold, James Hawley allowed himself a wry smile. Yes, there would be a husband for Isabel Kenton, though that husband would never be him.

Giving out the last armful of the presents Hewett Calcott had brought, Isabel returned a stream of Christmas greetings. Every single person at Woodbank House had received a gift. She glanced about the ward, seeing the men holding their parcels, reluctant to break open the wrappings. The child in each of them wanted to prolong the pleasure, to keep the magic of the moment, hold it in his heart. Tears threatening, she turned away, unable to join the general laughter that followed a nurse's saying: 'Santa Claus says you are not to open your present until tomorrow!'

Leaving the ward, hung about now with gaudy home-made paper streamers looped with red-berried holly from the garden, Isabel took the stairs to her room. She would have to tackle that last-minute shopping she had been promising herself to do for a week or more. She needed to buy a gift for Owen and of course one for Hewett, but each day so far had come and gone without her doing so.

What was wrong with her? She sank on to the bed, sitting stiff and upright though her fingers writhed together, refusing to be still. Why did she feel so empty, so incomplete? She had received no letter from Mark, but the feeling that held her was more than worry for him alone. It was like a vacuum, a hollow-ness that nothing seemed to fill, and still the cause of it eluded her. She was not ill, Kenton Engineering was functioning well, she was engaged to be married and had a friend in Hewett. Apart from Mark's return home, she had everything she could want. Absently reaching into the drawer set into the small table beside her bed, she took out the gift Hewett Calcott had made to her. He had not waited for her to open it, not long enough even to receive her thanks or be rewarded by a smile. He strode directly from the house as if angry. She traced a finger over the soft leather box, admiring the rich colour. Why had he left so abruptly? They had talked so easily together, enjoying each other's company.

She twisted the box in her hand, tilting it to catch the light from the fire, watching it play over the gold tooling. Hewett Calcott had shown no sign of displeasure, not until . . . She looked up quickly, her gaze drawn towards the dancing flames in the grate. Until Owen had walked in on them! Was there something between them? Had Hewett, like James Hawley, known Owen previously and perhaps had some altercation with him? It couldn't be, Owen would have told her. She stared into the fire's brilliant heart but the question in her own burned brighter. Were the man she was to marry, and the man she loved as a father, enemies?

The man she loved as a father! The box slipping from suddenly nerveless fingers she rose to her feet, the answer to her feelings solid as a stone in her stomach. Isabel Kenton had everything she wanted. Everything except a father! She felt the tide of emptiness rise up to swallow her. *Our Mutual Friend*. The title of the book that still held that damning letter danced before her eyes. Friend or not, they had both known the man to whom it had been written. Her mother and Luther Kenton, both had known the identity of the man who was Isabel's father, and both had died without revealing their secret. Somewhere in the depths of her memory that hated laughter rose to mock her yet again. Luther Kenton had won after all.

'But, my dear, I would much rather you did not go out alone.'

'It will not take very long, Owen.' Isabel lifted her cheek for his kiss.

'Then take the girl along with you.'

Drawing on her gloves, she used the moment to avert her eyes from his as she realised the kiss had done nothing to assuage the emptiness inside her.

She smoothed the gloves slowly over each finger, warding off the need to recognise the new fear beginning to grow in her. But it was not truly new, only the facing up to it was new. She had been so sure, so absolutely certain. So why did she feel no joy in his touch? Could it be that it was not love she felt after all, had she made a terrible mistake in promising to become Owen Farr's wife?

'There is really no need.' Prolonging the moment serving only to feed her fears, she looked up at him, looked into eyes green and bland as a mill pool, eyes that told her nothing. 'Besides, Mary is much too busy helping in the kitchen.'

'Then let your shopping wait until I can accompany you. As your fiancé I really cannot allow . . .'

He could not allow! Memories of her old life taunted her. Luther had so often '*not* allowed'. Was her life with Owen destined to follow the same pattern, to be nothing more than the obeying of his orders?

Seeing the small frown draw her brows together Owen realised the inadvisability of his choice of words. Isabel Kenton had been her own woman for three years, he would need to be careful in the way he phrased things, but only until after they were married. Then it would be his decisions that mattered, and only his, and he would phrase them any way he pleased. Smiling he reached for her, hands holding her upper arms as he looked into her face. 'I cannot allow you to torture me with worry for your safety. That is why I beg you, my love, please do not go alone.'

It was nicely done. Seeing her frown dissolve he congratulated himself on the speed and suavity of his reaction.

'I am no longer a child, to be afraid of the dark,' Isabel replied, wanting to believe in the genuineness of his concern for her but somehow failing to convince herself.

'If only I did not have these damned papers to deal with!'

Releasing herself from his grasp, Isabel returned his kiss and touched her fingers to his cheek. 'But you do, Owen. And as you have said before, the Army is an impatient master. It will not wait.'

Relieved that at that moment the doorbell rang, releasing her from the need to say more, she turned as Mary scurried through from the kitchen, hastily smoothing down her 'upstairs' apron that had been covered by an all-enveloping one belonging to Mrs Bradshaw.

'The mistress be just 'ere, please to come in.'

Isabel smiled and this time the pleasure behind it was real. 'Mr Hawley, good evening.'

Returning her greeting, his glance passed to Owen Farr standing at her back, but he made no repetition of his words.

'You call again . . . Sergeant, wasn't it?'

At his sides James Hawley's hands curled into fists. If only Farr were outside he would knock the insolence from that face. As it was he replied coldly: 'Mr Hawley will suffice now.'

Lifting a hand, Owen Farr made a thorough inspection of well-manicured finger nails. 'Yes, yes, I understand your reticence. Coming up from the ranks, not the same as a commissioned officer, eh, old chap?'

'As you say, not the same.' James Hawley's voice was like chipped ice but a smile curved his mouth. 'But then, you and I are hardly the same sort of man, are we? We are different . . . in more ways than one.'

Behind Isabel, Owen Farr drew in a quick breath. Feeling the tension between them quiver like a bowstring, she stepped forward. 'What can I do for you, Mr Hawley? Have you some business on Mr Calcott's behalf?'

'No, Miss Kenton.' The ice melted from his eyes as he turned his gaze back to her. 'I took the liberty of calling to wish you and your . . .' the pause that followed was tiny but marked '. . . household a Happy Christmas.'

'Thank you.' Isabel's smile deepened. 'A most happy Christmas to you too.'

'Hold on a minute.' Owen came forward, eyes nakedly taunting and malicious. Isabel Kenton might be oblivious to this man's feelings for her but Owen Farr was only too aware of them. James Hawley loved the woman *he* was to marry. The knowledge pleased Owen. He could use it, use it to strike this guttersnipe down! 'Perhaps if Mr Hawley has no business of his employer's this evening he might do us both a service?' Ignoring the hand Isabel placed on his sleeve, he went on, 'He might be prepared to escort you to the town, my dear. What do you say, Hawley?'

For a moment James did not answer. There was something behind Farr's request, something only his devious mind would think up.

326

'No.' Isabel filled the gap quickly. 'No, I would not dream of inconveniencing Mr Hawley.'

'You would be causing me no inconvenience, Miss Kenton. Escorting you would be my pleasure.'

She felt the rush of warm blood to her cheeks. She had walked with this man three years ago after he had hauled her from the midst of that crowd, and had enjoyed walking with him then. Blush deepening she glanced down, fiddling with her gloves, ashamed to own she wanted to take such a walk again. 'No,' she said, a sudden hammering in her heart making the words sound stilted, 'I couldn't, but thank you . . .'

'Then I will leave the damned papers, the Army can whistle for them!'

'No, Owen!' Isabel glanced anxiously at him. 'That will only cause trouble.'

Inside he smiled. He had played his trump card and had won. 'I will just have to take that chance, my dear. I would sooner face the wrath of the military than have you in the town alone at night. Though it will mean Doctor Seaton's reports not reaching headquarters on time . . .'

'Doctor Seaton?'

'Yes.' Owen's smile was smooth as oil on water but his eyes laughed as they met those of the other man. 'Doctor Seaton and I have to work together a couple of times a week, reporting the medical progress of each patient, that sort of thing.'

'Owen, we cannot let Doctor Seaton down.' Isabel began to draw off her gloves.

'And I will not have my fiancée disappointed.' He laid his hand on hers, preventing her from removing her glove completely. 'If you will not allow Mr Hawley to escort you, then I must.'

Embarrassed and confused, Isabel forced herself to look up. 'Mr Hawley, if you are sure it will be no inconvenience then I should appreciate your company to the town.'

'It will take some time to harness Janey to the dog cart,' she apologised as they left the house.

Looking up at the sky silvered by a bright winter moon, James knew he did not want to ride, did not want anything to shorten the time he had with her. 'Why take Janey out of her warm stable? It is only a five-minute walk to the town. But perhaps you do not care for walking?'

'I don't mind.' Isabel smiled as he glanced down at her. 'But, Mr Hawley, do you think we could ride the tram? I have never taken a ride on one and they look so exciting.'

Moonlight on her upturned face, her lovely eyes soft pools of beckoning shadow set his heart racing. If only he could take her in his arms, touch his mouth to hers, if only . . . He swallowed hard. Such dreams were for children. 'Then a ride on a tram you shall have,' he said, 'though I guess it is already on its way through Moxley so it means a sprint.' Grabbing her hand, he ran with her along the drive and out of the gate, the ache in his injured leg forgotten.

He had not wanted the ride but as they clambered breathless on to the tram, her eyes sparkling with pleasure, he felt that never in his life would he be able to refuse her anything.

'Them's pretty rosy cheeks.' The blue-uniformed conductor smiled down at Isabel as he came to collect the fare. 'Be the colour put there by the cold or by that young man o' yourn?'

Selecting two halfpenny tickets from a variety of coloured bundles clipped to a board fastened by a black leather belt to his waist, he inserted them into the punching machine beside it. 'That be a penny.' He held the tickets out for James to take then dropped the bronze coin into a flat leather bag also held up by the broad belt. 'That be a pretty wench you got there.' Isabel dropped her head but that did not deter the conductor. Twiddling the corners of his luxuriant moustache, he grinned. 'You wants to marry her soon, young feller me lad, or I might just make the offer meself.'

'Are they all like that?' Isabel whispered as the man passed down the aisle between the wooden seats.

'No.' Resisting the urge to touch her pink cheeks, James followed the progress of the conductor. 'He is one of the old ones. Conductors these days are mostly women, the men having been conscripted. The women are pleasant enough but you don't get the chatter – I suppose that's due to their worries about their men and families.'

'I can understand that.' She turned her head to the window, looking out into the darkness. It was the same darkness that would be covering Mark, but out there on the battlefield the pinpricks of light would not be shop windows glimmering or the flickering of carriage lamps. They would be the swift flash of tracer fire that heralded bullets.

'Try not to worry, Miss Kenton.' James tried to forget the throbbing in his leg, not yet fully healed of its wound. 'Your brother will come through all right.'

Her eyes still on the window steamed up by the warm breath of the passengers, Isabel nodded but one gloved hand hid the sudden tremor of her mouth. She so much wanted what he'd said to be true.

Reaching across her, he traced a finger over one corner of the misted pane. 'Look,' he whispered. 'Your brother is smiling, that means he is well.'

Looking at the caricature of a round smiling face, its tiny finger-blob eyes slanting sideways, Isabel's own smile returned.

'Bull Stake.' At the rear of the tram the conductor called out to his passengers. 'Terminus, all off!'

'What about him?' Isabel pointed to the small round face smiling from the mist.

Reaching out his hand, James rubbed the glass clean, his mouth turning down as he looked at her. 'No one appreciates art any more.'

'And such a great talent too.' Isabel giggled. 'How a man must suffer!'

Helping her from the narrow bench-like seat that ran down the side of the tram, the mock sadness faded from James's face but his heart was cold and heavy. His murmur lost beneath the noises of people shuffling along the aisle, he added, 'Yes, how a man must suffer!'

It was all so different. Isabel remembered the night she had been caught in that last awful air raid. The shops had been lit then too but soon the dim light of their windows had been increased a thousandfold as the falling bombs had exploded, encasing the buildings in flame. Since then there had been long months when no light had been allowed to show at night. 'Black out' the people called it, which was what it had been: apart from the light of the moon streets had been left totally dark. But there had been no bombing raids since, no silent shape floating overhead carrying death and destruction, and gradually Darlaston had relit its lamps. Now they gleamed everywhere. Candles in jars wrapped around in coloured cellophane glistened like myriad jewels; red, blue, orange and green, they hung in every shop window and draped every doorway, casting a veil of magic over the night.

Watching the almost childlike pleasure flit across her face, James Hawley felt his own misery cut like a knife. If only . . . But there could be no 'if only' for him. Isabel Kenton was far beyond his reach, the man she was meant for someone else. In the darkness his mouth set. Isabel Kenton would never be his – but she would never be Owen Farr's either!

Opposite them, wrapped in scarves and hats, the glow of the lanterns held in their hands golden upon their faces, a group of carol singers began to sing.

'Once in Royal David's City . . .'

Royal David's City! Isabel glanced again at the ribbons of softly glowing colours glistening against the shadows. Surely even that place was no more wonderful than this town looked tonight?

'It is all so beautiful.' She turned as the final notes of the carol drifted away into the night. 'Do you not think so, Mr Hawley?'

'Yes.' Emotion filling his throat, James Hawley looked down into the face of the woman he loved. 'Very beautiful.'

'O little town of Bethlehem,
How still we see thee lie,
Above thy deep and dreamless sleep,
The silent stars go by . . .'

The voices rose again and as she listened Isabel's eyes lifted to the sky, stars thrown across the void like carelessly strewn diamonds. Keep him safe, she prayed silently. Keep my brother safe.

'Where to first?'

The question broke her silent plea. 'I would like to stay here all night,' she answered quietly.

Taking her arm, James drew her from the path of a busy shopper, head swathed in a shawl, arms weighed down with baskets of vegetables. 'Then in the morning they would find you like a beautiful ice maiden . . .'

'. . . claimed by the Ice King as his bride?' She laughed up at him, eyes rivalling the stars. 'Taken to live with him in the Land of Snow forever. How very romantic!'

'Maybe. But does the Land of Snow have shops?'

'Or candle jars wrapped with coloured paper?' Her laugh subsiding into a smile, she turned toward Appleyard's drapery shop. 'Let's not chance it.'

Walking beside her, James smiled. She had not freed herself from his hand.

'My goodness! Have I really taken up so much of your time?' At the far end of King Street, Isabel came to a halt as the clock of St Lawrence's church chimed nine. 'I am so sorry. I . . . I'm afraid I got carried away. I must not keep you a moment longer. Please leave me, I can get a hansom to take me home.'

'Is your shopping finished?'

Isabel glanced at the parcels held in his hands, then at the

walking stick hooked over his arm. She had forgotten his
wound! Lord, how could she have been so insensitive?

'Yes.' She made to take the packages from him. 'It was
thoughtless of me to take so long, I apologise.'

'A man grows a little tired of apologies.' He smiled.
'Especially when he is enjoying the company he is in.'

'Have you enjoyed shopping . . . really?'

'Truth?'

'Truth!' Isabel watched the smile curl about his lips, lifting
one corner of his mouth just a fraction higher than the other,
the way it had so often . . . Suddenly her mind seemed to stand
still; only her heart moved, turning a somersault in her chest.
She had watched that same smile so many times in her dreams,
but why his . . . and why not Owen's?

'Not the shopping . . .'

The smile curved again, and again Isabel felt her heart
lurch. '. . . but being with the shopper, that I have really
enjoyed.'

Unable to speak for the strange sensation flooding through
her, Isabel signalled to a hansom standing at the corner of
Victoria Street.

'You have not seen the best,' James said as the driver guided
the horse across the road, coming to a halt before them.

'The best?' She queried.

Juggling the parcels, he opened the door of the cab. 'The
crib. You have not seen the crib yet.'

The crib. The Christ child lying in His manger of straw, His
mother smiling down on Him while kings and shepherds
worshipped. It was one of the highlights of the year. They had
always been taken to the church each Christmas Eve when they
were children, she and Mark; and there they had stood hand in
hand, silent, bound up in the wonder of the birth of the Holy
Child.

'I have not seen that since Mark . . .'

'Then why not see it now?' James asked gently. 'Who better
to ask for your brother's safekeeping? Who better to understand

your hopes and fears?' Placing the packages on the seat of the cab, he turned to her. 'Will you come?'

Nodding agreement, Isabel waited while he instructed the driver to wait outside the church, then walked with him into the building.

It was the way it had always been. The wooden shepherds knelt in their usual places; roughly carved animals poking their heads over tiny byres watched three kings in brightly painted robes lay their gifts at the feet of Mary, her gown as blue as it had always been. It was all so familiar, so much a part of her past. Only the feeling inside herself was new, the feeling that caused her breath to catch in her throat as the man beside her smiled again.

'Have you told Him your fears?'

'Yes,' Isabel answered faintly.

'Then He will put everything right.'

'What about you? Have you told Him yours?'

Turning, he led the way back along the darkened nave. No, he had not told Him, told of his wish to be with Isabel if only a little longer. That he had not asked for; it could not be granted.

Outside the night sky was heavy with stars, the full moon sparkling on a sprinkling of hoar frost which had turned the earth to crystal. James Hawley gripped the handle of his stick. He would remember this night all his life, for God could give him no more.

Beside him Isabel touched a hand to his sleeve. 'Mr Hawley,' she asked quietly, 'if you really do not mind, would you . . . might we walk back to Woodbank together?'

Chapter Twenty-Four

It had been a wonderful evening. Removing her warm mohair suit, Isabel hung it in her bedroom then slipped on the dress she wore for helping in the kitchen. The shops had looked so pretty with their festoons of candle jars, the carol singers and the stable scene in the church.

Smiling to herself, she glanced at the packages Mary had carried upstairs for her and then at the slim white ticket with its bold black print on the table beside her bed. 'For you, Miss Kenton,' James Hawley had said, pressing it into her hand. 'It will help you remember your very first tram ride.' But she would need no reminder. Every moment of that evening was engraved on her heart. Why had she almost never thought of Owen during the entire time she was out, and why the emotion that had almost overwhelmed her on occasion?

That one was easy to answer! Scooping the ticket into her hand, she crumpled it into a ball. Her first Christmas Eve visit to the town since Mark had gone away to university, then the memories of childhood . . . no wonder she had been a little shaky. It would have been the same no matter who her companion had been! Her fingers closing more tightly about the scrap of paper, she stared at the white-washed wall. Why had she even thought James Hawley could have influenced her feel-ings? They were simply business acquaintances, there was no more to it than that between them nor would there ever be. She was in love with Owen and would soon be his wife. James Hawley meant nothing to her. Uncurling her fingers, she glanced at the twisted paper. *Nothing.* With a quick, almost angry movement she tossed the ticket away. She was going to marry Owen! Staring at the crumpled scrap of pasteboard she fought the sensations sweeping through her, threatening her equilibrium as they had an hour ago. Slowly she picked up the ticket, smoothing away the creases. Opening the drawer of her bedside table, she laid it beside the beautiful leather-covered box. Then, grabbing her packages, she walked downstairs.

She placed the parcels beneath the tree Mr Bradshaw had set on the table in the hall alcove. It was not as big as the ones that had stood in the hall before the war but Braddy had insisted they have it nevertheless. 'A little bread be better than no bread at all!' she had declared. 'We must count our blessings. There be many a house this Christmas will be lacking more than a Christmas tree!'

Looking at the gifts, each of which bore a name, Isabel felt the sting of tears in her eyes. There was no gift carrying Mark's name. *Have you told Him your fears?* she remembered James saying. *Then He will put everything right.* She had to believe that, believe the war would end quickly and the world be put right again. But how did you right the world of those whose husbands and sons had been killed? Reaching a hand towards a branch of the tree, her sleeve caught a parcel, sending it toppling to the floor.

It fell to the back of the table. Annoyed by her own clumsiness, Isabel edged into the alcove, bending to retrieve the fallen package.

'Ruth, I love you, you know how much I love you . . .'

Hand still holding the parcel, Isabel felt her whole body turn to ice. Lost in her own thoughts, she had not heard the door to the study open or the soft footsteps crossing the hall.

'. . . soon we can be together, truly together. We will buy a house – not here in England. No, we will go to Italy or maybe Switzerland. You choose, my love . . .'

336

Hidden in the shadows, Isabel rose to her feet, standing like a statue carved from marble.

'. . . we do not have long to wait. Once I'm married to Isabel Kenton I will have money, and with a bit of luck that brother of hers will never return from France. That will mean all old Kenton's property will be hers . . . ours. Think of it, Ruth, enough money to last a lifetime. A lifetime together.'

Ruth? Isabel's blood ran like iced water in her veins. Owen Farr did not love her! He only wanted her for her money! She should move, run upstairs, anything so she would not have to hear any more. But somehow her feet seemed frozen to the floor.

'No, Ruth, you don't mean that . . . you love me . . . you *must* love me.'

The words, though said in little more than a whisper, carried into the alcove.

'I can't live without you . . . I love you, Ruth, I love you . . .'

Isabel's fingers tightened about the package, crushing the wrapping, but still she could not move.

'It's him, isn't it?' Owen's voice sharpened, the feeling in it striking her like a physical blow. 'Him . . . Hawley. He's been talking to you, hasn't he . . . *hasn't he*? I should have known!'

James? Isabel wondered. Did he mean James Hawley, was *he* the man to whom Owen was referring?

'Well, he hasn't got the Army to protect him this time.'

'Wait!'

'I've waited too bloody long already. This time Hawley is going to pay!'

Hidden by the gaily decorated tree, Isabel felt herself grow faint. She had heard the threat in Owen Farr's voice, heard the slam of the door as he left the house, but it was that one word, 'Wait!' that rang in her head.

It had been said softly yet loud enough to reach her, and just loud enough for her to recognise the voice.

Doctor Seaton's voice!

*

Swinging the motor carriage out through the gates of Woodbank House, Owen swore viciously. 'Hawley – that foundry rat!' He had been the cause of all the trouble in France; had it not been for him none of it would have come out. And now – now he had been to Ruth, probably threatened to go to Isabel Kenton. But Hawley would never speak to her. After tonight he would never speak to anyone again.

'Watch out, you mad-headed bugger! You be like to kill somebody!'

The words came at him out of the glow of the headlights but Owen did not even glance at the figure that leaped into the hedge for safety. All he could hear was Ruth: Ruth telling him there could be no life for them together.

But how . . . how could *he* cause an accident to happen in a steel works? A lawyer had no business . . . no need to be in the works. Yet that was how it had to be, the only way. His thoughts turned as fast as the spinning wheels of the motor carriage. No one would flicker an eyelid at a man being killed there: a crucible tipped too soon, wagon loads of iron ore running out of control . . . there were many ways. But how to implement one of them?

The cries of women frightened by the speed of the motor carriage, the angry shouts of men waving their fists, made no impression on Owen as he swung the racing vehicle sharp to the left. He could not do the job himself but there would be those who would. After Pinfold Street the road became narrower, streets twisting and turning, box-like houses almost touching the sides of the motor carriage.

Bumping against one as he followed the maze of unlit thread-like streets, Owen's sanity returned. Motor carriages were not a feature of areas such as this; his would be remembered, perhaps recognised. He had to find a man who worked in the foundry Hawley managed, a man who would do what was required and ask no questions. But he must take care. Anger led to careless-ness and thence to mistakes. Easing his foot off the accelerator,

Owen breathed long and slow, the sharp bite of the night air clearing his brain.

What a pity this had not happened a week ago! A cold smile settled on his lips. He could have arranged an unexpected gift for Hawley, a gift to be delivered on Christmas Eve. Well, that gift might be a day or two late but it would still be delivered!

Catching a glimpse of the lamp that burned off toxic gas from the sewers, lighting the crossing point for trams, Owen turned the motor and followed the road to the Bull Stake.

'You should have kept your mouth shut, Hawley!' he muttered, bringing the carriage to a halt outside the Cross Hotel. 'You should have kept quiet . . . and lived!'

The motor carriage would not seem so out of place here, the hotel was a regular haunt of the town's businessmen, a place where they enjoyed more than a glass of wine and a light supper. Owen leaned against the hard leather-covered seat, both hands still holding the steering wheel. The type of man he was looking for would not be found in this establishment. He needed to know the names of a few of the less reputable beer houses, drinking parlours likely to be frequented by men not too choosy as to how they might earn fifty pounds. Across the street a group of men, laughing and calling bawdily to each other, stepped from a dimly lit public house. Owen's cold smile returned. A place such as that.

The engine still throbbing, he reached forward to turn it off. That would mean cranking the thing again when he was ready to leave but he could not draw attention to himself by leaving it running. His finger on the switch, he froze. There, coming towards the junction! Was it him? Eyes narrowing, focusing on the tall figure, a long overcoat not quite hiding his limp, Owen watched as the man passed the lighted window of the hot pie shop. There was no question, he would know that face anywhere.

His hand jerking back from the switch, he snatched at the

hand brake, jamming his foot down hard on the accelerator. He would need no hired killer, he would do this job himself!

Beneath him the motor carriage swayed as the powerful engine roared then shot forward, careering towards the crossing like some crazed animal.

In the darkness that was his conscious mind, Owen heard the screams of women as they grabbed their children, pulling them into shop doorways or holding them against the buildings, shielding them with their own bodies; but none of it made any impression, only the figure turning now to stare into the glare of the headlamps was real to him.

'Seems there's been an accident,' said Arthur Bradshaw, stepping into the kitchen. 'A man has been injured along of the Bull Stake, pretty badly as I heard. They've brought him here, miss, this being the closest 'ospital. It were here or the Sister Dora, and Walsall be a fair step away.'

James! Breath catching in her throat, Isabel remembered the words Owen had flung behind him as he had stormed from the house. Standing in that alcove, stunned by the disclosure of his true feelings for her, she had thought the call for him to wait had been made by Doctor Seaton. But she had been wrong, that had been an illusion, a trick played by her mind, for when she had stepped from the shadows the hall had been empty. Whoever Ruth was had followed Owen from the house. Forcing herself to cross the hall, she had gone to the kitchen, avoiding the piercing look that told her Mrs Bradshaw knew something was wrong.

'What sort of accident?' Now Letty laid aside the knife with which she was carving ham, glancing across to her husband as she wiped her hands on her apron.

'One of them motor carriages.'

'I might 'ave known!' Letty said, shaking her head disparagingly. 'I said it afore and I'll say it again: them there things be dangerous. They shouldn't ought to be allowed, not on roads where people has to walk. Folks is bound to be killed.'

Killed! Isabel felt her hands tremble. Had James Hawley been killed . . . was that what Owen had intended when he had said he was going to pay?

'Was . . . was anyone else involved?'

'I don't rightly know, Miss Isabel,' Bradshaw answered. 'I didn't see the folk who brought the chap in, they went with the doctor apparently, it was one of the nurses told me what happened. Her mumbled something about the motor carriage making straight for a fellow on the other side of Pinfold Street, but that be foolish talk. More like something went wrong with that machine, they don't be so easy to handle as a horse.'

'If that be what they call progress then it might be better for folk if progress hadn't been made!' Taking a loaf of bread, Letty began to add more slices to the pile Mary was buttering. 'Best get the big teapot, Sarah. Strikes me there will be a few extra wanting a cup of tea by the time this be over.' She glanced over to where her husband still stood. 'No good standing idle,' she said tartly. 'If you've no more to do out there then I can find you plenty here.'

'I was seeing to the stoves, stoking them up for the night. Promises to be a cold one, the moon be high and almost white.' At the door that led to the yard he turned. 'If I be needed, send Mary to give me a shout.'

'Do you think that man be hurt bad, Mrs Bradshaw?' Mary glanced up from her task.

The housekeeper let out a long breath. 'I don't know, wench, but this much I do know – it's going to be a sorry Christmas for some poor family.'

'Excuse me, Mrs Bradshaw, may I come in?'

'Of course you can.' The last of the bread sliced, Letty laid aside the knife as she answered. 'Is there summat I can do? We heard as how there had been an accident.'

The nurse stepped further into the kitchen, the light of the gas lamps lending a lemony tinge to her high starched cap and stiff apron that reached to the hem of her grey skirts.

'Will the fellow be all right?'

'Doctor Seaton is still with him.' The answer was non-committal but the woman's eyes told it all.

'Eh, the Lord help him,' Letty sighed again.

'Do the people who brought him here know who he is?' Isabel leaned against the table, holding on to it for support. 'Have they said his name?'

'I'm sorry, Miss Kenton, but I can't give you any information. Doctor Seaton will make a full report in due course.'

A full report? Isabel wanted to scream. Was that all they thought about, making a full report! Was that the way of the Army? Make a report and damn people's feelings!

'Miss Kenton,' the nurse said again, 'Sister sent me to tell you the injured man is asking to see you . . .'

Isabel swayed, the colour draining from her cheeks. They had enjoyed a pleasant evening together, laughing over the silliest things; his eyes had been so soft and warm as they'd stood before the stable scene in the church, so full of kindness as he had spoken of Mark. And now . . . she felt her throat fill with nausea . . . now he was dying.

'She also said to tell you that should you feel you are not up to it . . .'

Forcing herself upright, Isabel answered. 'It . . . it's all right. Of course I will come.'

Following the quick-footed figure of the nurse, she heard the low murmur of men talking in the rooms she had turned into hospital wards, heard the occasional chuckle over a shared joke – a sound she would never hear again from James Hawley.

'Doctor Seaton and the patient are in Ward Three.' The nurse pointed to the large sitting room. 'The bed at the end.'

Left alone Isabel hesitated. How could she go in, how could she talk to him? But how could she not? He had not turned from her when she needed support, she must be strong for him now. Pushing open the door, she walked into the ward, the greetings of the men falling away as they saw the pallor of her face.

At the far end screens that two schoolgirls had covered in pretty checked cotton were drawn around a bed. Behind them there was silence. Drawing a last deep breath, she pulled them slightly apart.

'Miss Kenton.' Doctor Seaton straightened up, the stethoscope he had been using falling against his chest. 'Thank you for coming. The patient . . .'

But Isabel was not listening. She was staring at the man standing on the opposite side of the bed. She was staring at James Hawley. He was not dying! Her brain reeled, her mouth fell open. He had not been knocked down by a motor carriage!

'Miss Kenton, I told nurse to say you did not have to come.' Voice crisp as her starched uniform, the Nursing Sister caught her elbow, steadying her as she swayed. 'Let me take you back to your room.'

'No! No, thank you.' Isabel's eyes lifted to Sister's calm, authoritative gaze. 'I wanted to come.'

'If you are sure?' Releasing her arm, Sister stepped back, making room beside the bed.

'Isabel . . . Isabel, I . . .'

Mind still reeling, she looked down at the figure in the bed, only his face showing above a white sheet that was slowly being stained red. 'Shh!' She touched her hand to a head of tousled blond hair. 'Rest now, Owen,' She whispered, 'we can talk later.'

'There . . . there will be no time.' The swollen lips hardly moved but the words were distinct. 'I have to tell you – I was going to take your money. I . . . I was going to rob you.' He laughed then gasped with the pain of it. 'I was going to rob you, like a common bloody thief!'

'No, Owen.' Isabel smiled, her sight blurred by gathering tears. 'You would not have robbed me, you would never have hurt me.'

He laughed again, making a gurgling sound in his throat. 'Ever the faithful fiancée, Isabel. But you are wrong. I *would* have

343

hurt you, as I hurt Ruth . . .' Eyelids closing, he breathed rapidly, short shallow breaths that rattled in his lungs; then he was looking up at her again, green eyes unnaturally bright. 'It was not Ruth . . . never blame Ruth.' The words came soft and faint on his last faltering breaths. 'It was me, I was the one . . . Ruth did not want . . . want any part . . . but I . . . I forced myself on . . .'

Lifting one hand, he reached towards her, but at almost the same moment it fell to the bed. His eyes closed and his head slipped to one side, a trickle of blood oozing from his mouth.

'Isabel' he murmured, 'tell them . . . I lied. I was to blame, only me. Tell Ruth . . . tell . . . I'm sorry.'

But Isabel did not answer. She was staring at his throat above the dislodged sheet. Staring at the chain from which hung a tiny red-gold bell. The necklace that had been a twenty-first birthday present from her brother, the necklace that had been snatched from her neck weeks before. *I could not resist it.* She seemed to hear Mark's words as he had placed it around her throat. *A bell for Bel.*

'Owen.' It broke quietly from her lips. 'Oh, please . . . no!'

'Come, Miss Kenton.' Sister took her arm again as Doctor Seaton drew the sheet upward. 'There is nothing more you can do.'

It was *her* necklace. Isabel walked slowly up the stairs, eyes seeing nothing but the tiny golden bell hanging from Owen's throat. He could not have stolen it, it was not he who had snatched it from her neck in that bombed out shop, not he who had been about to rape her, of that she was certain. Yet it was her necklace, the one Mark had given her. So how had Owen come by it? Had he perhaps bought it from the man who had stolen it?

Going into the cramped room she had assigned herself, she leaned against the closed door. That had to be the answer. But would he not have recognised it as belonging to her? He must have seen her wearing it. She raised one hand to her throat, fingers touching the high collar of her dress. Perhaps not. She had taken to wearing it beneath her clothing since Mark had been posted abroad, as if by doing so she could somehow guard him from harm, as if she were holding him safe. And she *would* keep him safe. Folding her hands, she closed her eyes in silent prayer.

Somehow she would keep him safe.

Hi, Sis!

Drawing a startled breath, Isabel's eyes flew open, her hands falling to her sides.

'Mark!' She stared into every corner of her shadowed room. 'Mark?'

But nothing moved among the shadows, no voice marred the silence. A half sob falling from her parted lips, she stumbled to the bed. The voice had sounded so clear, so real! But it was not real. The words had been spoken only in her imagination.

Don't worry, Bel.

Sinking to the bed, she listened to the voice in her mind, the sound so real to her that Mark could almost be standing at her side. At that moment she felt she could reach out and touch him, put her hand in his as she always had when they were children.

Don't worry about anything.

Holding her breath, afraid that to release it would dispel the beloved voice, Isabel sat perfectly still.

We have each other, Bel, nothing will ever change that. We will always be together, we are part of each other. I love you, Sis.

Tears sparkling on her cheeks, she whispered, 'I love you too, baby brother.'

'Can I go now, sir?' The small man twisting his cap in his hands stood awkwardly in the doorway to the study. 'I've told you all I know. The motor carriage come hurtling from King Street way, straight across where Pinfold Street meets the junction of Walsall and Wednesbury Roads. Straight across he come, and the tram . . . well, that couldn't stop, not that quick. Slammed right into that automobile, it did. Hit it sideways on. I reckon that bloke in there,' he gave a sideways movement of his head, 'well, it be my opinion he never seen the tram. Wherever he was in such a hurry to get to, I bet it was no 'ospital bed.

'I helped get him out from under that carriage and do you know what he did? He grabbed my wrist and laughed. It be true – he laughed! 'Tell them,' he said, 'tell them it were not Ruth, it were me to blame.' Then he passed out and that gentleman over there helps me to put him on my wagon and we brought him here, you being the nearest doctor like. So if it's all right with you, sir, I'll be off 'ome.'

'Thank you.' Seaton nodded. 'I have no doubt the police will be wanting a word with you.'

Twisting his cap nervously, the little man glanced at the desk. 'Arrh, well, I've put where I lives on that piece of paper, and if I ain't there then my Molly will know where it is I can be found. So I'll say goodnight to you. Goodnight, miss.'

Waiting until James Hawley returned from seeing the man out, Isabel said: 'I overheard Owen talking in the hall after returning from shopping this evening.'

'Then you knew?'

'About his wanting my money not me? Yes, Doctor Seaton, I knew.'

'And the rest?'

Isabel glanced over to where James Hawley sat hunched in a chair. 'If you mean, did I hear him speak of Ruth, then yes. But that is all I know. I could not hear the other person's voice clearly, except for one word that carried quite distinctly. I . . .' She turned again to Seaton. 'I could have sworn, just for a moment, that the voice I heard then was yours, Doctor Seaton. I apologise for my thoughts.'

'Don't apologise. You were correct in thinking I was the one to whom Owen was talking.'

'But I do not understand?' Isabel frowned. 'He called the person Ruth, he was talking to a woman.'

Holding up one hand as James made to intervene, Seaton

gave a sad smile. 'No. Don't let's hide things away any more. I *am* Ruth. My name is Rutherford. Rutherford Seaton, known to Owen as Ruth. It is a long story, Miss Kenton, long and rather painful.' Lowering himself into the chair behind the desk, he placed his hands on its polished surface.

'It began in France over a year ago. I was the medical officer assigned to the unit in which both Owen and James served. The trenches were under constant bombardment, even at night the troops received little rest from the fear of yet another attack and even less sleep from rats milling about their feet, nibbling away at corpses not yet cleared from the trench. There was so much fear . . . so much stress that when Farr's behaviour began to deviate I conveniently labelled it under the same heading. Stress manifests itself in so many different ways, I did not look for any other cause.'

'Seaton, you were not to know . . .'

'Then who was?' Bowing his head, the doctor was silent for a moment before adding: 'I was the doctor, I should have recognised his behaviour for what it was instead of hiding things from myself behind a diagnosis I knew to be wrong.'

'You did it to save the man's neck!' James banged his fist against the arm of his chair. 'You can't blame yourself for that.'

'There is no one else to blame.' Seaton looked at him bleakly. 'And now the man is dead.'

'Doctor Seaton.' Isabel leaned forward, touching his hand across the desk. 'There is no need to tell me anything of what happened in France. What is passed is passed.'

'Passed!' He gave a soft hopeless laugh. 'Passed but not dead. I don't think it will ever die, at least not until I do.'

Pushing himself out of his chair, James walked across to the bookcase, staring at the neat rows of books inside. 'What good will talking about it do? Raking over dead ashes never lit a fire.'

'No, it did not.' Seaton smiled. 'But it clears the grate. And that is what I need to do – clear the grate, so to speak. And if you do not mind, Miss Kenton, I would like you to stay while I do so. Will you?'

347

She did not want to stay. The horror of all that had happened in so short a time was undermining what little remained of her self-control. Any moment now the slender thread that held her together might break, but she had to take that chance. Risk her own sanity to help this man whose face displayed a need greater than her own. Touching his fingers once more, she nodded.

His hands remaining on the desk as if to steady him, he drew in a long breath. 'Farr began calling into the hospital tent on a regular basis: a headache, a sore foot, all trivial things. At first I took no notice. Then, when no one else was present, his attitude would become over friendly. Again I told myself the man was suffering from stress, trying to compensate for the lack of a mother's comfort.

'Then he started to invite himself into my personal tent. I would wake and find him there beside me, vowing that he loved me. No sort of advice seemed to work on him. When I threatened to have him placed on report, he broke down in tears. Of course I know now I did not help him by not reporting his behaviour, but there was so much out there to send a man over the edge! I believed that having him up before the top brass, possibly court martialled, might lead to just that or worse. I kept telling myself the war was all but over, that the next day would see an Armistice and Farr would be among the first shipped home. But of course that did not happen.

'Then came the day of the first push for Thiepval Ridge, a day that brought the wounded pouring in faster than I could have them transferred to the field hospitals; but for all the ones that dragged themselves or were carried back, I knew there were more, many more, still lying out on the battlefield, waiting for the help that could not reach them . . . and . . . and I'm afraid I broke.'

For a brief moment Isabel stared at him, perplexed. Was he telling her he was a coward, that he had deserted his post, run from the line leaving wounded and dying men to fend for themselves? That could not be true. This man was the very soul of kindness, his devotion to the patients in his care shone from him like a beacon. She said gently, 'You said yourself, stress is shown in many different ways. You must have been under the most severe kind. Anyone can be forgiven for breaking under such terrible circumstances.'

'Yes, he told you stress makes men do many things they would not normally do,' James intervened, his face drawn with anger and tension. 'What he has not told you is that he went out alone to treat those men still lying in the field; that all night and most of the following day he stayed with them, treating where he could, comforting where treatment was no use – and all the time he was under enemy fire. Shells bursting too close, sniper's bullets whistling past his ears, death poking its finger in his back, every minute of every hour!

'What he has not told you is that *I* found him, the man he had been trying to save already dead on his back, but still the doctor would not let him go. He was crawling with him, trying to get him back to our lines! Is *that* the behaviour of a man who broke? The only breaking Rutherford Seaton did was to give in to the compassion that was in him. And then when we got him back, that swine . . .!'

'James was the one got me back,' Seaton went on as the other man seemed unable to continue. 'It seems that in my absence Farr went a little crazy. I was told afterwards by one of my orderlies that James got him away before any officer could witness it. But that did not stop Farr. He came back night after night, always waiting until I was alone. Then one evening the Divisional Commander chose to pay me a visit. Farr declared to the end that someone had informed . . .'

'That someone being me!' James laughed hollowly. 'But it was not. I wanted to inform but I couldn't stand the thought of the consequences.'

'No, it was not you, James.' Seaton smiled thinly. 'It was me!'

'You!' Dark brows pulled together in disbelief, James Hawley stared at the man whose life he had saved. 'You informed Division?'

Fingers pressed against his lips, the doctor nodded. 'I came to see there was no other way. Farr's illness had gone too far. If he had transferred his obsessional behaviour from me to someone else, there could have been serious consequences. The next recipient might not have been so ill disposed to it. I asked one of the orderlies to report to the Officer of the Day and put forward my request to speak with the Commanding Officer. But I did not expect to see one of such high rank. It seems a report of my going over the top without orders had reached head-quarters, and they wanted a word with the doctor whose brain seemed to have gone absent without leave. I was still pretty sick, the wound to my shoulder had become infected so I had been given a dose of something to put me to sleep, but Farr must have thought I was unconscious, maybe dying. That was the final thing that really tipped him off balance. Somehow he got my arms fastened about his neck and was holding me in his, weeping and vowing his love, when the Commander walked in.' Seaton looked across at Isabel. 'The outcome was Farr's dishonourable discharge for action unbecoming. He was drummed out of the Army.'

'Then Owen was not wounded?' She whispered.

'No, Miss Kenton. That was another fantasy of his.'

On the mantel shelf the clock ticked loudly. 'And you, Doctor Seaton?' Isabel asked at last.

'Yes.' He laughed quietly. 'What of me? The Army could not be sure, you see. In their eyes I was as suspect as Farr. So I too was sent home, though due to a chronic shortage of doctors I was not dismissed the service.'

'But surely they believed you? You reported what was happening, you would not have done so had you . . .'

'Had I welcomed Farr's attentions? Or maybe I had reported him only when I felt things were getting too hot. That was the line the prosecution took. That had there been no question of complicity, agreement to what took place, I would not have allowed it in the first place, much less let it go on for so long. Their argument seemed feasible in the absence of proof to the contrary. The Army could not be sure. My posting to this country was not a dishonourable dismissal, so they told me, but I was removed from my post nonetheless.'

'And sent here!' James snorted. 'Christ, have they no sense at all? Didn't anyone have the gumption to check on where Farr lived?'

Pushing himself wearily from his chair, Seaton crossed to the door. Opening it, he said over his shoulder, 'That will no longer be a problem.'

Chapter Twenty-Five

There were four of them. Isabel flicked the corners, her eye following each as it slipped beneath her thumb. Four letters fastened together with a length of tape that might once have been white but now was brown with splashes of grey. Four letters from Mark. She had carried them to her room, wanting to be alone when she read them, not wanting Braddy and the others to see the tears she knew she would be unable to hold back.

She riffled the corners of the envelopes again. She had waited so long for word from Mark yet now, perversely, did not want to open his letters. Was that feeling born of fear or simply of wanting to prolong the pleasure of expectation? She had done the same as a child: longed for the gifts of Christmas or birthdays then delayed the opening of them, wanting the delicious thrill of not knowing to go on and on. Mark had always snatched away the wrappings from his gifts, eager to get to the contents.

Turning the bundle of letters in her hands, she looked for some official note of explanation as to why they had all arrived together. But there was none. There must have been a hold up somewhere; Mark would not write four separate letters to her only to send them all together. Loosing the tape she felt the cold waters of fear lap the warmth of her joy.

Opening the first envelope, she slid out a folded sheet of

paper. It was dated December. Four months ago! The coldness gathering in her, she began to read.

'*My dear sister . . .*'

Isabel felt her heart turn over. He always began his letters to her with the same cheery 'Hi, Sis'. Why not this one?

'*I went to visit Goosey's grave today.*'

Stunned, Isabel stared at the words. Mark's friend was dead! Slowly, her hands shaking, she read on:

There are so many little cemeteries, each planted with row after row of crosses. So many crosses! And each all that is left to mark a man, a life! The buried dead sleep in their pitiful graves while the unburied dead cry out to heaven. Why are we doing this, Bel? What has driven the world to madness? What evil drives man to kill man, country to destroy country? All around me I see the faces of men tortured by the pain of seeing comrades snatched away, friendships severed by the cold hand of death. So I say to you: Cherish your friends, Bel. Do not turn away from those who wish you well for one day you may lose them as I have lost a good and true friend, one I miss with a pain too deep for tears. Every night I ask: How much more, oh God, how much more? But with every new dawn the guns awaken.

Yet with each new day there comes also the chance of a letter from home. Without that to hope for the agony of mind would be more than I could stand. Your letters give me hope, and I await each one with the same gladness. That you at least, dear Bel, have not let go of a proper perspective on life; that your faith holds good. That is the beacon which, God willing, will one day light me home. I implore you, never lose your hold on life, never let the unhappiness of this war close itself about your heart; do not allow its bitter seeds to take root within you for the fruit of that tree is withered and dry.

It is growing dark now, a sunset beautiful as any I have seen paints the western sky. (So much like the glow that lights the skies of Darlaston when the furnace gates are lifted.) But when

*it is gone and all is shadows, I shall quote the words of a poem
written by a fellow officer.*

> *Deep in the slumbering night hide me away,*
> *Where I may gaze upon unmoving stars,*
> *And feel the scented airs around me play . . .*

> *Pray for me, Bel, pray for me!*
> *Your loving brother,*
> *Mark*

Holding the letter close to her breast, the tears fell
unchecked. What was happening out there, what were those
men living through, what hell were they dying in? There was so
much in Mark's letter revealing his untold misery that she could
not bring herself to read the others. Not yet. She could not read
them yet. Her soul would not contain any more tears. Opening
the drawer of her bedside table, she slipped the letters inside then
stood looking at the leather-covered box and the tram ticket
beside it. *Cherish your friends, Bel. Do not turn away from those who
wish you well . . .* Mark's voice seemed to echo in her mind. But
was that not exactly what she had done? Turned them away. She
had continued the business of the works, but any meetings with
Hewett Calcott or James Hawley she had kept brief to the point
of rudeness. She had closed herself off, built a barrier to hide
behind. But *what* was she hiding? She touched a finger to the
white ticket. A broken heart? No, she had not loved Owen, that
much she had already realised before hearing his words that
terrible night. Injured pride then? No, not even that. Slowly she
closed the drawer. Her own pride she could overcome, but not
the taint of bastardy! She would have told Owen. Risked his
noising it abroad, using it as the reason for their marriage not
taking place. And she could have expected nothing less; he
would hardly have told friends and family that the woman to
whom he was engaged no longer loved him. But now she would
tell no one. Never again would she come that close to a man.

Tears still wet on her cheeks, she lifted her head. 'Laugh, Luther,' she murmured. 'Laugh as you always did, as you always will.'

'I'll put it to you plainly, there is no point in beating about the bush!' Hewett Calcott looked squarely at the man whom he had made manager of his Darlaston steel works. At first he had wondered whether his action might not have been a little rash, such a young man being put in charge. But Hawley had proved himself more than equal to the job and to handling the men; they had accepted him, the few older and more experienced, those exempt from Army service, recognised his knowledge and skill with steel as being equal to their own, while the younger ones, those serving time until they were of an age to be snatched away, respected the firm but fair treatment he gave them. Recognition and respect. No wonder he had been given such rapid promotion in the field.

'I intend to expand the place I bought from Jago Timmins's sister,' Hewett told him now. 'Probably demolish the house, I will never live in it. I thought of putting up a factory on the site, possibly producing engines or gear boxes for motor carriages, for much as I dislike them I fear they will not go away. They are a part of the future, one we must accept. The point I am making is this: I need a partner. Someone who knows steel, can handle men, and above all someone I can trust. I am offering that partnership to you.'

'To me!' James was thunderstruck. A partnership? It could not be true, he had heard wrongly.

'That is what I said.'

Outside the small office the clang of steel leaving the rolling beds rang in rude harmony with the shouts of men stripped to the waist except for the sweat-cloths circled about their necks, bodies glistening as they shovelled coal into the glowing maw of a furnace or strained to tip a crucible. James heard it all unconsciously as he struggled to comprehend what his employer had said.

'Well!' Hewett picked up his tall hat. 'Do you want it or don't you? It shouldn't take that much thinking over.'

'Mr Calcott.' James forced himself to concentrate. 'I don't understand. You know my situation. The money I earn is the money I have . . . *all* I have. There is none with which to buy myself into the smallest business, much less a partnership in yours. The fact is, sir, I have nothing to bring to such an agreement.'

After placing his hat on his head, Hewett drew each glove slowly over his fingers. 'James,' he said, easing the last one into place, 'I made no mention of money because money is not what I need. What I *do* need I have already listed. You possess each of those qualities. I have found you honest, trustworthy and hard-working. Those are the attributes I wish to bring to my business. Those and those alone are all I would take from any man in exchange for a partnership. And I would very much like that man to be you.' Lifting his glance, he held the younger man's still dazed eyes. 'So what do you say . . . can we make it Calcott-Hawley Steel?'

'Sir, I . . .'

'Not "Sir".' Calcott smiled as he held out his hand. 'From now on it is Hewett.'

Outside the spring sunshine glistened on dust-covered roofs and turned chimney stacks to gold. Following Hewett Calcott across a yard that seemed no longer to be cluttered with heaps of rusting metal and clinkers, the waste drawn from the coal fires of the furnace, James wondered if what had happened inside that office was as much of an illusion. A partnership with Hewett Calcott? Real . . . or as fake as the gold on those stacks?

'I see by the look on your face that you still do not believe me.' Hewett smiled. 'But tomorrow, when the papers have your signature, then you will. Meantime, come with me and look over the house that goes along with the position.'

Built a little way from the town and its belching smoke stacks, the house was of fine red brick. Its own chimneys, tall and graceful, rose from a slate roof that topped windows of an elegant bow top design, while around it poplars were showing the first signs of leaf.

'It will be a bit of a ride from here to the works.' Climbing from the carriage, Hewett entered the door already opened by a maid in a white apron, her brown hair coiled neatly beneath a frilly lace cap. 'But then the Leys be a prettier part of Darlaston, with cornfields in place of steel works.

'I furnished the place and set a staff to run it,' he went on as he handed his hat and gloves to the maid. 'But that you must do over. Fit the house up to suit yourself.'

'I can see nothing I would want to change.' James followed him into a large airy room filled with light from spacious windows beyond which could be seen the garden.

'Well, maybe not, but chances are your wife will once you are married. They like to set their own stamp on things, which is why I left the garden for . . .'

For his own bride to design? Were those the words he had left unsaid? Despite the beard, James saw the other man's jaw set. Had he bought this house thinking to share it with a woman, and had she refused him? Was it Isabel Kenton who had refused him, or was it this house she had refused? Hewett Calcott's voice entered his ears but the gates to his consciousness were locked against it. She had begun to receive visitors, so Seaton informed him one evening when they'd played chess together. It seemed she was finally over the shock of Owen's death. But why refuse Calcott? The man loved her, a blind man could see that, and Isabel Kenton was not blind. Besides which she had strong feelings for the man. So why refuse him?

'. . . I think it has all it needs should you wish to move in straight away, but that decision is yours to make. Keep what you will, chuck out what you don't like.'

They were already back at the front door, Hewett taking his hat and gloves from the girl who bobbed him a curtsey.

'The house has no name yet.' He took up the reins as James climbed into the carriage. 'That too I thought to leave for . . . for you to choose.'

Not me, James thought as the carriage rolled away. You had not thought it to be me would name this house. No, nor any man.

It promised to be a good summer. Isabel watched the rays of the setting sun spread gold and carmine against a sky cloaking itself with purple. *As beautiful as any I have seen.* Mark must have watched a sunset such as this. Pray God he was watching this one safe somewhere. She had read the other letters but that one written last as proved by the date, had plagued her heart with its pathos. Mark had lost a good friend, and only his letter had prevented her from doing the same. But that had not happened. Hewett Calcott had shown no resentment of her seeming coldness towards him during the weeks since Owen's death, and neither had James Hawley.

Owen! The sadness was still there, not for his betrayal of her but that one so charming and amusing should have come to live a life that brought such misery to himself and others.

The breeze across the garden was warm with scents that promised summer. Poor Doctor Seaton! He had seen it all as somehow being his fault, saying he should have left as soon as he knew Owen was here, living so close to Darlaston. He had applied for a transfer, the senior nurse had confided, but had been told there was no replacement for him. So he had stuck things out for the sake of his patients, yet still he blamed himself.

Everyone is so kind and patient, she had told Mark in a letter. They think I have lost the man I loved, but the truth is I was not in love with Owen Farr. I bitterly regret his death but I realise that to have married him would only have brought us both unhappiness. She had been about to write how confused she was, how much she needed him to help sort out her life. But in the end she had written neither of those things. Mark had enough to contend with, he needed to hear that all was well with her, she could not tell him it was not. She could not tell him that the confusion of finding herself in love with two men had never really left her. She loved Hewett Calcott, that was clear, but it was not a love born of longing, of waiting to hear his voice, wanting the feel of his mouth on hers; nor was that the kind of love she had held for Owen. He had been amusing and courteous, paying attention to her until she had thought herself to be in love, but that love was an illusion, a dream from which she had awakened. So now she could tell Mark all was indeed well with her, that Isabel Kenton was not in love with any man.

Taking one last look at the sky slashed by the sinking sun, she turned towards the house. Those words too she would not write, for in her deepest soul she knew them to be a lie. But that was a lie she could live with, as living her life as Luther Kenton's daughter was a lie.

'Don't you ever take notice of what you are told?'

Isabel turned at the sound of that voice.

'I said once before you would catch cold, standing out here without a coat.'

'James . . . Mr Hawley!' Suddenly she was breathless, heart pounding as it had when she had raced Mark around the grounds. 'I did not hear you come into the garden.'

'I admit my sin.' James Hawley's smile seemed oddly tight. 'I walked across the lawn.'

'That *is* a sin.' Isabel tried to return his smile. 'But I promise I will not tell Bradshaw.'

'Since that will make us partners in crime, perhaps I might prevail upon you to call me James?'

'Partners should be on first-name terms.' Isabel managed a little laugh. 'But should Bradshaw catch you out in any more sins, I shall deny having any part in them.'

'I will defend you to my dying day.'

The words were said lightly but in the dimming light Isabel caught a look in his eyes that twisted her heart.

'You sound like my brother,' she said quickly, afraid of the tumult building inside her. 'He was always saving me from the penalty of some escapade or other, or at least so he would have me believe.'

'Have you heard from him recently?'

She nodded and in the twilight he saw the unhappiness that stole her smile. If only he could take her in his arms, kiss away the anxiety that suddenly tightened her mouth. But that was a joy and a privilege that would never be his. What had a foundry worker to offer the daughter of Luther Kenton?

'I had a letter from Mark yesterday,' she said, tears trembling on the edge of every word. 'He tries to sound cheerful but underneath I read the misery he is living through, the fear and despair at what is happening all around him; he must be living in hell . . .'

'They all are.' He stepped closer and then somehow she was in his arms, her face against his chest. 'But you must not let him know your fear. It is you who will be keeping him from giving way to madness, just as you did me.'

'You?' Lifting her head she looked into his eyes, her strength almost failing her at the depth of love she saw there. 'I kept you from madness?'

What did it matter if he told her? The worst she could do was to laugh and walk away; it could add no further misery to his heart than was there already.

'Yes,' he said, wondering why she did not step away from him. 'It was remembering how soft and gentle your voice was that helped deaden the sound of gunfire. It was the image of your face I carried in my heart whenever we went over the top. You were the one I was willing to die for, you were the one I wanted to live for. Would to heaven I had not!'

Her arms going instinctively about him, Isabel held him close, feeling the earth lurch beneath her feet at his words, yet at the same time feeling a great songburst of happiness, a surge of emotion that flooded every part of her as she realised she loved James Hawley. This time there was no tiny murmur of doubt, no uncertainty. This was the man she had loved all along.

'James.' She stared up at him, all the love in her heart plain to see. 'James, please never say such a thing again.'

'But it is true!' He lifted his face to the sky. 'It would have been easier that way. How can a man live without a heart?'

'But you have a heart, James. You have mine.'

For several seconds she felt a great stillness in him, a frightening heart-rending stillness, then a long shudder of emotion that forced the words from his mouth. 'Isabel, you mean . . .'

The smile that was in her heart spreading to her mouth, she whispered shyly, 'Yes, James. That is exactly what I mean. I love you. I think I loved you from the moment you hauled me away from that crowd.'

'Oh, my love!' The words were little more than a groan before his mouth took hers.

'But I thought you and Hewett Calcott . . .' he said when at last he released her long enough to speak.

Isabel laid her head against his chest. 'I do love Hewett,' she said, 'but not this way, not as I love you. I love him as a friend or as a daughter might. I hope always to keep his friendship.'

'Isabel.' His arms dropping away from her, he stepped back, staring into the darkness that had descended over the garden. 'You should take Hewett as a husband. He will be able to keep you as you deserve, give you all and more of everything your father gave you. Everything I cannot give you.'

A spasm of pain shooting through her, Isabel gasped. Was that what James thought she wanted? Did he think she saw love as but the acquiring of a comfortable home?

Everything her father had given her! Were it not for the pain inside her, Isabel would have laughed. Fighting to keep the emotion from her voice, she said quietly, 'I do not want Hewett Calcott as a husband, nor do I want his wealth. This house was bequeathed to me on . . . on my father's death. That also I do not want. Under the terms of the will, I was to live here or the property would be sold. It is now in fact technically no longer a home but a hospital. I do not pretend to understand the ins and outs of legal wranglings. I have given the house, and everything inside it away. All I have left are three treasures I could not bring myself to part with. One is a brooch that belonged to my mother, the second is the bracelet Hewett gave to me at Christmas, and the third . . .' she hesitated, feeling her mouth tremble '. . . the third is a rather crumpled tram ticket.'

With a strangled cry, James reached for her, his arms tightening as though never to let her go.

'I want nothing of Luther Kenton's!' Her voice throbbed as she spoke. 'Everything he ever gave me is sold and the money will endow the house as a hospital forever.'

She had nothing! James felt his whole being grow light with gladness. Then he could ask her, safe in the knowledge that the disparity in their fortunes could not affect the answer. Her body tight against his own, his lips touching her hair, he asked softly: 'Isabel, will you marry me?'

In the silence that followed he heard her sobs. 'No, James,' she said finally. 'I will not marry you.'

Stunned, his arms fell away from her once more. 'I beg your pardon?' he muttered. 'I thought . . .'

'You spoke of all the things Luther Kenton had given me,' Isabel said as he turned away from her. 'It is true he gave me every comfort. But those comforts were dearly paid for, not only by my mother's money but by her happiness and that of her children. The truth is Luther despised both myself and Mark, gave us nothing but harsh words and misery all of our life.

'But surely you must know I would never hurt you?' He moved towards her but she stepped away, avoiding his touch.

'Yes, James, I do know, and I could never hurt you. That is why I cannot marry you. You see, Victoria Kenton was my mother but Luther Kenton was not my father. You would be marrying a bastard.'

'Is that all?' James laughed, pulling her once more into his arms. 'I thought for one awful minute you did not really love me.'

'There have been enough lies in my life, James. I will not add another to it by saying I do not love you.'

Looking down into her face, he touched his finger to a tear shimmering like a diamond on the soft curve of her cheek. '*You* were all I dreamed of in France, *you* are all I dream of now. It makes no difference to me who your father was. Once we are married it will be my name you bear. Take it, Isabel, and give me back my heart.'

Isabel stared at the letter.

It had been sent to the wrong person. It was not meant for her. She had Mark's letters there in the drawer beside her bed, she had received several together less than a fortnight ago. This one was wrong, it was not hers!

But it was. The deadness in her heart told her it was. She had prayed so hard, so many times, prayed he would come home safely. But Mark would not come home, he would never come home.

Tears coursing down her face she lifted the letter she knew by heart. It had been telegraphed from the Western Front and signed by Mark's commanding officer.

'My dear Miss Kenton,'

Blinking away tears that blurred the words on the sheet of buff coloured paper, Isabel read the letter again, searching every line for something that would tell her it was a mistake.

'I write to you regarding the death of your brother, No. 96655 Flying Officer Mark Kenton.

I regret to inform you that he was killed during a raid over enemy lines near the village of St Christ on the west bank of the River Somme, now in the hands of the Germans.

The plane he was piloting was hit by enemy fire and seen to burst into flame before crashing into the ground. A communiqué from the German Officer Commanding at St Christ, reports that none of the crew of the aircraft survived.

I have to inform you that no further information is at hand and close with deepest sympathy from his comrades and from yours sincerely.
  Sir William Aynsley
  Wing Commander
  633 Squadron
  Royal Air Force.'

Folding the letter, Isabel carried it to the drawer beside her bed, laying it with the last letters she had received from Mark. It was such a little, all that was left of her brother, just a pile of letters.

'Mark!' The cry coming up from the furthest depths of her, she sank to her knees beside the bed, hands covering her face. It must have been his spirit, calling to her the day that Owen died. How could she have lost them both? 'Oh Mark, I love you so, you were all the family I had.'

Beyond her bedroom window the sun lowered from the sky in flames of crimson glory. Lifting her face to it, Isabel saw none of the beauty of the sunset, but only her brother's plane falling in flames to the earth.

Chapter Twenty-Six

Satisfied the knot in his necktie was suitably tied, Hewett Calcott reached for his coat. He had done the right thing in taking on James Hawley as a partner, he would find no better. And the house on the Leys? That had been the right choice too. It had been specially built, a place without memories, a place he had hoped to bring *her* to, a place where Isabel Kenton might forget the past, a place they would share together. Then had come Owen Farr's announcement, the words that had knocked the bottom from his world. Isabel was to be another man's wife.

He had left Woodbank with his hopes shattered and his dreams in pieces about his feet. Perhaps that was the way it was meant to be. Touching the pocket of his coat, he smiled sadly. The gift he had given her that same day had not been the one he had wanted with all his heart to give.

Drawing out the small box he had taken to carrying with him always, he stared at the gold-tooled design impressed into dark blue leather. Had she accepted what this box held she would have been his; but he had not offered it . . . it had already been too late. But what of now . . . was it still too late?

His fingers closing over the box, Hewett Calcott felt the smile fade from his mouth. Isabel Kenton may have no fiancé but she was in love, perhaps more so than before. He had realised that more and more with each meeting, seen the veiled sadness in her courteous welcome. She was in love with a dead man!

What had he felt those few days before Christmas? Hope, elation, promise? Yes, he had felt each of those, but most of all he had felt love. And this – he stared at his hand almost swamping the box – this was to be the proof not only of love but of . . . Lifting his head sharply, mouth thinning to nothing, he thrust the box back into his pocket. It was not to be! His hopes had come to nothing. Isabel Kenton would never see what was in this box, nor ever know what was in his heart.

James Hawley was already there when he arrived at the Chamber of Commerce and Hewett greeted him warmly. Tonight he would present his business partner to Darlaston's men of steel. He smiled inwardly. That should set a few tongues wagging!

Making their way to the meeting room, acknowledging the nods and greetings of the assembled men, they took their seats at the table.

'Ready, James?'

'Yes, I'm ready.'

Hewett smiled. 'Then let's give this lot the news. It'll be the surprise of their lives.'

'Before we do,' James touched the other man's sleeve briefly, 'I would like to tell you *my* news. Isabel Kenton has agreed to become my wife.'

For several seconds Hewett sat stunned by what he had heard. Isabel was to be married! And to James Hawley. Was he the one the unhappiness in her lovely eyes had been for? Was he the man she'd loved all the time and not Owen Farr?

'You don't approve, sir?' James saw the tension in the set of the other man's mouth. 'I . . . that is we both felt you would be happy for us. I love Isabel, have loved her for years. There will never be any other woman for me.'

There will never be any other woman for me. Hewett himself said the exact same words all those years ago. His heart had been breaking then as it was breaking now; and until he had met Isabel

Kenton it had known no solace. Then he had thought at last it would be over, that once more the world would smile for him, that she . . . But he could not tell her now, could not cast a shadow over her happiness. He would go on as he knew he must, go on living without love.

'. . . I know what people will think,' James went on, 'a foundry man and the daughter of Luther Kenton . . .'

'No!' The word was snapped out, sounding harsh and cold. Beneath his fine brows, Hewett's eyes were frozen. 'Luther Kenton was . . .'

From the other end of the room a murmur of voices broke out and he stopped speaking as Isabel walked towards them.

The pallid look had gone from her cheeks yet still the sorrow of her brother's death shadowed her eyes. Hewett Calcott felt the tug at his heart as James handed her to a seat between them and Isabel smiled at him. There could be no doubting it: James Hawley was the man she loved. There would be no place in her life for Hewett.

'James has told me of his great good fortune,' he murmured as she sat down.

A smile still touching her lips as she turned to him, Isabel answered softly, 'It is my good fortune too.' Then, her smile dimming, she added, 'If only I had realised sooner, Owen might not . . .'

'Ifs are shifting sands.' He touched her hand lightly. 'You cannot build on them. Forget what has gone before. Look to the future, my dear, and be happy.'

'We have a deal of business to discuss.' The chairman's voice rose above the rest, bringing them all to silence. 'So best get on with it.'

'Arrh, sooner we be done the better. There be places more inviting than this where a man can spend his time!'

'Arrh, and we all know where *they* be. The Cross being only one!'

Face red with the effort of calling the laughing men to order, the chairman shuffled awkwardly, his glance deliberately excluding Isabel.

'Manners, gentlemen!' he reprimanded. 'There be a lady present.'

'And a very beautiful one.' Seated opposite Isabel, dressed in a lavender grey coat over a maroon silk vest, the son of Joseph Hayden fixed his nut brown eyes on her face. 'I say we take advice from our chairman and remember our manners. Ladies first . . . eh, gentlemen?'

Nodding agreement, his glance still avoiding direct contact with her eyes, the chairman answered briefly. 'You have the floor, Miss Kenton.'

'Thank you.' Amethyst blue velvet suit moulded close to her slender body, gaslight lending her deep auburn hair a halo of fire, Isabel rose to her feet. Glancing at each face in turn she began, 'I asked your help once before, now I ask it again.'

'Not another 'ospital!'

'No.' Isabel's glance travelled to the man who had interrupted. 'Not another hospital, though with the number of wounded coming home one is sorely needed. However, that is not what I wish to ask of you.'

'Then what do you want?' Nut brown eyes played languidly over her.

Giving James a quick smile, she turned once more to the assembled men. 'Yesterday I signed Woodbank House over to the people of Darlaston, to serve as a hospital for them once this war is over. I ask your help in maintaining it as such.'

'What do Darlaston want with another 'ospital? The Sister Dora be a fine place,' came an irate voice from the far end of the table.

'Yes, the Sister Dora is a fine hospital,' Isabel answered. 'But it is in Walsall, several miles from this town – miles that may well prove fatal to a patient as we have often seen after accidents in the foundries. Then there are children and pregnant women . . .'

'Women and children? Pah! What be they needing a hospital for? Kids have been falling down for years and no harm done. As for pregnant women – that be nature and nature don't need no help from us!'

Her eyes suddenly glacial, Isabel allowed them to rest on the florid face of the man now leaning forward, one forearm thrown challengingly on to the table's gleaming surface. 'You would know, would you? You have kept a count of the number of women who die in childbirth; the number of young men barely out of childhood who suffer burns or are crippled from accidents every year in our steel works? Or is it that you close your eyes to those things? What the eye does not see the heart does not grieve for! Is that your philosophy?'

'Ain't my fault so many women get themselves pregnant . . .'

'No, but you does your share!'

Waiting for the roar of laughter to subside, Isabel stood her ground. She would say what she came to say and these men would hear it, like it or not.

'Miss Kenton.' The chairman spoke up. 'I fail to see how . . . how women in that condition can be our responsibility . . .'

'You fail to see!' Isabel retaliated. 'Every woman who finds herself "in that condition", as you so delicately put it, is there because of a man. I do not say the doing is entirely his, I know it takes two to make a third, but neither can any man deny his part in it or his share of the responsibility!'

'Come now, Miss Kenton,' another man intervened. 'We have all taken care of our wives when they have been . . . that way, as we have taken care of our children. I think I can speak for every man here who has a wife and family when I say we afford them the best care possible.'

'I do not question that,' Isabel returned coolly. 'What I *do* question is, *how* do you afford them the best? Where did the money come from that bought them every care? And I will tell you from where: it came from the sweat and labour of the men who worked twelve hours a day in your foundries, and comes now from the sweat and labour of women and boys, those

371

mothers and children who have kept your factories going when conscription took away your workforce; kept your profits rolling in so that *your* women and children could continue to be well cared for.'

'We never asked no women to come into the factories nor no lads to work the steel!'

Isabel rounded on the speaker, glance deprecating as it swept over his florid face. 'You did not keep them out either, did you? You did not refuse their labour, because to do so would have closed your works.'

'They knowed it was their duty to take on their men's jobs, to keep the munitions and the steel going.'

'Oh, yes.' Isabel's tone was scathing. 'They knew their duty better than many men here know theirs! It was the duty of the women and boys to keep the steel rolling and the armaments factories working. But where will I find *your* wives and children? Which factory or steel foundry are they performing *their* duty in? Or is duty only the responsibility of the poor!'

'Miss Kenton.' The chairman waved one hand to quieten the angry retorts from the assembled businessmen. 'Maybe you would tell us exactly what it is you want? That way we can avoid any further unpleasantness.'

Isabel nodded. 'A few minutes ago I said I had signed Woodbank House over to the people of this town to serve as a hospital. Doctor Seaton and others of the medical staff have agreed to stay on and run it. There are funds for several years but once they are used up . . .' She hesitated, feeling the antagonism all around her. They saw her as a meddling female, best put in her place. Well, that was their prerogative, but before they pushed her into their chosen slot they would see that not all women fitted the mould so easily. What she had to do was little short of begging, but she was not too proud to do it if it meant keeping the hospital for Darlaston. Lifting her head, she glanced again at the antagonistic faces all around her. 'Once that money is used up the hospital will need your help to survive.'

'Oh, arrh!' a man sneered. 'So now we come to it. It be our

money Kenton's wench be after.'

'Yes, it is your money!' Isabel faced him, defiance in every inch of her slender body. '*Your* money and *your* gratitude.' Then just as suddenly the coldness and defiance died from her eyes and her shoulders slumped as if in defeat. 'It would be little enough in return for what the people this town have given you,' she said softly. 'A small amount from each of you is all it would take, and it would mean so much to them.'

'Miss Kenton is right.' James was on his feet as Isabel sank back into her chair. 'A hospital where local people could be treated quickly would be a godsend to Darlaston.'

'Arrh, mebbe it would.' The man's florid face turned a shade darker and the sneer returned. 'So let God send the money to keep it going!'

'The sum involved would cause little hurt to any of you, but for some it seems the pain of parting with it is too much.' James met the red-faced man's glare full on. 'As, no doubt, was the pain of facing up to conscription! For my part, I pledge my share here and now.'

His eyes murderous from the sting of James's words, the man breathed in deeply. 'Oh, you do, do you?' he snarled. 'You pledges your share. And just where do a foundry rat get that kind of money?'

'A foundry rat with a full partnership in Calcott Steel has that kind of money and to spare.' Hewett's words rang around the room, stunning his audience.

'Partners!'

'*Full* partners.' Hewett emphasised the word as the gasps of surprise subsided.

'But . . . but he be nowt but . . .'

'A foundry rat?' Hewett smiled briefly at James. 'Yes, that is what you call men who have lived and breathed steel from boyhood, who have worked and sweated doing a job you do not understand enough about even to talk intelligently on the subject. It is the foundry rats who have built this town, they who keep it going; *their* knowledge is the foundation on which the steel industry is built. Their blood and sweat the cement that binds it together. It was that skill and knowledge I wanted for my steel works. That plus the grit and reliability only a true foundry rat could give me. Those were the qualities I demanded from a partner – ones I found lacking in so many so-called steel men. And from today anything James Hawley contracts or pledges will have my full and total support. Which includes a yearly subscription to the Darlaston Hospital.'

'Of course it do.' His face still flushed with anger, the sneer back on his mouth, the man who had opposed Isabel laughed in Hewett's face. 'Of course you supports the Kenton wench. You will give her the money she asks for, but not because you be a bloody philanthropist! We all knows what be behind your generosity . . . you be in love with her! You love Kenton's daughter and be all set to marry her!'

Along the line of its trim beard, the muscles of Hewett Calcott's jaw twitched and tightened. Beneath the cover of the table his fingers clenched and unclenched as he rode waves of emotion that threatened to engulf him.

'Well, Calcott!' The laughter rang out again, mocking and derisive. 'Tell me if I be wrong . . . or could it be Kenton's daughter has refused?'

'You are not wrong. I *do* love her.'

Across the table the low laughter came again, bringing with it a tide of feeling Hewett no longer wanted to suppress. One hand touching the pocket of his coat, he rose to his feet, ignoring Isabel's soft cry and the look on James Hawley's face.

'Yes, I love Isabel,' he said, so loud not a syllable could be missed. 'I love her, but asking her to be my wife is something I will never do.' Drawing the blue box from his pocket, he laid it on the table before her. 'I would if I could but it is not possible. You see, Isabel Kenton is my daughter!'

*

374

Isabel looked once more at the photographs inside the beautifully engraved locket. Herself and Mark as small children on one half, and on the other a faded brown snapshot of their mother and a young man, a man who was without doubt Hewett Calcott. Staring at it for several moments, she blinked away the tears before snapping it shut. Then turning it over she read again the words engraved on the back. '*Here, my darling, we can be a family*'. Her mother's name followed.

'But why?' She looked up into a face filled with love and pain. 'Why?'

'Why did I not return to your mother?' Throwing back his head, Hewett dragged in air, his mouth parted as if to scream his agony. 'I never knew she was pregnant. Every letter I wrote her brought no reply. The fear she had stopped loving me, and the desire I had to be with her, finally grew too much for me to bear. But by the time I got back she had married Luther Kenton. I think I lost my reason then. I left Darlaston and travelled God knows where, doing God knows what, but it seems I made money. It took nigh on ten years for me to come to accept what had happened but when I did I came home. That was when I received this.' Taking an envelope from his pocket, he handed it to Isabel.

Her hands shaking, brain still reeling from the shock of what he had said earlier in the meeting room, Isabel looked at the name and address written upon it in a hand she knew so well. Lifting her glance, her eyes rested on the bookcase. *Our Mutual Friend.* Even from this distance she could clearly read the title of the book that still held a letter written in that same flowing script; and from a distance infinitely greater she clearly heard that old mocking laugh.

'Read it, Isabel, you have to know.' James, whom both she and Hewett had asked to stay behind at Woodbank to hear his explanation, came to her side, touching a hand to her shoulder.

Slowly, every beat of her heart sounding like the pounding of a drum, Isabel drew the sheet of paper from the envelope.

'*My dearest, truest love.*'

Tears burning against her eyelids, she forced herself to read on.

> *Seeing you once more was a gift from God, the only gift apart from my children, our children, I ever really wanted; whatever the Lord now has in store for me I can face without demur.*
>
> *I begged of you when you came to me not to reveal to them your true identity; I asked you to help me shield them from the scandal that would follow them for the rest of their lives. This I ask again. Let our secret rest with us and die with us. Please, my dearest love, do not bequeath it to our innocent children.*
>
> *It will be hard for you, Hewett, watching them grow, being unable to hold them in your arms, but try to be strong for their sakes and for mine. Luther Kenton took me when there was no one else and for all I never loved him I would not see him made a laughing stock in the town, for that would destroy him utterly.*
>
> *When you are lonely or sick at heart, take out this locket which I send you. Breathe the names of the children that are yours and mine. And, Hewett, know that they would have loved you as I love you, my one dear love, and keep them in your heart as you have ever been in mine. God keep you safe and in His mercy grant that one day we may be together.*
>
> *Victoria*

'How could I act after reading that?' Hewett turned away towards the darkened window of the study as Isabel's hands dropped to her lap. 'How could I refuse her anything, though it broke my heart? How could I bring shame on the woman who was my whole existence? I knew when I saw her that she was dying, and I wanted to die too.'

Touching Isabel's arm as she made to move, James gave a quick shake of his head. Hewett Calcott would never heal until all the hurt and bitterness had poured out of him.

'And then, when it was all over, I saw the two of you standing beside her grave, one on either side of Luther Kenton, your hands in his; his adored children. But you were not his!

376

You were mine and my heart cried out to me to take you, my daughter and my son. But my promise to your mother had been given. You would go on being the children of the man who had married her not for love, or to keep her from scandal, but for the one thing I would not take . . . her money!'

He turned about and Isabel's heart contracted as she saw the pain in his eyes.

'Then tonight, in that room,' he went on, voice thick with tears he would not allow to fall, 'I could no longer deny . . . I broke my promise to your mother and you . . . you will have to live with our shame. I'm sorry, Isabel, I'm so very sorry!'

'No.' Jumping to her feet, letter and envelope falling unheeded to the floor, she ran to him, throwing her arms about him, her own tears sliding unchecked down her cheeks. 'Don't be sorry, not for calling me your own! It was no fault of yours that you and my mother did not marry, the blame lies with Luther Kenton. He stole a letter that was meant for you, did it for his own selfish ends.'

Releasing him, she opened the bookcase and drew out the book that concealed her mother's letter. 'She knew of this before she died,' she said softly, not knowing whether or not her mother had spoken to him of it. 'She knew you had not deserted her.' Pressing the yellowed paper into his hands, she returned to stand beside James, leaving Hewett to read it.

'Oh my God!' The words were whispered quietly as he finished reading, the heaving of his shoulders displaying the grief that overtook him.

'If only Mark could have known.' Isabel glanced at the photograph of her brother.

'He did know, Isabel.' Hewett picked up the silver frame, touching a fingertip to the handsome smiling face inside it. 'I could not bear to think that he . . . he might never know. I wrote him a letter telling him everything and enclosing a copy of your mother's letter to me, but I asked him to say nothing to you. I said that when he returned I would tell you, but only when he was here to be with you.

'I enclosed my letter in another addressed to his Commanding Officer with an explanation that also requested he respect my confidence. I asked that Mark's letter be given him only should it be considered that the contents would not upset him so much he might lay himself open to more danger . . . go off the rails somehow. I left that decision to his superiors.' He traced the smiling face again. 'It seemed Mark could handle the situation for I had a letter in reply, one which began, "Dear Father".'

'Oh, I am so glad!' Isabel went to his side, tears shining like stars in her eyes. 'And I know Mark would be also. Thank you for telling him.'

'I lost you both once before.' His voice husky with emotion, Hewett looked into the face of his daughter. 'Please, Isabel, please don't let me lose you both again? God has taken my son, that I must live with, but if you turn from me . . .'

'I will never turn from you.' Standing on tiptoe, Isabel kissed his cheek. 'I love you, Father. It is over now.' Placing her hand on his arm, she pressed it gently, her smile soft and warm. 'We can take the words from the locket and turn them into reality. We can be a family. There will be no shame for me in that. I want the world to know our true relationship.'

Catching her in his arms, Hewett pressed his lips to the shining auburn hair so close to the colour of his own. 'Isabel! Oh, my child,' he murmured, 'I wanted so much to tell you, dreamed so many times of hearing you say those words. I love you, my dearest girl, I love you so much.'

Pressed against him, her heart swollen with happiness, Isabel smiled through a veil of tears. 'I love you too, Father,' she whispered.

Releasing herself, she took a hand of each of the two people she loved most in the world, the man she was to marry and the father she'd thought never to know, and in the silence of her heart she listened.

But there was no answering laughter.

If you enjoyed BITTER SEED, here's a foretaste of Meg Hutchinson's new novel, A LOVE FORBIDDEN:

Chapter One

'You be nothing but a trollop – a dirty, stinking, bloody little trollop!'

Leah Bryce's already narrow face seemed to become even narrower, her sharp features more drawn, her usually colourless eyes blazing with old hatred and new spite.

'Who have you been with? Lying out on the heath with some man, giving yourself like a whore! Or be it more than one? Be it that you have lain with so many you don't know who has left you with his bastard?'

'Mother, please, it wasn't like that . . .'

Leah's hand lashed out, catching her daughter's face, hurling her sideways against the dresser, sending plates toppling from the shelves. 'Wasn't like that?' she spat, thin lips drawn back in a snarl. 'Wasn't like that! Then what *was* it like?' Grabbing the girl's shoulders, she hauled her upright. 'Don't be telling me I'm wrong, that you don't have a child inside you. There were no cloths from you last month and none the month before that. No show of blood for almost a three-month and you regular as night following day since you were ten year old. Ain't nothing but a man causes that to stop, so don't be telling me you don't be carrying!'

Her shoulders slumping, the girl pressed her hands to her face, sobs shaking her thin frame.

'I knew I was right!' The vindictive gleam in her eyes

changing to one of triumph, Leah drew a paper from her pocket, slamming it on to the table that half filled the kitchen.

'I guessed what this was the minute I found it. I knew then that what I suspected was true. Well?' Leah's open palm came hard down again on the table. 'Look at it. Look at the marks you yourself have made on it, then tell me those marks don't number the days since last you had a flow of blood! Look at it!' The last was screamed as she grabbed a handful of the girl's hair, savagely twisting it about a closed hand, yanking her head back on her neck and forcing her to look up.

The pencil marks blurred into one long continuous line, the tears in Miriam Bryce's eyes seeming to make it move and slide across the paper like a thick black worm. The paper had been hidden beneath the flock mattress of her bed, but not well enough from the prying eyes and poking fingers of her mother.

'Yes, they mark the days sure enough.' Leah pushed with the hand that was folded in the girl's hair, throwing her once more violently against the heavy oak dresser. 'But they don't mark *all* the days of your sins, I'll be bound! It's my guess you've been at your dirty little games much longer than is written there.'

'No!' Eyes green as newly sprouted grass sparkling under dew, Miriam looked through her tears at the woman who not once in her memory had ever given her a loving word. Who since the earliest time she could remember had shown her only harshness – a harshness that since she had grown into a beauty had turned to spite. 'I am not what you accuse me of being. I am not a whore.'

'Then what would you call yourself?' Both hands coming palm down on the table, Leah leaned forward, glaring at the girl who cowered on its other side. 'You ain't what I accuse you of, so what are you? Any woman who lies with all for the asking be a whore in my book, and in that of any other decent body.'

'I do not lie with any man for the asking.' Miriam's head came up, sun slanting in at the room's one window, sprinkling the rich russet of her hair with threads of gold. 'There has been only one.'

Slowly drawing herself upright, Leah Bryce's mouth curved

into a cold, loveless smile. 'So, there has been only one, and that makes you less than a whore! Go ask the priest at St Matthew's if lying with just one man outside the marriage bed makes you less than a whore. Ask him if a seventeen-year-old girl with a bastard in her belly be any better than a trollop.'

'Yes, I am pregnant,' Miriam said with quiet dignity. 'And I do not defend what we have done. We both know it to be wrong, but the child I carry will not be born a bastard. We are going to be married just as soon as the banns can be called.'

'We?' Leah's thin lips tightened. 'You say *we*. Just who is the man can't wait for his pleasure but takes it afore placing a ring upon your finger?'

'You know him well enough, we have loved each other since being children. We always intended to marry. His name is Saul Marsh.'

Across the table Leah Bryce's eyes glittered above that cold smile, giving her narrow face the look of a fox with a fresh kill. Marsh! His mother was a widow the same as herself and she too had only the money her son earned to keep her from the workhouse. Now he was about to bring home a wife and soon a child. Two more mouths to feed and probably one more each year. Inside Leah the smile widened. Perhaps the workhouse would soon be called upon to take in more than one old woman!

'Then Marsh knows about his love child, you have told him?' She caught the look behind her daughter's eyes, one that told her all she wanted to know. He had not yet heard of the child.

'I . . . I shall tell him this evening, when his shift at the mine is finished.'

'Then tell him this an' all,' snapped Leah. 'You have four years before you be of the age to marry without my given word.'

Miriam's eyes widened and her words tumbled out in a rush. 'You . . . you would not deny us?'

Leah sank to the floor, gathering the pieces of broken china slowly into her apron. Behind the shelter of the table she heard the girl's sharp intake of breath, and the smile that rose to her own lips was warm with the pleasure of spite. She wanted nothing more than to have the child she loathed taken from beneath her roof; nothing more except the satisfaction of seeing her suffer. The girl could marry, but only after her father's dues had been paid.

The pieces collected, Leah rose to her feet, malice burnishing her dull brown eyes to the colour of beaten copper. 'You will not have the condoning of what you have done from me,' she said evenly, eyes fixed on the girl's stricken face. 'That which is in your belly will come out a bastard and that it will remain, till you be twenty-one. By that time Marsh may have another wench in the family way, one who can marry afore you.'

Her lovely face crumpling, Miriam stared at her mother. 'Why?' she asked, tears coursing down her cheeks. 'Why do you treat me the way you do? What have I ever done to make you hate me so much?'

Holding the apron bunched about the broken china, Leah's fingers tightened and her eyes flashed venom.

'You lived,' she said quietly. 'You *lived*.'

Ralph Bryce placed the last of the numbered tokens on the tub he had filled with newly hewn coal then called for the donkey boy to push it along the rails to the shaft bottom. Using the strip of cloth wound about his neck to wipe the sweat from his eyes, he squatted on his haunches, leaning his bare back against the coal seam glittering like black diamonds in the gleam from his Davy lamp. It was well named 'the deep seam'. Thirty feet thick and running for miles beneath the ground, it had yielded a rich harvest for the coal masters, and today he felt as though he personally had dug every ounce.

'Another shift finished, Ralph lad.'

'Arrh,' he agreed wearily.

'Then let's be getting up above. We be spending that much time down here my old woman be getting to think I've got meself a fresh 'un!'

'Now what could you be doing with another woman?' Hands hanging tiredly over his knees, Ralph smiled, his teeth gleaming white in the pool of light cast by the lamp.

'Not a lot, Ralph lad, not a lot for sure. It be all I can manage to keep my Sarah happy. Once a week it has to be, but I tells her that more than that sends you blind!'

Chuckling low in his throat, the other man gathered up the pick he had laid aside on the ground and, bent almost double against the tunnel that was less than half his height, began to shuffle his way back towards the shaft.

Pushing himself up from his haunches, the shovel with which he had loaded coal into the tub grasped firmly by its wooden haft, Ralph followed, his head almost on his chest to avoid striking the jagged outcrops of coal jutting from the roof only inches above it.

'Will you be laying the dust along of Banjo's?' his workmate asked.

'Not this shift,' Ralph answered, spitting out the coal dust raised by the other man's feet. Since the wage paid by the owner of the Grace Mary mine had been reduced by six shillings a tub, a tankard of ale at the beer house was one of the things he must do without. Keeping the house and feeding three mouths left little over to pay for ale. Saturday evening was the one time he made an exception, and then two tankards was all he allowed himself.

Reaching the end of the tunnel that the two of them had burrowed through the massive vein of coal over the months, they stepped into the iron cage, Ralph tugging the rope that rang the bell in the winding house.

Rising slowly through darkness so deep their lamps were helpless against it, both men held their silence, each feeling relief seep through him at the end of a fifteen-hour day.

'You'll be needing no bath tonight,' the man winding the cage remarked as it reached the surface. 'It be raining heavens hard.'

'In that case, I reckon I'll take the time to drink a second tankard at Banjo's.' Ralph's shift mate grinned, blinking against the purple evening that both men found brilliant after the stygian blackness of the mine. 'It'll mean less time spent listening to my Sarah chuntering.'

'That wife of your'n might do her share of grumbling, but you would come off badly without her!' the winder called as they trudged across the yard towards the checking shed, hurriedly slipping on shirt and coat that had been removed at the coal face, their hob-nailed clogs squelching in the slimy clay of wet coal dust.

Removing the brass disc hung about his neck, Ralph handed it to another man who barely glanced at it before draping it over one of a line of nails driven into the brick wall and equally sullenly took the lamp, placing it on a long wooden bench that ran beneath.

Calling a goodnight that received no answer, they stepped from the shed, turning up their collars against the rain before setting off on the mile-long walk across the empty heath, following the track that would lead them safely past mines whose disused shafts lay open, ready to claim any who did not have the sixth sense born into miners.

Snap tins wedged under their arm, bottles that had held their drink of cold tea shoved into a coat pocket, the two bent their heads to the driving rain and trudged in silence, steps quickening as they reached the surer ground of Gypsy Lane. Passing the boiler-making works that loomed black and huge out of the night, they crossed Fishers Bridge spanning the canal.

Coming to the tramway that skirted the village, Ralph took his leave, turning in the direction of a house that stood some distance away across the heath while his workmate went eagerly in the direction of the beer house.

Glad to be alone, Ralph slowed his steps, lifting his face to the rain, wanting it to wash away the misery lodged like a stone in the pit of his stomach. He should be used to the pain of it by now, it had been with him for years, growing as he watched her grow. But the sting of it cut deeper with each new day that dawned; days that brought the fear of losing her to another man, the agony of thinking of her in someone else's arms, in someone else's bed. It was a fear and an agony that was ripping the heart from him, that made his life a living torment, yet it was a torment he could not end for what could come of the love that filled him, that kept sleep from him night after night, the deep needful love of a man for a woman? The love that no man should have for his sister.

Across the darkness of the heath the yellow glow of oil lamps spilled from the window of the cottage that had once stood surrounded by fields of crops and animals. But the dairy cow had long since gone, the plough horse been sold and the corn and wheat fields reclaimed by gorse and broom. Only the chickens kept by his mother remained of the life that used to be.

Would it have been more pleasant? he wondered as he walked on. Working by the light of day, seeing her go about her chores, watching her lithe young body as she brought his midday meal to the fields, sun glinting on her russet-coloured hair, seeing her lift her lovely face to smile into his eyes? Feeling the pain surge afresh in his chest, Ralph knew that way of life could only have worsened the hurt inside him. Far better for him to be shut away in the dark bowels of the mine; shut away with his shameful secret.

'You be fair soaked.' Leah turned from emptying a kettle full of boiling water into the tin bath set before the fire. 'Let me take that coat from you.' Placing the huge smoke-blackened kettle on the hob of the shiny blackleaded grate, she eased the wet coat from Ralph's shoulders spreading it across the back of a chair drawn over to where the fire's heat would reach it. She had seen many such nights as this and was well prepared. A bath to wash the dirt away and put warmth into her son's bones, and lamb broth with suet dumplings to satisfy his hunger.

Taking the striped twill shirt as he pulled it off, she felt a surge almost of pride sweep through her. Her son was a fine figure of a man. There were those in Brades Village would be proud to have him as a husband. But he had shown no interest in any girl. She crumpled the shirt in her arms. None except . . .

'There be cold water in the pail.' She indicated a bucket stood in the hearth. The same cold fear gnawed in her stomach, one she had felt for the last ten years. 'Give a shout when you be finished, and I'll bring you in a clean shirt.'

'Where's Miriam?'

Leah's heart sank. If she told him the girl had not been home all evening then Ralph would insist on going out to find her, out into the rain and cold again, and all for a dirty little slut.

'We were out of flour and I need it for tomorrow's baking.' The lie came easily from a tongue long practised in the art and no blush stained her cheeks.

'You sent her for flour . . . in weather like this!' Ralph hesitated, one boot half unlaced.

'It were not raining when her went.'

He lifted his eyes to his mother, experiencing the same rush of suspicion he always did when Miriam's whereabouts were in question. Too many occasions in childhood on which he'd found his sister with weals red on her arms, or marked across her face, had taken the trust from him and even now they were both older it had not returned. There was something about his mother, something that caused her to hate her own daughter; he had seen it often in her face, heard it in the way she spoke to the girl. It was unnatural, and more than that it was dangerous. One day that hatred would become too strong, one day it would threaten all their lives.

'What time was that?' he asked, lowering his foot to the floor.

'Not much after three.'

Ralph glanced at the enamelled tin clock on the mantelshelf. 'That's nigh on five hours ago. She should have been back long since.'

Leah saw the quick leap of concern darken his eyes and the coldness of her own fear mounted. They were both worried over Miriam but not for the same reason.

'I asked her to look in on Martha Lloyd.' She hitched the shirt in her arms before letting them come to rest under her flat breasts. 'Her Isaac has not been at all well since Advent. The cold and damp plague his bones. It be likely they be pressing her to wait of their lad coming in from the pit so he can fetch her home.'

'Happen you're right.' Ralph lifted his foot again, fingers busy with the leather bootlace.

'Of course I be right. Give the lad time to wash the coal dust from his body and take a bite to eat and he'll bring her.' Turning towards the door that gave on to the stairs, Leah felt hope quicken within her, easing some of the cold fear in her stomach. The girl had been gone long enough for her tears to give way to hunger and cold, to have begun the return home, to cross the heath in the dark . . . With luck she was already lying at the bottom of some pit shaft!

He would come. Miriam drew her shawl closer about her shoulders, shivering in the damp night air. Saul would know where to find her. They often came to this hollow they had found at the foot of the straggling limestone hill, its entrance hidden by clumps of gorse. Here they could be together, and for a short precious time she was free from her brother's watchful, suspicious gaze, and the acid tongue of her mother. Why was it that Leah hated her so? It had been that way ever since Miriam could remember. Many times after her father's death she had cried herself to sleep, her back stinging from the bite of the belt he'd never used on her but which her mother had kept especially to beat her with. Often her mouth had bled from the sharp slaps her mother would give without the need for reason; blows she still inflicted whenever Ralph was not home.

Feeling the blood pound in her veins Miriam pressed deeper into the hollow, knowing the tremor was not solely due to the cold. Ralph had always defended her, protected her from their mother's cruelty whenever he could, yet there was something in him that frightened her, something she did not understand but saw in his face each time he looked at her; a sadness that haunted the depths of his eyes. Yet when she smiled at him he turned from her as though she had struck him.

But would he defend her now, seeing the sin she had committed, or would his anger blaze forth as their mother's had done? Would he too turn from her? But even should he not, he could only shield her from Leah's vindictive spite when he was at home, and that was for just a few hours in the evening.

In the distance a vixen screamed, the sound ringing over the silent heath, and Miriam pressed a hand to her mouth to hold in a frightened cry. The folk in the village said the screams and calls heard on the heath at night were the spirits of men lost in the mines, trying to find their way home.

They were old wives' tales, Ralph had said when he had heard her sobbing in the night. Told to frighten wayward children. There was no truth in what they said, there were no such things as ghosts and spirits. Nevertheless Miriam had stayed a long time awake, needing the reassurance of his arms holding her fast. But that had been long ago in childhood. Her hand closed over her mouth, her eyes wide with fear she pressed backward until her spine came flat against the rock, her stare fixed on the entrance to her hiding place, blood curdling in her veins as the fox screamed again.

What if Saul did not come? Sobs she could not hold back escaped through her fingers, echoing from the rock face, their sound joining together like the voices of some unseen choir, blending and rising, the noise filling her with terror, tracing her spine with icy fingers.

What if he did not truly love her after all, if he had merely used her and now wanted no more to do with her? Thoughts tumbled through her mind, adding fresh fuel to the fear that riddled her. Maybe he would refuse to accept that the child she carried was his. He too might think, as her mother did, that she had lain with others beside him. But she had not. Dear God, he must believe she had not!

But if he did turn his back, refuse to marry her? The thought refused to be banished. What would she do? Would her mother allow her to stay at home? And if she did, would the child be subject to the same cruel treatment that had been meted out to Miriam?

'No!' she cried aloud. 'Don't let that happen to our child. Please, Saul . . . don't let that happen.'

Drawing up her legs to her chest, arms folded about them, she let her head sink down until it rested on her knees.

'Please,' she sobbed quietly. 'Please send him to me.'